THE WISEGUY

PIPER STONE

Copyright © 2024 by Stormy Night Publications and Piper Stone

All rights reserved. No part of this book may be reproduced or transmitted in any form or by any means, electronic or mechanical, including photocopying, recording, or by any information storage and retrieval system, without permission in writing from the publisher.

Published by Stormy Night Publications and Design, LLC.
www.StormyNightPublications.com

Stone, Piper
The Wiseguy

Cover Design by Korey Mae Johnson

This book is intended for *adults only*. Spanking and other sexual activities represented in this book are fantasies only, intended for adults.

CHAPTER 1

"You should never trust a wolf in sheep's clothing. Because the only thing the wolf will ever want to do is break you."

—Rachel E. Carter

Maddox

Forbidden.

There were about a dozen reasons that word continued to drift through my thoughts and had since I'd stepped foot in this goddamned city.

New York.

The fucking danger capital of the world. At least in my mind. The only damn good thing about the crowded city was the food, which I'd had my share of. However, I couldn't wait to get out of the place, the people making my skin crawl.

Tonight was no exception.

I was on edge, scanning the ugly bar, itching to use my weapon on someone. Maybe because my testosterone had surged, my balls aching. Still, I could smell danger all around me, my extensive training providing a sixth sense for such things. Unfortunately, I couldn't put my finger on why.

Confronting danger was always a priority in a world where men pretended to be kings.

The statement had been something I'd remembered from years before, long before I'd become the Wiseguy for one of the most notorious and powerful crime syndicates east of the Mississippi. I was the enforcer, a man both feared and respected by men within our organization as well as within the ranks of our enemies.

Threats were a way of life, no matter how legitimate certain aspects of our operation had become. And they were never to be taken lightly. That's why I'd been tasked with coming to New York. To keep the peace.

To keep anyone from destroying our operation in any manner.

To annihilate anyone who tried.

Given I had no regrets for anything I'd done in my career, killing some asshole who dared try to hurt such a precious commodity would be easy. And enjoyable.

A smirk crossed my face as I swirled the drink in front of me.

I relished being called the Boogeyman, taking my job seriously. I also valued the friendship I shared with the Kingpin of the Thibodeaux family, the man I considered my brother. There wasn't a single thing I wouldn't do for Arman, including taking a bullet for him. I'd done that on more than one occasion. I'd also hunted for him, scouring cities to locate assholes who dared get in our way or betray us.

Those were easy deeds to handle, bloodshed certainly not something I shied away from. I was a lethal man after all, my methods of eliminating problems making me legendary.

As if that mattered.

However, the request he'd asked me to handle personally was... difficult as fuck. And why? Because it involved a beautiful woman, one I couldn't have, the single woman considered forbidden. But dear God, my thoughts weren't just impure, they were downright sadistic. Tying her to my bed would just be the beginning of defiling her. I certainly understood the ramifications of what I was thinking, let alone if I acted on the fact my cock suddenly had a mind of its own.

Get a grip, dickhead.

She was fucking off limits, the epitome of forbidden.

Arman would likely cut my dick off with a dull knife, shoving it down my throat until I choked. I was here to keep watch over his most precious possession of all.

I tossed back the cheap liquor, the biting taste sliding down my throat doing little more than reminding me that death was a great equalizer. I almost laughed at the thought, yet as the piano player returned from a short break, my entire body stiffened. The truth hit me hard between the eyes. Death meant nothing. What did?

Uncontrollable lust.

That's what I was experiencing, something I'd worked very hard to ignore. I'd succeeded, refusing to think about my desires for even a single second. Granted, I'd filled the majority of my days with work or going to the gym in order to keep my mind on everything else but the reason for my potential demise. Now that was impossible since she was only thirty feet away. Thank God for the darkness of the club or my needs would become impossible to ignore. I'd had over forty years of being able to shield my thoughts and my desires from those lurking in the shadows, determined to bring down the Thibodeaux family.

Tonight, it seemed as if the armor I'd positioned around myself mentally was tarnished.

All because I wanted to fuck her, claim her as my own.

Arman's only daughter.

Fuck me.

Zoe Thibodeaux was stunning in every way, her long raven hair shimmering in the lights the only decent thing about the joint where she was working a gig. She'd left a mafia princess, a young girl with big dreams. She'd return to her hometown as a woman, which didn't bode well for curtailing my thoughts.

Or my raging desires.

As she eased onto the stool in front of the aging baby grand, I took another sip of my drink, holding the cheap liquor in my mouth. Watching. Forever watching her. The week I'd spent guarding her had allowed me to study her every move, her lovely nuances something I hadn't noticed before. Sure, she'd been nothing a kid to me before she'd left, a girl I'd tried to remember with pigtails and a coloring book in her hand.

Now, that was impossible.

I'd noticed how sultry her laugh had become, how she ate her food gingerly, and when she loved something, her eyes rolled into the back of her head. She was serious about almost everything, walking quickly from building to building while attending classes. Shit. I'd stood outside her dorm as rain had pelted my skin, using the excuse of remaining her bodyguard when all I'd wanted was to catch another glimpse of her.

The word possessive came to mind.

Or maybe I should use the term obsessive.

In my depraved mind, she belonged to me.

My actions had shifted from bodyguard to stalker, including hiding from her as Arman had requested. Shit. This needed to end. Thank God, his fucking flight was due in tomorrow. I'd lose my mind if I was forced to stay another day.

I laughed and threw back the rest of my drink, almost slamming the dense tumbler on the bar. As soon as she started to play, I took a deep breath, instantly mesmerized as I'd been before. She had no idea what the music did to me, luring the beast from deep inside out into the open. I was forced to shift my cock, trying to keep it from being pinched in my zipper. The throb remained, the tightness in my balls becoming critical.

At least this was her last set. She'd return to her dorm, sliding under the covers and I'd retire to the hotel where I'd spend another sleepless night, up at the crack of dawn to use their worthless gym. At least I could burn off some testosterone.

Or so I hoped.

I'd be leaving in two days, just after Arman and Raven arrived for her graduation. Then I'd collect my shit before the three of them returned.

She was such an amazing performer, but the way she was feeling the music on this night was entirely different than the last concert she'd been required to perform at her college. Then she'd been graded for her final exam, choosing to wear black as she handled the classical concerto with professionalism.

On this night she allowed her emotions to show, her body movements adding to the passion of the selected piece. While the male customers leered at her, licking their chops as if they had a chance with her, no one was appreciative of her talent.

And I wanted to crush all of them like the fucking cockroaches they were.

As her fingers tickled the ivories, I leaned my head against the wall, trying to shove aside the sexual images that had formed the moment I'd laid eyes on her after almost five years. Unfortunately, they continued to pulse in my mind's eye, refusing to allow me any peace.

Her naked body under a shower of water.

Cupping her full breasts in my hands, squeezing her nipples until she cried out in pleasurable pain.

Licking her sweet nectar as she writhed underneath me, calling out my name as ecstasy rolled through her.

Driving my throbbing cock deep into her tight channel, filling her with my seed.

I fisted the glass once again, only this time I heard a slight crack as the tumbler succumbed to the pressure. Moments later, I opened my eyes, realizing more time had passed than I'd realized. Almost instantly, I lost my cool as I noticed some guy hanging around the stage. While in his hands were flowers, blood-red roses to be exact, I sensed the very danger that had kept me alive during various assassination attempts over the years. Christ. The asshole was swaying, obviously drunk. That he'd gotten the flowers at this time of night was the reason for my concern.

Still, making a scene wasn't necessary until it was, even if the hackles on the back of my neck were raised.

Inching closer, I continued to stay in the shadows even though it was all I could do not to wrap my hand around the offending asshole's throat. The last thing I needed was for some unknown drunk to trip my wires, alerting Zoe to my presence. Arman had been clear about reminding me she was not to learn I'd been sent to watch her.

The fact I was here wasn't unusual given children and wives were considered the single weaknesses of powerful men such as Arman. However, the timing was. The seemingly out of the blue request had raised a red flag, yet my best friend had simply shrugged off my concerns. That had pushed me to an edge that usually meant someone would face my wrath. Maybe tonight it would be the dude with the gray hair attempting to lay his filthy paws on the beautiful princess.

Almost nothing about Zoe surprised me at this point, including her tenacious attitude, the rebellious woman reminding me of the perfect combination of her mother and father. Yet as I moved closer, I could smell her fear. That did surprise me. She'd just ended the short set, now standing and facing the man offering her flowers.

While she took them at first, I gathered from the look on her face that she was concerned enough about the gesture to place them immediately on the top of the piano. Whatever she'd said to him obviously annoyed the son of a bitch by his crude facial expression but fortunately for him, he turned and walked away.

Much to Zoe's relief.

She waited, pressing her hand against her chest before walking off the stage in the opposite direction toward the small employee locker room that I'd already checked out. I waited for a full five minutes for her to return. When she didn't, I sensed she'd slipped out the back door, possibly to avoid the asshole who'd bothered her.

I yanked out three twenties from my wallet, tossing them on the bar before pushing my way through the crowd toward the exit, running toward the subway. As soon as I noticed her heading down the flights of stairs, I realized the same guy was following her, even glancing over his shoulder before he moved behind her.

The street wasn't deserted yet one of the man reasons I loathed New York was that no one would care if she was accosted, looking the other way instead of getting involved.

That was all I could take. I raced forward, snapping my hand around the man's jacket, yanking him backward by several feet.

After issuing a punch, I expected him to stay down on the sidewalk where I'd explain to him that following pretty young girls wasn't in his best interest. When the fucker made the mistake of struggling to his feet, even taking two swings at me, I had to grin. He actually believed in his inebriated state that he could best me.

I grabbed him by the throat, driving him across the sidewalk, slamming his body against the wall. His breathing was rancid, like a brewery mixed with a French whorehouse. Men with no self-respect pissed me off almost as much as those I considered treacherous bastards.

"What... do you want?" he asked gruffly.

Instead of answering right away, I reached my hand into his jacket pocket, easily finding his wallet.

"You're robbing me? Just don't kill me."

I released my hold from his neck while I yanked out his driver's license. "Lucas Marciano." After reading off his name, I purposely dropped his wallet on the cracked sidewalk before yanking the Glock into my hand and pressing it against his temple. "Now, I'm giving you a choice. You can either walk away from here and live to see another day or attempt to follow that young woman any further. It's entirely up to you. I'm a fair man."

"I wasn't doing nothing. I swear to fucking God."

While there was a slight slur to his words, the fact he knew exactly what I was referring to irritated the piss out of me. "You have three seconds to decide." When his eyes barely registered I was speaking to him, I shoved my other arm into his throat, cutting off his air supply. "Two seconds."

He coughed, doing his best to nod.

I drove my arm against his vocal cords, cocking my head and sneering at him. I could easily snap his neck if I wanted, but I wasn't here to cause any more of a scene than necessary. When I released my hold, he tumbled to his feet.

"I know your name and where you live, Mr. Marciano. I'm giving you a piece of advice and I suggest you take it. Stay away from pretty young women and you just might make it to your next birthday. If not, I will be back. And next time, I won't be so nice since I'll be forced to dole out punishment."

"Who the fuck do you think you are?"

I drove the barrel of my weapon under his chin, using every ounce of control not to fire off a single shot. Allowing things to get messy would only add to my workload.

"You can call me the Boogeyman."

CHAPTER 2

Two months later...
Maddox

Fucking July heat.

New Orleans was broiling, sweat beading across my forehead. Maybe because I was dressed in a goddamned suit. Even the air conditioning in my pricey sports car couldn't keep up with the relentless heat. Just before I was about to exit my vehicle, my phone rang and I answered without looking, ready to bark at the person on the other end.

"Maddox."

"She's home." Arman Thibodeaux's voice was distinctive as usual, but today the tone held a sense of relief. "She landed safely. Just got in an hour ago."

He'd insisted his only daughter return from New York, which would likely be a bone of contention for the stunning young woman with a brazen attitude and a mind of her own. "You finally convinced her to return." I'd been surprised she hadn't returned with her father. I doubted her decision to remain in the city longer had been met with Arman's full approval. Granted, the girl did have him wrapped around her finger and always had.

"No. I insisted she come home for the summer at minimum. Pick up a dozen roses. Will ya? No, make that two dozen. And they need to be red."

Red roses. I loathed the flower more now than ever. Especially the color, but for him, I'd make an exception.

I shook my head, Arman's request driving a smile to my face. He was my boss, considered the most powerful man in New Orleans. The ruthless syndicate leader known as the Kingpin was also my best friend.

And I was his Wiseguy.

He rarely asked for favors, preferring to handle his business and personal needs himself. This made number two for the day, the first being to hunt down a rat who'd dared steal from the organization. That one had been easy, the smarmy dude's inability to keep his trap shut the very reason it had taken me all of one hour and four minutes to track his sorry ass to his on-again, off-again girlfriend's place just outside of the city.

The second favor wasn't difficult, but it did remind me that his daughter, the luminous Zoe Thibodeaux, was headed back to town after several years of being away. She'd been little more than a kid when she'd left for college, a typical eighteen-year-old with a chip on her shoulder, flirtatious as hell. It had been easy then to ignore the crush she'd developed on me. Several years had passed since then but after Arman had recently requested that I shadow her in New York given his growing concern for her welfare, everything had changed. Desire had reared its ugly head, making it almost impossible to block the girl out of my mind.

I'd stood in the shadows after stalking her for over a week, watching as she performed in what I considered a seedy club on the west side of town. An adventure far removed from both the required protocol of her life and of her status as princess of one of the most powerful mafia families within the United States. It was a secret she kept from her father. I was certain of it. Who was I to interfere? She was a woman after all.

Damn it.

The thought of seeing the sweet, innocent, and vulnerable Zoe again was like having a dagger driven into my heart. Sighing, I rubbed my jaw, realizing it was as tight as my chest.

Just thinking about her made my cock ache, my balls tighten. That couldn't happen. Period.

There were rules in every business, the ones inside the Thibodeaux organization brutal yet fair. However, among friends there was a code of ethics that shouldn't need to be written down or clarified. Thou shalt not entertain lurid thoughts about your boss' and best friend's daughter. Unfortunately, I'd been a rule breaker my entire life.

Why stop now?

Because Arman would fucking kill me. "Anything else?" I asked as I tapped my fingers on the steering wheel. Even though I had the windows closed on my Charger, I could still hear the thumping bass drum from the blaring music the asshole was playing. How the hell could her neighbors stand to listen to that crap? Great. Now I was showing what Zoe had often called my advanced age.

"She adores Kristal champagne. That's not what we're serving. Why don't you pick her up a bottle."

"You're allowing her to drink? I'm in shock."

"Pu-lease. She's been living on her own for years. She's a full-grown adult, something she continues to flaunt in front of my face."

Yeah. He shouldn't remind me of that. Since returning from New York, I'd done everything possible to keep visions of her stunning face and voluptuous body out of my mind. That had included hours spent in the gym pumping iron and boxing until exhaustion had taken a significant toll on my muscles. Hell, I'd even gotten another tattoo. Yet the lurid fantasies had remained, lingering in my mind alongside visions of a thick rope ready to be wrapped around my neck. Fuck me. "I'll be happy to. Incidentally, I found Blockhead with his gal," I told him, trying to draw the conversation back to business. We'd taken to calling the stupid Italian that since he'd been given a second chance after fucking up a direct order less than a year before.

At this point, it was best to keep my mind on the business at hand.

"You are the man, which is why I sent you to handle this."

"Don't lie to yourself, buddy. You sent me because that lovely wife of yours would kick your butt straight to Texas if you didn't help her with the final events for the party."

He groaned and all I could do was grin. "Okay, fine. You're right."

If anyone had told me that a gorgeous woman would have the merciless, savage man wrapped around her little finger so tightly all she had to do was give him a heated look and he'd jump, it would have been a call for a bloody battle. But Raven had managed to soften the guy, his young son adding fuel to the family fire.

That wasn't the kind of thing that I could allow to happen in my life. I was the enforcer, the man who kept the peace in a city full of demons and witches. My reputation suggested I commanded Black Magic. Who was I to alter our enemies' train of thought?

"Haven't you figured out that I'm always right?"

Arman laughed. "Handle business as you see fit but don't be late or Raven will have your hide. The roses are important."

"Stop worrying. I'll be there with bells on."

"Yeah, yeah."

I ended the call, shoving the phone into my jacket. While I was certain Raven would admonish me for wearing black to a festive college graduation party, it was the color suit I always wore when handling business, a signature that had fit the term Wiseguy and the other moniker that was whispered in the darkness.

The Boogeyman was back in action. Maybe a little violence would soothe the savage beast inside. It was worth a try anyway.

I'd been given the feared moniker years before because I usually struck in the middle of the night, easing from the shadows and killing my victims without a second thought. I'd enjoyed the earned reputation, the terror that I'd instilled in the hearts of our enemies. The cloak of darkness had protected me over the years, not that anyone would dare go against me. I glanced at the waning light in the sky and sighed. Today was an exception only because the party was being held early evening, allowing Zoe to get settled after her flight from New York arrived.

Before stepping out of my car, I grabbed the brass knuckles, a recent birthday gift from Arman. I rolled the rough pads of my fingers over the thick brass, appreciating the feel. I'd yet to use them but my knuckles were bruised from the beating I'd given a disobedient soldier only a day before.

I wasn't getting any younger, my ability to heal not nearly as fast as it had once been. I rolled my eyes as I checked the ammunition, slapping the magazine back in place on my Glock. After exiting the vehicle, I scanned the street. If anyone was paying any attention, I'd never know it.

And they certainly wouldn't be stupid enough to contact the police.

I crossed the street, thinking about how I wanted to handle this. Time was of the essence, which would prevent me from engaging in my usual enjoyable activities. That didn't mean the pipsqueak wouldn't suffer first. It just meant I couldn't carve pieces off his body as I preferred to do. Besides, I had his girlfriend to contend with and she was a handful and a half.

Plus, I wasn't into hurting or killing women, no matter the bad deeds they'd done in their lives. It was all about respect, women vital in the world of powerful men. In truth, they ran the show. I grinned as I headed toward the small house, the dilapidated home fitting of the rundown neighborhood. If Ricky and Gina didn't shoot up their earnings, placing it in stocks as I'd done, they'd be able to afford a nice place, a decent car. But no. Heroin was their proclivity of choice.

Everyone had one.

Mine was killing people.

The grin remained as I reached the front door. Goddamn, the people had the worst taste in music, the singer screeching out lyrics that made no sense. Whatever. I wasn't here to critique their choice in music. Even if I bothered knocking on the door, there wasn't a chance one of them would hear me. At least the loud volume would cover up any noise made, including Gina's screams. The girl took being a screamer to new level.

The door was unlocked and as I walked inside, I slipped on the brass knuckles. They weren't in the living room or the kitchen and they certainly hadn't been out on the sagging back porch. That meant one thing.

They were engaged in activities in the bedroom.

Great.

As I headed down the crowded hallway, boxes piled against the wall on one side, I felt taller than ever. The low ceiling wasn't something I was used to, my six-foot four-inch frame coming close to hitting the wooden beam. There were two doors, the cramped bathroom empty. The door to the bedroom was partially closed. I was amused the music couldn't hide the animalistic grunts and snorts coming from inside.

I was already reaching the end of my patience. Another few seconds and I'd lose my temper, which wasn't something Rick wanted me to do. Bad things happened when I did, violent and bloody things that no one could recover from. I had no intention of getting my suit bloody. That wouldn't bode well for the two hundred guests Arman and Raven had invited.

I kicked in the door, half laughing when the two lovebirds paid no attention. Gina was in full control of the moment, Rick shackled to her bed in silk scarves. After a few seconds of waiting and being ignored, I finally cleared my throat.

Gina reacted first, throwing her head over her shoulder, snarling as she glared at me.

"You need to leave, Gina. I have business with Ricky alone," I told her.

"Fuck off," she said, as if my sudden appearance was nothing more than a slight hindrance. She'd made no bones about the fact she didn't like me, even going as far as to threaten me on more than one occasion.

Without a second of hesitation, she allowed me to see how ambidextrous she was, spinning around then leaping off the bed like a goddamn cat. I was shocked she landed smack against my chest, immediately pummeling her small fists into my face.

I was forced to grab her wrists, tossing her off me easily, but she wasn't going down without a fight, throwing her body toward me. This time, I took a step out of the way, snapping my fingers around her wrist. At least I'd come prepared, dragging her out of the room and into the kitchen. By all rights, I should treat her just like I would any other asshole who accosted me, but I couldn't do that. Maybe I was growing soft in my advanced years. The thought brought another snicker to my lips.

"Get off me, you fuckhead!" she screamed.

"That's not going to happen. However, you will need to calm down."

She had the nerve to rake her nails down my cheek. Now she'd pissed me off. I snapped my hand around her throat, pushing her up against the edge of the counter. While she continued to fight me like a wildcat, I managed to rip out the handcuffs I'd brought myself, slapping one around her wrist, the other around the handle of the oven.

Before she had another chance to cause more blood, I backed away, shaking my head. "You should learn not to fight with the Boogeyman."

"When I get loose, I'm going to kick your ass. You're nothing but a cockroach that I plan on fumigating."

The girl truly believed she was tough. Well, good for her.

"Whatever you say."

"Goddamn you, prick. You bastard. I will fucking kill you."

She was screaming obscenities as I took long strides out of the room, wincing when I touched my cheek. The bitch had drawn blood. Great. I'd need an antiseptic and likely a rabies shot. Just what I needed.

I returned to the bedroom, shocked to find that Ricky had managed to get himself out of the restraints, trying to fit his oversized body out the small window. It would have been a comical sight had I not been in such a pissy mood.

I wrapped my hand around the back of his thick neck, yanking him back onto the bed. I could tell instantly he was hyped up on drugs, his bloodshot eyes the first indication, the second the fact that he was stupid enough not to take his beating like a man. When he lunged for me, taking two wild swings, managing an undercut to my jaw, I hissed then kicked him square in the chest.

He tumbled backward, sliding across the slick sheets, his body slamming against the wall. Taking deliberate steps around the bed, I yanked him up by the throat, issuing two brutal punches. The music might be loud, preventing me from hearing the moment his nose was crushed, but given blood spewing toward me, it was easy to see what I'd done.

Fortunately, I was quick on my feet, dodging the gore seconds before it landed on my jacket. I issued one more to his kidneys then allowed him to slide down the wall. He stared at me with fear in his eyes and while I'd originally wanted to make this as painful as possible, I'd grown weary and bored with the fight.

"You fucked with the wrong people, dickhead. Didn't you know stealing is against the law?"

He blubbered something I couldn't understand.

"Sorry. I can't hear you." I replaced the birthday gift with my weapon, sighing when he beckoned me to come to his level with his hand. Fuck. Seconds later, I dropped down to a crouched position, chastising myself for playing with my target. "What is it, Rick? Are you trying to apologize, begging for another chance?"

He took gaping breaths, blood running into his mouth. As he started to wheeze, I cocked my head. Somehow, he managed to grin.

"Go fuck yourself."

His words and the sentiment were clear. He hadn't given a shit about loyalty or respect, which was why I wouldn't show him any remorse.

I placed the barrel of the weapon against his broken nose and pulled the trigger.

"Fuck me." As blood splattered onto my jacket, I cursed a blue streak.

It looked like I'd be forced to make a pitstop to change my clothes after all. I hated when targets made me late.

Especially for this event in particular.

CHAPTER 3

Zoe

"A wolf in sheep's clothing. That's what that sinfully gorgeous man is, and you know what they say about men like that, don't you?" Maggie had asked me after being abruptly turned down by the powerful, dangerous man.

"No. What?"

"They will always find a way to eat you alive, driving their sharp canines into your rapidly beating heart."

She'd laughed after issuing the words, acting as if her thwarted advances no longer meant anything to her.

But I'd known better.

We'd been barely eighteen, both of us believing that we could conquer the world. That had been the night she'd gone after my father's right-hand man with exposed claws, draping her voluptuous body over his in a way that most men couldn't ignore.

Maddox had done so easily, which I'd secretly been thrilled about. I'd never told my best friend that the powerful hunk of a man was the single person I'd had a crush on for years. Sadly, Maddox had always acted as if I would remain a little girl and nothing more. Granted, I hadn't filled out completely even at that age, certainly not like Maggie, who'd had every boy in high school after her.

I'd changed since leaving for college, barely able to recognize myself any longer. Sadly, I had a strong sense that my fully developed curves wouldn't sway my father's best friend. Maddox Cormier was someone who'd protected me since I could remember, his sense of duty and loyalty to the family first and foremost in his mind.

I stared at my reflection in the vanity mirror, blinking several times before glancing at the photographs I'd taped to the edge, stupid pictures of fun times in high school, girlfriends that I'd thought would remain in my life. Now the events and fun times seemed like a lifetime ago. So many changes had occurred in the almost five years I'd been gone, the time and distance altering me as a person. Or maybe I'd just tried to become anyone but who I was, which was impossible. No one would ever allow me to forget I was a Thibodeaux through and through, a princess to be cherished.

Including by my bodyguard.

I was home, a festive party getting ready to start. I'd laid out four different dresses, still unable to decide which one was perfect. For some crazy reason, I felt sick inside, my nerves raw. I'd be lying to myself if I pretended not to know the reason why. After over four years it was possible that I'd be forced to see Maddox again.

Forced was a harsh word, but the last conversation I'd had with the man had nearly destroyed me. I wasn't the same girl any longer, much stronger and more resilient given my college experience, but I still wasn't certain how I'd handle seeing the man in person after all these years.

I'd purposely not come home while attending college, pretending that I was too busy to enjoy family celebrations. That had prompted my overprotective father and the beautiful woman he'd married to come to New York, refusing to leave me alone for the holidays. This time, I had no excuses. None.

Home.

After hanging in New York for a few weeks after graduation, my father had insisted I come home and stay the summer before deciding on which career I wanted to pursue finding a job in, nursing or music. He'd had a sense of urgency in his voice, yet when I'd asked if anything was wrong, he'd ignored the question. He'd simply said he wanted to spend some quality time with his daughter before I entered into the workforce.

Even if I had yet to make up my mind what I wanted to do with the rest of my life. I certainly couldn't remain a mafia princess forever. The thought brought a laugh to my lips.

Maybe I'd try my hand at singing, pursuing a music career that had nothing to do with my classical training. Now I rolled my eyes at the thought. Performing in less than stellar environments for cash hadn't been the most delightful experience after all. I'd run into winos and drug addicts.

And men watching me as if I was their prey.

The thought of the jerk I'd seen watching me entered my mind. Maybe I'd been overreacting, but I'd seen a lone figure standing outside my dorm room, another time hanging out at the club where I'd once worked. Maybe that's why I'd reacted the way I had with the guy who'd tried to bring me flowers. Why was I thinking about that tonight? That was the past, the city I'd once thought I'd thrive in in my rearview mirror. My ineptness had seen to that.

I raked the brush through my hair, making ugly faces at my reflection. Fuck the girl staring back at me.

I'd wanted to pursue my dream, including auditioning for the New York Philharmonic, which had me insisting to my father I had to finish a menial job prior to returning home. The lie had been easy, the single girlfriend I'd had in college allowing me to stay at the small apartment she'd rented after our graduation. The audition, on the other hand, had been a disaster.

I'd forgotten the piece altogether, something that had never happened before. And why?

Because of the threat arriving the night before. My mind had issued a blank. So when my father had called, insisting I come home, I'd caved into his request. Now I felt like I'd lost the backbone I'd gained while living in New York.

I hated myself for being weak, for allowing some asshole who didn't even know me to scare me off from my dreams.

I'd pursued both interests, earning degrees, but music had been added on after being discovered at a little bar where I worked as a pianist and singer for extra money. I certainly couldn't tell my father that I'd moonlighted as a singer, or he'd have a cow.

The dual major had kept me in school a few months longer, but it had been worth the extra time and effort. I'd been fortunate in that my father had allowed me to pursue whatever I'd wanted, protective yet not domineering. Although I'd sensed music hadn't been his first choice. That's why I hadn't told him about the audition.

Then again, I wasn't certain he was fond of nursing either, even though I'd always wanted to help people. Maybe that had been because no one had saved my mother. Still, his promise to allow me to decide had been a huge surprise given he was considered a brutal, vile man to almost everyone who knew him or of his reputation.

Here I was, home as required, forced to face the one man who I couldn't have. For about a bazillion reasons I was nervous, so much so the second glass of wine I was in the middle of consuming wasn't doing me any good. There were far too many memories in my old room. I glanced at one of the pictures of my mother, her smiling face reminding me of my own. Daddy had told me I looked exactly like her, which I'd come to realize had initially been difficult for the man who'd grieved for years, only Raven able to bring him out of the darkness.

Now, as I stared at my reflection, I was the one who felt the grief even more and I wasn't certain why. There were other pictures I'd saved, birthdays and a special visit with Santa. It was strange to see me at eight or nine, Maddox looming in the background, allowing my father to bask in the moment of his only child getting photographed on the lap of some unknown man dressed as Santa. In truth, I hadn't saved the picture because it was a favorite memory. I'd saved it because it was one of the few I'd had of Maddox. I'd forgotten to pack it when I'd left for the airport the day I was headed to New York.

I'd been glad I had given the horrible conversation I'd had with the man who'd always been my bodyguard. My bodyguard. No one had ever called him that. He was far too important in the Thibodeaux organization, the third in command after my father and one of my uncles, but he'd always been there protecting me.

A hot flash rushed through my chest, heading to my face. There was no reason to be embarrassed yet that's what I felt. At least it had changed from thinking of myself as a stupid little girl with a ridiculous crush. I shifted my attention to the other pictures, able to smile.

I ran my fingers across one photograph in particular, Maggie someone I'd missed after moving away. We'd called each other a few times, had promised to stay in touch. Maybe it had been my fault our friendship had fallen apart. It had been my turn to play catch-up by calling her. I'd been busy, or so I'd told myself. The truth was I'd wanted to end another connection to New Orleans. Not doing so was too painful, especially when she always actively talked about the man I'd had a crush on since I could remember.

She'd known all along everyone who worked for my father was considered off limits to me, so why not pursue Maddox like the little vixen she was? According to our last conversation, they'd hooked up more than once. I still wasn't certain if she'd been trying to gauge my reaction or tossing the news in my face for a darker reason.

I found the possibility of their tryst hard to believe, but I didn't know Maddox that well, the man so private that I'd developed fantasies about his past. Still, the ugliness of hearing the details had pained me to the point I'd hated her. Maybe I still did. That wasn't healthy. Neither was returning home, but I had no excuses any longer to refuse the party my father and his wife had insisted on throwing me.

Not showing up wouldn't be polite. Plus, he'd hunt me down, requiring one of his soldiers to drag me back home kicking and screaming. And he would have likely chosen his most trusted soldier and best friend.

Maddox.

My personal bodyguard and the man who couldn't give a shit about me or the way I felt about him. "There you go again. Shut it down, girlfriend." Damn if my voice didn't sound hollow.

I closed my eyes, groaning as I dropped my head into both hands, cringing when I heard a knock on my bedroom door. "Yes?"

When it opened, my father stepping just inside, I plastered on a smile. He could never know that I'd once made a promise to myself that I'd only lose my virginity to the stunning, rough and tumble man I adored. To date, I'd never allowed a single man to go past first base. Maybe the career I should choose was becoming a nun.

"You're not dressed," my father said, his dimples showing as he smiled broadly.

"You mean the fluffy pink robe won't cut it?" I adored my father. He was brilliant, ruthless, yet loved his family fiercely. He was also the kind of man the majority of people were terrified of, especially after getting on his bad side. His reputation had preceded him even in New York, most people shying away from me as if I had the plague. I could resent him, but I'd grown up in a life of privilege, never wanting for anything.

Well, with a single exception.

His laughter boomed into my room, the mischievous look on his face showing his age. Not that he was old, something he would never admit to anyway, but I did like to tease him. "There are some people I'm eager for you to meet."

Uh-oh. I knew exactly what that meant. I was still a mafia princess, a valuable commodity. While he'd never treated me as if I was a possession, something to be sold off to the highest bidder, I'd always known that strong alliances made between two families were like winning the lottery. Power and influence, wealth, prosperity, and utter control. I'd heard those words more than once. While Arman

Thibodeaux was already king of New Orleans, he wanted to be king of the world.

"You mean you have a few eligible suitors you'd like me to entertain, perhaps gaining a marriage proposal."

He looked hurt for a few seconds, his eyes flashing a strange emotion that evoked a moment of fear deep inside. He was anxious, worried enough about something that he was masking his fear. "It's important that you find the right man."

"I'm not ready to get married."

He took a deep breath, glancing out my window. "You know I'd do anything for you in my life. Don't you?"

"Yes, of course."

"Sometimes there are difficult decisions to be made, especially in my business. I just want you to know that I love you."

He was frightening me more than he'd ever done, the hair on the back of my neck standing up.

"Daddy? Is something going on?"

"Of course not, sweetie. I just always want what's best for you." Now he appeared drained, the look in his eyes haunting.

"I know you do." I walked closer, noticing the pulse on the side of his neck was rapid, the cords thick with tension. I knew better than to try to get him to confide in me. He'd always tried to keep the ugliness of business away from me, and from Raven. But I sensed the burden was significant.

"You can introduce me to anyone you want. I'll play the hostess with the mostest."

I knew enough about my father to know that he wouldn't tell me whatever was going on, always shielding me from business because he believed me to be just his little girl. A princess.

Just like he'd called me so many times.

He laughed again, trying to slide his suit of armor back into place. I'd always believed my father invincible. Now I was beginning to wonder if the cracks in the thick steel were increasing. What wasn't he telling me?

"You are going to give a small recital for our guests, aren't you?"

Now he had a puppy dog look. "And if I say no?"

"Then you won't be entitled to your surprise. I'm just sayin'." He waved me off, closing the door but I could still hear his laughter.

At least my father could still make me smile, almost as giddy as when I was a little girl and he pretended to be Santa. I moved away from the mirror, glaring at the dresses I'd selected. Red was my choice for the night. Why not be daring? I had nothing to lose.

Or did I?

CHAPTER 4

Zoe

Maddox.

I couldn't get him off my mind, scanning the entrance foyer then the hallway as I headed to the kitchen. He was nowhere to be seen. Maybe he wasn't coming. We weren't friends after all.

I laughed at the thought as I entered the room, smiling the moment I saw my new stepmother, although she was only a few years older than I was.

"Look at you!" Raven tugged on my forearm, twirling us both around in a circle. As she pulled me into her arms, I felt more at ease being home.

"How are you doing?"

"Fantastic. We're glad you're home."

I backed away, shaking my head. The caterer they'd hired was barking orders to her staff, putting the final details into place. "You mean Father dearest has wanted to keep an eye on me."

"Nonsense," she cooed. "However, you know how your father is." She winked as if it was a joke we shared. Yes, I knew exactly how my father was. He'd be spitting nails laced with poison if he knew the lurid thoughts I had.

"Yes, more than most. Is something going on I should know about?"

Raven narrowed her eyes as she folded her arms. "What are you talking about?"

I shrugged, glancing at the bustling catering crew, the incredible scent of luscious foods making my tummy growl. "Daddy seemed tense when he came to see me."

"I'm not sure why. It's just business as usual. Granted, he's had some difficult clients lately, which has made him more irritable than normal. He's been working a lot of overtime so he's a bit exhausted. Nothing to worry about." She looked away, her brow furrowing.

There it was, a confirmation that something was wrong, although she was a very good actress, doing her best to act like her worry wasn't heightened. "Well, hopefully he'll come around. Everything is wonderful, the house beautiful. Thank you for putting this together. You really didn't need to go to all this fuss."

The look of relief on her face was torturous. "Nonsense. Your father and I wanted to do something special. You've been working hard for years, the accomplishment something you should be very proud of. Now, go enjoy the festivities. Just so you know, there are some hot-looking young men here." She winked, giving me a heated look.

Groovy. I was being set up. I knew it. "Oh, no. I've sworn off men for a few years."

"Uh-oh. You'll need to tell me that story."

"Nothing to tell worthwhile. Men are nothing but big children."

"You just realized that?" she teased, which allowed us both to laugh.

There was no story, at least not one I could tell anyone about. I'd all but ignored boys since leaving for college, the few dates I'd been on turning into disasters. I'd even been called an ice queen by more than one of the bastards. That wasn't just because I'd refused to put out for them. As soon as they'd made the connection to who my father was, they'd run like scared rabbits.

I almost walked out when I couldn't help myself, even though as soon as I asked the question, I regretted it. "Oh. Is Maddox here?" I tried to sound nonchalant, but I wasn't certain it was working.

"He had something to do for your dad. I'm not certain he's going to be able to make it."

That meant he wasn't coming and hadn't planned on it. And the something was handling a difficult situation, which usually meant someone was going to end up on the punishment end of Maddox's fist. Disappointment swept through me like some crazy tidal wave. "Oh." I couldn't even look at her. That I'd thought he might break through the gruff exterior, attending a party for me was nuts. He didn't want me. I wasn't good enough for him. It was time I got over my foolish crush.

Past time.

"Hmmm... Is there something you're not telling me?" Raven asked, a coy look crossing her face.

"Why would there be?" I was a better actress than I'd given myself credit for. "He's just the hired help. Right? I just wondered if he was going to be following me around like a lapdog."

She lifted a single eyebrow, a sly smile crossing her face. "Ri-ight. Whatever you say. Why don't you have a glass of wine. I'm thinking maybe you need it. You're the one who seems tense. I'll let you know if I run into Maddox." As she handed me one from a tray about ready to be served, a slight grin crossed her face.

Giving her a wide-eyed look of total innocence, I accepted the gesture, growling on purpose. "Why ever would you say I'm tense?"

"I wasn't born yesterday. You like him."

"Who?" I did my best to act as if I had no clue who she was talking about.

"Maddox."

"Are you kidding me?"

"Uh-huh. Just be careful. You might be playing with fire. But your secret is safe with me."

The way she threw up her hands, spinning around in a circle created a heated flush floating from my neck to my cheeks.

"You've got it wrong. He annoys the hell out of me."

"Okay. Have it your way," Raven half purred as if she knew something I didn't. "However, we *will* talk later." As she headed out of the kitchen, I tried to keep the smile plastered on my face, losing it the second she'd cleared the doorway.

There was no doubt my acting skills sucked.

I grabbed a piece of cheese before leaving the kitchen, milling through room after room to try to shove aside any and all thoughts of him.

Another wave of disappointment slipped into my system when he didn't suddenly appear out of the shadows. He wasn't required to come to family celebrations, although he used to come to them all the time. Things might have changed, our last words terse. I'd been a foolish little girl then, acting as if a man of his stature could want me. He'd made certain I had no problem getting on the plane.

More guests were arriving, so many of them people I'd never seen before. I'd been completely out of touch with what had occurred in New Orleans over the years, trying to forget who I was. As I passed through a crowd of men, I could tell several of them were eyeing me as if I was a luscious snack. Okay, so they were cute, some even handsome, but I wasn't in the mood.

I threw back half the glass of merlot, almost choking in the process. I exchanged the heightened level of disappointment with a moment of sadness that I hadn't allowed myself to experience for years. It was from being back in the house I'd grown up in, the one I'd shared so many good times with my father. And Maddox.

I'd always known my lurid thoughts and desires were wrong, completely taboo, forbidden in every way. I wasn't a fool. If my father believed there was anything going on between Maddox and his only daughter, his baby girl, he'd put a bullet between Maddox's eyes. He had all but said those exact words the day I'd turned eighteen, although he was talking about almost every boy who dared glance in my direction.

A half laugh bubbled to the surface, but it sounded bitter. The fantasy had been spectacular, keeping me warm during long, lonely nights, but it wasn't real life. It could never be. Not in any language or in any country. Even if we were an item, there wasn't a single place on earth where we wouldn't be hunted.

Maybe coming home was a huge mistake, even if my father had made it clear that I had no other choice.

I should hate Maddox for his frank words on the day I'd left, but all I'd done was pine away for him even more.

"You're going to do great in New York," Maddox said.

I'd been given a rare moment to be alone with the man considered my bodyguard, my father speaking with the pilot. I'd insisted on leaving for New York alone, trying to act like I was all grown up, even if I remained terrified inside.

"What if I don't want to go?" *I asked, trying to sound alluring.*

"Why would you say that?" *He scratched his head, acting as if he was bored, looking everywhere else but into my eyes.*

"I thought maybe there was a reason to stay."

I walked closer, crowding his space.

"Nah. You need to live your life for you, Zoe."

The bastard still wasn't looking at me.

"That's exactly what I want to do. With you."

Maddox slowly turned his head, narrowing his eyes. "What does that mean?"

God. Men could be so dense, as well as pigheaded. Exasperated, I did the only thing I could think of that would grab his attention. I rose onto my tippytoes, gripping his jacket with both hands and capturing his mouth. Almost instantly he stiffened but didn't budge at first. Until I pushed my tongue past his lips, exploring his heated mouth.

He grabbed my arms, pushing me away forcefully, gasping for air as he threw a look toward the direction where Daddy had gone. "What the hell do you think you're doing?"

"Kissing you. What does it look like?"

As he stretched his arms out, pushing me backward by another foot, I glared at him.

"You're a child. This can't happen," he growled, his fingers digging into my skin.

I jerked away, humiliation creating a horrific wave of nausea. "I'm not a little girl any longer, Maddox. I'm eighteen. I've fully grown."

He rolled his eyes, breaking the connection completely and taking another step away from me. "You need to get on that plane, Zoe. You have your entire life ahead of you. You'll find someone better suited to your needs. I am not that man."

With that, he'd turned away from me. I'd been crushed beyond belief, barely making it onto the jet before tears had begun to fall. Yeah, he'd made certain I'd known he didn't want me. God. I was such a fool. It would be easier to hate him. That's what I needed to do. If he didn't want to even acknowledge my significant accomplishment, then fuck him.

Stop it. You're acting like a child.

I'd blame it on the wine I'd already consumed but that would be a lie.

I shored my shoulders, greeting the guests as I continued moving through the house, doing everything I could to shove the fucking asshole out of my mind.

"You look lovely, dear," an older lady I didn't know said as I passed.

"Doesn't she now? She's all grown up," her companion added, although the tone sounded haughty to me. "A perfect image of her mother."

"Thank you both for the compliment," I said politely, although the bad girl inside of me wanted to be catty, clawing out their eyes. Great. Now I had murderous thoughts about unknown guests at my own party. I needed to grow up. Maybe I needed to sidle up to one of the good-looking guys that I'd passed. At least I'd been noticed by a couple of them.

"The apple of her father's eye," the first woman said, and I could swear they were sizing me up. I wasn't certain why they were here other than it was apparent this was the party of the year. Or maybe I should say spectacle.

My father had certainly invited the most powerful and influential people in the city. The mayor. The chief of police. Well-known artists. There were even a couple of celebrities and musicians. I'd often wondered if they attended the events my father had thrown out of enjoyment or because they knew not accepting the invitation wouldn't be good for their health. I'd known most of my life people were terrified of every male within my family. I'd found it mostly amusing, although I'd heard enough stories to know how dangerous they were.

Especially Maddox. He was the Wiseguy of the organization, the one man you didn't want to cross. Maybe I just had a thing for bad boys. It suddenly felt as if everyone was staring at me, something I'd always hated.

Without being asked, I moved to the music room, the lovely location overlooking the pool. I headed to one of the sets of glass doors, peering outside. There were twinkling lights in all the trees, the warm evening inviting, several of the guests enjoying the festive atmosphere outside. I'd never felt so lonely in my life or so out of place. It was strange to be home after almost five years. The fact my father hadn't changed anything about my bedroom since I'd left for college was a stark reminder of just how much time had gone by.

I ran my hand over the smooth surface of my baby grand, tickling the ivories as I took a deep breath, placing my wine on top. A recital, huh? Well, at least Daddy hadn't tried to coerce me into playing something he preferred. This had always been one of my few happy places, somewhere I could pretend I'd grown up in the perfect nuclear family. A mother and father, a baby brother or two. A normal life. That just hadn't been in the cards. It never would be.

I was a mafia princess after all. My father could put a spin on the world I'd grown up in, but the standoffishness of everyone at my graduation party was just a stinky reminder that I'd always be inside a glass cage being studied as if I was a science experiment. Escaping to New York hadn't done me much good. It hadn't been any different there. I'd come to realize that I'd never be able to lose the name or my family's reputation.

"I missed you, old girl," I whispered. And I had. My beloved piano had gotten me through times of depression and worry, loneliness, and my own heightened level of anxiety. Music had been the healing force, not having a mother taking a significant toll on me. More than I'd ever let my father know since his grieving had almost destroyed him. I was thankful every day that he'd met someone like Raven.

If only I had a strong force in my life.

There was no reason for me to be sad on this day. I'd just graduated from college with a double major, even if the combination was bizarre. I had my whole life ahead of me. Then why was I melancholy? I sat down, taking a few seconds to think about what I wanted to play. After placing my fingers on the keys, I closed my eyes.

Music was in my heart, buried in my soul. I didn't need my eyesight to feel the music, to bask in the moment as I got lost in chords and adagios. As I began to play, the peace that always accompanied the moments I was able to steal for myself washed through me.

There was no one else. No sound. No worries.

Just the music.

And that was okay by me.

CHAPTER 5

Maddox

"Jesus Christ," I muttered when I pulled into the driveway leading to Arman's estate. Vehicles had lined the street, more parking on both sides of the aggregate surface. I'd heard he'd invited everyone who was anyone from Texas to Miami, but I didn't think that many would attend a freaking graduation party. It wasn't as if the girl was getting married.

The thought brought another horrific taste in my mouth.

What would I care anyway if that were the case? I'd been her bodyguard. I was certain I'd do that again when necessary. Especially given the recent issues Arman had faced. Granted, I wasn't surprised he'd insisted on Zoe returning home for the entire summer. It was much easier to keep an eye on her when she lived under the same roof instead of a couple thousand miles away.

He'd sent me to New York for a week, fearful that she'd be abducted or worse, used against him. I made certain Zoe hadn't seen or heard from me, remaining her shadow the entire time. It was something that I'd perfected to an artform, the ability to hide in plain sight when necessary considered an attribute in our world of organized crime.

It didn't matter the corporation had gone mostly legit. A significant portion of the money earned still came from more lucrative ventures no one could call on the straight and narrow. I was forced to return to the street, finding a parking spot three blocks down. That alone was enough to keep me in a piss-poor mood.

After parking, I checked my watch. The party had started over an hour before. Stopping to change, purchase flowers and the exact brand of champagne the precious girl deserved taking me more time than I'd allotted. Fuck. I hated to be late for anything.

I'd been forced to contact our cleaning crew to handle the situation at Gina's house, sending her packing in the process with a tidy sum of cash in her hand. I wasn't worried the woman wouldn't accept her good fortune. She was being provided more than enough to start a new life in another city. But her hatred of me fueled her, something I'd need to keep in the back of my mind.

I grabbed the flowers and champagne, scanning the street before heading toward the house. The moonless, humid night seemed more oppressive than normal, the absence of noise, including from the usual insects, odd. There was usually nothing quiet about New Orleans even in the summer months, especially when a party was in full swing.

While my weapon remained in my suit jacket, it wouldn't be in good form to walk the upper echelon neighborhood brandishing a weapon. The thought allowed a smirk to cross my face.

As I took long strides toward the house, a tightness formed in my chest. The reason had nothing to do with the recent unrest in the organization, although I'd had a terse conversation with Arman only days before.

I refused to think about it as I finally made it to the driveway. More guests were arriving, everyone in a festive mood. While I could easily see soldiers surrounding the house, it was obvious they'd been told to remain in the shadows as well. There was nothing that could break up a party faster than being terrified of a gunman.

Once I was near the house, I noticed Landry in a suit near the front door casually smoking a cigarette. He remained where he was as I approached. He was Arman's other trusted man, someone who'd come up through the ranks from being nothing more than a gopher to sharing the same title of lieutenant as I did. However, I had full seniority, my rank considered third in line of power. As if either Arman or Francois would give up the reins. "Anything going on?"

"Just a lot of people preparing to get drunk," he said, taking another puff. "And some fucking reporters showed up. Bastards."

The family had been in the news dozens of times, lately more for their philanthropic actions versus the early days of being treated as a family kin to the devil. A lot of changes had occurred over the years, most of them beneficial to both the family and the city. However, there were reporters determined to get their fifteen minutes of fame by scraping up dirt on the family. I refused to allow that to happen. "Make certain none of the fuckers get into the house."

"Don't worry. Tony is casing the grounds, making certain every single one of them is leaving. You know how he is."

Tony Teracino had started working for me only recently. Given my workload had increased, my promotion to vice president of operations keeping me away from Arman's estate more often than not, Arman had assigned the man to remain by my side. While Tony was trustworthy, we'd yet to develop a rhythm, Tony's idea of a chain of command and mine completely different. At least in this regard, his instinct had been on the money. Tony was considered a high ranking made man, the old term something Arman's grandfather had used and it had stuck through the generations. The two men I'd hired were low ranking members on the totem pole, unacceptable to be my main man according to Arman.

As my best friend had grown older, he'd become more like his father, whether he wanted to believe it or not. He'd challenge me to a brawl if he knew I was even thinking that way.

"Good. Keep an eye out for anything out of the ordinary. Let me know if you see anything."

"Is there a reason to be concerned?" Landry lifted his head, studying me intently.

I scanned the well-lit area, every tree sparkling with twinkling lights for an added festive nature. "I just have a bad feeling churning in my gut." And I did. Arman had been acting odd lately, keeping things to himself. That wasn't like him, the man sharing just about everything with me. Plus, there was talk of trouble brewing, various sources on the street acting cagey as fuck. That didn't bode well for doing business on any level, legitimate or otherwise.

"Well, fuck. When you do that usually means some kind of explosion." Landry grinned although he was right. My instinct had almost never steered me wrong.

Snickering, I moved toward the front porch, stopping just long enough to chastise him. "Those things are going to kill you."

"Yeah, maybe if I lived long enough to see that happen. Did you know the average life span of a made man inside a mafia organization is forty-five years old?"

I rubbed my jaw, thinking about his statement. He was the master of often useless details. It would be great fun watching him on an episode of *Jeopardy*. I had a feeling he'd clean up. "Think of it this way. You have six more years to fuck up your lungs."

He burst into laughter, and I shook my head. Within a couple of years, I'd hit that magical plateau. It was a good thing I had my will in order. I rolled my eyes at the macabre thought.

As soon as I walked in through the front door, Arman appeared as if he'd sensed my arrival.

He had an amused look on his face, a drink in one hand. "You're late. Complications?"

"Let's just say his girlfriend was difficult."

"Mmm…" He walked closer, glancing at the scratches remaining on my face. "I can see that. You have a way with the women, my friend."

"You've turned into quite the comedian."

Laughing, he grabbed the bottle of champagne from my hand. "Zoe is in the music room. The concert I asked her to perform is about over. Why don't you take her the flowers when she's finished?"

"I thought you were planning on doing that yourself."

There was something disconcerting about the way he glanced in the other direction. "Unfortunately, I have a phone call to make."

"Business, tonight? I'm surprised after all the fuss you made."

He clapped me on the arm. "The fuss? I never make a fuss."

While he laughed, I sensed there was something else going on. "Yeah, you do when it comes to your wife or children."

"Okay. Guilty as charged, my friend," he said, trying to act nonchalant. "However, as you well know, owning a business is a pain in the ass. The call is a necessity and one I can't get out of. And the call might take some time. Make certain everything goes as planned. This party is important and I want Zoe to feel at home."

"What's going on, Arman? First, you had me take out…"

"Nothing. Stop worrying."

"Uh-huh. Do you need me?" Important. He'd all but insisted Zoe come home for the summer or longer. I didn't need to be a rocket scientist to know he was concerned she'd be made a target. However, he was keeping things close to the vest and that pissed me off.

"No. Assholes I can handle easily. Now, go be with my daughter. Make certain she's okay. Just don't leave her side. Do you understand?" The concern on his face was palpable.

"No problem. I won't," I told him, concerned given I had no clue about whoever he was having a conversation with. He usually told me everything, bouncing off ideas and concerns. That he wasn't now meant he felt he didn't have a handle on the situation, something that he couldn't stand. "Did something else happen you're not telling me about?"

"Let's just say that I refuse to be caught in a weak moment. Go. I can handle this bullshit." He continued scanning the front door as if anticipating trouble would walk straight in.

I glanced over my shoulder, bristling. "Understood, Arman. I'll make certain no riffraff bothers her."

He lifted his glass in appreciation. "You're a good friend."

"Something for you to keep in mind," I said, grinning, trying to lighten the mood even though I remained on edge.

"Very funny."

"Have Francois and Louie arrived?"

"Unfortunately, Louie is locked in a tedious surgery, both kids sick with the croup, so Sara is stuck at home as well. Francois is here with Delaney and Edmee is without Zane, who couldn't get a flight out of Paris where he's conducting business due to a horrific weather system."

"Still, it's a full house." The Thibodeaux family was my family as well, but there was something as odd as the night air about the way he'd mentioned who was here.

He grinned. "Only the best for Zoe. Everybody missed her. I'm thinking you included. I'll be back as soon as I can."

My jaw was clenched tighter than ever. I watched him walk away, noticing Tony out of the corner of my eye. He headed toward me, his jaw as tight as mine as if he'd had an altercation.

"What's wrong?" I asked as he approached.

"Reporters. There's one that refuses to leave. I made the mistake of pushing her. It's that Sandra something chick."

"Let me guess. The folks Ms. Wells is working with caught your disagreement on camera."

"Might have occurred."

Fucking great. "You need to learn to hide your temper. Landry will handle her if she continues to be an issue. Stay inside and make certain the Thibodeaux women are protected, little Gabriel as well." I didn't like the fact Raven and Arman's little boy had been kept here, but Arman had insisted it was safer than any alternative.

"Sure. You got that look, boss. Are we expecting trouble?"

"So I've been told but I hope to hell not," I barked.

"Uh-huh. I'll keep my weapon nice and close just in case. By the way, nice flowers."

There was no special reason Tony's laugh irritated the hell out of me, but it did.

I shoved my nasty thoughts aside, weaving my way through the thick crowd of people, far too many guests in my opinion, but both Arman and Raven enjoyed splashy parties. I grabbed a scotch from one of the six or so bars, already consumed by the music Zoe had selected to play. I wanted to down the entire thing to calm my fucked-up nerves.

I couldn't remember the number of times I'd been invited to one of her private concerts starting when she was eleven or so. Arman had always been the proud papa, indulging his baby girl, wanting her to feel like a princess. She'd always wanted to play music, becoming a concert pianist. That hadn't been on Arman's radar. If the man had his way, she'd remained locked in her room instead of forging her own way. Zoe would never stand for it.

As I neared the music room, I gathered a sense of awe amongst the guests. While I'd been standing in the auditorium in New York during her last solo performance with the school's orchestra, the music had been selected by her professor. However, that was the moment everything had changed. I'd stopped thinking of her as my boss' daughter, a freckle-faced teenager, and had started seeing her as a beautiful, vivacious woman.

I'd burn in hell for doing so and Arman would be the one to put me there.

I walked closer, loathing the fact I was fully aroused. I'd never been that much into music, perhaps because I was almost always working, but everything Zoe selected was breathtaking, tonight's music no different.

However, the piece she was playing was as dark as the night, almost as ominous as the quiet had been outside. The sound was haunting, so melancholy that no one in the room was moving. With her long fingers and expressive actions, almost always playing with her eyes closed, she was mesmerizing to watch. She'd selected a classical piece but one emphasizing the bass chords. She was completely into the music, her body swaying, her long hair shimmering in the LED lighting.

And there wasn't a single person in the room untouched by the sensuality of the music, the choreography undoubtedly embellished by the artist playing it. It was easy to fall under Zoe's spell, wishing the moment wouldn't end.

At least from where I stood, I was able to catch a clear glimpse of her. Zoe was stunning in a bright red dress, her long dark curls sweeping more than halfway down her back. She'd always had radiant skin, the kind of woman who never needed to wear makeup, but tonight she was glowing. Sighing, I did my best to look away, cognizant that Francois was about to flank my side. His arrival made me tense even more.

He waited to say anything and when he did, his voice was hushed. "Amazing, isn't she? I know I'm her uncle, but that girl has talent."

"Yes. Her performance is incredible."

After swirling his drink in his hand, he chuckled from seeing what I held in my hand. "Roses. Nice touch. From you?" There was a slight admonishing tone in his voice, which wasn't unusual for the gruff man.

"Not my idea," I said through gritted teeth.

"Ahh. I should have guessed. Arman's. Daddy always comes through. He worries about Zoe far too much in my opinion. The girl is brilliant and savvy. She can handle herself in the big bad world." Francois was close with Arman, his true second in command and Capo, but I was closer in some aspects, the secrets and desires we'd shared over the years entirely different.

"You have a child prodigy yourself, Francois. One day she'll be old enough for you to worry about her future."

"Who says I don't worry about her now? You'll learn one day, my friend. As soon as you've discovered your wife has conceived, your entire world will change, nights of worry just part of the routine."

"I doubt I'll find anyone as special as what you and Arman have. That's fine by me."

"Never say never."

"If I hear that phrase again, I'm gonna puke."

He laughed. "Finding someone will do you some good. In my humble opinion."

"I doubt that."

"Said every man before the right woman came along. I know. Shut the hell up," Francois snorted. "Since you're here guarding the prodigal daughter fiercely, I'm grabbing another drink."

All I could do was nod. As with any crime syndicate, wives, lovers, and children were considered weaknesses, protection starting from day one. As I studied her from a distance, a tightness developed in my chest.

I was even more uncomfortable than before, memories of how I'd reacted at the airport sending a dull ache behind my eyes. I'd been gruff with her on purpose, something I wasn't proud of, but there'd been no other choice. Allowing her to think I was anything other than her protector was akin to a death sentence. There still wasn't any other choice but to keep her at arm's length, but this time it was my problem. When she'd refused to come home on more than one occasion, I'd had a feeling it had to do with my crass behavior. Fuck. Now that I had men working under me, I'd assign the duty of protecting her to someone else.

Somehow, I had to get her out of my system.

When Zoe finished the song as well as the requested concert, she slowly lowered her head, keeping her fingers on the keys. Only when she lifted her hands, placing them in her lap did the cheers and applause break out. As several guests rushed toward her as if she'd earned celebrity status, I noticed two men watching her from the other side of the room. The way they were looking at her brought a stab of anger to the forefront of my mind.

I powered down the remainder of my scotch, slamming the dense glass on one of the tables before pushing my way through the crowd. Right now, the goddamn roses were a hindrance. When one of the two men started to approach, I threw him a look. Given I stood taller than almost everyone else in the room, the mystery guest could easily see the anger riding my face.

He made the right choice to back off, but I had a feeling I hadn't seen the last of him. Arman's suggestion that he find a suitable husband for his daughter had shocked the fuck out of me. He'd told me on more than one occasion he'd never do that to her. The sudden change of heart should have been the first red flag. If I had to guess, I'd say he'd asked a few passable suitors to the party for her to meet.

My jaw was clenched, my anger turning into rage as I neared the piano.

"Thank you," she said more than once, the warm flush on her face a clear indication she wasn't comfortable with the amount of praise she was receiving. I took a deep breath, sidestepping the mayor and the man's wife, waiting as they congratulated her.

"That was incredible, my dear," Mrs. Kingsford said.

"There aren't enough adjectives to describe that performance, Zoe." Mayor Kingsford kissed Zoe's knuckles. The mayor was considered an ally, a man who'd been elected likely because of the sizeable contributions Arman and his family had made to the campaign.

"Thank you, sir. I really appreciate the compliment," Zoe said.

The moment I moved behind her, she immediately bristled, standing taller. I wasn't used to seeing her wear heels, the girl usually in jeans and sneakers. While I'd seen her during my week in New York, I hadn't gotten any closer than ten yards. Being this close was dangerous, enough so it would take every ounce of control I had to shut down the longing that lingered, even if it meant taking a sledgehammer to my head.

She remained stiff and as the Kingstons moved away, she slowly turned around to face me. There was defiance in her eyes, a hint of anger and hatred similar to what I'd seen seconds before she'd boarded the jet. The word stunning came to mind, her beauty and grace more distinguished than I'd captured before.

The moment was frozen in time, as if no one else was in the room. She didn't blink, didn't move a muscle, but the intense frown on her face told me she wasn't happy to see me at all. When she glanced at the flowers, I could tell she was bothered by the sight of them.

"If they're from you, I don't want them."

"They're from your father."

"Aw. Still his lackey I see. What's with the scratches on your face? Did you piss off some woman as you tend to do?"

Jesus. She'd come out swinging. I gave her a hard look, concentrating far too long on the way she dragged the tip of her tongue across her lower crimson-stained lip. It was obvious college had changed her. In my mind what she needed was to be taken over my lap for a brutal spanking. At least the thought dragged my mind out of the quicksand.

I kept any retort to myself, placing the bouquet on the piano. "Welcome home, Zoe. Congratulations on your successful graduation. I hope you enjoy your night."

With that, I walked away. Perhaps it would be easy to keep my distance after all.

CHAPTER 6

Zoe

How dare the man walk away from me! How dare he act as if I was nothing.

Seeing him again had made me crazy.

I fisted both hands, wanting nothing more than to go after him, issuing a hard crack of my hand across his face. His chiseled, strong jaw. His… His gorgeous face. I looked away, trying to swallow the lump in my throat. A part of me wanted to trash the roses, even if they were incredibly gorgeous. I'd been rude, something I almost never was, but the hurt remained after all this time.

Sadly, I wasn't certain what that said about me.

A few seconds later, I snagged the bouquet, bringing the two dozen gorgeous red roses to my nose. The fragrance was incredible. I rolled the tip of my finger along a petal then down to one of the stems. "Ouch."

A thorn had pricked my finger. Another wave of anger almost pushed me into tossing them across the room. As I brought the tip to my mouth, I watched him slowly walking toward the doorway of the music room. He'd changed in the years I'd been gone, even more muscular than before, filling out the dark suit in an insanely attractive way. A hint of gray at his temples had added to his debonair appearance, but his eyes remained haunted, dark and cold. The look of a true predator.

Even though he'd acted as if he couldn't care less about me, he remained in the doorway as if standing guard, scanning the perimeter as I'd seen him do hundreds of times. His muscular frame was filled with more tension than I'd ever seen, coiled as if waiting to strike at a moment's notice like the predator he was. The man acted as if he was a lion pacing his cage, ready to pounce on anyone who got in his way. Some people had no clue just how dangerous he was, but I did. I'd seen it in action more than once, admonishing him for his brutality.

Yes, he was insanely good at his job, his ability to protect as well as his strong sense of loyalty something that my father admired, their friendship lasting longer than any other Daddy had had. But to me, Maddox would remain nothing more than the hired help. It had to be that way.

Right. Tell yourself another lie.

Oh, girl. What are you doing? What are you thinking? This isn't high school and that man isn't going to give you a second thought.

How many times had I said that very same thing to myself? By now, it should be the only thing I accepted.

An ache had formed in my temple, one that threatened to make the rest of the evening miserable. I refused to allow it. This was my party and I planned on enjoying it to the fullest degree possible. Why was it that I couldn't take my eyes off him? Fury at myself lashed at my brain and my heart and I did my best to look away.

Everything about the man was insanely gorgeous. Tonight, he looked as if he'd walked directly off a *GQ Magazine* cover, rocking the sharp linen with gusto. Between his long, shaggy hair that covered his collar and the two- or three-day scruff adorning his strong jaw, I could have easily remained mesmerized by the first sight of him.

However, my resolve was intact. He continued to think of me as nothing but a little girl. I'd seen it in his eyes. Well, I'd find a way to show him what he was missing. That should do the trick to purge him from my system. As I turned to grab my almost empty glass of wine, I noticed two rather handsome young men studying me intently. It was obvious they were talking about me by the constant glances they were issuing. Hmmm... *There you go. Perfect.*

At least I could provide a sexy little show for Maddox. Maybe then he'd finally see me as a woman.

I offered a sly but sexy smile, flipping my hair over my shoulder before walking toward the door, forced to pass within inches of the man I'd coveted for far too long. Even his scent was alluring, far too provocative for a goddamn soldier. On purpose, I stopped short, giving the two fine-looking gentlemen another quick but seductive glance, dragging my tongue across my bottom lip in an exaggerated manner.

"Here. Put these in some water, will you, Maddox?" I asked, slapping the bouquet against his chest without bothering to look him in the eye. "I'm getting another drink. Oh, and next time you select flowers for a lady, make certain you rip out all the thorns or she just might use them on you." After holding up my bloodstained finger, I didn't give him time to object, heading away from him with a sway in my hips. I'd never been very good at walking in heels, my Converse sneakers more my style, but I did my best sashaying out of the room, heading for one of the many bars that had been set up.

The damn flowers reminded me of the ones I'd ignored in New York a few nights before my graduation. The guy had been drunk, the same dude I'd seen more than once during my six-month stint at the little jazz club I'd worked at. He'd been harmless, but after the ugliness of thinking I'd been followed, his gesture had been unwelcome.

By the time I made it to another room, I felt sick inside, hating the way I'd treated Maddox. I didn't bother looking behind me, fearful that I'd see his chastising face. What was I doing? It was a lost cause to begin with.

"That performance was insanely incredible," Edmee said as she rushed toward me. "I'm so glad you're home."

As my aunt threw her arms around me, I noticed Maddox had followed me into the library, obviously determined to keep an eye on me. I needed to get away from him or I was going to lose my mind. "Thank you. Just a few favorite selections I enjoy playing."

"The piece was so sad though, dark and dangerous. You should be happy, ecstatic that you're a free woman." She laughed, rolling her eyes.

"Are we ever truly free?" Dark and dangerous. Maybe I'd selected it with Maddox in mind.

"Maybe you're right, although you're far too young to be so philosophical," Edmee countered, laughing as her eyes twinkled. "I'm sorry Zane couldn't make it. He had to fly to Paris for business unexpectedly and is currently stuck in the airport."

"Oh, I'm sorry. Why don't I grab you a drink?"

She gave me a sly look and placed her hand on her stomach.

"You're pregnant?"

"I know. Can you believe it after all this time?"

I'd heard horror stories of the two lovebirds trying. Children. Something I was determined never to conceive. Why should I bother? They'd be subjected to scrutiny and protection their entire lives. "I'm so happy for you."

"Don't tell anyone. It's a surprise for Zane when he returns home."

I zipped my lips with two fingers before pulling her into another bear hug. "Everyone is happily married."

"Not everyone." She glanced at Maddox then back to me. She'd been the single person in my family I'd told about my wayward crush after she'd found a stupid love note I'd written him when I was much younger. Well, it was really just a valentine from one of those crazy packages meant for kids to dole out to their classmates, but I'd added some sparkly hearts that I'd taken time to draw. I'd chickened out giving it to him, which had allowed her to find it years later in one of my drawers. Why I'd kept it I wasn't certain, but she'd teased me relentlessly for months afterward. Now, with Raven suspecting, I'd need to keep my distance from the man for the long haul. God. How was I supposed to do that?

"Whatever. Maybe because he's such an asshole."

"Whoa. You know Maddox has a tough job following around after your father. Lighten up, girl. Life is too short. Have that drink."

"I think I will. Then I have a few sexy men to flirt with. Do you have any idea where Daddy is?"

"Not a clue. I'll see if I can find him for you."

"That would be cool." She squeezed my arm before walking away, her wink making me tingle almost as much as the moment I'd laid eyes on Maddox. I threw him another look then purposely turned toward the bar. "Another glass of merlot, please. And don't skimp on the size of the glass."

"Yes, ma'am."

As soon as the bartender slid the glass across the wooden surface, I wrapped my fingers around it, chugging a good half of the expensive wine. "Top it off if you don't mind." I threw a look over my shoulder, trying to curtail my aggravation that Maddox had obviously been told to follow me. I was a grown woman. I should be able to walk around freely in my own house. Damn him.

"Thank you again," I told the bartender before I walked away, trying to keep from saying something nasty to Maddox, which I knew wasn't fair.

Thankfully, the two fine-looking young men both walked in my direction.

"Well, hello there," I said. "And just who are you?"

"I'm Franklin and this is my friend Dante."

Dante was clearly either of Italian or Spanish descent, his chocolate eyes and raven hair more attractive up close. Or maybe it was the effects of the wine that allowed me to think of either one of them as cute. I pressed my hand against Dante's chest on purpose, unable to keep from throwing a look over his shoulder at Maddox. "Franklin and Dante. What are two fine-looking men doing at my party?"

"We were invited," Dante said in a sexy voice.

"Fabulous." When Maddox gave me a stern look, I took a deep breath. Perhaps it wasn't a good idea to cause a scene. That would be disrespectful to my father and to Raven. I could hate Maddox all I wanted but this was my father's house. "Maybe I'll see you around, boys. Thank you for coming." I sensed Maddox's anger, his clenched jaw a clear indication.

I wanted to laugh in his face, but I had to admit that I was slightly ashamed of my behavior. Instead of following through with telling me I was a bad girl, he turned around and walked out of the room. So much for making him feel jealous. I wasn't certain what the hell I was doing.

"You play beautifully," Dante said, lifting his glass and giving me a nod.

"Thank you very much. A true passion of mine."

"Passion. We understand the concept well," Franklin said under his breath, a slight growl making the moment uncomfortable. They glanced at each other and I had the distinct feeling they'd shared a woman before. Oh, no. That wasn't the kind of girl I was at all.

"I'm certain you boys have passions of your own." I glanced toward the door, butterflies continuing to swarm into my stomach. I felt a moment of disappointment bridging on despair when I didn't see Maddox's larger than life frame in the doorway.

"Oh, we do, princess. Don't we, Franklin?" Dante said, his tone even darker than before.

"Absolutely, including requiring beautiful women to surrender to our needs." Franklin laughed, as if this was nothing more than a game.

That's the moment I became incensed. My anger reared its ugly head, and it had nothing to do with wine. I hated men who believed women should kowtow to them, surrendering in any manner. "First of all, I'm no one's princess, nor will I ever surrender to a single man. Second, the two of you are rude. Have an enjoyable evening."

When I started to walk away, Dante had the nerve to grab my arm.

"Where do you think you're going, princess? You only leave when I tell you to leave."

I snapped my head in his direction, glaring into the man's eyes. Why did he seem familiar all of a sudden? "Take your hands off me." I tried to keep from making a scene but as his fingers dug into my skin painfully, I hissed, ready to launch into a battle if necessary.

Instead, he inched closer. "Not until I decide to do so."

A strange tingling sensation rushed through me, a jolt of current that could only be caused by one thing. Maddox.

"The lady said to get your hands off her. I suggest you do so." Maddox was glaring at the man with so much hatred that I was swooning. He stood at least six inches taller than the two boys, the anger in his eyes sparking more than just my full attention. If I didn't know better, I'd say a jealous streak ran through him.

"Get lost, fuckhead," Dante made the mistake of saying, stupid enough to turn his back on the powerful man.

I'd seen Maddox smashing a man's face before when he'd dared try to abduct me years before. I knew exactly when he reached the breaking point, his eyes darkening and his nostrils flaring. Very few people understood that underneath his sophisticated attire and boyish grin was a man possessed, one full of rage when necessary.

Maddox wrapped his hand around the back of Dante's neck, digging his fingers in and tossing the asshole as if he was a ragdoll. As Dante's body was slammed against the wall, the man slowly sliding to the floor, Franklin remained in shock, his eyes opening wide and his mouth hanging open.

I almost retorted he should be careful not to suck down a fly but held my tongue, curious as to how far Maddox would go.

The moment Maddox turned toward him, he threw up his hands, tossing half his drink onto the floor.

"I suggest you get the fuck out of this house without any delay, or I'll do much worse," Maddox said in his commanding voice, barking like a dog when Franklin remained in shock.

Unfortunately for Dante, he made a huge mistake by struggling to his feet, daring to pull out a weapon from his pocket.

"Look out!" I screamed.

As I'd seen dozens of times, Maddox's reflexes were quick. He turned abruptly, snapping his fingers around Dante's wrist, bending it to the point I could swear I heard bones snapping. As he issued two brutal punches to the asshole's face, there was no doubt Maddox had crushed his nose.

Dante howled and Franklin all but ran out of the room. Within seconds, two of my father's soldiers rushed into the room.

Maddox stood over Dante, shaking his head. "Get the fuckers out of here," he snarled, issuing a command to the soldiers.

"You got it. Happy to," one of the soldiers said.

"You son of a bitch. You broke my nose," Dante huffed as one of the soldiers jerked him to his feet. He yanked his arm away, giving me then Maddox a nasty look. "This isn't over."

"Like hell it's not," Maddox snarled. He remained turned in the opposite direction, following the trail as the soldiers grabbed Dante by both arms, dragging him out of the room. When he turned toward me, his chest was still heaving from rage, not from exertion. With a single long stride, he closed the distance, lifting my chin with a single finger. "Are you hurt, Zoe? Did those fuckers injure you in any way?"

"No. I'm fine." I was still stuck in a fog, longing to find the right words to thank him.

The moment was captured in time, frozen as if we had no clue what to say to each other. I couldn't help myself, dragging my gaze down from his face, swallowing hard as I fought the desire spinning like a tornado all throughout my system.

He rubbed my cheek and the feeling and warmth was entirely different. He'd rarely touched me, had done everything in his power to keep his distance. I couldn't help tingling from excitement, fighting the nerves and uncertainty.

"I could have killed that bastard," he said in a gruff voice.

"You're not a killer, at least not really."

"If you think that then you really don't know me."

"I know enough." *I want to learn much more.* I dared not say that to him. The sweet moment lingered, his touch becoming more heated than it had been before.

When he took a deep breath, the beautiful spell was broken, the rugged man pulling his hand away as the mask was shoved back in position.

"Go enjoy the party, sweetheart. I'll handle the fuckers. My way." Now there was a sharp edge to his voice, his chest rising and falling from continued anger.

Nodding, I started to walk away then without thinking about it, I pressed both hands against his chest, rising onto my tiptoes and kissing his cheek. When I pulled away, he turned his head and our lips brushed together. I was caught in the moment, unable to move. He instantly tensed just like he'd done years before and I took two purposeful steps back, trying to break the mesmerizing hold. "Thank you." As I walked out, I refused to look at him again.

But dear God, I hungered for him, the longing leaving me aching inside. I had a chance to tell him how I felt, doing what I could to help him see that I was a woman now, but I'd chickened out.

Some defiant, brave girl I was.

Stupid. Stupid.

I headed away from the room, needing some air and time to myself. There was only one place that I could achieve both, as well as a little peace. I moved toward the kitchen, easily able to make my way to the back corridor leading to the laundry room and the exit toward the garden. There was so much activity that no one paid any attention as I slipped through, opening the door and disappearing outside into the darkness.

The light breeze allowed scents of night-blooming jasmine and other flowers to tickle my nose, the twinkling lights in the trees providing enough light to make my way to the cobblestone path. My favorite place in the entire world was the greenhouse that I'd heard my mother had adored as well. There was something so special about seeing flowers grow from seeds or tiny plants to the point they were almost taking over every shelf, adding color and warmth to the typically austere environment.

I glanced over my shoulder before moving inside, softly closing the door behind me. There was no need to turn on the light. I preferred the natural glow provided by the full moon, the shadows the darkness provided allowing me to hide like I used to so many years before. "How are all the beautiful plants today?" I asked, as I used to do as when I was younger. I milled through the aisles, touching one then the other. I'd learned about plants, enjoying digging my fingers in potting soil and dirt for as long as I could remember. My father used to tease me about appreciating mud pies, whatever that meant.

They were good times, simple times. The memories had followed me to college. I'd been so eager to forge my own way, I'd almost forgotten how much I loved this place, the beauty and tranquility offering me solace. I turned in a full circle, trying to figure out why everything seemed so difficult lately, including making choices for my future. After a few minutes, I finally sat down on the small bench my father had built for the younger version of me. It creaked from age, but it was as comfortable as I remembered. The corner setting was my favorite place to hide since it was located in the back of the greenhouse, hidden by the tropical plants and flowers.

Maybe I hadn't chosen my career because in truth, I'd always wanted to work in my family's business, continuing on with the legacy started generations before. My father had forbidden me, as if by being a woman, I was too fragile. I knew he wanted to protect me, but I was quite capable of handling whatever was tossed in my direction. Some moments of my life brought far too many memories, fear of the unknown regarding my future always present.

I wasn't certain how much time had passed but almost as soon as I closed my eyes, I sensed a presence and jerked to a standing position. The slight creak of the greenhouse door wasn't something I'd imagined, the closure a noise I recognized. Since I couldn't make out the entrance from where I stood, the hair on the back of my neck stood up on end.

The place was much closer to the outskirts of the estate property, the road leading into the city of New Orleans just behind us. My father had always warned me not to come out here at night. Even though he'd installed cameras, there was a thick forest surrounding a good portion of the estate, allowing for the ability to remain hidden while easily firing off a weapon. Fear skittered down my spine and I was resistant to call out, terrified that Dante or the other asshole had found me, making good on his ugly threat.

Swallowing hard, I noticed a few tools in a rack only a few feet away. I moved quickly and silently, grabbing a long spade with my shaking fingers. As I crept forward, I held it with both hands, prepared to strike if necessary. I moved down one of the aisles, trying to step quietly across the gravel path. I heard nothing else, but I knew someone was there. Hiding. Waiting.

Ready to pounce.

I rounded a corner and the second I noticed someone in the shadows with a gun in his hand, I swung the implement, cracking the asshole directly in the center of his back. Down the fucker went, the gun flying out of his hand. I leapt over him, trying to get away before he had a chance to regroup but he was too quick for me, snagging my ankle, bringing me to my knees. The spade flew out of my hands, and I watched as if in slow motion as it turned three times before tumbling to the earth.

Yelping, I fought to get out of his hold, kicking and connecting with my other foot.

He easily flipped me over, pressing the full weight of his body against mine, yanking my arms over my head. "Stop fighting me, Zoe."

His deep baritone was recognizable anywhere, the sound floating over me like a warm blanket on a cold winter's night. I was lost in the moment, the trickle of moonlight allowing me to see the darkness in his eyes. But this time there was more than concern or anger in them. There was lust, complex and unbridled lust.

I took gasping breaths, my throat tightening as I stared up at him. Maybe I believed in fantasies or possibly a little bit of magic. Or maybe I was a little bit cuckoo. Whatever the case, the feel of his chiseled body, his rock-hard cock throbbing from the same intense electrified desire coursing through me left nothing to the imagination.

He could no longer deny the way he felt about me.

I'd never experienced that moment when all time stood still, the very second where the world ceased to exist around me.

Until now.

And in those few beautiful seconds, I was no longer the daughter of his best friend, the young girl he'd been sworn to protect, I was a woman in his eyes.

Then the unthinkable happened, the one beautiful moment that I'd longed to experience for so many years.

He crushed his mouth over mine.

CHAPTER 7

Zoe

I'd been kissed before by boys over the years, but the passion Maddox exuded, the masterful way in which he managed to snag both my wrists in one hand while cupping my jaw with the other left me tingling all over. My pussy throbbed, so much so I sensed the increasing dampness between my legs. My nipples were hard as tiny pebbles, pressing into my dress, which was clinging to his suit jacket.

Maybe I'd fantasized about him too many times, but this was one of those cases where reality was much better than the fantasy. His actions left me breathless, the way he swept his tongue back and forth, dominating mine leaving me in a state of shock.

And the taste of him was spectacular, the combination of scotch and cinnamon teasing every nerve ending, my throat parched for more. I wiggled under him, maneuvering one leg free so I could press my bent knee against his thigh. The intimate moment took on a surreal set of sensations, and I prayed the few seconds of passion would turn into something else entirely. Even the way he was digging his long fingers into my cheek was exciting, allowing me to envision us in the throes of a wicked tryst.

There was nothing more I wanted than to have his naked body pressed against mine, to bask in the heat of our needs while we surrendered to our desires.

When he suddenly broke the kiss, I couldn't keep from whimpering, darting my eyes back and forth across his as I struggled to arch my back.

He released his hold on my wrists, the powerful man taking deep, gasping breaths. I was certain he would come to his senses, admonishing me for temping him. When he eased onto his knees, I was certain of it. I remained stunned, unable to blink or even breathe. When he yanked off his jacket, pitching it aside, I was floored.

"You ran away. You knew better than to do that."

"I needed some space, a little air."

A slight growl erupted from deep in his chest, his look as admonishing as I knew it would be. "You know better than to try and get away from me." When he pointed his index finger at me, I sensed the desire coursing through him was at a point of becoming uncontrollable, the electricity we shared crackling like live wires dancing in a thunderstorm.

That left me breathless, incapable of thinking clearly.

"How did you find me?" I managed, shivering to my very core.

"You think I don't know you, Zoe? You really believe that after all these years I have no clue about the woman inside? This is your hiding spot, the place you always went to when you were upset. I used to stand outside watching you, ensuring your safety."

"You did? I didn't think anyone knew."

Huffing, he eyed me carefully, as if uncertain what he wanted do. When he rubbed his knuckles across my cheek, an audible moan escaped my mouth. "I know everything about you. Every. Single. Detail."

Oh, my God. Talk about fantasies coming true. "You still think I'm a little girl?"

He half laughed. "You're a woman, alright. A dangerous, beautiful, forbidden woman," he muttered, the tone so low and husky that I had to strain to hear what he was saying. Lowering down, he opened his hand, brushing the tips of his fingers down my face to my neck, his chest rising and falling as he agonized over the moment. He had no idea what he was doing to me, the tingling sensations that clouded everything else.

"Damn it. This is wrong," he said, starting to pull away. I grabbed his hand, pulling myself up by a few inches.

"Why? I've wanted this for years."

"Don't say that. I'm all wrong for you, Zoe, and it's not just about the fact I'm your father's best friend."

"Maddox. Please. No one needs to know." There. I'd said it. I'd finally found the courage to break free of the protective shell.

The expression on his face darkened even more. I was certain the man was going to ravage me. And that's exactly what I'd hoped for. He continued to hesitate, his wheels spinning. Then I had a feeling there was no going back, the line we'd crossed dangerous yet one we'd both wanted. I was light as a feather, giddy and so into the man that I was certain nothing could ever break us apart.

Yet the moment he yanked down the thin straps of my dress, exposing my breasts, I was in a complete state of shock. He was brutal in his actions, as if there wouldn't be any chance of saying no.

As if I could do that.

"I'm going to destroy you," he said with a dangerous tone wrapped around his voice.

"Then do it."

"Help me, God. For I'm about to sin."

I pressed my hands against his shirt, taking shallow breaths as I stared up at him. As soon as I wrapped my fingers around his shirt, clutching as if my life depended on it, he issued a rugged growl and dipped his head, cupping both my breasts. Every touch was rough, a wash of pain gripping my muscles as he pinched both fully aroused buds.

"Oh. Oh, yes." I no longer recognized my voice.

"Perfect."

I arched my back even more, mewing as he wrapped his wet lips around my nipple.

"Oh, God." Nothing could have prepared me for the heat of his breath or the scintillating rush of emotions and dazzling sensations coursing through me like a raging storm.

Moaning, I fought with his shirt, ripping it from his trousers, struggling to reach his cock. The moment I was able to slide my fingers across the thick bulge, I was thrown into a powerful rush of adrenaline. Every sound he made fueled the fire between us, the man turning into a crazed animal as he sucked and nipped my tender tissue. I was crazed with need, longing to feel the heat of our bodies pressed together.

Stars in the brightest colors floated in front of my eyes as the rush of excitement turned into an almost desperate need we both shared. I was crazed with longing, managing to slide my hand under his shirt. The single touch of his skin seared the tips of my aching fingers. We tore at each other's clothes, and I was certain I'd popped a button on his shirt. What did I care?

He was so authoritative when he wrapped a finger around the edge of my thong, snapping his wrist forcefully. His grin was almost entirely evil, but I loved his sudden recklessness, the barbaric state he was in, something the organized and controlled man had never allowed me to see. After shoving my nicest pair of red lace panties into his trousers, he shook his head.

"You are a bad little girl."

Experiencing his playful side was also entirely different. I'd once told him to get the stick out of his ass. It had been my sweet eighteenth birthday party and I'd been showing off for friends, finding an open bottle of liquor. By that point, the four of us were headed to a long, drunken night and visits to the toilet. He'd yanked the bottle from my hand, glaring at me before muttering something about turning me over his knee and spanking me. According to him, that's exactly what had been missing in my life.

"Do you remember my eighteenth birthday?" I asked out of the blue.

He narrowed his engaging eyes for a few seconds before lifting a single eyebrow. "How could I forget? I had to pump coffee into you so your father wouldn't find out you'd been drinking. You called me every horrible name you could think of. Come to think of it, your girlfriends did as well."

"Oops."

"Uh-huh. I still owe you a spanking for that ugly behavior."

I laughed, the sound happier than I could remember in a long time. "See. You wouldn't dare since I'm all grown up."

Maddox moved to my other nipple, flicking his tongue back and forth before biting down. "Careful, little girl. You're not in charge. And daring me isn't in your best interest."

Why did his possessive words thrill me as much as they did? "Oh, yeah? You won't touch me."

Maybe a huge part of me had wanted him to spank me that night, to treat me like a bad little girl. As he pulled away, sitting on the rocky floor, I almost started to laugh. But the second he grabbed my arm, yanking me over his lap, I was torn by the rush of desire and shock. He jerked my dress up to my waist, exposing my bottom. I was stuck in the haze of shock, whimpering like I was a small child.

He didn't hesitate to make good on his promise, bringing his hand down in rapid succession. Holy crap. I was shocked how much it hurt, and he was only using his hand.

If I remembered correctly, he'd threatened the use of his belt all those years go. Okay, so my behavior had been completely reckless and he'd managed to keep me from facing my father's wrath, but it was the night I'd told him I hated him with all my heart. Meanwhile, the truth was it had been the first moment I'd embraced the crush I had.

Especially after my girlfriends had all but thrown themselves at him. When he hadn't responded, only speaking to them gruffly, all three of them had been convinced he was gay. What bullshit.

When he brought his palm down repeatedly, I wiggled in his lap, humping the thick bulge between his legs. The insanity of what he was doing kept me in a state of awe, the pain turning into pure agony.

"You'll need to learn that rules are important," he said gruffly, although there was amusement in his voice.

"I play by my own rules."

He chuckled as he'd done before, the sound adding another series of chills. "You'll learn. I'm just the man to teach you."

I closed my eyes, involuntarily throwing back my arm, pressing the back of my hand across my aching bottom. The heat had already built, the sting something I knew would remain all night long. And dear God, I was so wet, my pussy throbbing. I had a feeling his trousers would carry the burden of my longing for at least a couple of hours. It served him right for spanking me.

He grabbed my arm, pressing and holding it against the small of my back. "None of that or I will give you the spanking I promised you on that adventurous birthday."

Why was it that his words excited me as much as they did? I shuddered as the spanking continued, yet the agony had already started to morph into something else entirely.

It was almost as if I was enjoying the heated round of discipline. Still, I bucked against him, pushing my other hand into the dirt, even digging my nails into the surface.

"Take your punishment like a good girl."

"Oh, I'll get you for this."

His throaty laugh became a strange reward, but the real treat was the fact the man was letting go. When he caressed my aching skin, I sensed his desire was getting out of control, his breathing more ragged than before. "I think you've had enough."

Sweet Jesus, I didn't recognize the sound of his voice. The moment he let go of my arm, I scrambled off his lap, pretending as if I was going to try to run away from him. He didn't hesitate, snapping his fingers around my leg. Not only did he yank me back by several feet, he turned me over, straddling my hips.

"You're not going anywhere until I tell you that you are."

It had been the gruffness to his tone that night years before that had gotten to the other girls. Just like it was doing to me tonight. He stared down at me as if I was sizzling meat on a silver platter, ready to be feasted on by the brutal man. As he lowered his body down the way he'd done before, I pressed my hand against his chest.

"Oh. Yes…" I laughed from nervousness, kneading his insanely perfect abdomen as I fought to free his cock. Suddenly, he grasped my hands again, shoving them against the dirt, his breathing more labored than before.

There was a sudden primal urge surging between us, a need that couldn't be denied. As he rose onto his knees, I sat up, grasping his belt.

As his brow furrowed, his chest rising and falling, a heated smile crossed his face as I fumbled to try to free his cock. I was panting and moaning at the same time, darting my eyes into his face.

The moment he grabbed my dress, ripping it over my head, I'd never felt so naughty in my life and I loved every second of it. I scrambled to my knees, finally managing to unfasten his belt, ripping at the button and zipper of his trousers. Every action became more frantic, as if we were both making up for lost time.

He cupped both sides of my face, growling again as he dropped his head, capturing my mouth as he'd done before. This time, our tongues dueled, but he refused to allow me to have any control. I was on fire, incapable of thinking clearly, nor did I want to.

The kiss was even more passionate than before, pushing me into heated bliss as he raked one hand over my shoulder, running the rough pads of his fingers down my spine. When he broke the kiss, he kept his lips close, his whisper dancing across my skin.

"This shouldn't happen."

"I know."

"But I will have you," he muttered, nipping first my lower lip then my chin, raking his tongue from one side of my jaw to the other. "So fucking beautiful. All mine. Always mine. No one else will ever touch you again."

His sentiment stunned me even more than his actions, my heart racing from hearing his possessive words.

Tickling vibrations coursed through me as I freed his cock, shuddering the moment I managed to wrap my hand around the base. He was thick and hard, so large that I was filled with glee. Everything about that moment left me breathless, a nervous laugh bubbling past my lips. The way he rolled his hand under my buttocks created another lingering wave of wetness between my legs, my pulse racing.

I pumped his shaft, rolling my hand up and down, creating friction. My mouth watered to taste him. He moaned the entire time, every muscle tensed. When he ripped his shirt over his head, I gasped from the sight of him. I'd seen him without a shirt before, but he was even more magnificent, his muscles carved as if out of the finest stone.

"You are... Oh, my." I knew I wasn't making any sense, but it didn't seem to matter. He grinned, his eyes flashing in the stream of moonlight.

"You could have killed me."

"I thought you were Dante."

He laughed, the sound dark and ominous. "He will never have a chance to touch you ever again."

I shuddered from the thought of what could have been done to him. There was no way I was going to ask, but I had a feeling if Dante remained alive, he would never forget his encounter with Maddox.

"No more talking," he commanded, pushing me down once again. He pulled one leg around his hips then the other, his body shaking as he stared down at me. Without hesitation, he placed the tip of his cock against my swollen folds. The moment he thrust the entire length inside, I issued a sharp cry, the sensations tearing through me dazzling.

"Oh. Oh. Oh." I'd never thought I'd be able to experience something so incredible, the feel of having him buried deep inside a dream come true. I was quivering all over, the anticipation and fantasy not nearly as good as the real thing. My pussy muscles stretched to try to accommodate him, the ache even more intense, the lust I felt turning me into a wild animal.

It was the same for him, the man throwing back his head with a possessive roar. I squeezed my thighs against him, the weight of his body so sensual. So protective. I remained lightheaded, excitement and need building to a precipice. As he slowly lowered his head, I was struck by how incredibly handsome he was, as if I was seeing him for the first time.

I rolled my hands over his shoulders, tingling the entire time from being able to touch him. I hadn't realized how many scars he had, the roughness of his skin telling me a story, one that I wasn't certain I wanted to hear. How many times had the brutal, amazing man jumped in to save a member of my family? In how many ways had he risked his life? I was so thrown by the series of emotions that I wasn't certain anything would ever be the same again.

He pulled almost all the way out, the look on his face turning more carnal, highlighting his true predatory nature. "Baby. You are so damn hot. I want to fuck every hole, take everything that belongs to me."

There was no way he had any idea what his filthy words did to me, the scintillating vibrations that refused to stop.

The way he yanked my arms over my head, intertwining our fingers together was special, as if the electricity we shared, the connection we'd built through the years was strengthening.

It was another beautiful moment where all time stopped. There were no sounds but those of our rapidly beating hearts, mine echoing in my ears. He used his hold on my hands to push up from the rocky surface, studying me intently as he fucked me. I'd always believed Maddox to be devoid of most emotions, as if the acts he'd been required to commit over the years had changed him.

I wasn't a fool. I'd learned early on about who and what my father really was, Maddox performing some of the most heinous deeds, but the emotion I saw in the man could rival any woman.

Including me.

I remained unblinking, digging my nails into his skin as the sensations dancing through me became overwhelming. Within seconds, my body was reacting entirely different than any other rush of excitement I'd felt.

As he lowered his head, pressing his lips against my cheek and ear, his heated words and breathless whisper could easily push me into a trance.

"Come for me, my little lamb."

His little lamb. The term was something he'd used so many years before. There was something cathartic about him using it at this moment. Or maybe it was a reminder of how forbidden our breathless moment in time truly was.

When I said nothing, his nostrils flared. "You will learn to obey me. Come for me. Now."

Everything about his change in behavior was startling, his obsessive need something I thought only dreams were made of. And the strangest thing of all was that I wanted to obey him. The thought was crazy, so much so that the moment my toes started to cramp, actual shock tore through me. The orgasm soaring through me arrived so quickly and with so much force that it could be considered violent.

I was thrown by the lights dancing in front of my periphery of vision, the fact that my mouth was open in a perfect O but there was no sound. None. It was as if I'd floated into an alternate universe, incapable of speaking, remaining in suspended animation.

And nothing had every felt so exquisite in my life.

Maddox pumped deep inside, his actions becoming more savage.

Finally, it was as if the dam had broken, another raw and intense moment of rapture cutting through me like a razor-sharp knife. I could feel my blood pressure rising, my pulse skipping several beats and in the next few seconds, I was completely lost in the blissful feeling of rapture.

"Oh. Yes. Yes. Yes…"

"My beautiful baby. My little lamb."

As his words filtered into my eardrums, I sensed he was close to releasing, every muscle in his powerful body tensing. Every action became rougher, his entire face shimmering in the moonlight as beads of sweat dripped from his brow to mine. His scent was incredible, woodsy with a hint of dark spice, and I prayed it lingered, staining my skin.

Maybe I was a silly girl, but I didn't want to take a shower, remaining with his seed filling my womb.

A series of growls cascaded from his throat seconds before he erupted deep inside.

I never believed this would happen.

I'd done everything I could to stop imagining it.

I'd wanted so badly to hate him for the way he'd treated me.

For the most part, I'd been successful.

Until he'd walked into that room with roses in his hands. Then all had been lost. But now, as he lifted his head, the light that had burned so brightly only seconds before dimmed. He'd all but shut down and shut me out.

I didn't need for him to tell me this could never happen again. I knew it in my heart and soul.

And that was the most crushing feeling I'd ever experienced.

As soon as he opened his mouth to speak, I placed my fingers across his lips. "Don't ruin it. Please. That's all I ask."

Before he had a chance to respond, a sickening feeling, a gut instinct ripped at my mind. The moment I opened my eyes wide, he sensed something was wrong.

Then all hell broke loose as the sound of gunfire shattered the magical spell.

CHAPTER 8

Maddox

What the fuck?

Pop! Pop! Pop! Pop!

The gunfire was rapid and while the sound wasn't close to the greenhouse, I immediately pulled Zoe further into the shadows, covering her with my body. Fuck me. While I'd been losing my mind, engaging in carnal activities with the one woman that wasn't allowed in my life, the entire world of the Thibodeaux family had just been thrust into chaos. From what I could tell, there had to be at least four gunmen, but my guess was that there were more. Shit. My thoughts drifted to the little prick who'd attacked Zoe.

If I had to guess, I'd say the Italian and his buddy had been used as decoys.

Or perhaps worse.

There was no chance Arman had invited the little pricks.

I shoved my cock into my trousers, disgusted with myself for losing control.

"Stay calm and stay down," I instructed in a hushed whisper.

"Oh, my God," Zoe moaned. I pressed my finger against her lips, sensing movement outside. She understood what I was trying to tell her, nodding once. "Who would do this?"

The answer wasn't one I was ready to think about just yet. Whatever Arman had found himself in the middle of likely had something to do with the surprise attack. The question was why? "Just stay right there." Scrambling to my feet, I kept low to the ground, scanning the glass for any sign of activity.

Seeing none, I moved toward the door, glancing through the frosted panes. When I noticed no movement of any kind, I headed back to her, dropping down and raking my hand through my hair. "Are you okay?"

She nodded, her body still shaking. She'd sat up, doing her best to reach for her dress while covering her breasts. Her eyes highlighted terror, which added to the rage that continued to build.

My gut had told me that Dante and his sick buddy had been nothing more than sentries, but I'd yet to be able to ask Arman if they'd been invited to the party. It wasn't like invitations were being checked at the door, which was something I'd advised.

Arman had refused, as if the sentiment was repulsive. Maybe he'd learned to listen to me after this.

"What's happening, Maddox?" Zoe asked, shivering underneath me, her fingertips digging into my forearms. "Who's shooting?"

"I don't fucking know, but you need to listen to me, sweetheart. Get dressed. Stay out of the light and whatever the fuck you do, you will not leave this safe zone. Do you hear what I'm saying?" I'd never felt so out of control in my life. It wasn't a good place to be, my absence one reason the assassins had managed to get past our security. Rage rolled through me, the kind that would lead to bloodshed and violence. I needed to rein in my emotions, or I'd lose all sense of control.

She was staring toward the glass, her lower lip quivering. When she said nothing, I was forced to grip her chin, tugging her face toward me.

"Listen. To. Me. I need to hear you say you'll stay right here." The girl had always had an issue following rules, but this time it could get her killed.

"What? My family. Everyone is inside. My little brother. You need to make certain they're safe. You have to, Maddox. Please." She clung to me, almost becoming hysterical. While she and other members of the family had been taught how to handle a crisis of this nature, it was entirely different when facing it for real. "Please. Please!"

"Calm down, little lamb. I *am* going to fix this. I promise." I backed away, grabbing her dress and tossing it in her direction. "But you will fucking follow my rules, Zoe. Do you hear me? Right now, I'm your only lifeline."

The best she could do was nod, her eyes darting back and forth. I sensed there were things we both wanted to say but now wasn't the time or place.

I rose to my feet, yanking my shirt from the floor and struggling to get into it. Shit. Where the hell had my weapon gone?

She nodded, still shaking as she crawled to her knees, fighting the material as she slipped it over her head. "Please be safe, Maddox. I can't lose you."

"Go to the back of the greenhouse and stay. No matter what you hear, remain in hiding. Okay? I promise I'll come back for you." Lose me. Her words cut into me like a rusty knife.

"Okay. Please don't forget your promise. My family is important."

"Remember your training. It might keep you alive."

"I remember. You taught me what to do." She tried to act resilient, but I could smell her fear. Hell, I didn't blame her.

For all the bravado the beautiful girl always tried to show, the attitude that I'd known had been a cover for missing her mother and growing up with guarded friends terrified of her father, she seemed exactly like the little lamb I'd called her.

The sentiment pulled at everything inside of me. I was a bad man for what I'd just done, taking advantage of the situation. But the moment I'd seen that fucking son of a bitch pawing her as if she belonged to him, something had broken inside of me, shattering my last resolve.

I'd craved something that I couldn't have more than I'd wanted to breathe. Now people would die for my ridiculous choice. I felt it in my gut.

I found my weapon, prepared to leave the greenhouse when she lunged for me, wrapping her arms around me.

"I'm afraid. I'm terrified."

Her admittance just about broke me all over again. A part of me wanted to tell her that she should be, but being as asshole right now was about the worst thing I could do. Besides, I wanted nothing more than to protect her, to lock her away so no one could ever hurt her. I gripped her chin, peering down at her, the hunger yet to abate. "You're going to be fine. I will return. You have my promise of that as well."

"Don't make promises you can't keep."

I grinned on purpose before snatching my jacket from the floor, placing it around her shoulders then standing. "I don't intend to. Don't underestimate me. Now, go hide in the shadows."

Zoe was slow to respond but finally scampered away, but not before stopping and throwing a look over her shoulder. It was too dark to see her expression, but I didn't need to. She was as concerned as I was.

I moved to the door, listening for any sounds as I opened it, carefully going outside. Almost as soon as I managed to take a couple of steps, another round of gunfire tore into the night sky, screams following. I took off running toward the house. Within seconds, I noticed one of the gunmen. He wore dark clothes and a ski mask, but the fucker had tripped the motion sensor lights outside, drawing my attention. Now he was a perfect target, and I took advantage, firing off a single shot.

As usual, my marksmanship was on the money, the long-range hit gunning him down with a bullet between the eyes. I raced toward him, determined to gather any information. After reaching him I dropped to my knees, yanking off the mask. I'd suspected there would be no instant identification, but it still pissed me off. I patted the son of a bitch down, finding nothing on him except for another magazine of ammunition.

I scanned the perimeter. Whoever had sent the brigade of assassins had balls. After confiscating his weapon and additional magazine, I lunged forward, trying to remain as silent as possible.

When a shadow suddenly appeared from my right, I dropped and rolled, about to fire off another round when Francois staggered toward me. Jesus fucking Christ. He'd been hit, blood covering seeping through his crisp white shirt.

"Francois," I growled, keeping low to the ground as I headed toward him. He dropped to his knees, taking gasping breaths, pressing his hand against his injury.

"Just a shoulder wound," he insisted, but his breathing remained ragged.

"What the hell happened?"

Francois glanced over my shoulder, wiping his face with his bloody hand. "I don't know. I heard gunfire then there were several screams. Suddenly, there were two masked men in the house. I managed to shoot one of them, but my lieutenant is down, at least two guests. Everybody panicked at that point."

"Where the hell are the women?"

"Tony has the girls and little Gabe. He's taking them to the safehouse. Arman disappeared."

Fuck. "Any idea how many gunmen?"

"At least ten, maybe more. They just came out of nowhere. It was a coordinated attack, disguised by the party. Where's Zoe?"

"She's safe, in hiding. Get back to the house," I instructed. "See if you can find Arman. I'm going to handle these fuckers."

"Don't get yourself killed."

Another flash caught my eye and both Francois and I snapped our weapons toward the intruder, firing indiscriminately. "This ain't a good day to die, buddy," I told him.

He laughed, struggling to get to his feet. "You got that right."

I stayed low to the ground as I headed to the side of the house, keeping both hands wrapped around my weapon. I could still see the greenhouse and I remained unnerved. As I rounded the corner, I could tell guests were rushing out, hysteria settling in. I took off running, forced to drop and roll as another gunman came out of nowhere.

Pop! Pop!

The masked man was down in a second. I didn't waste any additional time trying to secure an ID. That wasn't going to happen at this point in time. I moved to the house, noticing Landry as he sprinted around from the other side. He had a gash on his forehead, likely from a weapon.

"What the hell?

"A car pulled up and before I knew what was happening, four men jumped out, ambushing me. I blacked out for a couple minutes," Landry said, still panting. "What the hell is going on?"

More guests were piling out of the house, the commotion getting ridiculous. "That's the question of the goddamn day. We need to take them out."

"Look. I think they were searching for something in particular," Landry added.

"Why do you say that?"

"Because before I blacked out, I heard one of them say find her. Her? Who the fuck are they talking about?"

Her. My instinct shifted into overtime. "I have a feeling it's Zoe. Get in the house. Get all these people out of here. Secure the house."

"Where the hell are you going?"

"To protect the person they came for." Taking Arman's daughter would be a surefire method of damning the entire family. I bolted back the way I'd come from, sprinting toward the greenhouse. I came within twenty yards when I heard her high-pitched scream.

No. No. No!

I was running as fast as possible, gasping for air as the anger ravaged my system. The second I rounded the corner of the garden building I could see her struggling with her captor. While she was in imminent danger, the direction they were taking her led through the woods toward the street backing up to the edge of Arman's property. There were two of them. I tried to remain quiet as I approached, realizing that I had about two minutes before things would get dicey. I jerked out the weapon from the dead assassin, using the fact I was ambidextrous to my benefit.

"Let her go and maybe you get to live," I commanded, pointing the guns at each masked man.

As expected, the jerk holding her spun around, pressing the barrel of his gun against her forehead. She hissed, her eyes darting back and forth as she struggled with the arm that had been placed around her neck.

The one thing I had to count on was that Zoe had been trained. She knew how to deal with a situation like this. I'd taught her subtle hand and facial commands, which would need to come in handy.

"I don't think so." The man's voice had no accent. As with the other assholes I'd dropped, there were no discernable features. They were just hired guns sent to disrupt the party and create chaos. If they'd wanted to kill anyone, including Francois, they'd be dead. The intent had been all about capturing Zoe.

"Nice subterfuge," I said as I walked closer.

The second asshole tried to take a step away, as if I'd allow him to get the drop on me. That's the moment things were about to get dicey. I made a hand sign with the weapon in my hand, grinning as I kept my eyes locked on Zoe.

My concentration was spot on as I leveled the weapon in my left hand at guy number two, issuing a loud bellow as Zoe stomped on the assailant's foot using everything she had. It was just enough to break the man's hold. She threw her elbow into his stomach for good measure before lunging away, dropping to the ground and scrambling into the darkness.

Just like I'd taught her to do.

Then I fired off three rounds in rapid succession.

Zoe yelped seconds later, and I took long strides in her direction, crouching down and pulling her into my arms. "I got you. It's over."

"I was so afraid," she managed. "But I knew you'd come."

When I looked up, Tony and another soldier were racing toward us. "Jesus Christ." The first soldier spun around in a circle, ensuring no one was trying to get the drop on us.

"The last of the fuckers ran off. They're gone." The second soldier had been with Arman for years, well-seasoned in every aspect of protection.

I pulled Zoe onto her feet. "That's exactly what they had planned. We need to get back to the house. Call the cleanup crew. I want this mess taken care of."

"What do you want me to do with them?"

"Put them on ice. If one of them is alive, keep him that way."

Tony nodded. "I'll have them rounded up. You know the police are going to show."

"I'll handle it. Just get going."

Zoe clung to me as I wrapped my arm around her. "They wanted me. Why?"

"To use against your father." I started walking us toward the house, still scanning the perimeter. What troubled me the most was that the fuckers had almost managed to get away with it. Security had slacked off, the fact no one had attacked the house for years allowing everyone's guard to fall, Arman's included.

"Bastards. You saved me. I knew you would. You've always been my hero."

Her words almost carved a hole in my heart, one large enough I was pulled into another layer of darkness. I knew why she'd made the statement but at this moment, I felt like nothing but a failure. I'd allowed my dick to interfere, something I'd promised both myself and my best friend would never happen. I'd made a blood oath to protect Zoe with my life, something that had been done more years ago than I could count. I'd blurred the lines. I'd endangered her life.

"Come on. Let's get you inside," I told her, ignoring the giant elephant in the room. I'd need to ensure she knew what we'd shared could never happen again, but only after the situation was locked down tight.

As we entered the house, an eerie quiet instantly put me on edge.

Then I heard a commotion as soon as we moved into one of the hallways. Landry was racing toward the kitchen.

"What the hell is going on?" I growled, seeing the horror on his face.

"It's Arman. He struggled with one of the intruders. He's shot. And it's bad."

CHAPTER 9

Maddox

Hospitals.

It had been a long time since I'd been inside one, but the old feelings of loathing the cold and stark facilities had returned. I stood with my hand on the wall, staring out the window toward the bustling parking lot. I'd remained deep in thought since arriving at the facility, memories of the past drilling into the forefront of my mind.

I glanced at the Styrofoam cup in my hand, the bitter taste of the cheap coffee all I deserved even if I wanted a shot of bourbon or a fucking bottle. Arman had been immediately taken into surgery after arrival, the bullet nicking his lung. That's all we'd been told, other than his injuries were considered life-threatening.

It was my fault and mine alone that Raven could lose the man she loved, the father to her beloved child. She was as strong as they came, but not on this day. It was supposed to have been a celebration, a festive event with family and friends. It had turned into a nightmare. She'd yet to look at me or say a goddamn word, but I'd sensed she blamed me for not being there by his side.

Hell, she should.

Guilt wasn't something I was used to feeling, remorse not in my vocabulary, but on this night, I was drowning in it. Even Zoe had kept her distance, which was pulling at the man inside of me, the one who wanted to wrap a cocoon around her. I rubbed my eyes, the dull ache behind them remaining after popping Tylenol like candy. How many fucking hours had passed? I checked my watch. It was already two-thirty in the morning. While I was no doctor, the surgery had lasted far too long. That had to mean the chances of Arman surviving were slim to nil.

Goddamn it. I wasn't a praying man but at this moment, I'd try just about anything. What I was certain of was that I planned on hunting the person responsible down like a dog.

There was no news on the people truly responsible, no claim from the darkness as enemies often chose to do. The silence was the worst, the not knowing pushing everyone to the edge. The last thing we needed to do was react without learning the full details. However, there were far too many emotions involved, enough I was fearful damning decisions would be made.

Francois flanked my side, his anger as intense as mine. He'd refused to be admitted, pushing the EMTs aside when they'd offered assistance. His arm was in a sling, but knowing the man, that wouldn't last long. For now, he was the head of the family until Arman recovered. He stood staring out the window as if one or both of us could find answers when at this point, there were none to be found.

"You did your best, Maddox," he stated, exhaustion in his voice.

"Yeah? My best wasn't good enough."

"You saved Zoe. You made certain Raven and Gabe were protected. Hell, your instinct kept my beautiful wife and my sister from being caught in the madness. You're a goddamn hero, Maddox, and it's time you started acting like one."

"Fuck that!" I exclaimed too loudly, capturing the attention of Landry and a few of the other soldiers. I shook my head, the fury only increasing.

Francois clapped his hand on my shoulder. "I know you're worried but Arman is tough. He'll make it through."

"I don't know." I'd shoved everyone away, pressing my hands on the wound as others had called 9-1-1. He'd almost bled out on the way to the hospital. I'd been left there to pick up the pieces, to ensure that the shit was cleaned up, forced to handle the police as they arrived in three squad cars.

Sure, we had them on speed dial, most under our control in one way or another, but when you had shots fired at celebrities, two politicians injured in the process, that didn't bode well for keeping the peace or the alliance intact. At least they'd taken the report and left, but I had no doubt they'd be required to return.

"Did you call your father?"

"Yeah," he said. "Mom and Pops are returning from Italy as soon as they can."

"How are they?"

Francois shook his head. "You know Pops. He's threatening to burn down New Orleans to find the people responsible."

"Who was Arman on the phone with?"

He narrowed his eyes as he turned toward me. "I have no idea. What did he say to you?"

"It's not what he said but what he didn't say."

Snorting, the Capo of the family faked beating his head against the wall. "Arman thinks he can handle everything his way. He doesn't understand we have old enemies who want nothing more than to slide into New Orleans."

"He gets it. He just refuses to believe it could be an issue." The patriarch of the family had made enough enemies during his reign that it would be next to impossible to pick just one contender for the attack. While I'd tried to keep track of them over the years, even I'd grown complacent given the change in the business model by going legit. I'd been a fool all the way around.

Francois nodded, catching the eye of his wife, Delaney. "The South Americans swore revenge after the last war we had with them."

"That was years ago. Fucking years. Alturo's entire world imploded after the shit that was pulled in Key West." Raphael Alturo, the brutal dictator of a South American cartel had nearly destroyed the Thibodeaux Empire several years before, coming closer than anyone had at dismantling the organization. Shipments of diamonds had been stopped for some time, but Arman had refused to allow the newer lucrative and very legal business to remain idle but for so long.

While we'd used alliances to clean house in Cartagena, nearly rendering Alturo's powerful empire useless, it had stuck in the back of all our minds that one day someone would pick back up where the destroyed regime had left off.

Only this didn't feel like the South Americans. It felt closer to home.

"Yeah, but we can't discount the possibility," Francois said. "Once we know about Arman's condition, we'll have a meeting, including with Pops."

"Someone from his past?"

He snickered. "Maybe. Dad made a hell of a lot of enemies over the years, Arman trying to become the peacekeeper."

"Something you couldn't stand."

There was a strange look passing across his face. "Let's just say I would handle things entirely differently."

Yes, he would, which irritated Arman and was the single reason they argued as brothers.

THE WISEGUY

"You need to rest and gather your strength. You might have your chance at doing just that." I turned toward him, giving him a hard look.

"You know what's funny?" he asked absently, his voice riddled with exhaustion. "That's not what I want. Not in the least. Maybe it's because since being with Delaney, I understand more about what Arman has been trying to accomplish."

"And what is that?"

He thought about his answer before providing it. "Normalcy. If there's such a thing in our world. A place where our kids don't need to look over their shoulders or have bodyguards. That's what Arman has been trying to accomplish and he's been telling it to me for a long time. I just didn't get it."

"Yeah, well, the lack of security added to the horrible event."

"Maybe so, but bad shit can happen to anyone at any time. I can't blame him for wanting his daughter's return to be everything he'd hoped it would be. I'm sending Thomas to Texas to handle business there."

I nodded, noticing the man was pacing the hospital corridor, trying to console Raven, his daughter. He was also like a brother to Arman, growing up with him until he'd left the family fold about the same time I'd entered the picture. Once believed to be a traitor, the former FBI agent had taken an executive role within the company years before after leaving his former position.

"That's a good idea. He needs to check and ensure that Devin Carlos hasn't reared his ugly head again." The man had caused us difficulties years before, playing a hand in almost getting both Raven and Zoe killed in a horrific warehouse fire, trying to lay claim to our Texas stronghold at the same time. I'd blamed myself for not being there for Zoe as I should have been, but things had gotten dicey. Just like they had with Alturo, the South American dictator who remained in seclusion. I'd tried to convince Arman to eliminate both enemies, but he'd chosen otherwise.

At this point, I'd already created a mental list of the most brutal enemies the family empire had faced during the last few years. The two names came to mind quickly, the others incapable of planning a revenge operation like we'd just experienced.

"I doubt Devin would be that stupid."

"Are you willing to put the life of any family member on that bet?" I eyed him carefully.

"No, you're right. I'll have Thomas look into Devin's current situation and see if there's any unusual activity in South America."

"Good. The sooner we rule out those potentially responsible, the better."

"Agreed. Go to Zoe, Maddox. She needs you. In case you haven't noticed, the sun rises and sets when you walk into a room, the girl lighting up." He nodded toward the opposite end of the waiting room. "She's taking this really hard."

What the fuck? I wasn't certain what to say. "She sees me as some fucking hero when I'm not."

"There you go again not taking enough credit. Be her hero. Especially if something happens to Arman."

Something. He meant if the man took his last breath. If that occurred, I'd never forgive myself. Then I'd become the one who burned down the city if necessary to find the culprit.

"If that tragedy occurs, I'll need you by my side. Is that understood?" Francois said far too casually in my opinion. "You are vice president."

"If you're worried that I'll shirk my duties, don't be. I'm a consummate businessman."

"That's not what I'll need you for, my friend. Your brawn and hacking skills are worth every penny my brother pays you." He lifted his head, locking eyes with mine.

While I wanted to argue with the man and his logic, I sensed he had a reason for what he was saying that had more to do with his distrust of someone else inside the Thibodeaux Empire. There were always possibilities that someone was bought off, blackmail used to get them to turn coat, but it had been a long time since that had occurred. And with the business going almost one hundred percent legit, the timing was strange.

Except for Zoe's return, which I continued coming back to. Was there any possibility this had more to do with her than any one of us realized? I couldn't ignore the possibility. Maybe I could find out if she'd been in the middle of a situation with my computer skills.

Hacking had started as nothing more than a pastime, a way to garner information when I was in my twenties. I'd become damn good at it, able to slide under the radar of almost any organization's security system, no matter how strong they believed them to be. That included the military, the CIA, and the DEA. It didn't matter. However, lately, the pastime hadn't been necessary.

"Understood," I told him, not ready to raise an alarm about Zoe in particular. He was as concerned as I'd ever seen him, more so than when he'd been forced to go head-to-head with Alturo to save Delaney's life.

He headed off, returning to where Delaney was sitting on one of the uncomfortable couches. Another quick glance in Zoe's direction and I realized she'd disappeared. What the fuck? She'd been given strict instructions to always keep her ass in this room unless she had an armed escort. And I was her fucking bodyguard.

I moved toward the corridor, glancing one direction then the other, noticing her long dark hair swinging behind her as she headed to God knows where. I started jogging, shoving my way past too many people for this time of the morning. There was a sudden emergency, a team racing alongside a man on a gurney, forcing everyone to the side. It was shit like this that assassins took advantage of.

They'd been on an important mission, one they'd paid damn well to accomplish. At least two, maybe more of them had gotten away, and they'd die instead of going back to the person who hired them emptyhanded. That's how heads rolled and blood was spilled. I pitched my body against a nurse's station, completely losing sight of her. The moment

THE WISEGUY

the doctors and nurses had passed, I took off running, constantly scanning the bleak corridor.

I skidded past another waiting area, something catching my eye. Stopping short, I backed up, taking a breath of relief seeing Zoe standing in front of a vending machine. Anger attempted to crowd out the swell of every other emotion. I took four long strides and wrapped my hand around her arm, shoving her against the wall beside the bank of machines.

"What part about not leaving the main waiting room did you not understand?" I tried to keep my voice down, but I was exasperated, loathing the fact control had been stripped away.

Her face pinched and she jerked her arm away. "I wanted a soda. Okay? That's all. This is a hospital, for God's sake."

When she tried to skirt around me, I planted both hands on either side of her. "You need to start listening to me."

"I am. Nothing is going to happen in here." She searched my eyes, shocked I'd suggest something so ridiculous in her mind. How the hell was I supposed to get through to her? Maybe being in New York hadn't done her any good after all.

"Did your father ever tell you about the time I took a bullet for him?"

"Only that you didn't hesitate in doing so. Why are you asking me that?"

"No, I didn't, because it was my job then as it is to keep you safe now. Arman knew the score. He was trained to handle the danger. That didn't mean the bastards who'd attempted to end his life to remove him from the pecking order of the family hadn't tried again. It was in this very hospital. I'd gotten out of surgery, and he made the fucking mistake of taking a walk by himself. He almost died that day and would have if his instinct hadn't kicked in at the last minute."

Her mouth was twisted in both frustration and a new appreciation of fear. In my mind that was a good thing. "I didn't know."

"No, you didn't. And do you want to know the lengths the person took to try and end his life?" I asked.

"Even if I don't, I'm certain you're going to tell me."

"Yeah, I am, Zoe. The man slaughtered a doctor, dragging his body into a storage room. Then he took the man's identity. Thank God, your father's instinct was spot on. You don't have those instincts."

"How can you be so certain?" She lifted her chin, her rebelliousness returning.

"Because your father did everything in his power to keep you away from the nightmare that reared its ugly head from time to time. In my mind, that was a mistake." Her scent was once again wafting into my nostrils, making it impossible to think clearly.

"You're wrong about me, Maddox. I'm stronger than you think. I understand who and what my father is, what you are."

"Do you? Do you really?" I waited to see if she'd answer, continuing when she kept her glare and nothing more. "It's not about being strong, Zoe. It's about being wiser than your years, being forced to grow through the worst experiences. No one wishes that on you or any other child within the Thibodeaux family."

"So that's all I am to you, a child? My father's daughter?" She was acting even more defiant than before, as if the danger and bloodshed that had just occurred hadn't happened.

"Right now, you're acting like a child."

"It's funny, Maddox. That's not what you said a few hours ago. I was all woman, capable of suiting your needs. Were you just faking it, using my body to get your rocks off?"

The haughty expression she wore was irritating but not nearly as much as the longing ripping through my soul. I leaned further in until our faces weren't far apart, our lips almost touching. God, I wanted the woman even now. What the hell did that say about me? She tried to crowd against the wall, slamming her hands against my chest. What we'd shared had to be shoved into a black hole or her life would be placed more at risk.

I refused to allow that.

"Hear me, Zoe, because I'm only saying it once. You're my best friend's daughter, the girl I swore I would protect at all costs. I can't do that if we're involved. Do you understand?"

"What I understand is that you used me. You fucked me and tossed me aside."

"You know better than that."

"Do I?" She pushed me again, acting as if she could get away from me. The woman was sin wrapped up in a sexy, ripped dress and blazing eyes the color of the finest whiskey. She had no idea what I wanted to do to her right now. The vision of dragging her inside a closet and fucking her brains out was clouding everything I needed to do. It was hurting my job and risking her life.

I took a deep breath, looking away. She took that moment to slide under my arm, taking long strides away from me. I easily snagged her again, the force I used in jerking her backward more than I intended. She was slammed against my chest, gasping for air as she tilted her head. There was far too much desire electrifying the moment, her breathing skipping several beats.

"Don't do this, Maddox."

"Do what, Zoe? Care about your welfare? Ensure you make it to your next birthday?"

We both heard someone clearing their throat and I slowly turned my head. Francois' glare was questioning what the fuck was going on. Well, he needed to take a number. So was I.

"Yeah?" I barked.

"Good news. Arman is out of surgery and he wants to talk to you."

I slowly turned my head toward her and she blinked several times before glancing down at the floor. "Come on, Zoe. Let's see about your dad."

Instead of answering, she jerked her arm away, bolting past both of us. Francois took a full three seconds, shaking his head as he studied me.

When he walked away, I exhaled. The shit was getting out of control.

Why did I have a terrible feeling the worst was yet to come?

CHAPTER 10

Maddox

The bleak hospital room was similar to the one I'd been in all those years ago. It seemed very little had changed. Even the machines checking Arman's vitals had the same sound. The only difference was that I had no memory of the light level or the color of the walls. Now, with the pitch blackness outside, the drab gray paint made the entire room seem ominous. As if death was right around the corner.

I stood just inside the doorway, staring at my buddy, the man I'd shared dozens of bottles of booze with over the years, commiserating about whatever enemy we had to face or new business decision Arman had wanted to kick around. We'd shared stories about women, both hoping and searching for someone we could consider special, realizing that bringing anyone into our lives on a permanent basis was not only risky, but would also place that person in harm's way.

Shit, we'd gone to baseball games together, munching on hot dogs and guzzling beer. We'd even been in a softball league together after college, pretending we didn't have a care in the world. I'd grown rich being a part of the Thibodeaux family, which had meant a hell of a lot to me given I'd all but been abandoned as a child, my mother a drug addict, my father absent for most of my life. Which in truth was probably a good thing. It was likely that I would have turned out a thug like the man my mother had coveted, surrendering to an abusive marriage before he'd left with some floozy he'd met at a bar.

Arman had been like a brother. We'd stood against bullies in high school, frat boys in college, both of us feared and revered at the same time because of who we were. And more important, how dangerous we could be. We'd done some bad shit, things neither one of us were proud of. Hell, his father had gotten us out of trouble more times than I could count on one hand. I was considered family. Somehow, I had a feeling that wouldn't be the case if any one of them knew what I'd done with Zoe.

I rubbed my jaw as the memories came rushing into the forefront of my mind. I wasn't certain why it seemed important to go down memory lane other than this was as close to death as Arman had been. I couldn't stand seeing him just lying there with an IV dripping into his arm, monitoring devices keeping a close eye on his blood pressure and oxygen stats. Fuck me.

Anger tore through me more than I'd experienced before, the situation ridiculous. I knew it was mostly because of the guilt, but that didn't change the fact the entire security system needed a rehaul, including hiring different men. I would work on that later once Arman was stable.

And while I understood Francois had to be ready to take over the helm, that didn't mean I was going to discount Arman's desire to live. He had every reason to get better. Goddamn the situation.

I finally gathered up the courage to walk closer, standing beside his bed. After a couple of minutes where he didn't stir, I decided it was best to allow him to rest. I'd come back later. Before I had a chance to turn, he opened his eyes, even managing to provide a slight smile.

"Hey, buddy. What's the... ugly... expression for?" Arman asked. I was shocked his voice sounded surprisingly strong, barely winded.

"Maybe because my boss looks like shit."

He laughed then starting coughing. "Yeah, well, you don't look so good yourself, buddy. Did you get all the bastards?"

"Unfortunately, two of them got away that we know of."

I could tell he was enraged by what had occurred, yet what I hated the most was the look of desperate concern in his eyes. "What were they after?"

The truth was I didn't want to tell him.

"Maddox. Tell. Me."

"They tried to take Zoe."

When he acted as if he was going to get out of bed, the monitors went nuts. "I'm going to fucking kill them."

"No, you don't," I said, gently pushing his shoulders. "I'm going to protect her. I won't allow your daughter out of my sight. I'm also going to figure out why."

"You know why. To get at me."

"By whom? Do you know?" His hesitation was a red flag, but I had a feeling he wasn't ready to confide in me. "Devin? Alturo?" I kept my eyes locked onto his, but they didn't flicker when the two names were mentioned.

"No, and I seriously doubt either one had anything to do with the attack. However, the list of candidates is significant. You told me that more than once. I should have listened."

"Yeah, you should have. The question is, did any of them have the capabilities or the balls to go against you?"

"I don't know but I suspect their armies were building while ours were turning legit. My father warned me to keep my finger in the dike, ensuring our enemies were kept locked down and so did you. I should have listened."

I closed my eyes briefly, the headache getting worse. "You need to get better, Arman. Save your strength." There was definitely something he was holding back. It was my job to figure out what that was while he was incapacitated.

"Fuck that shit. My daughter is not safe here. You know that. They will come for her again. Just like what happened before with Raven and Zoe all those years ago. I can't go through almost losing them again. I can't allow it to happen."

"This isn't the same."

"No, it's worse. I feel it in my bones." Arman was becoming exasperated, his pulse increasing.

"Yeah, I know." I glanced out the window into the darkness, uncertain what I could say to make him feel any better. "You have my word I'll protect her with my life. I won't leave her side." The pangs of guilt were gut-wrenching, like sharp, jagged edges of a knife cutting into me.

When he gripped my hand, squeezing with more pressure than I thought him capable of, I took a deep breath.

"No. That's not good enough. Take her away, Maddox," he said, the tremor in his voice one of rage.

"What do you mean?"

"Take her out of New Orleans. Go to your house in St. Barts. Lock her down."

I was shocked by his suggestion. He had to be under the influence of the drugs used in surgery.

"That's crazy, Arman. With you recuperating, Francois will need help. And I need to tighten security. I'm the only one who can do that."

"No. My daughter will not be taken. You're the only man I trust to keep her safe. You have Tony, and Landry knows what to do. You can rely on them. Zoe needs you more now than ever."

Jesus Christ. He had no idea what he was asking. The exasperation in his tone was as confusing as it was alarming.

"You want me to take her out of the country without any backup? That's not smart and you know it."

"Don't argue with me!"

Whew. I took a deep breath, holding my tongue. "What is going on?"

"I'm sorry I jumped on you. You need to let me figure this out."

"Jesus Christ, Arman. I'm your best friend."

"Which is why I need you. No one knows you own that house except for family members. No one. Just take her there until I can… Until I can get a handle on this."

This. What in the fuck was he talking about?

He was as concerned as Francois was that the abduction attempt had been partially because of someone's assistance on the inside. "Yeah, I know, but I don't like the odds." Arguing with him was pointless. The man was as hardheaded as they came.

"The odds are better if you take her where no one knows where you've gone."

"What about Raven and Gabriel?"

"I have an alternative plan to keep them safe. Just do what I say, Maddox. I need to be able to rely on you. Besides, they aren't the target."

What the fuck wasn't he telling me and more important, why?

I shook my head, trying to find an appropriate excuse for denying his request. "I don't like it. There's too much at stake."

"Yes, there is, which is why you need to do this. It's a command, my friend. You won't go against my wishes. Will you?"

"Why do I have the distinct feeling you're not telling me something?"

Arman exhaled, pulling his hand away and fisting his fingers. "Just do what I say this time, Maddox. You need to trust me."

"This isn't about trust and you know it. It's about having your back. This isn't a good idea. If you were thinking clearly, you'd see it."

"Just do it!" The way he snapped indicated fear.

The tension between us was unusual, his eyes imploring mine. Fuck. I shook my head, struggling to find the right words, if there were such a thing.

"Fine. I'll leave once I know you're going to survive this."

He adjusted himself on the bed, rolling his eyes as if my suggestion otherwise was ridiculous. "I'm fine. You can leave when it's light."

"Jesus Christ." I knew better than to continue arguing with him.

"Just take care of my baby girl, Maddox. She's important to me. You don't know how much my children mean."

"I think I do, buddy. I understand. I'll care for her as if she was my own. However, I will put my foot down that I will not take her out of the country until your father arrives. He needs to be questioned and debriefed." The man knew when I wouldn't budge from something.

"Fine, but not one fucking minute longer. You will do this. It's my one favor I'll ask."

"Yeah, well, I doubt that," I said, trying to lighten the moment. "Rest and heal, Arman. I won't fail you."

"You're the only one I know for certain who won't."

Another pang of guilt tore through me. As I walked out, I wasn't surprised to find Francois standing outside his brother's door. The way he stared at me was a look of knowing, as if the man could see right through me.

"What did have to say?" he asked after at least ten seconds had passed.

"He wants me to take Zoe to St. Barts."

Francois studied me, nodding a few seconds later. "He has his reasons. That includes his complete trust in you regarding her welfare."

"Yeah, so he said. I need to handle a few things before we leave in a few hours. Plus, I want the opportunity to talk with your father." I started to walk away until he spoke, keeping his voice low so only I could hear.

"My brother trusts you with his little girl, Maddox. In all ways. I think you know what that means. You're a man of honor."

Honor? I'd crossed a line that could never be recrossed.

His words meant keep my fucking hands off her. That was exactly what was going to happen.

So help me God.

* * *

With Arman's estate considered a crime scene, his father had opened up his home, which would be considered the location of operations, at least until more details were discovered. There were employees bustling about the house, preparing the rooms to include the majority of the family as guests for the time being. It was a good idea to lock everyone down until more was known about the person behind the attack.

At least some of my advice was being taken.

Jean Baptiste was still a formidable man, his reign in the family ending less than a decade before. However, the Frenchman hadn't retired completely, keeping his fingers in the wealthy Thibodeaux pie. While he'd aged, his hair turning almost entirely gray, he'd always had an aura of dark power, as if he could crush a man with his fingers.

Not today.

As the early light of dawn broke through the horizon, he remained at the window staring out into the still darkened skies, his appearance frailer than I'd remembered.

A half dozen soldiers remained at the hospital including Landry, ordered to guard Raven and Arman with their lives. Delaney was caring for Gabriel, the little boy finally taking a nap after asking dozens of times about his father. Even Edmee remained at their father's house given Zane's absence. Everyone would hunker down until further notice.

While Louie had come out of surgery to learn about Arman, he'd yet to arrive with his wife and children, something his father had demanded. Louie was the brother who wanted nothing to do with the family business, but over the years had been pulled more and more back into the fold. It was entirely possible any family member could be made a target when it was discovered Zoe had been taken out of the city.

"A somber group," Thomas said as he eyed my entrance.

"It's to be expected," I answered back.

I glanced at Francois, who was finally starting to show his exhaustion. Several of our trusted soldiers were in the room, not only awaiting orders but in position as security if necessary. In my mind, it was too little too late.

"What the fuck do we know?" Jean Baptiste barked, throwing back his scotch. It didn't matter what time of the morning it was, all of us had alcoholic beverages in our hands. That's what war did to a man, especially when caught as off guard as we'd been.

"I'm checking some of my old contacts," Thomas offered. "Francois has already asked me to head to Texas. I'll keep an eye on Devin Carlos."

"At this point, we don't know enough to initiate a war," Francois said.

"He's right," I added. "There's no scuttlebutt on the street, no claims of ownership."

"And no gloating either," Francois added, lifting his eyebrows as he shifted his gaze from Thomas back to me.

We were all on edge, Jean Baptiste even more than usual.

The patriarch turned toward his other son, darting a glance in my direction after doing so. "What the fuck are you doing to try and find out?"

"We're hacking every enemy operation we know exists," Francois snapped in rebuttal. He didn't like being treated as if he wasn't capable of running the operation.

"I'm checking with every old contact within the FBI," Thomas added.

I took a deep breath, walking toward the other set of windows in the massive office.

"What say you, Maddox? I want to hear your thoughts on who's behind this."

Jean Baptiste should know me well enough to know I spoke my mind. Especially when asked.

"I think we need to go down a list of every potential enemy, including during the time you were leader of the family organization. This attack was definitely revenge based. We need to narrow down that list as soon as possible to prevent an even worse attack." Christ. I made it sound like we were already embroiled in a war. "And that needs to happen quickly. We need to determine who has the most to gain from destroying the family." I didn't bother turning in the patriarch's direction. He knew when I wouldn't take no for an answer.

"That will take a good deal of time," Francois said, which I already knew.

"It's prudent we go into this with as much accurate information as possible. You're well aware of that, Francois. It's what Arman would want."

"He's right," Thomas offered.

"What he wants is his daughter protected," Francois countered, his anger increasing.

"We will not bicker," Jean Baptiste hissed. "Maddox is right. We have enough computer-savvy soldiers to track the whereabouts of our enemies. I'll provide everything I have, including files from my office. Thomas, ensure that Devin is under full control. Texas has become vital to our operations."

"Don't worry. I will."

I sensed Thomas was as surprised by the man's attitude as I was.

It was always believed Jean Baptiste kept what might be affectionately known as little black books on every single enemy. From methods of operation to known hideouts, he'd always seemed to know where to strike when necessary.

"Good," I said, my tone overpowering. "I'll check with various connections we have throughout the world. We can't rule anyone out at this time. In addition, I think another prudent choice is to check into Zoe's background. There could be unknown enemies attached to her given the years she lived in New York." This time, I turned toward Francois.

His eyes opened wide, a smirk on his face. "You've taken to being vice president, Maddox. A fascinating and very good idea. Why don't you task Tony to run down everyone who was close to her?"

That was the perfect use of the man's time. I nodded, shifting my gaze toward my man. My thoughts drifted to the time I'd spent in New York. Other than the drunk, I'd seen no evidence anything had been off about Zoe, her friends or classmates. That didn't mean I hadn't missed something. If she was the target, it was likely her movements had been targeted for some time.

"I'd be happy to," Tony said. "Do you want me to head to New York?"

"Not unless we determine doing so is necessary. Set up operations here," I told him. "Check the known syndicates in New York however. Just in case."

"This isn't New York based," Jean Baptiste snapped.

"We're not ruling anything out, Pops." Francois nodded his approval in my direction while his father hissed under his breath, hating the fact his authority was being undermined. Francois knew I wouldn't allow any stone to go unearthed. Not under any circumstances. He'd been around me for far too long.

"We need to determine the person responsible as soon as possible. I have a bad feeling this is only the beginning of a long nightmare," Francois said more casually than I would have believed.

"You have good instincts, son," Jean Baptiste said. "We need to work together. We need to use the old ways."

The old ways. Tracking and killing if necessary. I wasn't opposed to the thought, even if Arman would be.

"There's something else you need to pay attention to," Thomas stated as he pulled his iPad from the coffee table.

"What now?" Francois barked.

"Evidently there was a reporter at the party?" Thomas eyed me carefully. He'd yet to arrive from Texas when the party had commenced, only arriving after the tragedy had struck.

"Sandra Wells. She's an investigative reporter from one of the local channels. Why?" I moved closer and as soon as Thomas handed me the tablet, I cringed. While the sound was on, the blonde going on about what she called the crisis in the Thibodeaux family, it was the headline that had grabbed my attention.

Is the Great Thibodeaux Empire Ready to Fall?

The report started with the incident between herself and Tony, continuing with scores of guests racing away from the party after gunshots had been fired. And finally led to an interview with the two politicians who'd been struck by bullets.

Francois was looking over my shoulder and I sensed his growing rage.

Just like mine.

"She's painting us once again as a violent mafia family, corrupt in all aspects," he said with no inflection in his voice.

"She hung around after being asked to leave. If I had to guess, I'd say she was tipped off about events ready to occur." I lifted my head, glancing from Jean Baptiste back to Thomas, who was rubbing his jaw.

"We were set up," Thomas said quietly.

I nodded. "That's apparent. Whoever wants to destroy us was ready to do so in any method possible."

"That means the reporter will likely continue to snoop." Francois moved toward the coffeemaker, glancing at the bar as if determining which choice was applicable. I couldn't blame him for wanting to drink so early in the morning. We'd become too complacent as an operation, allowing an enemy to enter our space without realizing it.

It didn't matter about our business operations being legitimate or not, what we didn't need was people sticking their noses in our business. We had enough illegal activities still ongoing that we could easily be railroaded into prison terms. That wasn't going to happen.

"Thomas. I think you need to use your connections to determine if she has any allies that might be of interest," I suggested.

"Good idea," Francois said as he selected coffee as his drink of choice. "We may need to have a conversation with the woman as well."

I walked closer to him, lifting an eyebrow. "I think you should wait until we know more. It's obvious she has some inside information."

Francois slowly lifted his head, eyeing me carefully. He knew what I was suggesting. He nodded and looked away. "This could turn into a nightmare."

"It already is," Jean Baptiste said, his voice more haunted than I'd heard in a hell of a long time.

"It's time I take Zoe to the safehouse," I told everyone. "Whatever Arman is concerned about, his instincts are spot on."

"Yeah, I agree with you." Francois gripped my shoulder, squeezing as if in camaraderie. "Stop worrying, my friend. Take care of my niece."

"I will."

Jean Baptiste nodded. "Are you certain you don't want a brigade of soldiers with you?"

"Not at this time." The last thing I wanted to do was to allow anyone outside of the family to know where we were going.

At this point, Zoe's life might depend on complete anonymity.

Especially since my instinct told me we'd been compromised by one of our own.

CHAPTER 11

Zoe

Shivers continued to course through me, even more so than during the horrible gunfight. Maybe because I was in a tiny plane thousands of feet in the air, the on and off turbulence making my skin crawl.

Or maybe because I was being taken from my family. I'd felt as if the attack had been my fault. Why would I be singled out? Nothing made any sense at this point and the man sitting in the pilot's seat wasn't saying anything.

"How come I never knew you were a pilot?" I asked out of the blue, still marveling at the fact. I'd slipped into the small cockpit, refusing to remain alone in the back. While the small jet was well equipped, I'd felt every wind shear, which had exacerbated my fear of heights tenfold. My stomach churned, my mind still stuck in a horrific fog.

"Because you never asked." He threw me a look over his shoulder.

We'd flown into Cuba to refuel, my protector not allowing me to get off the plane.

"That's because it's not something normal people bring up in conversation. Hey, what other crazy hobbies do you have other than hacking into people's secure computers? Wine? Women? Flying airplanes?"

He laughed, which was the first time since seeing him again. We'd been through too much trauma in the last twenty-four hours, the horrible images of the shooting and the masked intruders trying to abduct me never far from my mind.

Alongside my father's condition, the tubes stuck in his arms horrifying.

"Well, we aren't normal people. Are we? I've wanted to learn to fly since I can remember. I woke up one day and decided I wasn't getting any younger. So I signed up for lessons. Then I bought my first plane."

"This is yours?"

"My pride and joy, a Cirrus vision jet."

"Which means?"

His grin was boyish, more so than I was used to. "Which means I don't need a copilot."

"Hmmm…" I wasn't certain what else to say. The plane was small but there were drinks and snacks on board and I'd gotten a chance to try out my flight attendant skills, which

I'd been forced to admit I sucked at given the amount of turbulence we'd had.

Sighing, I shook my head as he concentrated on flying, my thoughts drifting back to my mother's photograph I'd looked at just before Maddox had escorted me out of my father's house to his Charger, insisting I lie down in the back seat until we'd left the city. It was all so cloak and dagger.

I wasn't certain why I'd been thinking about my mother during the flight. Maybe because this was one of those times I wished for comfort. It was silly given my age, but I wanted to be able to ask for advice. Raven would have been happy to sit and talk with me, but the fact she wasn't that much older than I was somehow changed things.

I'd only been four years old when my birth mother had died, what few memories I had more like flashes of light versus the kind of images and thoughts I could wrap my mind around. While I adored my father, the man doing everything in his power to become both mother and father until he'd met Raven, he'd been embroiled in grief for many years. So much so that he'd kept pictures hidden away, the pain of losing her too intense. I'd had one by my bed, which I'd left there when I'd moved to New York for college. Maybe I'd believed that I was too old to be pining away for my dead mother.

Maybe my melancholy thoughts were because she'd been my age when she'd passed. Or maybe because I'd been taken from my injured father at his insistence, landing on a goddamn tropical island as if two lovers were going on a paradise vacation.

I rolled my eyes, doing everything I could to keep from glancing over at the powerful, gorgeous man as he drove. He was dressed more casually than I could remember ever seeing him do, the light-colored linen trousers and tight polo accentuating his insanely good looks. His hair had been tousled in the warm breeze, the hints of gray at his temples drawing my attention more than before. There I went again, lusting after someone I couldn't have.

Everything about being forced to leave my home irritated me, but especially since Daddy had insisted that Maddox be the one to take me to safety. Of course I hadn't been able to express my concerns when he'd ask why, insisting I tell him.

I'd never been able to get away with anything my entire life. He had the uncanny ability of knowing when anyone was lying. As Maddox rolled around the curves of the two-lane road in the middle of the tropics, I wondered whether that also applied to my father's best friend.

Okay, so engaging in carnal sin with the man hadn't been my best decision for about a dozen reasons; the fact Maddox was doing everything to ignore me like I was with him was clear indication of the horrific tension. It was so palpable it could easily be cut with a knife. Hell, maybe a spoon. Even the crackle of electricity we'd shared before was entirely different.

Sadly, the desire for the man remained, even though I refused to acknowledge it on the surface. I stole a quick glance, forced to admit I hated the silence. He'd said maybe ten words since we'd left the hospital, quickly putting together suitcases before the powerful man had whisked me to a private airport located at least thirty miles outside of the city. I understood the reason for being cautious, why he'd ensured no one had followed us and few people were told where he was taking me. I'd been brought up a mafia princess whether I wanted to believe it or not.

My father had been the sole reason the Thibodeaux Empire had shifted away from illegal activities, becoming almost entirely legitimate. However, that didn't mean that the old tactics of security and methods of protection weren't required or used. My grandfather had insisted on that, Maddox believing wholeheartedly that every aspect of caution had to be taken.

But I'd sensed he wasn't happy.

"How was your time in New York?" Maddox asked out of the blue.

"Fine. Challenging. Why ask me that now?"

"Because I need to figure out what we're dealing with."

It took me a few seconds to realize what he was saying. "You think the attack had everything to do with me. Don't you?"

"I don't know what to think, Zoe. There isn't a single clue of what we're dealing with other than the men sent to try and abduct you were pros. They were on the premises for a sole reason."

"Me." I shuddered intensely at the thought. "Oh, God. Why? I thought this was about business."

"I'm not saying it wasn't. Did you have any threats while there, anyone suspicious following you?"

Swallowing hard, I tried to think about what he was asking me. "I had almost no friends while I was there, Maddox. They were too afraid of who my father was."

He nodded, but I could tell by his fisted hand how much tension he was under. I also wasn't entirely certain he believed me. In truth, I'd often felt as if I'd been followed, including during my last week at school. I'd looked over my shoulder more than once but had seen nothing.

"We're going to be landing soon. Go strap yourself in. We could be in for a bumpy landing."

"Okay." I folded my arms as I returned to the seat, fighting the heightened nerves. Seconds later, the change in altitude was apparent. A single tear slipped down my cheek, the only one I would allow. I was stronger than anyone gave me credit for.

Maybe that's why I hadn't been honest about the threat I'd received.

* * *

My eyes were heavy, my pulse still racing. The landing had been solid, but I'd remained terrified until he'd cut the engine. He'd insisted I wear a hoodie until we were safely nestled in his Jeep. The gesture had been a stark reminder that it didn't matter where we were, my life was in danger.

I was simply exhausted, unable to sleep on the plane, terrified my father wouldn't make it. Just seeing Raven sobbing uncontrollably had nearly broken me, my little half-brother confused as to what was happening to his daddy. It was all insane, including the fact I'd almost been abducted.

Exhaling, I leaned my head against the headrest, staring out the open window of the Jeep. Not only did Maddox have a private plane, one of which he was the pilot, he also had a secure and conditioned storage unit near the tiny airport where he kept the vehicle and a lot of trunks that held weapons and ammunition. It shocked me how much he'd amassed. When he'd loaded an assault rifle and two handguns, along with a case of ammunition into a duffle bag, I'd stared in shock. It was as if the man was anticipating a war.

The sun was setting, a flurry of vivid colors crisscrossing the insanely perfect sky, the eight-hour flight bumpy as hell given a thunderstorm we'd rolled through. Now my stomach was in knots, my mind foggy as I continued to wonder about why I'd become a target. Other than for money.

Or revenge.

"Did the men who tried to take you say anything?" Maddox asked, his voice gruffer than before.

"Just that I was coming with them. And no, I didn't recognize their voices. They didn't have accents either."

"That's what I guessed."

"You killed them. Didn't you?"

"Not all of them."

"That's why I was sent away. You and my dad think I did something wrong."

Maddox shook his head. "Don't overreact, Zoe. No one thinks you're to blame for a fucking thing. Whatever is going on, your father refuses to have you as a target."

"I'm worried about Raven and little Gabriel. Did you see her face?"

"Don't be so concerned. They will be well taken care of, surrounded at all times."

"That's no way to live," I insisted, to which he said nothing. I continued to glare out the window, thinking about the odd threat that I'd tried to ignore. The man's voice had been disguised, mechanical, but the words were ones I'd never forget.

"You belong to me now and always."

Then the bastard had hung up the phone. I'd tried to tell myself that the asshole had simply called the wrong number since no one but my family and Maggie knew my number. Now I wasn't so certain of anything. The older man at the club for several nights. I'd sensed I'd been followed after leaving the club, then the man had disappeared. Nothing made any sense. Why me? Why now?

Stop doing this to yourself. This has nothing to do with you. It's all about your father.

My inner voice was correct. I wasn't the target, not really. Then why were my hands clammy, my heart racing? I glanced at Maddox. Just seeing the anger on his face kept my pulse spinning out of control. What was happening to my family?

"I don't know why I couldn't have stayed. My father might have needed me. Why did you take me away?"

"I'm just following orders."

"Orders? You're friends with my dad, Maddox. You were the best man at his wedding to Raven, for God's sake. You went to high school with him."

"He's also my boss."

"Ah, yes. The Kingpin and the Wiseguy. Right?"

I'd sensed I'd angered him all over again. I hated the mafia aspect, always wishing my father had been a doctor, lawyer, or something else less dangerous. But as my father had reminded me more than once, I didn't get to choose what family I was born into.

"We're really in danger," I finally said, barely recognizing my voice.

"Yes, Zoe. We are. Don't worry. I can and will protect you."

"I know."

I took a deep breath, the open roof on the Jeep allowing me to inhale various fragrances from the dazzling flowers and salt spray from the close proximity of the ocean. I'd been lucky enough to grab several sightings of the cerulean blue water, but even that hadn't taken away the heavy anxiety. I was surprised he hadn't forced me to lie down in the back. A bitter laugh threatened to rise to the surface. I was starting to lose it.

Maybe the reason I remained in a grumpy mood was the fact I'd been dumped in the middle of paradise with the man of my dreams and he hated me. Or maybe I loathed myself. As he shifted into second, rounding another corner more slowly, I sat up in my seat. Every muscle ached including my heart.

"Are we getting close?" I asked.

"Less than a mile away." I also hated that there was a coldness in his tone, as if he'd shut down with me completely. I'd sensed his annoyance in playing my babysitter, forced to leave the situation. He was a control freak and always had been, a man who took his need to dominate seriously.

"I didn't know you owned a property in the islands."

"There's a lot of things you don't know about me, Zoe. I'm certain I know very little about you."

That was a true enough statement. "Is your cottage a place where you come to find peace or maybe salvation?"

He acted as if he was choking, throwing me a look as he made a turn. "Do I need salvation?"

"I think you do. You've had demons inside of you for all the years I've known you. It's as if you can't or won't make peace with who you are. That's very sad."

I was certain his deep exhale was the only answer I'd receive. I was wrong.

"Your father has enjoyed coming here alone and with Raven. They honeymooned here."

"At your cottage?" Granted, from what I'd seen both before and after landing at the French-controlled island, I could tell the place was as magical as it was tropical. However, I never figured my father as a flip-flop wearing beachcomber. Maybe there was a lot I didn't know about him as well. That's what being sent away to school had cost me.

"Technically, it's called a villa." His grin was laced with mischief, another attribute I was certain I'd never see again. My curiosity as to why was answered only a few seconds later as he pulled the Jeep close to another breathtaking view of paradise. The moment he slipped the gear into park, I rose to my feet, sticking my head out the open roof, staring at the 'villa' with my mouth wide open.

"Are you kidding me?"

"I'm not sure what that means," he said as he cut the engine.

"This is... spectacular. I had no idea you owned something like this."

"As I told you before, little lamb. There's a lot you don't know about me."

There was no adequate way of describing the stunning view of the house or the rolling waves of the ocean slicing against the crystalline pearl sand beach, the backdrop of oranges and various shades of purple and pink highlighting a private, pristine setting. In front of me was a wide set of white stone or concrete steps leading to a narrow curving set of steel steps coated in what had to be white epoxy. They led to a two-story expansive home in a style that could only be described as a posh island retreat. The entire setting was lined with palm trees and huge hibiscus in various colors.

From where I stood inside the vehicle, I could just make out a second structure, smaller like a bungalow with another set of stairs leading to what appeared to be a private beach. The house itself was nestled in a cove setting, midrise mountains surrounding the property with no other structures in sight. I couldn't have been more floored, the slight tingling sensations prickling my senses.

"Gorgeous. How long have you owned it?"

"About twelve years. Believe it or not, the property was in disrepair, previously owned by a drug lord who hid out here. Renovation took three full years, especially since I had to deal with the French historical society." He climbed out, immediately grabbing our bags.

I eased onto the stone driveway, drinking in the setting as I inhaled the sweet fragrance of flowers. The breeze had picked up, blowing my hair everywhere. I grabbed the long strands, turning in a full circle to see the entire place. "How often do you come here?"

"Not as often as I'd like, but I've been busier than ever since being promoted to vice president."

"Congratulations. I forgot to tell you that."

"It's an honor to be considered your father's most trusted friend outside of his family."

His statement was another reminder that we could be nothing more than pseudo friends. I cringed inside but had come to terms with the way the situation stood. "I'm sure it is." Another moment of tension settled between us, one palpable enough I could hear my irregular breathing.

"Come on. I made certain I had some provisions dropped off, but it's likely we'll go out for more tomorrow."

"You mean you're going to allow me outside of the house?"

He chuckled as he headed for the stairs. "No one knows who I am or who I work for down here. The place is registered in a bogus company name that has nothing to do with Thibodeaux Enterprises. Arman hired an attorney to make the transactions anonymous. The man did an excellent job. The few who see me around know me as Rourke."

"Rourke?" I asked as we headed up the stairs. "A fake name too? Isn't that a little too over the top?"

"Not when safety is involved, and Rourke isn't fake. That's my middle name."

"Maddox Rourke Cormier. I like it. Very powerful."

He lifted his eyebrows as he threw me another amused look. "Well, I'm glad you do."

I shielded my eyes from the last vestiges of glowing rays as I stared at the house. It was modern in design, the flat roof no doubt made of metal as well, the wide eaves covered in what appeared to be molded aluminum. And as one would expect from a tropical setting such as this, there were very few walls that weren't made of glass, allowing me to catch a slight glimpse of the interior covered in shadows. The front door was located on the second floor, a thick metal railing overlaying the massive outside foyer covered in marbleized stone. I stood gawking at the backyard, even more shocked than before.

The water was feet away, lapping gently against the beach. I was in awe, barely able to turn away.

"I still cannot believe you own something so spectacular. It's as if there aren't any other houses here."

"There are, just over the mountains. The privacy is one reason I fell in love with this place. There are six miles on either side of the beach and tropical forests, only a few houses in other gated locations anywhere close." When he flanked my side, his body less than an inch from mine, I could feel the building heat and it added to the apprehension.

I wasn't entirely certain how I was supposed to spend a few days with the man entirely alone. "You have a pool," I whispered, trying to keep from reacting to his closeness.

"Yes, and a hot tub. Other amenities as well."

"What are we going to do while we're here?"

He chuckled as if I had no understanding of living in a beach environment. "Sail. Snorkel. I'll teach you to dive. Shelling. Surfing. Walking. I have an exercise room, a state-of-the-art movie theater, and a billiards table under a veranda. I doubt you'll be bored."

"What about a piano?"

"Come with me, little lamb." He pulled out a set of keys, backing away toward the front door. As soon as he walked inside, flicking on a series of lights, I was certain I'd walked right into another fantasy.

All my life I'd wanted to live in a beach setting, something I'd told my father over and over again. He'd take me to the water in New Orleans, the beaches in Galveston, Texas whenever he could, but it wasn't what I'd dreamt of so much of my life. I was happiest with my hair up in a ponytail, wearing shorts and tank top or a bathing suit, donning fuchsia flip-flops and sunglasses while listening to tropical or reggae music. It was a fact that very few people knew, including Maddox. He'd always been so formal around me.

Maybe we'd have a chance to get to know each other. Or maybe I was dreaming.

He dropped the bags just inside the door, shoving his keys back into his pocket, moving through the open floor plan through the incredible living room to the glass windows. Only they weren't windows but sliding doors. As he unlocked and swung them open, I gathered another incredible whiff of the salty sea and couldn't stop a slight moan from escaping.

The front sitting area was incredible, complete with a stone fireplace, gorgeous furniture, and throw rugs that were works of art. As he beckoned with a single finger, a grin crossed his face. This had to be his happy place, somewhere that he allowed his hair down.

A pilot and maybe a pirate. The thought made me smile.

I followed him into another set of rooms through a wide-open doorway. The huge living room led into an almost as large kitchen. The walls, cabinets, and high tapered ceilings added to the openness of the layout, the muted furniture and artwork doing the same. Color had been added through accents located almost everywhere: red tropical flowers in a huge low vase on the wood coffee table, red throw pillows and accent rug. There were red towels in the kitchen, and another vase on the island.

That also allowed a homier feel instead of being stark and cold. My eyes were drawn outside as he also opened the sliding doors, letting in the fresh air. The roofed patio was complete with at least a dozen columns, allowing a view to die for, the ocean so close it felt as if I could reach out and touch it. There was a table near a covered grill, a massive bar that I bet was stocked with everything imaginable, and another seating area that could easily accommodate twelve or more guests.

"Go on. Go outside," he encouraged as he shoved his hands in his pockets, taking a few steps back and nodding toward the outdoors.

I took careful steps, holding my breath as I walked onto the intricate stone, staring at the pool. There were also cabanas, one with a pool table and another with yet a third seating area complete with a stone firepit. Lounge chairs were on two sides of the pool keeping the amazing view unobstructed. And surrounding the area was a long strip of rolling perfectly green grass flanked by palm trees. This was the kind of place where dreams and fantasies were made a reality.

"Look to your left, Zoe."

His command was darker than before and when I did, I threw my hand over my mouth, literally scampering toward the baby grand painted in red. "Oh. My. God. This is incredible." I ran my hands over the surface, my heart fluttering from seeing such an incredible instrument. "You keep this out here?"

"Only when me or one of my guests are here. I had the cleaning staff push it outside. I thought you might enjoy the inspiration."

"I don't know what to say or think."

"I want you to be comfortable here. My house is now your house." Why was it his words were so stilted?

"I have no doubt I will." I ran my fingers over the keys and sighed. "Do you bring a lot of guests here?"

"Very few. Almost no one."

There was a strange sadness in his tone, the sound forcing me to turn and face him. He'd moved to behind the bar, already pulling glasses from one of the glass shelves behind him. He didn't look at me, but I could tell he was deep in thought. I'd seen the guilt on his face more than once, especially after talking to my injured father after his surgery. What we'd done was eating Maddox alive.

"Women?" I immediately regretted asking him that.

I held my breath when he didn't answer. "No, Zoe. There's been no one for a very long time. And there can't be anyone in my life."

"Why is that, Maddox? Why are you forced to live the life of a monk?" I moved closer, curious as to if he'd bother answering.

I sensed almost immediately he was annoyed since I continued to dig at the reasons he'd shoved me away.

"If the shit that went down the past day didn't explain the reason with vivid clarity, then I'm not certain what to tell you." He poured a glass of wine for me, plopping two ice cubes in a glass and pouring some private label bourbon for himself. Then he shoved the glass toward me in an exaggerated gesture, his glare expressionless.

"Okay then. Why did the attack happen? Do you have any idea, other enemies in mind?"

"No, but I think your father might. Either him or your grandfather. While I'm hiding away in paradise, your father is on his own facing some unknown enemy." He moved out from behind the bar, turning his attention toward the water as if he was attempting to dismiss me.

"Is that why you're so angry, because you're forced to babysit me?" When he didn't answer, instead walking toward the stairs leading down to the pool, I jumped in front of him. "Answer me."

"I'm angry because I allowed my guard to fall. Protecting you is part of my job."

"Because of me your guard fell. Because of feeling something for the first time in your life. Right? Just a job. I don't know what to say."

His jaw was so clenched I was certain he was going to crack it. He said nothing yet his silence screamed volumes. When he finally spoke, I was incensed. "Don't put words in my mouth, Zoe. I'm doing what is required."

And for some reason, I lost my cool and my patience. "Required? Fuck you, Maddox. I'm stuck with a man who used me to get a few jollies, someone I looked up to at first before I fell down a rabbit hole of cravings. Did you know

I've had a crush on you since I was a teenager? Did you know that I did all I could to save myself for you?" His look of horror made me laugh. "Don't worry. I wasn't a virgin. I allowed a single boy to touch me and hated every moment of it. That's where I got the term ice queen. Yeah, and I know. That makes me a stupid little girl, or what you call a little lamb. I get the danger. I understand the distraction I caused by coming into town irked you, forcing you to be on edge. That's fine, Maddox. I'll stay out of your way while I'm here. That way I can do everything I can to hate you. In truth, that shouldn't be too difficult given you're a grumpy asshole with no zest for life."

Mr. Silence struck again and I was sick inside. Yet as soon as I tried to storm away, he grabbed my arm, swinging me back around just as he'd done inside the hospital.

He fisted my hair, yanking back my head by a couple of inches, his hot breath cascading across my face as he lowered his head. The way his chest was heaving, I was certain he was going to have a heart attack.

"Don't test me, Zoe. You won't like me or what happens if you do." He dropped his head even more, leaving his lips tantalizingly close, my mind spinning with the longing for him to kiss me. When he used his leash-like hold on my hair to shake me, I knew there was no turning back the clock.

"Let me guess. You're going to spank me again like a bad little girl?" I mocked him by using my seductive voice, even purring afterwards. The flash in his eyes tore at my senses, sending wave after wave of explosive vibrations into every cell and muscle. The love/hate situation between us was already getting on my nerves.

"If necessary."

"I'd like to see you try." I shook my head, gazing down the length of him as he'd done to me a thousand times. "You're right in that you're nothing but a savage monster, a true Neanderthal."

He cocked his head slightly and I dragged my tongue across my bottom lip just to tempt and tease him. Somewhere in the back of my mind, I knew I was playing with fire, but I honestly didn't care. It would seem my life had been turned inside out on a permanent basis.

"You will follow my rules, Zoe. You will do exactly as I tell you to do."

"This isn't the fucking military." He was sexier than before and I could tell he was completely aroused, the thick bulge in his pants a dead giveaway. However, I was humiliated that my panties were soaking wet, the sparring turning me on like little else had done. We were like two kids in sandbox, tormenting the other to cross the line that we'd already done before.

"You're right. It's about keeping you alive and I'm the only man who can do that. As I said, you will follow my orders. Do. You. Understand?"

"Yes," I hissed and instead of placing my hand on his chest to steady myself, I did exactly what I'd wanted to do before.

I slapped him.

CHAPTER 12

Maddox

I reared back, the hard hit shocking the hell out of me. When the feisty woman tried to walk away, I fisted her hair, dragging her back.

"Let go of me," Zoe snarled.

"Not a chance, sweetheart. Following the rules doesn't include slapping me." The way she pushed her palms against my chest continued to torment the hell out of me. I was hard as a rock, longing to drown myself in her perfume and fuck her like the bad girl she truly was. But that option was off the table.

And I would do everything in my power to keep it that way.

However, punishment wasn't.

"I'll tell my father on you."

"Really? You're going to share with your father the tryst we've had? You're going to break his heart on purpose?" Goddamn, the woman could push my buttons more than any other had in my life. Maybe it served me right for succumbing to temptation, tasting the forbidden.

The way her mouth twisted was as tempting as everything else about her. So much so, I was about ready to lose my mind all over again.

"Fuck you," she snarled.

"Yeah? We will see. Now, you're going to be punished and I will continue to do so until you realize that your behavior won't be tolerated and that I'm the only man who can keep you alive."

Her laugh was meant to irritate me. All it did was entice me even more. Stars were floating in front of my eyes, ones that were leading me into more dangerous decisions. When the vixen tried to slap me again, I snapped my hand around her wrist, issuing a tsking sound.

"That wasn't very nice of you, Zoe. Now, you're going to take your punishment like a good girl."

"And if I don't?"

"Then I'll lock you in your room. I don't think that's something you want to have happen. Do you?"

"I was right. It's easy to hate you."

That's exactly what I was hoping for. "Good." I tugged her across the veranda toward the piano, hating everything about the moment. But it was the only way to keep her alive and strong. Maybe I was doing it because around her, it was almost impossible to keep my resolve. When I let her go, she backed away as if I'd burned her, the look of hatred on her face tearing at me as everything else had. "Undress."

"What?"

"You heard me." When I reached for my belt, she glared at me in horror.

"You can't do that."

"I can and I will. This isn't a democracy, Zoe. The quicker you realize that, the better."

She narrowed her eyes, her voluptuous chest rising and falling. She had no idea how close I was to fucking her over the back of the expensive musical instrument. "Fine. But I will find a way to repay you."

The girl had chutzpa, which could help keep her alive. I'd also sensed there was something she wasn't telling me. That she'd stopped trusting me was troubling, another reason for shutting down my feelings.

A hard flush crept up both sides of her lovely face, embarrassment for being placed in an uncomfortable situation riding her. However, her eyes remained full of venom. She turned away, dropping her head as she fumbled with the button on her jeans. The fact she'd shut down her emotions had bothered me almost as much as our carnal behavior.

Now I was able to smell her fear, a scent that was undeniable. I'd been trained to recognize the scent by Jean Baptiste, who'd insisted all his boys, as he liked to call us, learn the first sign that someone was lying to us. That had been the moment I knew I wanted to work for the family.

I couldn't help but notice her body was shaking as she ripped her shirt over her head, revealing a sexy lacy bra that I shouldn't be paying any attention to.

When I heard her muttering curse words as she peeled away the dense material of her jeans, it was impossible not to smile. Now I was the one looking away on purpose, slowly tugging the thick leather strap from my belt loops.

I'd sent Tony a text, letting him know to dig into her professors, everyone in her classes, and to check her phone records. If the little lamb was hiding something, she'd soon learn that it wasn't in her best interest to do so.

When she stood in only her underwear, blushing pink in color, my mouth watered as my balls tightened. As she'd done before, she folded her arms across her chest, turning to face me with all the defiance she was known for.

"Underwear as well." I forced myself to look away after a few seconds.

"Bastard."

"When you're finished undressing, place your hands on the piano and spread your legs." I took my time folding the thick leather, trying to control my breathing. I could still hear her curse words even as she followed my orders.

Only when I didn't hear any other sounds did I finally turn toward her, holding my breath. My cock was now pressing hard against my pants, enough so my balls were pinched. Seeing her in the light was breathtaking, my mind pivoting to all the filthy places in my mind that shouldn't exist.

I moved closer, taking several deep breaths before pressing my hand on the small of her back. "Stay in position. Thirty strikes should be a perfect reminder."

She threw me a look but said nothing, only her ragged breathing a continued indication she was furious with me.

As I brushed my hand to her bottom, she sucked in her breath, this time the sound exaggerated. It had been a long time since I'd used a belt when spanking a woman. What unnerved me almost as much as the moment that was unfolding was that it dredged up dark desires and sadistic needs, which had been my undoing before.

I took a step away, twisting my hand around the leather. When I brought the belt down twice in a row, she didn't react at first, which surprised the hell out of me.

Seconds later, she shuddered visibly, kicking out her leg. But I sensed her continued defiance, her determination to hate me as strong if not stronger than before. I brought the belt across her sit spot four times. The slight cry she issued was quickly stopped, but her shoulders heaved as pain washed through her.

A tightness in my chest formed, an ache that shifted all the way down to my feet. This was the last thing I wanted to do but knew it was necessary.

In order to break the hold.

In order to keep her alive.

My next breath was rattled, so much so spots formed in front of my eyes, but I continued the spanking, bringing the belt down six times without hesitation.

She finally yelped, throwing back her head and gasping for air. "I hate you so much." She twisted her pelvis, the sharp cries continuing.

"That's fine by me." But it wasn't. That was the last thing I wanted, but goddamn it. What else was I supposed to do? I moved closer, pressing my hand against her back to try to keep her calm. That was the moment I gathered a whiff of her continued desire, her pussy lips shimmering with wetness.

Christ. It was all I could do to keep from thrusting my cock inside. I brushed my hand from one side of her reddened bottom to the other, hating the way she flinched from my touch.

"Just get on with it," she said a few seconds later, her demanding tone bringing a smile to my face.

My fingers came dangerously close to her pussy lips, enough so I jerked my hand away. As I started again, it was all she could do to keep from racing away from me. But the woman stood her ground, refusing to give into temptation or allowing me to see a single weakness.

If only she knew how strong I believed her to be, so much so that I was tense, shaking as I continued doling out the strikes, one right after another. There was something entirely too cathartic about what I was doing, acting as if I was in total control over her body and soul.

The truth was I wanted her full surrender. The thought was wearing on me, so daunting that this needed to end before I lost my shit.

When I was close to the end, I rubbed my hand over her heated buttocks a second time, savoring the rush of adrenaline as much as the tingling vibrations jetting through me. I dared allow myself to slide the tip of my index finger down the crack of her ass, brushing it against her slickened folds.

When she tensed, issuing a sharp moan as her hips undulated, I knew that was all I could take. I backed away, doing everything I could not to gasp for air. "You've had enough. I'll take your things to your room downstairs. I suggest you try and get a good night's sleep." I purposely turned away, furious with myself more than before.

As I shoved my belt back through the loops, I gathered another whiff of her longing and bit back a growl.

Seconds later, I heard the rustle of clothes and walked away on purpose. The woman was everything I'd ever wanted and nothing I could have again.

* * *

I touched my face and almost laughed. Somehow, I could still feel the effects of Zoe's slap even though two days had passed.

Two fucking days of absolute misery.

Being in such close proximity was driving me bat shit crazy. The sooner I got off this goddamn island, the better.

"Pops has made an additional list. I'll send that to you," Francois said.

"I'll work on it as soon as you do. Nothing that you've sent me up to this point raised any red flags." While Zoe had done everything in her power to ignore me, I'd spent time in my secure computer room, doing what I could to hunt down the aggressor.

It was fascinating that so many of Jean Baptiste's very formidable enemies had died, some by being murdered, and others from cancer or other natural causes. Tony hadn't found anything either, but he'd yet to receive Zoe's phone records, although they were expected at any time. I'd asked her once again if there was any chance she'd developed enemies of her own and she'd barely managed to provide a single word answer. No.

She was lying to me and had now had every reason to distrust me. I wasn't handling the situation as I should but there was no other recourse now.

"Fuck. It's like looking for a needle in a damn haystack. There's nothing on the street either. However, Arman is on the mend, doctors amazed he's doing so well."

"That's good to hear," I told Francois, relieved that Arman would make a full recovery. "When is he going home?"

"A few days, or as long as the hospital staff can keep him tied down. He was ready to leave last night, and they almost put restraints on him. They're forbidding him to make phone calls, but he's been driving me crazy."

I chuckled and took a gulp of coffee, gritting my teeth as I walked out to the veranda, staring out at the ocean. "He is hardheaded."

"Uh-huh. Like someone else I know."

"He's hiding something, Francois. We need to find out what that is before it's too late."

He took a deep breath. "You know how he is when he's trying to wrap his arms around something. He always manages to dig himself out of the muck."

"Yeah, well, I have a bad feeling the muck had turned into quicksand."

"I'll talk to him, but I can't promise shit. I might be his brother, but if he won't confide in you then I'm not certain what the hell you think he's going to tell me."

"It's all about that phone call. I feel it in my bones." The nagging feeling continued to pulse in my stomach, as if whatever I was missing would rear its ugly head at any moment.

"Like I said, I'll talk to him."

"Has Thomas left for Texas?"

"Not yet," he admitted. "He's taking some time to check with his old contacts from the FBI. Ms. Wells doesn't appear to have any skeletons in her closet but he's continuing to dig."

I rubbed my eyes, hating the exhaustion settling in. "Keep an eye on our business in South America. If Alturo and his family are behind this, they'll attempt to heist the diamonds."

"Yeah, I already thought of that," he said. "So far there's nothing drawing any red flags. I think whoever is behind this is waiting until our empire crumbles naturally."

"Just like years before."

"I remember, Mr. Boogeyman," he said, teasing me about the moniker as he'd always done before. "Enough business right now. We will figure this out. We are a powerful empire just like Ms. Wells suggested. Now, how is paradise?"

Powerful empire. One aspect of business that the men of the Thibodeaux family never admitted was that once you were on top of your game, there was only one place to go. Given our expanded power swept now from Nevada to Florida, from owning sports and racing teams to nightclubs and the latest destination community just outside of Dallas, the empire was poised to take a huge tumble and would if the veil of decency was pulled out from under us.

That alone would tank the stocks, investors pulling out right and left. And if we were framed for any illegal activity, we might as well kiss our freedom goodbye. Whoever was doing this was a brilliant businessman, not necessary a thug like Alturo.

"Hot. Humid. Annoying. Perfect July weather." As Zoe walked out onto the pool deck from her bedroom, my cock reacted as it always did around her, stiffening to the point my balls ached. She purposely ran her fingers across the keys on the piano before giving me a hard look. She'd yet to sit down and play anything, likely on purpose since I'd spanked her there. My actions were still something I found difficult to accept, although I'd enjoyed every minute of it.

Every action methodical, she moved down the stairs and I couldn't seem to take my eyes off her as she placed a towel and bottle of water on one of the tables.

"See. As hardheaded as Arman is. For what it's worth, you're doing the right thing by staying there."

Right now, I couldn't care less about doing the right thing.

"Any thoughts from anyone on what we're dealing with?"

"Not yet. I've had men crawling the streets, including in Texas. There's been no outward threats, nothing on the street. There haven't been any unusual business activities either and I've checked everything from Texas to Key West. Whoever it is was toying with us."

"Tell me about it. This has to be revenge based. I feel it in my gut."

"I agree," Francois said. "It's just a matter of figuring it out."

"I think you need to talk to Jean Baptiste again, maybe privately." Arman had suspected that past enemies of his father's would come back to bite the entire family one day, especially since the man had been so brutal in handling business operations back in his day.

"I've tried. Pops is being… less than cooperative as well. Don't worry. He will sit down and talk with me. I'm like you. I have a feeling he has a general idea of who it could be. Either that or he and Arman are sworn to secrecy."

Fuck that. The one thing I had walked in on only a couple of weeks prior to the party had been a terse conversation between Arman and his father on the phone. It had been apparent his father had been attempting to coerce Arman into doing something he hadn't wanted to become involved in. That wasn't necessarily unusual given Jean Baptiste preferred keeping the more lucrative and illegitimate sides of the business more active. Now I was beginning to wonder if the attack had stemmed from that single phone call.

As Zoe moved toward the water, I tensed. I'd told her that she could have run of the house, even enjoying taking walks on the beach, yet when she had, I'd followed her, keeping my weapon out of sight but with me at all times. I shouldn't have any fear that we'd been discovered, although I monitored the security system, checking it three times a damn day. I felt as if we were living in a bubble, and at some point that bubble would burst in a way I couldn't control and I wouldn't be able to protect the woman I... I'd been assigned to keep safe. Fuck. I had the kind of feelings for her that were difficult to shove inside a box, even though that was exactly what I needed to do.

"Let me know what you find out, Francois. I don't want to be down here any longer than absolutely necessary."

"Think of it as a mini vacation."

"Right," I snorted. "That's not the way it works."

"Incidentally, when this is all over, Delaney and I need to have a few days in paradise."

"Any time you want, brother. After this is all over."

"Yeah, yeah. I got it. Delaney will be thrilled. Try and relax. Get on that sailboat of yours. Go water skiing. Do something to burn off the heady amount of testosterone. I'll let you know what I find. Keep doing what you do best in searching."

I'd yet to make contact, calling in a few favors, but that would soon become necessary if I didn't learn anything in the next forty-eight hours. I had a feeling the search was on to locate Zoe's whereabouts.

"You mean hacking. Very funny." Testosterone, my ass. Although he'd likely smelled my primal needs from across the room, I'd been so charged from the time spent with her. And relax? The man had to be out of his mind. I loved the house, the beach, and everything the water had to offer. I'd wanted nothing more than to cart the catamaran out, but wouldn't do so unless she came with me, which I highly doubted.

I took another gulp of coffee and glared at the cup, trying to keep from tossing it across the room.

Two days had passed of Zoe ignoring me. Two fucking days of the woman doing her best to act as if I didn't exist. Two days of me fuming because she'd seen through my armor, challenging me in a way no one else ever had.

Two days of her never bothering to look at me once. Shit, the woman had called me a fucking Neanderthal. Maybe I was.

At first, I'd congratulated her in my mind for walking away, dismissing me. I'd called her a good girl, praising her silently for recognizing that I was a monster. Now I was annoyed, even angered that she'd managed to keep her distance, ignoring the electric connection that was feeding on us like an alien boring into our blood cells. Great. Now I was comparing her to some creature from another planet. Or maybe that was me.

In truth, I'd never been this ignored by anyone, nor had I believed it was possible she could do so. I'd assumed that I'd be the one to shut her down over and over again. To realize that she had more self-control than I did was humbling. Great. Now I was analyzing myself like a freaking psychologist.

Maybe that's what I needed. I'd spent the last two nights tossing and turning, not losing sleep from worry about Arman or the Thibodeaux business, but because images of her voluptuous breasts and perfect nipples had battered my mind. I'd even imagined her soft moans coming from the other side of the king-size bed. I'd reached over to pull her on top of me more than once, which meant I was losing my shit.

I took another sip of coffee, staring down at the pool as she prepared to take her late morning swim. I had a coffee cup in my hand and I was barefoot and shirtless, sunglasses hanging from a neon cord around my neck. I was even wearing shorts for the first time in as long as I could remember. Yet I wasn't comfortable.

Because of her.

Being cooped up in a five thousand square foot tropical villa was more suffocating than I could have thought. I'd asked if she'd wanted to go sightseeing, or to purchase a few more groceries, although we were fully stocked. She'd just glared at me, walking away as if I'd said nothing. In truth, I'd wanted to spank her sweet ass for being so defiant, but I knew that would only make the situation even more difficult.

The coffee tasted sour, just like my mood. I headed into the kitchen, pouring the rest down the drain. As I planted my hands on the counter, staring out the window at the thick foliage, I realized that we couldn't continue this way. I couldn't protect her while we were fighting any more than I could if we were lovers. It was ridiculous.

Shaking my head, I stormed outside, heading down the stairs as I slipped my sunglasses into place. I could sense she'd heard me coming, immediately moving to the edge of the pool and diving in. She swam under the water all the way to the other side before breaking the surface. I crouched down, refusing to walk away for the fifth time. Her insolence wasn't going to be allowed any longer.

Whether she liked it or not, she was stuck with me.

"Zoe. Come here."

She didn't bother turning around or even looking in my direction. I wanted to be furious with her, but her rebellious attitude only increased the heat of the flames tickling my senses. If I wasn't careful, soon I'd been engulfed in them, incapable of making any rational decisions. That couldn't happen.

"Zoe. If I need to come and get you, I will. Then you definitely won't like me very much."

The way she spun around and the look on her face indicated she had a nasty retort ready. She swam toward me with intense vigor, as if preparing herself to slap me all over again. No other woman had done so in my entire life. Perhaps they'd known better, embracing my reputation of being nasty when I was angered. But this girl had no fear. At least of me.

When she was a few feet away but out of my reach, she stopped swimming, narrowing her eyes in another hateful glare. "What do you want? Did I break some unknown rule? Did I eat the last of your favorite cereal?"

It seemed all the anger and frustration were ripped away just by studying the sadness in her eyes. "I wanted to tell you that your father is going to fully recover. He'll be going home in a few days. That's it." There was no way to repair what had been done. I stood, taking a deep breath then starting to walk away.

"Wait."

"What is it, Zoe?"

"Thank you for letting me know. I'm sorry I've been acting so hateful. I do understand you're trying to do your job."

I cocked my head slightly, nodding a few times. "Both you and your safety are the only things I can concentrate on. I owe that to your father, my best friend. I hope that means something to you."

"Yes, it does. Why don't you come for a swim?"

"I have something better in mind."

"You do, huh? What's that?"

I turned around and lifted my shades, studying her intently. "How about a sail and snorkeling?"

She stared at me for what seemed like a full minute before answering. "I'd love that." She threw out her arm. "Friends?"

As I glanced down at her outstretched hand, I took a deep breath before crouching down, accepting her gesture. "Friends."

It was too bad the electricity coursing through us was so intense that we both sucked in our breath at the same time.

Yeah, as if this friends thing was going to be easy.

CHAPTER 13

Maddox

There was one thing my mother had told me that had stuck in my brain after all these years. In one of her rare, lucid moments, she'd reminded me that women had an innate way of getting under a man's skin.

That's exactly what Zoe was doing as she flaunted her sexy body in her skimpy bathing suit. Sighing, I forced myself to glance toward the horizon, scanning the perimeter, always on edge that someone would hunt us down. Without any backup, we'd be sitting ducks.

"This is incredible," Zoe said as she stood watching while I hoisted the sail, standing back as the wind began immediately to take her further into the cove.

"She's another one of my babies, but I don't get to spend nearly enough time on her."

"Her. Are boats always referred to as a woman?"

"Not always, but I always believed that sailing a boat was like handling a beautiful woman. You're required to learn every nuance about what she enjoys, and how she prefers to operate in order to make her purr."

Even in the bright sunlight, I noticed she was blushing, biting her lower lip to keep from laughing. Or screaming. I wasn't entirely certain. "That's actually… quite profound."

I was the one to laugh, already feeling some of the tension disappearing. She'd helped me pack a picnic basket and there was an even more private cove I'd found and explored where I would take her. The afternoon was perfect, barely a cloud in the sky.

"I don't know about profound, but this type of sailboat can be finnicky, enough so it took me some time to be able to operate her on my own. Once I did, I couldn't imagine being on another vessel."

"It's huge."

"Oh, little lamb. This is a small one in comparison to some of them." I'd used the endearing term, something I'd told myself I'd never do again. It didn't seem to faze or anger her. She was dancing to the reggae music I'd turned on, a lemonade in her hand. From where I stood, she appeared like an angel sent from the heavens, the golden light of the sun highlighting her dark curls and hourglass figure.

I forced myself to turn away before it became obvious I couldn't think about her without desire roaring in. Another moment of tension settled between us, which had constantly occurred over the last two days.

"Can I ask you a question?"

Suddenly, she was right behind me, the scent of whatever perfume she'd splashed on that morning already driving me crazy. "Sure. I need to keep steering so you'll need to follow me."

"Why do you work for my father?"

"Because he and I had the same vision as kids, the same burning desire to succeed in everything we touched."

"Is that really all?"

I laughed. "We were buddies, content to do everything together. He'd watch my back as I watched his. A few years turned into several more. We've been through a lot, he and I. But I wouldn't change the way my life turned out for anything."

"Did you know my mother well? I mean, if you were so close to my dad, you knew her from the beginning of their relationship. Right?"

I glanced over my shoulder. "Well enough. He kept a lot of their relationship private and I never bugged him about it. However, your mother was a bright star and brought your father a few incredible years. You remind me of her."

"Really?" Her face lit up more than I'd seen in a long time.

"Yes. However, I am very glad Arman found someone else. He's a much happier man and less of an asshole."

She burst into laughter. "Well, there's that. All because of a beautiful, feisty woman. Imagine that."

"Yes, imagine that." I threw her a look, half laughing once again. When she was playful, it seemed the world was a brighter place to be in.

"Why don't you have someone?"

"I told you why."

"But if my father can do it, then you can as well."

I shrugged my answer.

"See. There you go again refusing to tell me. Maybe all the girls jilted you. What are your attributes?" She was goading me, tapping her long finger across her lips. "Why don't I help you out? You're handsome in a rough and tough kind of way, trying to pretend you're all suave. You do look good in a suit, but I honestly think the festive shorts are much more you." She gave me a wry smile, lifting her sunglasses and waving her hand in front of her as if she was all hot and bothered.

"Uh-huh. Nice try."

"Oh, I'm being serious. Let me think." She hummed to herself, swaying her hips back and forth in such a way I had to try to concentrate on steering in the right direction. "You're a grumpy man, especially when you don't get your way, but you have an innate love of adventure. That's a plus.

You know your wines and champagnes and I have to believe that you know exactly how to treat a lady on a date. What would be the perfect date for you?"

She had no idea what her challenge was doing to me. Damn it.

"The perfect date, huh?" I asked, the amusement coursing through me a welcome difference.

"Yep. I doubt you know."

"Untrue. I'd prepare the perfect picnic basket and go on a sail to a private island where I'd already planned to have a fire in the sand. There'd be a bottle of wine or champagne, cheeses and we'd grill shrimp and oysters. Then there'd be a delicious chocolate dessert that we'd feed each other along with strawberries. I'd have a blanket so we could lie under the stars and listen to the music created by the waves, the moonlight and the fire our only light. We'd sail back at night to bask in the warmth of a hot tub with a nightcap. After that, I'd carry her to the bedroom where we'd enjoy a night of raw and blissful passion."

When I was finished, I turned my head in her direction. The look of shock and awe on her face was enthralling. She swallowed hard, pressing her fingers across her mouth. "That sounds amazing. Just perfect. And so romantic. I had no idea you had it in you." She threw her hand out before I could say anything. "You don't need to say it again. I realize now I know absolutely nothing about you. But I'd like to learn, Maddox. I mean as friends."

The draw to the beautiful girl was driving me crazier than before. "You can ask me anything, Zoe. Just know that I'm not the man you think I am."

"Meaning?"

"Meaning I'm not a good man, not by a long shot. I've done things that I'm not proud of, but they were necessary. And I would do them again." She looked at me with confidence, yet I could tell so easily that she carried bruises all over her soul as if trying to make them badges of honor. I fisted my hand around the wheel, my heart thudding against my chest a powerful reminder that she was off limits. Goddamn it. I was sick and tired of reminding myself of the obvious. It wasn't doing either one of us any good.

"I'm not the princess you think I am. I know the world I was brought up in, the brutality my grandfather enthusiastically pursued. I realize you've killed people before and will do so again. There are no illusions of grandeur or that my family hasn't crossed the line because I know better. For all the protection and safeguards my father placed around me like a bubble, I saw through everything. I don't want to live in a gilded cage, Maddox. I want to live my life, enjoying every moment because at any time my world could be cut short."

The girl was much wiser than I'd given her credit for. "Understood. Just know there are some things about my life I won't discuss."

"Like about the woman who tore you apart. It wasn't Maggie, was it?"

"Maggie? Who are you talking about?"

She shrugged but I could tell whoever the girl was, it bothered Zoe. "Do you remember my eighteenth birthday?"

"Vaguely." I remembered every single detail of the night she'd turned eighteen. Legal. No longer jailbait, the girl appearing more like a woman than I'd ever seen her in a stunning emerald-green dress that highlighted her curves, the softness of her skin. My cock ached thinking about the way I'd looked at her, as if she'd changed overnight. I'd been furious with myself, finding an excuse to leave the party early. It had taken every ounce of control to keep from taking her that night, claiming her as mine.

After that, I'd done everything in my power to keep from seeing her the few times she'd returned home, including ignoring her at Arman's wedding to Raven. At least that had been easy given her hatred of me because of what I'd said to her at the airport when she'd left for college.

Here I was, my dick aching, which wasn't the only part of me feeling the tight pull, the intensity of a need that would never be fulfilled. No longer could I walk away, pretending as if she didn't have a powerful hold over me. The tenseness we shared was as strong as the jolts of constant current, but she was living in a bubble if she thought I would be good for her. Fuck me. She had no clue what I was capable of.

"Oh, well, my best friend was there," she said, another blush cresting across her jaw as she threw a slight look in my direction. "She was so beautiful, perfect for you, but called you a wolf in sheep's clothing."

"Your friend would be right. I have a very dark side, one that should terrify you."

"I don't scare easily."

"Then maybe I'm not trying hard enough." I lowered my voice, giving her a dangerous look, drinking in her essence as if it was the only sustenance I needed to survive. The moment she dragged her tongue across her bottom lip as she'd done before, I forced myself to turn slightly so she wouldn't see the bulge between my legs, the building need that could easily get out of control.

"Maybe I like the darkness."

"Not my kind, Zoe. You need to find a good man, one with decent characteristics."

"You know what strikes me?" she asked as if in absolute control over the conversation.

"I'm certain you're going to tell me whether I like it or not." I didn't need to see her eyes to know she was rolling them. There was something sick about the fact I enjoyed pushing her buttons as much as she did mine.

She lifted her sunglasses briefly, the look she gave me capable of cracking granite in half. "Yes, I figure I have nothing to lose at this point. You see only truly bad men think they aren't. They call themselves decent when they probably carve up animals for sheer entertainment in their basements. They hide behind their arrogance and the lies they tell, sanctimonious in everything they do. Meanwhile, the good ones, those who embrace humanity even if they're forced to hide their decency, insist that they're horrible, so bad that they should be considered untouchable."

"While houses in New Orleans don't have basements, I've spilled blood in every other room imaginable. As I said, one day you need to find yourself attracted to a truly good person."

When she burst into laughter, it was far too disarming, the sound as sweet as any music I'd ever heard.

"That might not be what I want. Maybe I like to live dangerously because that's the only way to feel truly alive." When our eyes locked again, I was thrown by another series of vivid images of her writhing body underneath mine. "By the way," she continued, "Maggie told me months later that you two were... That you'd..." She laughed but the sound indicated how nervous she suddenly was around me. "That you were into her, enjoying spending time together."

"I assure you, Zoe, that I've never hooked up with an eighteen-year-old girl in my life. Not even when I was that age. I prefer women who can carry on a conversation, not just one who might be good in bed." While my words were truthful, I could tell they bothered her.

"Oh. Well, that's good to know. So it was an older woman who broke your heart then?"

I laughed and tried to ignore her words. That last thing I wanted to do was be reminded of my failures with women.

"I'm right. I can tell. Let me guess. She was five, no, at least ten years older, the one you lost your virginity to. She became your everything until she grew bored. Did you find her with another man, or did she simply walk into the sunset after leaving you a polite if not uncharacteristically icy note?"

Goddamn, the woman was good. She was brainy, beautiful, and far too observant for her own good. They were dangerous attributes.

"I suggest we keep our private lives private."

"Oh, you're afraid to be honest with me," she taunted.

"I just think there are some questions you don't want the answers to."

"Like how many people you've killed in your line of work?"

Half laughing, I shook my head. The girl was especially good at pressing buttons, something I should be used to by now. It was funny how I wasn't. "We'll be at our destination soon."

She sighed and walked toward the railing, peering over the bow. "I hope one day you can trust me enough to tell me things about your private life. I understand hurt better than most. Remember? Besides, you're my hero."

Hero. She had no business confusing an antihero with someone she could trust implicitly. "Stop saying that, Zoe. I'm no one's hero."

"You are to me. Isn't that worth something?"

"Let's just enjoy the day. Agreed?"

"Fine. Agreed."

The truth was that it wasn't about me trusting her but about not destroying her life because of who and what I was. That was the second greatest challenge, the first being the way I felt about her.

Somehow, I knew the temptation was too great. If I succumbed to the hunger, I had a feeling the two of us would be damned.

CHAPTER 14

Zoe

Darkness.

Maybe that was exactly what I craved as much as I did the man I couldn't seem to stop staring at. He was everything I'd ever dreamed of and more yet doing his best to remain closed off. After he'd spanked me like some bad little girl, I'd really believed I could easily hate him.

That wasn't the case.

I'd remained wet almost the entire time he'd taken the strap to me, which continued to shock the woman inside. Now here we were acting like there was no danger surrounding us, no need to worry about other types of boogeymen. I'd walked by his impressive computer and security room more than once, marveling in the amount of equipment he had, technology that appeared straight out of the future. I'd even dared venture inside the space, doing my best to keep from touching anything.

He was anticipating an attack. I could feel it in my bones. Here? In paradise? A cold shiver drifted down my spine at the thought. The fantasies about him had continued, even though I'd done everything I could to get him out of my mind.

Maddox stood in boating shoes and colorful swim trunks, the shirt he'd initially worn shed moments after he'd set sail. He was a feast for the eyes. His colorful tattoos and the way that the sunlight had already kissed his skin with a golden tan were keeping my pussy throbbing. I was reminded of a quote I'd heard years before and only just realized how well it applied to the description he'd given himself.

"The more we deny that we have a dark side, the more power it has over us." Sheryl Lee had made the phrase memorable, the words lingering in my mind long after I'd heard them for the first time. Maybe I'd captured the essence, locking it into the darkest reaches of my mind for a simple reason.

The darkness fed off my soul as well.

My father had even warned me that because I was so much like him, there was a hint of evil festering inside. I'd laughed because I only saw the good side to my father.

Just like I'd done with Maddox.

But in truth, we all had the kind of lingering turmoil, an unknown part of us that if we didn't embrace it, it stood the chance of eating us alive. While I was being far too philosophical on such a gorgeous day, I sensed I was trying to process the concept of just being his friend. What I couldn't tell him was that as of the moment he'd kissed me, there would never be another man who could rank even close to him.

He was also arrogant and annoying, but that was part of his charm, a curmudgeon with a heart of gold. I doubted I would get away with calling him that.

I removed my sunglasses, rubbing my eyes. Here I was in paradise, but nothing was real.

Crystal clear water, shades of aquamarine and cobalt blue were shimmering from the crystalline effects of the bright sun, highlighting the various vivid corals and fish.

Yellows.

Pinks.

Purples.

Reds.

It seemed every color was represented in the warm, shallow water the Caribbean Ocean had to offer. Maddox had ignored my comment on the woman that I sensed he'd been in love with, the one that had forced a shutdown of his system, instead educating me on the beautiful island of Saint Barthelemy located in the French Indies. I was fascinated that he knew so much about the history as well as the culture of those living year-round on what would be considered a postage stamp of only nine point seven square miles.

THE WISEGUY

I glanced over my shoulder, catching him watching me. His expression was entirely different than before, so unnerving that I found it difficult to swallow. Even though it was almost a cloudless day, I could swear thunderclouds were churning in ugly swirls around his head. Whew. If I didn't know better, I'd say he had x-ray vision. There was a shocking moment as the electricity we couldn't avoid between us fissured, crackling as if he'd managed to create a violent storm himself. The air around us became supercharged and suddenly, I couldn't breathe.

Wow. I rubbed my sweaty fingers down the side of my neck, the heat radiating off my body capable of keeping an entire city warm through a horrific winter. A laugh finally bubbled to the surface of my mouth from my ridiculous thoughts.

Get a grip, girl. He was very clear that there's nothing between you. Friends. Nothing more. Don't make this any worse than it is.

Oh, yeah. There was that. I continued studying the water, eager to dive in and hunt for treasures just like he'd promised were in crevices and the deeper water. I wanted to go exploring with him, to try to forget that my family was a thousand miles away, fending for themselves in sea of barracudas.

I almost laughed given our location.

Maddox was also an expert in navigation, the shallow reefs surrounded by ancient volcanoes perfect for the catamaran. I was inwardly smiling that he'd never had anything to do with Maggie, which was stupidly girlish. As I stood staring out at the ocean, it seemed we were the only ones on the island. There wasn't another sailboat in sight. I shielded my eyes from the sun, scanning the entire cove as he finished mooring us fifty yards or so from the shore of what appeared to be a small, very secluded beach.

"Are you ready to go snorkeling?" he asked, breaking the spell that had been holding me in a foggy haze.

"Do you want to know the truth? I've never been before."

"You're kidding me. Never?" He moved to a large box secured to the deck, opening it and digging inside. "I thought Arman took you to the beach a few times."

"He did but I was terrified of the water when I was little."

"You do know how to swim, don't you?"

"Oh, yes. He insisted I take lessons along with going to the firing range. In addition to ballet and piano lessons." I laughed given how ridiculous the combination sounded.

"A well-rounded girl is a good thing."

"Woman."

The way he looked at me as soon as I made the comment pushed another shiver down my spine. "Woman," he conceded.

Round fifty-two went to me. I bit back another smile.

He pulled out two masks and snorkels from the container, one in red and one in blue, grinning as he studied me. The fact we could stare at each other as we'd done at least fifty times since coming on this trip was... astonishing. I never wanted it to end, although there was always an end to everything whether I wanted to accept it or not.

"Which one?" he asked as he walked closer.

I hated the fact even after spending almost forty-five minutes in the direct sun, he smelled of exotic spices, citrus, and a huge dollop of pure sin. "Red. You know how much I adore the color."

"Then red it is." He handed it over and as I eased the mask over my head, he moved in front of me adjusting the band going around my head as well as the height of the snorkel. "Make certain you can take deep breaths."

While I did as I was told, I wondered if he heard the gaps in my breathing based on the closeness of his heated body. There was such a level of protectiveness in him with everything involving me that I should feel flattered. Only instead, I felt like the awkward girl I'd once been all over again, sheltered from anything that could hurt me. My father had even insisted that I turn seventeen before he taught me how to drive.

An unforgiveable sin in my mind, although I'd been a wild child during that period of time.

"Yes, of course I can. Are we ready?" I asked, immediately backing away and toward the three steps leading to the water.

"We're ready." He stalked toward me like the predator he was, and I found myself laughing, uncharacteristically joyful around him.

I couldn't seem to help myself around him, enjoying feeling free enough to tease him. I took a running leap into the air, only grasping my mask as the last minute to prevent it from flying off. Just as I entered the water, I could swear I heard a strange sound like…

Gunfire. Oh, God, no.

While I managed to gulp some seawater, I fought my way to the surface, coughing only a couple of times as I turned toward the boat after yanking the snorkel from my mouth. As I glanced at the vessel, I was forced to shield my eyes from the sun. Where had he gone?

"Maddox?"

Not only did he not answer, but he was also nowhere to be seen. I hadn't noticed him entering the water. I swam in another full circle, still not seeing him. The clear water should easily allow me to catch sight of his muscular body or some activity in the water. I almost panicked, shoving the rubbery mouthpiece back into my mouth and sticking my head into the water.

"Don't do this. Please." Shaking, I scanned the area around us, not seeing another boat or anything suspicious. That didn't mean there wasn't a sharpshooter somewhere. Oh, God. Now, I was drifting into paralyzing fear.

"Maddox!" Why was he doing this?

I started swimming away from the boat, every passing second making me uneasy. There were hundreds of fish, so many that it was difficult to see anything right in front of me. I powered through the water, puffing air as if I was a smoker. He had to be alright.

Another wave of terror skittered through me, a sick sense that he'd been shot.

When I felt a hard jerk, suddenly becoming weightless, I issued a scream, which forced the mouthpiece from my lips and water into my lungs. As I started to choke, I was lifted from the water, spun around to face the man who was purposely driving me crazy.

"No. Why did you do that? Why?"

"Whoa. Hold on. Are you okay?" he asked, his tone full of concern but the amusement in his eyes pushing a scowl across my face.

"No… thanks to… you." Another series of coughs erupted from my chest and I spit out salt water, resisting the urge to gag. I struggled to get away from him and he laughed until he saw my face.

"I didn't mean to scare you."

"Well, you did!" I snapped, trying to get away from him but he wasn't allowing it. "Don't you ever do that again. I was terrified something had happened to you." I was gasping for air at this point, hating the fact tears had formed in my eyes.

"Please, little lamb. I'm an excellent swimmer and know these waters like the back of my hand. I'm sorry. That was shitty of me to do."

"Yes, it was. Damn you."

Maddox smiled in a reassuring manner. "I said I was sorry and I meant it."

"Okay," I huffed, trying to tamp down the continuing trickles of fear. "What is it that you aren't good at?"

He wrinkled his brow as he spun me around in the water three times. "Let me think. Nothing."

"So modest. I don't know how you stand yourself."

"Oh, you might be surprised."

While his playfulness had returned, I pushed both hands against his chest and he let me go. But as he reached for my hand, his expression changed dramatically. "You really are a bastard."

"So I've been told. Come on. Let me show you Mother Nature's beautiful artistic canvas."

"Only if you promise not to tease me."

"I won't make promises I can't keep. Come with me, Zoe. I don't want to ask you again."

Why was it that his dominating side thrilled me so much?

We both shoved our mouthpieces past our lips and he led me out into deeper water until I finally dipped my head just under the surface. The colors of fish and coral were more explosive than before, so enticing that I was instantly relaxed. He pointed out various objects, watching my eyes as they highlighted the joy I was experiencing.

The warm water and the peaceful moment lulled me into a moment of feeling safe, as if being with him meant nothing bad could ever happen. I wanted the moment to last, but I knew as with all good things, they would soon be forced to come to an end.

He never let go of me, swimming as if in a practiced orchestration as we moved through the calm water. He pointed out various corals and fish, finally making hand signs as if he expected I'd know what he was indicating.

The time we spent with our heads nearly under water was some of the happiest moments I'd felt in a long time. I was relaxed, able to concentrate on breathing and enjoying the moment, basking in the sun and gorgeous colors of the ocean.

When we finally surfaced, I was shocked to see the sun had changed positions in the sky dramatically. I was giddy inside, immediately laughing as I yanked the mask down, blinking beads of water from my eyes. "That was incredible. So incredible."

He gave me a boyish grin, winking after removing his mask and before I knew what I was doing, I rushed toward him. I threw my arms around his neck, tangling my fingers in his wet hair, even daring to wrap one leg around him. In a shocking moment, I involuntarily pressed my lips against his. His body reacted almost instantly, his thick cock pressing into my stomach, his lips opening mine. We were both on fire, so much so that I was certain we'd combust, the electricity we shared more powerful than before.

I remained breathless, the longing sparking something that I knew would never end.

But only a few seconds later, his body tensed as it had done before.

Suddenly, we were reminded at the same time that what we'd shared was forbidden on one too many levels and both our bodies stiffened.

I backed away first, looking away as I treaded water, refusing to allow him to see how embarrassed I'd become. "I'm sorry. I was caught up in the moment."

"Mmm... do you see the shore over there?" Maddox asked from behind me, pointing over my shoulder.

"Yes." The small cove was exquisite, seductively tropical with palm trees and other thick foliage surrounding the perimeter. It appeared vacant, untouched, reminding me of an episode of *Lost*. As soon as my mind drifted to the television show from years before, a sudden shiver coursed down my spine. There'd been secrets galore on the show, murders and mysterious disappearances going unexplained. Crazy thoughts entered my mind about Maddox dumping bodies of former enemies in shallow graves in the dense forest.

I rolled my eyes, tensing as I felt his presence getting closer, the warm water lapping over my arms as I floated on the surface as if riding on a pocket of air.

"Swim to the shore for me and wait on the beach."

"Are you planning on leaving me there?" The question came out of the blue. I knew better. The man had far too much loyalty to my father to do something so stupid.

"Only if you're a very bad girl and continue not obeying my order." He laughed, the sound tantalizing in its huskiness, keeping my body aching more than before.

"What are you doing?"

"Perhaps I have a surprise for you. Now, swim before I change my mind. Trust me, little lamb."

I turned in a full circle, more than curious by what he had in mind. I did trust him, with my life.

But the problem was I wasn't certain I could trust either him or myself with my heart.

CHAPTER 15

Zoe

"Can I take a walk?" I asked without looking behind me. That was strictly forbidden.

"Nope. You're not going anywhere," Maddox answered rather gruffly since both of us were nestled in a secluded cove.

"And what if I do?"

"Then I'll hunt you down. I think you know what will happen if you try to make me capture you."

Capture. I shuddered at the thought of him doing exactly that, filthy images sparking the darkest parts of my mind. I had to shove away my lurid thoughts or I'd go mad from them. I folded my arms, the warm sun unable to prevent a chill from coursing through me.

Breathtaking wasn't the correct word for what I was seeing. Being able to stand on the shore, pearlescent sand between my toes, soft waves of aquamarine water lapping at my feet as I studied the once active volcano only a few hundred yards away was like a dream come true.

I was an ocean girl, even if I'd rarely visited a tropical location. I was more comfortable standing on a deserted beach than I'd been anywhere in my life. Part of the reason was that I was with Maddox, a man who'd stop at nothing to ensure my safety.

Even if it meant losing his life.

But there was more to the way I was feeling, the intensity of emotions sweeping through me like a tsunami. The truth haunted me, pushing me into an entirely different level of serenity, even if my feelings could never be expressed.

I was in love.

There was no doubt, no denying the way I felt about the man. He was my everything. I'd heard that said before in love songs and poems, celebrities and singers shouting it to the world only to break up with the man of their dreams weeks or months later. The way I felt about Maddox was for all eternity. Of that I had no doubt. He was the storm that kept me alive and awake, the sunshine that I could feel kissing my skin. And he was the rapid beating of my heart every time he was in the room.

Unfortunately, I wasn't allowed to have him. What did they call it? Unrequited love? I wasn't entirely certain what the phrase meant other than I wasn't allowed to taste the forbidden fruit more than once for fear of being poisoned.

This had to be what Romeo and Juliet felt. I wanted to laugh at all my analogies, but I was trying to make sense of the rush of sensations, the electric vibrations that neither time nor distance had squelched.

Maybe that was impossible.

What I knew without a shadow of a doubt was that there would never be another man for me. I'd never find a replacement and likely wouldn't bother. No wonder I'd all but saved myself for him, pining away for the impossible. I wanted to laugh but here we were together on a dangerous mission. All alone.

Yet we were both locked in a cage.

I heard crackling sounds behind me but resisted turning, enjoying the waning afternoon sun. My back and arms were slightly burned from the powerful sun, but it didn't matter. The day had been… perfect. Enlightening. Fantastic.

Oppressive.

But I wouldn't change the experience for all the rubies in the world. I bit my lower lip as I swayed back and forth, still shocked that Maddox had brought a picnic with all the goodies with him, swimming with the waterproof box to the shore while I'd been waiting for him.

He was still embroiled in the surprise, forbidding me to turn around. I was trying to be a good girl while he worked but the curiosity was killing me.

"How much longer?" I asked, maybe a little bit too loudly.

"Not long. Good things come to very good girls who are patient and obedient," Maddox mused, the sound of his deep voice skittering through me like rocket fuel.

"You obviously have me mistaken with some other chick."

His booming laughter sent another wave of chills through me. He had a way about him that was as infuriating as it was delightful. His signals with me were mixed, although I knew he was doing everything in his power to make me feel more comfortable. Instead, I was lost in the fantasy, refusing to give up on my tantalizing dream of being with him forever.

I knew I was being foolish, my youth showing every time I acted like a brat or had these kinds of thoughts but for the first time in as long as I could remember, I felt like me.

"No, I think I know the woman standing on the shore pretty darn well," he said, and it was obvious he'd moved closer.

Tensing, I did my best not to turn around, but I couldn't help myself, twisting my head to the side, struggling to see the surprise. Damn it. He'd hidden whatever he'd done pretty well.

"What do you think you know about me, tough guy?"

"Hmmmm..." He'd moved even closer still. "I know that you're an accomplished musician struggling with the fact you'd prefer to play music rather than become a nurse. Although you do have a natural instinct for helping people."

"Everybody knows that. You'll need to try harder to win me over."

"Is that what I'm doing?"

"I certainly don't think you want me to hate you."

He hesitated, his heated body so close I felt a buzz all around me, the current even more electrified than before. "No, Zoe. I don't, but if that's the way you need to feel, I will understand. As long as you can trust me."

"I do trust you. I just…" This was already going downhill. "What else do you think you know?"

"That you're exactly like your father."

"Meaning?"

"Meaning you're highly intelligent. You have a strong family and work ethic. You would give the shirt off your back to someone in need. You're passionate about everything in your life, refusing to take a back seat to anything or anyone. But the difference is that you still live in a world where you believe in the best in people."

"I hope I always will."

Suddenly, I felt the rough pads of his finger brushing against my shoulder, a drink appearing in an insanely adorable plastic glass seemingly as if by magic.

"I hope that for you too," he said gruffly, flanking my side as soon as I accepted the drink.

"And what is this?" I dared throw him a glance, biting my tongue to keep from saying anything else. He was even more handsome than before. If that was even possible. The sun had baked me, but his skin was more golden brown, adding another dimension to the aura surrounding him.

The way the light breeze tousled his hair forced goosebumps to dance down my arms.

"Just a little tropical concoction I created."

"If I didn't know better, I'd say you were trying to get me drunk."

"Only this isn't an alcoholic beverage," he said as he finally turned toward me. "Not until dinner."

"We're having dinner? Here?"

"Turn around."

The moment I did, I pressed one hand across my mouth. Seeing a fire going in the sand, rocks surrounding the flames, was incredible. "How did you do that?" There was also a blanket positioned just so on the sand, items placed on the surface. This was as close to paradise as I'd ever seen.

"I'm not giving away my secrets." He winked. "Come on. Are you game for making dinner together?" He backed away, grinning wider than I was used to seeing him do.

"What do you have in mind?"

"You'll see, but only if you come toward the blanket."

I gave him a saucy look, glad that we were both able to let go, if only for a little while. I sashayed closer, watching as he tugged out something from the cooler. It took me a few seconds to realize what he had. "Shrimp and oysters?"

"Only the best. Granted, it would have been better if we'd caught them ourselves."

"Beggars can't be choosers. I can't remember when I had seafood last. You know my dad is a huge meat lover."

He laughed, the sound trickling through my system creating another fire. "Yes, I know Arman's taste far too well. Did he ever tell you about the first time he tried a brand-new outdoor grill?"

"No. Spill it."

"Only if you get out the other items for dinner."

As I dropped to my knees on the blanket, another shiver drifted down my spine. For some crazy reason, I felt as if we were being watched, although that was next to impossible.

Unless the perpetrator had a telescope, which I was beginning to think was standard operating equipment for assholes attempting to destroy someone. My mind drifted briefly to the pictures that had turned up in my email, the scathing images doctored but the basis had been me in skimpy PJs standing in front of my dorm window.

While nothing had been done with them that I knew about, the fact someone had gone to such great lengths to try to humiliate me had kept me nervous for the last two weeks of school. I'd been waiting for the other even more horrible shoe to drop. The worst part about it? I'd lived on the sixth floor with no other buildings in close proximity. That was the only reason I didn't make it a habit of closing my blinds. There'd been no need to, no chance anyone could look in.

"Are you okay?" Maddox asked. The moment he touched my arm, I jumped.

"I'm sorry. Just lost in thought. So tell me about my dad and this grill."

He studied me intently, his eyes narrowing. "What did you think you saw?"

"Nothing." I continued to shiver, unable to shake the feeling.

I wasn't surprised when he jerked up, immediately taking long strides toward the edge of the water. However, I was shocked that he didn't magically yank a gun from a hidden pocket after having found a way to waterproof it. I was certain he had weapons on board the catamaran, although I hadn't seen anything while there.

His body was tense, one hand fisted as he shielded his eyes from the sun with the other, scanning the perimeter the same way I'd done before. I watched him silently for a few seconds before heading in his direction. The moment I placed my hand on his arm, we both had the same reaction we always did.

Slight shudders coursing through every muscle.

"It's okay. There's no way anyone is watching us. I'm just… I think the events of the last few days are finally kicking in."

He shifted his attention from the open water to me, placing a comforting, almost fatherly hand on my shoulder. The gesture was sweet but broke the sensual moment, shattering it completely. Another reminder I was his little lamb to protect and nothing more.

"You have every right to feel concerned and saddened by what happened. And I'm so sorry you were forced to endure something so tragic on such an important day."

"You don't need to feel sorry or upset. What happened wasn't your fault."

Maddox had always been so private that I'd made up stories about what he did in his off time, and it often seemed as if he had no life of his own. My wondering would continue as I doubted that he'd let me in on but so many additional aspects of his life. When he said nothing, I glanced at the water all over again.

"I understand your loyalty to my father and the reasons why but what happened between us was something we both wanted at the time. We're consenting adults. I know it can't happen again. And I accept that, although I want so many things, but please do me a favor and stop blaming yourself. Whoever is after this family, our family and you're a part of it, I have no doubt you'll discover the truth."

When I slowly turned my head, there was an entirely different look in his eyes, as if the man was seeing me for the first time.

He rolled his hand from my shoulder to my long strands of hair, fiddling with the ends as he took a deep breath. "Did anyone ever tell you that you're far too philosophical at such a young age?"

"Did anyone ever tell you that you're a huge curmudgeon at such an advanced age?"

His eyes twinkled. "No one who wanted to live."

"Here's the thing, Mr. I Almost Never Crack a Smile, I'm not just anyone."

"That I know, Zoe. And I do smile. All the time."

"Right. Tell me another lie, big boy. It would take a happy man in order to do so. You are not that man."

He grinned again and I wanted to melt right into the sand. "I'll have you know I'm very happy."

"How old are you again? Oh, yes. Very old."

"Your attitude could drive a man to drink."

"Better than having a stick stuck up your ass," I teased, chuckling from the sight of his face.

The way he pointed his finger at me made me giggle like a girl. "Careful there, little girl, or I'll be forced to punish you."

"Nope. That's not going to happen."

"It will if I say so. And I don't have a stick stuck up my ass."

"Coulda fooled me."

We both laughed as the scent of the incredible food wafted toward us, making my mouth water. But not nearly as much as the man standing in front of me. "Anyway, just stop beating yourself up. As you reminded me to do. Let's enjoy tonight at least."

"You're something special, Zoe. Don't let anyone tell you otherwise. And you're right. I will. If it takes my last breath, I *will* put out the fire."

Something flickered in my periphery of vision, an intense smell assaulting my senses. As soon as I turned my head, I gasped. "Maybe you could start right now!"

He caught my gaze, turning his head. "Ah, shit."

I wanted to laugh since the food he'd placed on makeshift grates over the flame had sparked into a large enough fire I wasn't certain he'd be able to put it out easily. For all of his organization skills, his careful attention to details, this was the first and if I had to guess the only time the powerful, handsome man would be off his game.

Unable to keep from doing so, I broke into laughter as he did everything he could to douse the flames, even attempting to save the ruined seafood.

If he only knew that I couldn't care less about food. The only thing that mattered was spending time with him.

The larger-than-life hunk.

The brooding, ruthless self-proclaimed killer.

And my personal hero.

CHAPTER 16

"*But you've slipped under my skin, invaded my blood and seized my heart.*"

—Maria V. Snyder

Zoe

Whoever said being friends was better than being lovers was an idiot, but as twilight began to set in, I was enlightened by the fact I'd prefer having Maddox as a friend than as an enemy. He was still the strong, brooding type but over the last couple of hours, he'd finally started to relax, telling me a few stories that both amazed and terrified me. They'd been devoid of emotion, a return to times when he was in full control of the situation. Handling business his way.

Killing when necessary, experiencing no remorse whatsoever.

"Do you believe in karma?" I asked.

Maddox chuckled. "Karma is a method of balancing good and evil, or righting wrongs. But in my mind karma has a hidden meaning."

I'd never known him to be so philosophical. "And that is?"

"To me the expression is one of hope, that whatever you put out in the universe will come back to you in the most unexpected ways."

"Only if you take a few chances along the way."

He grinned, which I also wasn't expecting. "Exactly."

I savored the moment, thinking about what he said.

"How many people have you killed?" I asked after there was a lull in conversation.

He took another swig of his drink, staring out at the ocean as he'd been doing almost the entire time since finishing dinner. The feast had been incredible even without the charred seafood. Breads and cheeses, other meats, and fruits. The selection had allowed me to see a more romantic side of him.

Yet as the light had begun to dim, the darkness had taken him other places, his mind lost in whatever operational maneuvers he required to calm the beast inside of him. He was even more on edge, as if my earlier concerns had flagged something within his psyche.

"Enough, Zoe."

"What does enough mean?" I bent my knees, folding one arm over them and leaning my head against both kneecaps as I studied him through the flickering flames.

"That I do what I need to do when necessary."

"I thought the great Thibodeaux Empire was all legit, following the rules and never daring to cross over that thin gray line."

The man stared at me incredulously. "Whoever told you that was either drunk or stupid."

His frankness continued to make me laugh, even if I could tell he was being deadpan serious. "Oh, come on now," I mused, pushing his arm. "You are many things but not a cold-blooded killer."

He took another sip of his drink, barely darting a glance in my direction. "Do you really want to know how many people's lives I've ended, Zoe? Is that something that's going to make you sleep better at night? Is this why you asked about karma?" When I didn't answer, he snorted. "I didn't think you really wanted to know. Leave it at enough. Or if you'd prefer, enough to know I'm a dangerous, lethal man. And I am certain karma will come back and bite me in the ass."

"You're a good man, even if you don't want to admit it."

"No, Zoe. I hate to burst your bubble. Why do you think your father warned me a hell of a long time ago to stay away from you?"

This was news. "He did?"

"Yep. He did." He took another swig of his drink, polishing it off then reaching for the bottle of scotch he'd brought. Meanwhile, he'd hidden away a split of Moet Chandon for me. While I was trying my best to save the bubbly, when Maddox clammed up like he was doing now, I wanted to drink from the bottle instead of the deliriously funny plastic glass he'd provided.

"Why?"

"Why do you think, Zoe? Because I'm not good enough for his only daughter."

I wanted to be angry that my father would do such a thing but that was Daddy dearest. No man would ever be good enough. "I think that's because Daddy is trying to hook me up with someone."

He slowly turned his head, narrowing his eyes, the flickering flames allowing me to catch a fleeting glimpse of raw, imposing rage. It was just like what I'd seen when he'd saved me from the two abductors. He'd wanted to rip them apart with his bare hands.

"What did you say?" he asked, although he sounded as if he was growling instead.

"He didn't come right and say it, but he told me at the party there were some eligible bachelors."

He took a deep breath, his mood darkening even more. The slight crack of the plastic glass in his hand allowed me a further indication of just how enraged he was at hearing the news.

"What is it? What's wrong?"

"He can't do that," he said with so much authoritativeness that I could tell my flippant comment had struck a nerve.

"He's my father, Maddox. I guess I'm worth more than I think I am." I tried to laugh it off, but not only did I realize it might have something to do with the reason I'd been attacked, whatever nerve I'd hit had also angered him significantly.

"Don't ever say that again. Do you hear me?" He grabbed my wrist, yanking me toward him.

I was more shocked by his actions than almost anything he'd done so far. I couldn't find the right answer, unable to say anything.

"Do you?" His command was darker than before.

"Okay. Yes, I hear you. I'm sorry. I was teasing. That's it."

His chest rose and fell, his breathing remaining labored. "You are a very special woman. He will not do that to you. I won't allow it."

It was the first time I felt as if he really cared, for a reason other than because I was one of his job requirements. "Forget I said anything, Maddox. I'm sure I'm wrong." Although I wasn't. I could tell by the hardline expression remaining on his face that he wasn't going to let it go. Shit. Shit. Shit. The last thing I wanted was to create a rift between Maddox and my dad.

He came close to polishing off another drink, but I had no illusions that the alcohol would affect him. I'd never seen him this angry.

"You're not being forced to marry anyone you don't want to."

His possessiveness was as startling as everything else about him. When he released his grip, I scooted closer. I could see his wheels turning once again, drifting back into the same aggravation as before.

"Daddy wouldn't let that happen. Would he?"

Maddox looked away, remaining stiff and on edge. Another wave of dreaded tension slipped between us and I couldn't stand it any longer. This felt like a merry-go-round ride and I was ready to get off.

Permanently.

"Do you know why the bubble is still there with regard to who you are, Maddox?"

The man did little more than throw me a quick look.

"Because you refuse to tell me anything about yourself. Not really anyway. You continue to act as if I'm made of glass, which I'm not. Don't do that. If there's something going on I need to know about, then tell me."

"Something going on? Do you mean like you almost being taken away from your fucking family?"

His anger was intensifying, enough so a lump formed in my throat. "I just want to know more about you. That's it."

"Fine. What is it that you so desperately want to know, Zoe? If I sleep with my gun on my nightstand at night? That answer would be yes, always. I also always have one in the bathroom with me. I don't leave the house without a fresh magazine of ammunition either. I'm an assassin for your family. That's not going to change because you want to see me as something else, something less ruthless." He half laughed under his breath as if I was a silly girl for thinking otherwise.

"Why do you do that?" Now my tone was demanding.

"Do what?"

"Act as if me asking you questions is such a big deal to you?" I heard the shift in my tone and huffed. Every time we got a little close, he pulled away, acting as if nothing mattered to him. Certainly not me.

"Because you don't deserve to learn the truth about me. You have this perfect man locked inside that big brain of yours. I'm not that man."

"Why? Do you beat puppies in your spare time or enjoy ripping away canes from old ladies at the bus stop?"

He stared at me with bug eyes, and it made me laugh all over again. "First of all, I don't think I've taken public transportation since I was a boy in school. Second, and more important, I doubt a puppy would dare get next to me."

"That's right. They do tend to sniff out bad odors."

"Are you telling me I stink?"

"Your attitude does."

"I'm just being honest with you."

"You've been everything but honest with me, Maddox. I told you I wanted to learn more about you, and you act as if I'm digging into your private life. I doubt you have a private life. You're like some Stepford soldier, a drone and nothing more." I jerked to my feet, taking a few steps away from the blanket. I hated the tension settling between us. I'd never been so frustrated with anyone in my life.

"Fine, Zoe. Then ask your questions by all means. Whatever you want to know, I'll be honest with you. But be careful what you ask for. For your information, I do have a private life."

"Right. Whatever you say."

"Ask. Go for it."

Goddamn the man. I pressed my fisted hand against my forehead, trying to keep from lashing out at him. "Oh, I don't know." I failed on the first try. "Let's see. Your favorite color. Your favorite food. Your favorite movie. Your favorite dog. Your favorite restaurant. How about if you could live anywhere in the world, where would it be? Or maybe, just maybe you could tell me what you do in your private time since you insist you have one."

As Maggie would say, honey was dripping from my mouth, luring the fly to my lair so I could eat him alive. I rolled my eyes from the thought.

"Okay. Orange. Seafood. *It's a Wonderful Life*. Anything that won't bite me. A little place called Cajo's on this island. St. Barts. And I enjoy reading when I'm not working."

By the time his answers settled in, I was certain he was lying to me.

Or making fun of my questions and the situation.

My reaction was without hesitation and fueled on the ugly frustration that refused to go away. I spun around, tossing the rest of my champagne into his cocky-ass face. "How dare you treat me that way. What a fool I was to think for a single moment that we could even be friends. You act as if you're holier than thou, as if I'm not good enough for you. Damn you, Maddox. Damn you for treating me as if I'm just a little girl. And damn you for making me fall in love with you."

Oh. My. God.

Shock tore through me, a sick feeling rumbling in my stomach. I slapped my hand across my mouth, blinking to keep tears from forming. Why had I allowed him to make me so emotional? To get to me?

I'd just exposed the exact way I felt about him. I was out of my mind completely. The horror of what I'd done settled into me, the look of shock on his face forcing another wave of embarrassment through my system. No. No. No.

Before he had a chance to say anything in retort, I bolted, racing down the shoreline toward the forest. At this point, I didn't care where I ended up as long as it wasn't near him. Why had I exposed my feelings, setting myself up for another chastising moment? I was such a fool. I hated myself that tears had not only formed in my eyes, the salty beads stinging, but that they were quickly sliding down both cheeks. He didn't deserve my tears. Not for a single second.

While I didn't bother looking behind me, I sensed him racing behind me, so I picked up speed, refusing to allow him to catch me. The last thing I wanted was to feel his hands on me ever again.

I ran even faster, managing to make it to the edge of the forest.

"Oh, no, you don't, Zoe."

His deep growl infiltrated every cell in my body, sending a wave of shivers all the way to my toes. When he grabbed my wrist, whipping me around to face him, I threw a hard punch to his jaw, shocking the hell out of both him and myself in the process.

"Let me go!" I screeched, pounding his chest with both fists.

"Not a chance. I'm going to protect you whether you like it or not."

"Just leave me alone. God, I hate you. I hate everything about you and this life. My father. You're right. No one is going to make choices for me. I'll run far away where no can find me."

"Then I'll hunt you down. There's nowhere you can run where you'll be able to get away from me. Do you hear me, Zoe? Nowhere." He was as exasperated as I was, even more so. His hot breath was cascading across my face, the musky scent of him creating a feeling of pure intoxication.

"No. I can't… You won't. I know you won't."

"Like fucking hell." The powerful man wasn't to be denied, his he-man protective side taking over, tossing me over his shoulder and trudging back through the woods.

"I'll get you for this." I refused to stop even when he smacked my bottom several times, the tingling sensations of pain evoking far too many emotions.

"I'm eager to watch you try." He smacked my bottom again, hoisting me even higher as he made his way back to the campfire. The second he lowered my feet onto the blanket, I did my best to scramble away. He refused to tolerate any additional antics, immediately fisting my hair, jerking me against his chest.

"Get off me!" I fought to drive my hands against his chest.

"Not a chance." He lowered his head. "I'm not letting you go."

"Why? Why are you bothering, Maddox? Tell me why you won't just let me go. Tell me why it matters to you. I'm nothing in your eyes, forbidden. Just a girl with a stupid crush." I continued to struggle in his arms, doing everything I could to slip free from his strong hold.

But when he slipped his hand to the back of my head, digging his fingertips into my skull, I had a feeling this was just the beginning. There was another explosion of energy between us, as if the entire world had just erupted into flames.

"Because you belong to me. And I swear to God. No man is ever going to touch you again. If they dare try, they will die by my hands. Do you hear me, Zoe? Do you?"

As he captured my mouth, every muscle in my body froze. There was such a sense of need building between us that I was driven to the very point of madness, the longing that intense.

His words were exciting, dangerous, and possessive. And I never wanted to be set free from his powerful hold ever again. He thrust his tongue inside, dominating mine as he'd done before, but as with everything about the structured, chiseled man, he was laying claim. As he shifted his hips back and forth, I was pulled into a darker moment, needing the intensity of our raging passions more than ever.

The fact his cock was rock hard, throbbing against my stomach sent a thrill of excitement deep inside, every nerve ending seared from the intensity of our connection. I was lightheaded and even with my eyes tightly closed, I could see vivid flashes of light spinning around my periphery of vision like a firestorm. Even the electricity shifting back and forth was more powerful, my extremities tingling from the white-hot sensations.

He tasted of scotch and strawberries, the combination as irresistible as the man. I allowed myself to become lost in the moment, swept up in the notion that this would mean something. As I slipped one arm around his neck, tangling my fingers in his thick curls, he pushed me backward, forcing me into an arc.

Within seconds, he eased me onto the blanket, straddling my legs as his kiss became merciless and unforgiving, as if the man were desperate to become intoxicated from my heated breath. The thought that all time stood still, that we were the only people left in the universe flowed through my mind. The idea was crazy, but one I hung onto as if by doing so, I could prevent cold reality from resurging, dragging us both into purgatory.

When he finally broke the kiss, he issued a deep, husky growl before dragging his tongue from one side of my jaw to the other.

I took gasping breaths, wrapping my hands around his shirt as I clung to him. I was terrified that if I let him go for even a few seconds, I'd realize he was nothing more than a mirage. He bit my lower lip before sliding the tip of his tongue down the column of my neck. I arched my back, the pleasure so intense I couldn't think straight.

He yanked the straps of my bikini top, easily exposing my breasts. As he untied the slender string behind my back, easily yanking the hindrance free, he whispered additional filthy words of longing. Every sound from his mouth, every guttural breath he took only added fuel to the already raging fire.

I rolled my hands over his shoulders, rubbing my palms down his back, marveling in the way his muscles felt underneath my fingers.

Chuckling darkly, he flicked his tongue across my already taut nipple, pushing another humming series of vibrations into my stomach. As soon as he pulled the tender tissue between his lips, sucking and biting down, a series of whispered moans escaped my lips. He took his time, the sounds he was making becoming more savage in nature.

Maddox cupped my other breast, squeezing before pinching my already hardened bud between his fingers. The flash of pain was exquisite, making me gasp for air.

"Oh. Oh, my."

"My little lamb enjoys a little pain. I'll keep that in mind."

"I'm not yours."

"Oh, yes, you are." He lowered his head to the aching nipple, biting down until I squealed. "All mine. The things I plan on doing to you are a complete sin. We'll probably go to hell for them."

"I don't care."

Seconds later, he settled between my legs and dragged his tongue under one breast then the other before dragging it down my stomach, taking his time to do so. His eyes never left mine, his heated breath keeping prickles on my arms and legs. After swirling the tip around my bellybutton, he dared lower his head, breathing across my bald pussy.

"You're so bad, so very bad," I muttered as I tossed my head back and forth.

"You haven't seen anything yet, sweetheart."

The moment he slid his fingers under the thin elastic of my bikini bottom, I closed my eyes and bit down on my lower lip. "What are you doing?"

"What do you think, little lamb? I'm going to feast on that pretty pink pussy of yours." He took an exaggerated breath, issuing another even darker and more dangerous growl than he'd done before.

If he was trying to excite me, I was already in the stratosphere, incapable of putting more than a couple of coherent words together. Breathing became next to impossible as he lifted and bent my legs at the knees, pushing them down to the blanket. I'd never felt so exposed in my life. My pulse was racing, my heart skipping beats. I was elated yet terrified, shocked by the sheer intensity of the combined fragrance of desire wafting between us.

I was so wet, my pussy throbbing, the ache leading to a rush of adrenaline. I couldn't seem to stop shaking as he settled between my legs, sliding his arms underneath and lifting my bottom from the blanket. Every sound he made was animalistic, intentional and I was lightheaded and crazed with desire.

As he dug his fingers into my skin, opening me even wider, I'd never felt so vulnerable in my life. There was no hesitation, only a sense of broadening need that was required to be filled. The moment he flicked his tongue back and forth across my clit, I let out an intense scream, pressing my hand across my lips only seconds later.

He swirled his tongue around in circle after circle until I reached for him, grasping onto long locks of his hair.

"Oh, no, you don't, little lamb. No touching until I allow you."

Even the darkness in his voice was entirely different. I floated on a blissful white cloud as he licked all the way down to my swollen folds, barely darting the tip inside. He was being gentle, tender, and it was almost driving me crazy. He continued taunting me for several additional minutes. I was so wet, so hot that I couldn't stop gasping for air. Now I was making the savage sounds.

When I shifted my hips, pushing up from the blanket, he lifted his head. I stared down at him with hazy eyes, fighting my racing heart.

"Is something wrong, sweetheart?" he asked coyly, the grin on his face far too mischievous.

"You're driving me... crazy."

"You have a problem with that?" The sexy bastard had the nerve to pinch my clit until another rush of excitement tore through me. "If so, tell me what you want."

"I..." Truth be told, I'd never had a man lick me before. Not once. But this... this was powerful enough I was a mess.

"Tell me." When he acted as if he was going to pull away altogether, I shrieked exactly what I needed for him to do. "Lick me. Dear God, lick me until I come."

His expression turned more carnal, predatory. "That's more like it." He instantly buried his head into my wetness, driving his tongue deep into my tight channel.

"Oh. My. God." As he licked furiously, I was thrown into another dimension, an orgasm tickling my toes for a few seconds. When he added a single finger, thrusting deep inside, I was lost in the moment. There was no other sound, no breeze or anxiety about what we were going through. Just sheer pleasure rolling through me like a tidal wave.

I pressed my back against the blanket, throwing my arms over my head. As I stared up at the bright stars twinkling in the sky, my muscles began to relax, tension drifting away. I could sense a smile had crossed my face as the sweet moment of nirvana drew near.

He added a second then third finger, stretching my muscles as he flexed his fingers open.

"So tight. Goddamn, you're so tight." His words were garbled, maybe because my ears were ringing.

I couldn't believe the amount of pleasure tearing through me, or the breathless wonder of what he might do next. He lifted my torso even higher, shifting his head back and forth, adding to the insanity of the beautiful moment with every deep and husky sound he made. No one could have told me that something so intimate could feel so good, but as his actions became more brutal, a climax began to curl my toes, sliding up both legs.

"I'm going to… Oh, God. Oh. Yes. Yes."

He licked even more furiously, pumping like a crazed man. I was thrown by how powerful the orgasm became, the rush of vibrations unlike anything I'd ever felt before. I could no longer see clearly from the heavy sprinkling of colors dancing across my field of vision. This was the most incredible thing I'd ever felt in my life.

As a single orgasm swept into a second, I was struck by the electricity shooting through every vein and muscle. He held me tightly, refusing to let me go until I stopped shaking altogether. I lolled my head to the side, laughing softly as he pressed kisses against one inner thigh then the other.

When I suddenly felt a swath of cool air, I snapped my head front and center. Maddox was standing over me like the true predator he was, peering down, his chest heaving.

"What are you doing?" I asked, no longer recognizing my voice.

He took his sweet time answering, a wry smile crossing his face as he pushed down his swim trunks. I was given a beautiful show, his long, thick cock making my mouth water all over again.

"What am I doing?" he repeated as he stepped out of his trunks, kicking them aside.

"Uh-huh."

"Now, I'm going to fuck you. Every. Single. Hole."

CHAPTER 17

Maddox

An arranged marriage?

Was she kidding me?

The ugliness swimming in my mind was intolerable. Would Arman do something that ridiculous, putting his own daughter in harm's way? Would he dare attempt to sell her off to the highest bidder? There was something off about the entire situation, just like I'd felt before. The fact he hadn't told me what he was dealing with alluded to the possibility my notions were spot on.

And I hated not being able to believe in Arman at this moment. Was it clouding my judgment, making me consider doing something that would tear a seam in our friendship that likely would never be mended?

Rage remained just below the surface, my gut telling me I was right. Why? Was the attack predicated by Arman's refusal to allow a connection to be made? I did my best to shove it aside for now, but I would revisit it in the morning.

"Maddox," Zoe whispered, dragging me back to the present.

I took a deep breath, holding it as I allowed my gaze to fall to her bare feet, almost as if seeing her for the first time. What I wanted to do was blasphemous, but there was no turning back. My anger was fueling my cock, shoving aside all rationality.

Hunger.

I felt famished and it had nothing to do with needing nourishment. At least my thirst had been quenched; the sweet taste of Zoe's pussy lingering in my mouth and throat only dragged the beast from deep within closer to the surface. I licked my lips in appreciation as I studied her voluptuous body, doing what I could to control the darkness swelling from deep within.

In laying claim to her, in shredding the forbidden veil that I'd honored, I'd placed her life even more into the danger zone. Keeping her safe could prove to be difficult. However, there was no turning back the clock, no chance of erasing what had been building since seeing her in New York.

The consequences would be difficult, painful, but were ones I would handle when necessary. Now I needed more, so much more that every muscle remained tense.

She tilted her head, her eyes shimmering in the firelight. She was the most beautiful woman I'd ever set eyes on. And she was truly all woman, every inch from her long legs and curved hips to her small waist and breasts that fit perfectly in my hands. I'd meant what I'd told her before. No man would ever touch her again or they'd face my wrath.

Her quiet purrs said volumes, the longing in her eyes full of hope for the future.

I'd laughed the first time I'd reminded myself I was a rule breaker, but here I was, tasting the forbidden again. Somehow, I knew the words I'd issued, the possessiveness I'd shown regarding the stunning yet aggravating beauty, would come back and bite me.

But I didn't seem to give a shit. I'd meant what I'd said: my ownership of her was just beginning. I wanted more and would take everything I craved. I wasted no time pulling her onto her knees. As I grasped both sides of her face, rubbing my thumbs roughly across her jaws, she looked up at me lovingly.

"You belong to me," I repeated as I stroked her face, marveling in the way she shivered at my touch.

"Forever?"

"Until the end of time."

I'd heard what she'd said, the love she'd expressed. There was still a part of me that knew I should continue driving her away, doing everything I could to make her hate me. She was too good, too innocent, and I was a vile man after all, the fucking Boogeyman that she should run from, terrified of what I could do.

Instead, the gravitational pull between us was only getting stronger, pushing me to do unspeakable and extremely filthy things to her luscious body. I had difficulty breathing or even thinking clearly, but as I brought her head closer to my aching cock, I sensed her increasing need.

"Suck me, baby."

Zoe rubbed her long fingers along the inside of my calves, taking her time to roll them up to my thighs. The look on her face was exquisite, mischievous in a way that was far too enticing. When she dared to blow across the tip of my shaft, I fisted her hair, pressing her mouth against it.

"Don't tease me. You won't like what happens when you do," I said in a garbled voice.

"Maybe I will," she purred, blinking as if the little vixen was in full control. She'd soon learn that was never going to happen. She continued to taunt me by dragging her tongue across my sensitive slit then down the side. As she slipped her hand between my legs, cupping and squeezing my balls, I pitched my head back, half laughing from the tremendous sensations. I was no longer surprised at how connected we were, the flashes of heat coursing through me resembling a wildfire.

She flicked her tongue from one testicle to the other, her actions forcing me to roll onto the balls of my feet.

"Open your mouth," I commanded, lowering my head and basking in the light shimmer covering her porcelain skin.

She did as she was told but I could tell the naughty girl had something up her sleeve.

"Now, suck." I pushed her head down, forcing more than just the tip inside. It was all I could do to keep from impaling her mouth until the tip hit the back of her throat. I couldn't stop thinking about the things she'd said in that she'd wanted to wait for me to be her first. She had no idea what that had done to me, the need building to a frenzied point. I couldn't seem to stop shaking, every muscle in my body tense as she swiped her tongue back and forth.

There was an imploring look in her eyes, every action she was taking the girl was questioning. As if she was uncertain that she was pleasing me.

"That's it, baby girl. You have one hot little mouth. You can be such a good girl when you want to be."

She opened her mouth even wider, encouraging me to take full control, to fuck her mouth. That's exactly what I did, driving the entire last few inches inside. When she wrapped her luscious lips tightly around my shaft, I pressed her head down even harder. The sadistic beast inside of me enjoyed the slight sounds of her gagging. Only then did I pull back on her head, allowing her to take a deep breath.

"That's it," I whispered, rolling my hips forward until I was thrusting hard and deep into her wet mouth. It was only a matter of time before I couldn't take it any longer, losing all sense of control. The headiness of taking her mouth, of making her mine was as ravaging as the moment, electrifying every cell in my body. Her mouth was hot, both of us on fire and at that moment, nothing else mattered but fucking her like the savage I was.

After pumping her mouth several additional times, I couldn't take it any longer, pushing her back by her shoulders. I stumbled back by a few feet, raking my forearm across the sweat beading on my forehead.

She licked her lips in an exaggerated manner and I wagged my finger at her.

"Such a bad girl."

"What are you going to do about it?"

"Take everything I want. That's what." I yanked her closer, sweeping her off her feet. Her squeal filtered into the night sky and as she struggled to grab onto me, I slid one arm under her bottom. When she was nestled in my arms, she wrapped her long, shapely legs around my hips, draping her arms over my shoulders. There was such devotion in her eyes, every action she took an attempt to please me even further. Just the way she tangled her fingers in my hair was enticing, but it was the seductive look on her face that kept me famished.

Leaning forward, she dragged her tongue from one side of my jaw to the other just as I'd done to her, easing back and issuing another husky purr.

"From lamb to a kitten. I'm not certain which I prefer," I told her, chuckling afterward.

"I might turn into a lioness."

"Then I'll need to tame you." I yanked on her hair, jerking her back into a deep arc. As I pressed my lips against her pulse of life, she shuddered in my hold, squeezing her knees against me. The heat of our bodies was sweltering, the current keeping us both on the very edge. I bit down on her skin, the taste of her almost as sweet as her pussy. I could spend hours exploring, tasting every inch of her, but not tonight. Tonight I needed instant gratification or I'd go mad. I nibbled on her chin, biting down on her lip before pulling away.

When I lifted her again, she didn't need to be told what to do. The feisty vixen took her time crawling her hand down my chest, wrapping her fingers around my shaft. When she placed the tip against her swollen folds, I lifted my gaze to her eyes, issuing a sly smile before impaling her with every single inch.

"Oh, yes." She threw her head back, digging her fingernails into my shoulders, her ragged breathing yet another delicious reward.

I gyrated my hips until I was fully seated inside, savoring the seconds her muscles pulsed, clamping then releasing around my cock. I pulled out, thrusting into her again, kneading her bottom as I repeated the brutal action.

"You're so strong."

"All for you, little lamb." I took two steps closer to the fire, appreciating the way she laughed in response. "Are you hungry for more?"

"God, yes. I want everything." Her voice no longer sounded the same, the huskiness matching mine. As she clung to me, I pumped like a wild beast, driving in and out in a practiced rhythm.

"So wet. So fucking hot." I rolled onto the balls of my feet again, the balancing act easy given the weight of her in my arms. There was nothing like holding her, having her so close, crushing her against me as I fucked her like a wild animal. "You're going to come for me."

"I don't think I can." Her laugh was subtle, whimsical. Before me the girl had never experienced a man giving her extreme pleasure. I would do that for days on end.

"Yes, you will." I thrust even more brutally, pushing her to the point of no return. When I dropped to the blanket, she gasped, her eyes opening wide.

Zoe leaned back, planting one hand on the soft material, using it to hold her position as she matched every savage thrust. The fact her eyes never left mine, her mouth twisting as passion erupted into raw bliss was a powerful draw. We were locked together in the moment in time, nothing else mattering around me.

"Come for me, little lamb. Come on my cock."

Her body shivered involuntarily, her brow furrowing as she closed her eyes. "You are… I don't think…" When she threw her head back, I pushed her all the way down onto the blanket, lifting onto my hands as I fucked her even harder. "Yes. Yes. Yes!" Her scream into the night sky, the way she quivered in my arms almost drove my control to the breaking point.

But I wasn't finished with her just yet.

I fucked her long and hard, driving her into a second orgasm. There was nothing like watching her face, the shimmer building across her beautiful skin, the tiny beads of perspiration forming over her luscious lips.

"Oh. Oh. Oh. Oh. Oh." She tossed her head back and forth, her long eyelashes skimming across her cheeks. As she raked her nails over my shoulders, digging them into the skin on my back, I threw my head back, gasping for air.

No woman had ever made me lose control. Not one. She was perfect in every way. I continued pumping until her body went limp, her breathing still ragged. When I pulled out, she squealed, her eyes opening wide.

"Where are you going?" Her question was laced with sadness.

As if I had any intention of leaving her.

Grinning, I pulled out, easing onto my knees. "Nowhere, baby." When I lifted her up, easily turning her over so she was on all fours, she gasped then laughed.

"You're such a mean man," she cooed as she tossed her head over her shoulder.

"You're just figuring that out?" I rolled the tip of my cock up and down the crack of her ass. Then I thrust it back into her slickened pussy, thrusting hard and fast several times. The moment I pushed the tip against her dark hole, she whimpered and dared to try to claw away from me.

"I don't think I can. I mean I've never. I mean..."

"Shush, baby. Relax and breathe. I promise you that you'll enjoy this." I'd never been a careful man, the few women I'd been with easily able to call me a sadistic bastard, but with her I wanted to be gentle. I longed to give her the kind of pleasure that she'd remember for a long time, craving what only I could give her.

I pushed an inch inside, the sensations rocketing through me unlike anything I'd ever felt. My body was shaking from the rush of adrenaline, the intensity of the still building need. The things I could do to her weren't just filthy but sinful. I wanted to break her down and build her back up again. What kind of monster did that make me?

I was blinded with lust, taking deep and labored breaths as I pushed another inch inside. I squeezed her hips as I pumped in slow and even strokes, still marveling in the heat as well as the way her muscles constricted around my thick cock. My balls were aching, so swollen that I knew I wouldn't be able to hold back but for so long.

"Oh, God. So big. I just…"

"Deep breaths, little lamb. Take deep breaths and it's going to feel so good. I promise you."

She did as she was told and within seconds, her back was no longer heaving, her sounds of discomfort turning into ones of sheer pleasure.

After driving two more inches inside, I stopped moving, allowing her to get used to my wide girth. "How does that feel, baby?"

"Amazing. Just… amazing." She laughed, lifting her head and arching her back. The moment she wiggled, I drove the remainder of my cock deep inside.

"Fuck. So good. So tight." I planted my hands on either side of her, pressing the full weight of my body against hers. Together we moved in harmony, savoring the moment of our bodies coupling together.

My sweet Zoe kept her head turned, as if trying to watch everything I was doing.

"I could fuck you all night."

"Then do it," she murmured, pushing back against me.

"Careful what you ask for." The sound of my laugh was almost evil as I thrust deep and hard into her, the sound of our bodies slamming together the sweetest orchestration of music. Taking her this way was primal, savage, but I would do it again.

And again.

I dropped my head, nipping her shoulder, my body tensing even more. This time as she pushed back against me, I knew I was losing all sense of control. In those beautiful moments of making her mine, of claiming what I'd already known belonged to me, I realized that even a brutal man like me could feel desperate need.

As well as love.

Sweet Jesus, I was falling hard for the woman.

Unable to hold back any longer, I released, throwing my head back and staring at the stars as I filled her with my seed.

"Yes. Yes. Yes."

And even though our combined sounds were ones of passion, I heard her sweet words all over again.

"I love you."

CHAPTER 18

Zoe

"Have you ever wanted to do something else with your life?" I asked as he opened the restaurant door, guiding me into the bright sunshine. The day was perfect, limited white fluffy clouds in the sky. The heat would normally be oppressive yet given the light tropical breeze and the closeness of the ocean, the term sultry instead of scorching came to mind. "I mean other than being a hero and a force of nature due to your power and ruthlessness."

Perhaps my choice of words was because of the man beside me. He was and would forever be my hero whether he liked the word or not. As Maddox pressed his hand against the small of my back, an instinctive quiver drifted down my spine.

"I was a wild kid, Zoe. I roamed the streets of New Orleans from the time I was eight or nine. I had no morals or values. At least that what I was told several times," Maddox stated, his voice completely devoid of emotion. He'd never talked about his former family, although I'd sensed for a long time he missed his mother.

"What does that mean?"

He yanked out his sunglasses, sliding them across his chiseled face as I watched. In all the years I'd known him, I could count on one hand the number of private aspects about his life that he'd told me, none of which shocked me or allowed me to catch a realistic glimpse of what made him tick.

"That means I was a little criminal, a kid who learned early on that only through stealing could I find enough to eat. I wasn't the kind of kid to scour through garbage, preferring to eat like a little prince."

"You stole?"

He chuckled as he threw me a quick look. "Yes, Zoe. I wasn't born with a silver spoon in my mouth."

"You never really mentioned your parents other than in passing."

"That's because there's nothing to tell. My mother was a junkie, my father abandoning us early on to take this job or that job. He lied every time about finding a break, coming home after squandering whatever money he'd made on women and gambling. The dude took criminal activity to a new level. That much I can tell you. He hated both my mother and me. He made that perfectly clear through years of abuse, beating us with everything he could get his hands on. The man took cruelty to an entirely different level."

Jesus. I had no idea. I'd seen a few scars on his back and a portion of his thighs, but I'd believed them to be from the years of working with my father. He was telling me his limited story as if standing on the outside looking in. That was the sign of a survivor.

I wrapped my hand around his arm, moving in front of him on the sidewalk. "I'm very sorry. I assure you that being born with a silver spoon in my mouth had its disadvantages, but I can't imagine what you were forced to endure."

The way he cupped my chin without hesitation, rubbing his thumb across my lips was scintillating, the move so unexpected, it surprised both of us. "I don't mean any disrespect, Zoe. I can't imagine what living in a cage felt like, the bubble around you required yet stifling."

"I can't complain, Maddox. You know my father. He did everything he could to be there when I was growing up, trying so hard to be my mother and father after Mama's death. And I had a wonderful support system."

"You do have an amazing family."

"I include you as my family," I told him, which seemed to have the opposite effect I wanted, his expression darkening even behind his dark sunglasses as he pulled his hand away. "So does everyone else. When was the last time you saw your birth father?"

"The day I pressed the tip of a butcher knife to his throat and told him that if he ever came around again, I'd kill him."

His admittance was so shocking and gut-wrenching that all I wanted to do was comfort him as he'd done with me. "I... What did he say?"

Laughing, he started walking again, his steps slow and easy. "That he'd hunt me down one day and see if I had the balls to follow through with my threat. But he left and I haven't seen him since."

"Where is he?"

"Rotting in prison somewhere. I couldn't give a shit where."

I was floored, uncertain what to say. There were so many things I wanted to ask him but the gift of allowing me into his life and his past was too precious to ruin.

"How did you get off the streets?" I finally asked after we walked a couple of blocks.

"Did you ever know your grandfather used to own a restaurant?"

Now I jumped in front of him. "My grandfather? He burns water."

His grin was wider than before. "He wasn't the chef, darling girl. He owned a very fashionable one in the heart of Duval Street. You should ask him about it at some point. From what I learned early on, the place was his pride and joy. It was also where he held his meetings, both with enemies and associates. He held court, sitting directly in front of the front window, allowing him to gaze on the activity on the street."

"How do you know so much?"

"Because the kid I was, fearless and a total hoodlum, decided it was in my best interest to steal from the restaurant late one night. I almost made it too with four hundred bucks in my hand, which was huge to me at the time."

This time, he stopped walking, crowding my space until I was forced against one of the colorful buildings. He placed his palm on the siding, lowering his head as his dazzling eyes danced back and forth across mine.

"You were caught," I purred.

"By your grandfather, red-handed. I thought for certain I was going to die. There wasn't a single person in New Orleans that didn't know who Jean Baptiste was or what he was capable of doing to anyone who stole from him."

"How did you get out of it?" I pressed my hand against his chest, toying with the thick material of his polo.

"Well, he asked me why I stole the money and for the first time that I could remember, I told him the truth including giving him my real name. I told him that I was starving and my mom used her social security to buy drugs."

"Oh, my God. I'm so sorry."

"Hey, it was a wakeup call. He gave me two choices. One, he'd call the police or two, I could work in the restaurant to pay back the money that I could keep."

"You worked for him? How old were you?"

"Fourteen and sure, it wasn't legal, but I started washing dishes then moved up to a line cook. After my mother OD'd, he gave me a place to live and introduced me to his entire family, including Arman. Instead of treating me like the vagrant I was, your entire family embraced the kid with the bad attitude."

"That's why you're so loyal."

"Absolutely, Zoe. Your grandfather saved my life. In turn, I saved his one day when some assholes decided to try and assassinate him. He never forgot that. There isn't anything I wouldn't do for your family. That's why keeping you safe is the only thing that matters to me at this point."

There was a moment shared between us that was entirely different, a sweet feeling of closeness that I hoped would last. I rose onto my tiptoes, taking my time before pressing my lips against his. I expected him to push me away, maybe more gently this time. When he wrapped his fingers around my neck, squeezing possessively as he pulled me to him, my heart fluttered.

The kiss was passionate, perhaps more so than the night before, yet there was so much more emotion involved, the moment tender as opposed to rough and desperate. He pulled me away from the wall, sliding his hand down my back, gently guiding me into an arc so I could feel exactly how he felt about me.

There were so many emotions coursing through me, another wave of sensations that might be irrational but were wonderful. I rolled my hands over his shoulders, clinging to the muscular man as if he was the breath of life, the only being I needed to survive. A number of vibrations tore through me, every nerve ending seared, and I was lightheaded. When he thrust his tongue past my lips, I didn't bother trying to fight for control.

I wanted to surrender to his dark commands, whether verbalized or completely physical. He had a hold over me that was more powerful than anything I'd ever felt in my life. I never wanted it to end.

When he finally broke the kiss, he nipped my lower lip before pulling away. "My perfect little lamb." His voice was darker than before, so husky that another thrill drifted all the way to my toes. "Come on. Let's keep walking."

He pressed his hand on the small of my back again, his steps more like swaggers as we moved forward, our sudden silence more about being comfortable with each other instead of the tension we'd felt earlier.

"I'm shocked you allowed me out of my gilded cage," I said casually as I glanced at his face once again. I bit back laughter seeing the expression on Maddox's face as soon as I called his gorgeous estate a cage.

"Hmmm…" he said, rubbing his stubbled jaw, the one that could drive me crazy with desire. He'd sailed back to the house, carrying me from the dock to the house. Then he'd dumped me in his bed, ravaging me all over again.

It was as if for a few moments we lived in a beautiful dream, something I'd never forget.

The surprise of taking me into the quaint little town was special, allowing me to feel more happiness than I'd felt in long time.

"Well, I guess then while we're here, I'll need to find a hardware store so I can get some locks for your bedroom. That way I can make certain you get the full prison effect of your stay with me."

I punched him in the arm, yanking out my sunglasses as we continued walking. Lunch had been amazing, the man insisting he take me to the restaurant he'd mentioned as being his favorite the night before. I could see why, the incredible delicacy of island and French cuisine some of the best food I'd ever had. "Very funny. Besides, I thought I was now staying in your room."

He laughed, more jovial than I'd seen him maybe ever before. He was always so on guard, including today, but the tension we'd shared had disappeared. Still, he was performing his job, scanning the streets as we walked down the busy street in front of several quaint stores. The buildings were colorful, just as with most island towns.

"Only if you're a very good girl."

"I'm always good. *Rourke.*" I turned around in a full circle, laughing once again.

He drove his hands into his pockets, studying me as intently as he'd done the night before. "Rourke, huh? Case in point. You're incorrigible."

"Yes, I am, thank you very much." I shrugged and continued walking faster until something caught my eye in one of the shop windows. As he approached, I pressed my hand on the glass. "You must be a regular at Cajo's. I was certain the hostess was going to offer more than just a table for two when you walked in."

"What are you talking about?"

"Come on. You're not blind. She was undressing you with her eyes."

"Does that mean you're jealous?"

"Should I be? I'm certain you have women everywhere vying for your time."

The sudden chill he emitted was a reminder that whoever he'd been involved with had kept him from attempting another relationship.

"There's been no one, Zoe. Not for a very long time. That's the way I wanted it so don't go digging."

"Uh-huh. I think you need to lighten up. And I have just the thing that might do it. Stay right here." I backed away from him before he could reach out and grab me, which I knew he'd try to do.

"What do you think you're doing?" True to form, he almost managed to snatch my arm but I slithered away from him, winking in the process.

"Purchasing you a little gift."

"You can't use your father's credit card. I don't want any possibility we can be found."

I spun around, planting my hands on my hips. "Oh, ye with little faith. I'll have you know that I do have my own money." Although I wasn't going to admit to him where I'd gotten it from. I could only imagine what both he and my father would do if either one learned about my former job. I'd never be allowed to leave New Orleans again.

"You know what will happen if you even consider trying to escape me."

"You mean escape your clutches? Not a chance, buster." I blew him a kiss and walked into the small shop.

"Can I help you?" The woman's French accent was lovely.

"I'm like to purchase the watch you have in the window."

"Certainly."

As she headed for the display case, I noticed Maddox had pulled out his phone, the look on his face strained.

For about a million reasons, I knew the beautiful bubble would soon burst. The dazzling island might be paradise, but I had a terrible feeling the location could become a war zone.

* * *

Maddox

"I'm sorry, Mr. Cormier, but Mr. Thibodeaux cannot receive phone calls," the nurse stated, her attitude snippy as fuck. If I were standing in front of her, I'd want to wipe her smugness off her face. Sure, she was just doing her job, but she had no idea what was at stake.

I needed to know if Arman had attempted or been successful in selling off his own daughter. The last thing I wanted to do was to mention it to either Thomas or Francois. And I especially didn't want to say anything about my suspicions to Jean Baptiste.

"It's important."

"I don't care if someone is dying, Mr. Cormier. Your friend has had a setback and the doctors are very concerned."

I glanced toward the shop where Zoe was, bristling from hearing the news. "What the hell does that mean?"

"That means a secondary infection has occurred. He slipped into a coma this morning."

"Fuck." I closed my eyes, my entire body aching. "Does his family know?"

"His mother and father are here." Her voice softened. "We're doing everything we can, Mr. Cormier."

"Please. Just take care of him." I turned away from the window in the store. The last thing I wanted to do was to have Zoe know how upset I was. She couldn't lose her father. Not now.

"Yes, sir."

I ended the call, holding the phone against my chest. What the fuck had I been thinking? I was going to yell at him, chastising my friend? Goddamn it. I would hunt the fucker involved.

"What's wrong?"

Hearing her voice directly behind me created constriction in my heart. I shoved my phone into my pocket before turning around. In her hand was a small gold bag, but it was the look of horror on her face that drew my attention. "Nothing is wrong, little lamb. Just checking to see if any progress has been made. What do you have there?"

"You're a terrible liar, Maddox. At least to me." She studied me for a few seconds before handing me the bag. "I wanted you to have something special to remember me by."

"You make it sound like you're going somewhere. In case you haven't figured it out, you ain't going anywhere out of my sight, sweetheart." I adored the way her cheeks flushed, her mouth twisting in both frustration and desire. I accepted the gift. The fact I knew where she'd gotten her money was like some dirty secret. At some point, I'd need to tell her that I'd been in New York. Sadly, I had a feeling she'd feel as incensed as I was in thinking she'd been betrothed to anyone.

At least her mischievous smile returned. "I wouldn't dream of running. Although it would be fascinating to see you on a hunt." She laughed, giving me another sly look until I reached into the bag.

When I pulled out the black box, I shifted my gaze toward the store. "What did you do?"

She threw on her sunglasses, looking anywhere but at me. "Nothing special."

When I opened the box, I was stunned from seeing the gorgeous watch nestled inside. "Zoe. This is too expensive. You can't do this."

"That's silly," she said, gently pulling the box from my hand, tugging until she managed to release the watch. "I can do anything I want. I am a princess. Besides, you used to buy me gifts all the time."

"Books. Dolls. Halloween costumes. Not expensive jewelry."

"Ugh. Don't remind me I loved wearing princess and bride costumes when I was young."

"You looked so adorable in them." The girl had a way of making me laugh. She had no idea how special she made me feel. And how much I longed to ravage her constantly. I allowed her to slide the watch into position on my wrist. As soon as she clasped the band, I noticed something out of the corner of my eye, instantly tensing.

"What? It looks amazing on you." She finally followed my gaze but by the point she did, the person I thought was standing and staring at us had disappeared into the crowd. Maybe the sun was playing tricks on my eyes.

Or maybe we'd been compromised. Whatever the case, I was eager to get back to the house. "This is incredible, Zoe, but honestly, it's too much." When I started to take it off my wrist, she placed her hand over mine.

"Please don't take it off. I know you have a lot of money and can buy anything you want, but I need to do this for you just to say thank you."

"I told you before, keeping you safe is part of my job."

"I don't want to just be a part of your job, but if it makes you feel any better, just think of it as an early birthday present."

"Hmmm... Well, when you put it that way." I scanned the area, doing my best to keep from allowing Zoe to see what I was doing. Worrying her needlessly was a ridiculous thing to do. "No one has ever given me anything so gorgeous before."

"Why do I doubt that?"

She tugged at my hand, backing up and requiring me to follow her.

"What are you doing now, bad girl?"

"Well, we didn't have dessert. I noticed a little ice cream store near where you parked. Game for a little ooey, gooey chocolate delight?"

"No, but how about a little strawberry instead?"

"You're no fun."

"What are you talking about? I'm a hell of a lot of fun," I teased in return, even though my heart wasn't into it.

"Prove it!"

I laughed and trailed behind her, taking my time while she flitted from one store to the other. I hated that my gut told me we had company on the island, praying I was wrong. Praying. I wasn't a praying man at all, but I did so for Arman. For all the times that had almost turned into tragedy, for all the bullets we'd dodged together, even laughing about a few of the instances over a stiff drink or five later, this time I had a sickening feeling pooling in my gut.

I'd even compared him to a cat with nine lives, bullets literally whizzing by him.

This time, I had a terrible feeling he'd used up his last life.

If so, there wouldn't be a city in the world, a cave in the jungles, or a rock where the fucker responsible could hide where I wouldn't find him.

He wouldn't just face my wrath; the bastard would be chained in a dark, cold place for the rest of his miserable life.

And I'd enjoy every moment of watching him suffer.

CHAPTER 19

Zoe

I'd witnessed Maddox talking in front of an audience of one thousand people without sweating. I'd seen him challenging enemies with a smile on his face. I'd studied the way he'd been cool as a cucumber in the face of atrocities, including the time Raven and I had been locked inside a burning building, the aftermath shaking all of us involved.

But not him.

And I'd seen his look of real despair at the hospital, the unshakable bond he shared with my father not allowing him to hide his emotions. Now I understood so much better the reason the two of them were close and it continued to create shivers all throughout my system.

THE WISEGUY

What I'd learned from silently reading the man while remaining in the shadows was that I knew instantly when he was telling a tale or flat-out lying.

He'd lied to me about something being wrong. Truth be told, whatever he was hiding was eating him alive. While I wanted to admonish him or perhaps beg him for us not to have lies and secrets between us, I couldn't do that simply because of what I hadn't confessed to.

"Sit right there. Do not move," Maddox instructed, pointing toward a small table outside near the door.

I did as I was told, tossing my hair just to tease him. He planted his hands on the table, leaning over and growling. "You don't scare me, big bad wolf."

"You'll learn, my little lamb, that I do bite."

"Don't excite me." I laughed and pushed his chest, watching as he shook his head before entering the small shop. If only I could figure out a way to keep the moment, capturing it as he'd done with me. I wouldn't mind finding a gilded cage if I could. Easing against the chair, I allowed the angst to fade, doing my best to enjoy the setting. We were on top of a knoll, the stunning waters of the Caribbean seeming so much closer than they were. The rolling waves were gentle, lightly kissing the pearlescent sand.

Even from where I was sitting, I could tell the beach was full of vacationers, the area populated with both fancy and intimate hotels. I felt so lucky that we were on the other side, protected from noise and people pollution. The street was crowded, so many people enjoying the fabulous weather and the dozens of quaint shops and restaurants. I could certainly enjoy living in a place like this, although I wasn't entirely certain what I'd do for a job.

Sure, there was my trust fund my father had established when I was a baby, a tidy sum built because of the financial advisor my father had hired, but I wouldn't be able to get my hands on that until I was twenty-five. Besides, I wanted to make a life for myself, to feel wanted and needed.

Especially by a man I could call my own. For longer than a getaway, an adventure full of danger. Giggling, I shook my head, finally feeling more relaxed. Maybe that was the greatest sin of all. My entire family was locked down in my grandfather's estate and I was enjoying gorgeous weather and the beach life. A pang of guilt crackled through me. I longed to talk to my father. Maybe I'd try calling him later, even if Maddox had explicitly told me not to use the phone, to keep it turned off.

My protector was certainly good at everything he did. Every. Single. Thing. Grinning from the wicked thoughts coursing through my mind, I closed my eyes, envisioning the night we'd shared, the intimacy that had kept us both silent as the passion had erupted.

He'd yet to tell me how he felt, at least not in anything other than sexual terms. Maybe I was expecting too much from the handsome man, certainly more than he was capable of giving. If that was something I had to live with, I was fine with it. The images came fast and furious, ones that could warm the cockles of any woman's heart, no matter if she'd been labeled an ice queen and fit the mold.

Which I didn't.

Certainly, if I had, Maddox had thawed me out with his soft lips and rough touch, his refusal to take no for an answer and the adorable dimple that rarely showed since he almost never smiled. Swooning was new to me, but not around the man of my dreams.

There I went again, acting as if I was some love-struck high school kid. Maybe that wasn't so bad, at least for now. I didn't need to adult all the time. Did I? I laughed softly to myself, more than enjoying the day and of course the fabulous company.

I was a girl in love and felt as if I could conquer the world. Giggling, when I felt his presence behind me only seconds later, I held my breath, refusing to open my eyes.

He placed his hands on my shoulders, kneading them as if realizing I'd been tense for days. Weeks. Who was I kidding? The fact he remained silent allowed me to keep my eyes closed, envisioning even more filthy things in the back of my mind. I felt his weight shift as he lowered down. His hot breath cascaded across my shoulders and I longed to reach up and touch him. Somehow, I had a feeling he'd retaliate in a playful yet forceful manner.

When he continued to remain silent, a single chill coursed down my spine. Then something happened that petrified me more than having shots fired, than having the two men dressed in black dragging me from the greenhouse.

The person standing behind me laughed. It wasn't just any laugh. The sound was full of anger and darkness.

And a promise.

I couldn't stop shivering, couldn't move or think straight. But when I opened my eyes and tried to scream, the feeling of his hands being on me wasn't there any longer. I jerked up, knocking over the chair, the table tipping precariously as I spun around. There was no one there. The closest people were sitting at a table behind me, now staring as if I'd grown a second head.

The woman rapidly spoke what sounded like French, appearing uncomfortable.

I pressed my hand across my mouth to keep from screaming.

"Zoe. What's wrong?" The question made me yelp, even jumping slightly.

When I looked back at Maddox, I couldn't speak.

He slammed the two cups of ice cream on the table, grabbing my wrist and pulling me against him, shielding my body with his. "What happened? Talk to me."

"I thought… I mean…"

"Baby. Calm down and talk to me."

"It might not have been anything. I heard a man laugh and it scared me. I thought I saw someone dressed in black."

He grabbed my hand, leading me away from the store and into the street.

"What are you doing?" I asked as I noticed he'd slipped his hand around to his back. That's when I realized he had a gun hiding under his shirt. Why hadn't I noticed it before? Oh, my God. This was real. This was…

"We're going back to the house. Did you see anything about what he looked like?"

"No, and I might have been imagining it."

Way to go. Several lies down, more to come?

My inner voice barked at me, but she was right. I just couldn't bring myself to tell him what had occurred in New York. He'd go ballistic.

"I doubt you were." He took long strides in the direction where he'd parked the Jeep, constantly sweeping the area. It was difficult to keep up with him even with the fear and adrenaline rush.

"Why? Did you see something?"

He didn't answer. I hated when he got into his brooding, security man phase.

"You did. Didn't you?"

"I'm always on the lookout, Zoe. I have to be. That's what will keep us alive. This isn't a game."

"I never said it was."

"Then don't act like it. Stay right with me. I mean it." He found a shortcut through a group of buildings and away from the crowd. When he came to a crossroad, he stopped short, throwing out his hand to keep me from moving onto the perpendicular sidewalk.

Just watching him peering around the corner created a wave of terror that was suffocating, my throat threatening to close.

"Fuck," he hissed, raking his hand through his hair. "Come on." He guided me across the street to an alley, constantly looking.

I still felt the man's hands on me. I couldn't have been imagining that. There was no way. What had the bastard been trying to do, terrify me? Send a warning that he was on the island? I breathed a sigh of relief when I saw the Jeep, but he remained tense, all but pushing me into the passenger seat.

Maddox jumped over the hood of the vehicle and into the driver's seat, starting the engine seconds later. He took off from the parking spot with such acceleration that the tires squealed. When he jerked out his weapon, placing it on his lap, I cringed all over again.

"Is he here?"

"I don't know, Zoe. But I need to make a few phone calls and find out. We may need to leave the island quickly."

"And go where?"

He exhaled, twisting his hand around the steering wheel. "I'm not sure."

I slunk down in the seat, struggling with the paralyzing fear.

Every few seconds, he checked the rearview mirror, which did nothing but make me even more nervous. Now I was the one who couldn't wait to get to the safety and sanctity of the house. His house.

In paradise.

When he slowed down seconds later, I glanced through the windshield. Someone in dark clothing was walking quickly down a sidewalk, constantly glancing over his shoulder. At least I thought the person was male. The fact he'd had a hoodie on when it was at least ninety degrees outside didn't let me confirm my suspicions or calm my nerves.

Maddox shifted the gear into fifth, throwing me one of his infamous looks that screamed I needed to remain calm and hold on for dear life.

I gripped the dashboard with one hand, the edge of my seat with the other, taking shallow breaths as he sped down the street.

Wind whipped through the open roof, the crowds of people meandering into the street making it next to impossible to make headway.

"What are you doing?" I finally asked.

"Finding out what the fuck we're dealing with."

"What if that's nothing?"

"There's only one way to find out, Zoe. Just hang tight." He continued to speed through the streets until he was finally heading away from town. I was shocked the person had made significant headway, pushing his way through the crowd of people on the sidewalks.

There was no doubt the person was running from something or someone. I couldn't breathe from the pressure on my chest, the fear that refused to abate. What if we had been found? Would we easily be able to get off the island? Where would we go? I couldn't think straight, constantly looking over at Maddox.

Suddenly, he picked up speed, racing through a yellow light, looking over my shoulder toward the sidewalk.

The person who was running was right there, trying to get past some construction debris. Snarling, Maddox jerked the steering wheel to the right, slamming on the brakes then throwing the gear into park. "Stay right here. I mean right here." He jumped out before I could say anything, keeping his weapon low and in both hands.

I watched as if in slow motion as he threw the person against the aging brick wall of some residence, slamming the person three times in rapid succession before yanking the hood away from the guy's face.

The person trying to escape was a male, but he couldn't have been more than sixteen or seventeen. I realized he'd been clutching something against his chest, dropping it after being almost assaulted by Maddox.

"What the fuck?" Maddox exclaimed. "Who are you?"

The kid was obviously terrified, shaking his head several times. Maddox proceeded to pat him down with one hand while he kept the weapon in plain sight with the other. "Who are you?"

When the young man spoke, it was in a language I couldn't understand. I realized seconds later that it was in Russian, which Maddox spoke fluently. I wasn't certain whether to feel relieved or even more terrorized than before. Maybe I really had succumbed to a taste of madness, imagining the person I'd believed to be there threatening me.

They continued conversing and I couldn't shake the ugly feelings, constantly looking from one side the street to the other. What if I was wrong? What if... The man's laugh filtered into my brain and I placed my hands over my ears.

Maddox finally shoved the weapon behind his back, nodding to the kid before heading back to the Jeep. I stared at him as he jumped in, shaking my head.

"What?" he demanded.

"You accosted that kid."

"He was running."

"So what? Kids run. They're in a hurry."

He started the engine, his grin returning. "Maybe so but that kid had also stolen some pretty pricy medications from the pharmacy."

"And you just let him go?"

Shrugging, he pressed his foot on the accelerator. "He needed them for his sick mom."

"And you believed him."

"Call me a softie."

"I'll call you gullible."

"You can call me the Boogeyman. Muah!"

When he laughed, that allowed me to relax.

For now.

However, the real boogeyman was out there. I was certain of it.

And he was coming. It was simply a question of when.

CHAPTER 20

Maddox

"He's not doing well."

Francois' statement sickened me, driving another dagger into my heart. "What are the doctors saying?"

"That's just it. They're not saying shit even though Pops had threatened them with a lawsuit already. I finally had to physically remove him from the hospital a couple hours ago."

"Do they know what's wrong?"

"Septic shock. Maybe. I honestly don't know. But his heart stopped for almost two minutes. At least Louie had committed his medical skills to assisting in Arman's care, which is the only reason Pops allowed me to take him home. I doubt that will last for long but at least he'd not hassling the doctors."

Fuck. I fisted my mouth, trying to tamp down the anger. Being so far away was pushing me to an uncontrollable point. I understood the reason why but with my patience waning, I knew I could lose my usual caution if I wasn't careful. "This is ridiculous."

"You're going to need to tell Zoe."

"She's already under enough stress. Something terrified her today. I think the situation is finally sinking in."

"Give her comfort. But not too much."

The sound of my laughter was bitter, hollow. "I'm not that kind of guy."

"So you tell me. I'll keep you informed. I'm heading back to the hospital now. Raven refuses to leave Arman's side, which means Thomas is reluctant to head to Texas. I may need to go there myself."

"I feel so bad for her and for little Gabriel."

"Edmee is taking care of Gabe. The kid isn't any wiser that his daddy was injured."

"He's two."

Francois half laughed. "The kid is bright like his uncle."

"Raven needs a shoulder to lean on. You know that."

"Yeah, but she's strong. Just like my niece. Tell Zoe what's going on. She won't forgive you if you don't."

That much I knew. Not that it made telling her any easier. "I'll do my best. If you find out anything, give me a call."

"Yeah, I will."

The news couldn't be any worse at this point. The ache only continued to increase as the call ended. It felt as if a heavy weight was placed squarely on my chest, the pressure mounting unlike it had done before.

The same hospital where Arman had taken up a vigil, willing me back to life. I'd been in a coma for two days, although I could swear the man had talked to me the entire time. Now I wasn't there to do the same for him.

Hissing, I held the phone up, almost tossing it against the wall. I'd never felt so out of sorts, so incompetent in my life. I'd been in control of everything, making certain details were clear and easy to read, that signs were followed up on if I was worried about something going on with the family or within the corporation.

The anger still buzzing like the flow of electricity I shared with Zoe, I glanced at the computer monitors one last time. She'd offered to help search for whoever was responsible. Perhaps that was something we would do together the next morning.

I'd purposely wanted to abide by Arman's rules in keeping her away from as much of the ugly side of the business as possible, but it wasn't feasible at this point. Plus, in truth, I could use her help. With Arman's condition worsening, my guess was that no one in New Orleans was paying much attention to the threats at hand. While I'd gone under the assumption that Arman's injuries were from fighting with one of the perpetrators, it was entirely possible the injury had been planned to keep the family off their game.

Goddamn them for forcing me to keep her safe outside of my own environment.

I pulled out the duffle bag I'd brought from the storage unit at the airport, placing it on the table in my office. As I headed toward the cabinet where I had additional ammunition, I thought about the Russian kid. While he could be a plant of some kind, I doubted he had any involvement. He'd been too freaked out I'd caught him, begging me to allow him to heal his mother.

What I hadn't told Zoe was that after telling her my sad tale about when I was about his age, the kid's story had resonated with me, and that the money I'd taken was for food and to try to keep my mother alive. I'd known a guy back then who'd sold pills that were supposed to counteract the effects of heroin. Of course, they hadn't worked, the two hundred dollars spent a waste of money, but I'd tried.

After that, I'd tried again. Nothing had worked.

I hadn't thought about that ugly time in my life for a few years. Zoe brought out the longing for family more than being with Arman or Francois ever had. They were like brothers, but it was never far from any of our minds that I also worked for the family. They'd never lorded it over me, had never made me feel as anything but family, yet I'd felt it within myself, the inability to get close.

Now all I wanted was to be close to someone, to build a family. That was a strange realization for a man like me.

THE WISEGUY

Maybe it was my version of a midlife crisis. Maybe I wanted someone to worry about me when I was gone.

Snorting, I grabbed my glass of scotch, tossing back a good third of it as I shoved aside my ridiculous thoughts. What I was sharing with Zoe couldn't last for a half dozen reasons, the biggest one having nothing to do with Arman, although that was a close second.

The fear that losing her, or anyone I cared about, could quite possibly break me this time.

Just like it had almost done when I'd lost my mother.

As well as the woman I'd transferred my adoration to only a few years later.

Since then, I'd ignored anything but my most base needs, those that could only be satisfied by fucking a beautiful woman. But walking away was what I was good at.

And I'd do it again.

Zoe certainly didn't need a broken-down guy with a dangerous attitude and an enjoyment of killing. Chuckling, I slapped the fresh magazine into my Glock, placing it on the table with the other weapons, the array some of my favorites, including the hunting knife I'd had for years. The shimmering bezel of the watch caught my eye and I stared at the gift, tensing all over again. The stunning piece had cost her a pretty penny, something she'd yet to explain though I knew she wanted to keep the white lie about working at the shithole of a club.

I couldn't get over the notion that Zoe wasn't telling me something, especially seeing the look of terror in her eyes. It was time to have a sit-down conversation with her, likely one she wouldn't enjoy, but the feeling remained that we weren't alone on the island. However, leaving wasn't possible unless absolutely necessary.

Plus, I had to find a way to tell her about her father's updated condition. That wasn't something I was looking forward to.

I'd spent the better part of the evening in my office, attempting to trace the recent activities of Raphael Arturo as well as others in my attempt to rule them out. So far, I'd managed to cross out seven, including a cartel located in Miami who had an ax to grind and wouldn't mind doing so with either Francois or Arman. I'd discovered they'd dwindled in size, likely given the DEA had been tossed crumbs anonymously, which had led to the arrest of their esteemed leader.

Granted, if they'd learned that Francois had been the bird singing their praises, it was a solid reason for revenge, but given only Arman, Francois, Thomas, and I were in on the dangerous ploy, that was highly doubtful.

While Alturo and his family were still in complete control of Cartagena as well as other parts of South America, there were zero indications a trip had been made to the United States recently or that he'd hired someone to carry out the deed. Still, I left him in the maybe category for now, refusing to mark him off completely.

I'd leave Devin Carlos to Thomas for now, but if he didn't learn something quickly, I would pull out every contact I had from Mexico through Texas and the west to plot an itinerary of his recent whereabouts and business activities. Hell, I might even head to Texas myself.

At this point, without catching a break or without Francois finding an informant willing to talk, we remained in the dark.

My patience was wearing thin.

I left my office, grabbing my scotch and turning off the light. As I headed into the living room, I was surprised not to find her curled up reading a book. For a few seconds, nerves kicked in, but I'd studied the camera surrounding the house more than once. I would have known if someone had crossed the property line.

And I gathered a sense that my little lamb wouldn't dare leave the property any longer. She'd said very little at dinner, picking at her food as she'd stared off into space.

I moved toward the back door, noticing her sitting in the dark staring out at the ocean. She had nothing in hand, just sitting calmly staring out at the water as if searching for answers. After watching her for a few seconds, I headed to the bar, refreshing my drink while pouring her a glass of wine.

As soon as I moved onto the deck, I expected her to react to my presence, but she remained quiet, unmoving. I eased the glass of wine in front of her and it took a few seconds for her to grasp it. At least she did, immediately bringing the rim to her lips. Exhaling, I moved to the railing, staring out at the water as she'd been doing. The night was beautiful, stars twinkling in the sky, the nearly full moon covered by a blueish hue, which created a slightly eerie atmosphere.

"My father is dying. Isn't he?"

Her question hit me hard, more so than I thought it would. The dull ache I'd felt both behind my eyes and in my gut increased almost instantly. Lying wasn't something I could do, certainly not about her family. "He fell into a coma because of a secondary infection. He's possibly septic. I don't know his prognosis, Zoe. I would tell you if I did."

"He has sepsis? Do you know what that means?"

"I'm not a doctor."

"Well, I'm trained to be a nurse. It's not good. How did you find out?"

"I called the hospital trying to talk to him. Then I spoke with Francois a little while ago."

She slowly turned her head. I caught the movement in the periphery of my vision. "And you're just telling me now?"

"I didn't want to worry you."

"There you go again acting as if I'm a child. He's my father, Maddox. No matter what you think about having a huge family, he's my everything. He was the one who consoled me when I cried, kissing all my booboos when I fell. He encouraged me to continue with piano lessons when I hated them as a teenager. He was there when I was stupid enough to try out for cheerleading, which I sucked at. But he made me feel like a princess by taking me to dinner after I failed the tryouts. What I'm telling you is that there is no other bond like that of a parent and a child. It's entirely different. Maybe one day you'll realize that. I only hope it's not too late."

Her words rang loud and clear. "I hope so too, Zoe. I want a family."

"Really? You could have fooled me. You act as if you don't need anyone."

"It's not about not needing or wanting someone. It's about whether or not caring about that person will place them in harm's way, just like what happened to you."

Zoe snorted as if I'd just made a joke. "A wise man once told me that it was better to take risks and live my life versus hiding in the shadows."

"Who told you that?"

She jerked up from her seat. "My father. And I know what you're going to say. I'm here with you because of his concern for me, so he meant everyone but his own daughter, but that's the way I've wanted to live my life. Taking risks. I'll do it again. Maybe you can't do that. Maybe you can't love someone, but I think you did and whatever happened killed your spirit. How very sad, Maddox. I want to be with you more than anything but not if you can't let go with me."

I sensed she was waiting for some big proclamation. I wasn't the kind of man to give one. So I did what I always did; I ignored her comment.

When she started to walk into the house, I bristled.

"Does it feel good standing on the outside of life looking in, Maddox? I know you cared about someone. Whoever she was killed your spirit."

The barb was justified. "Shutting down has been necessary."

"I feel sorry for you."

"Don't. The need is my fault. My penance."

"Penance? Why?"

"Because I broke off the relationship with her and learned the next day she'd overdosed. Just like my mother."

The quiet settling between us was worse than it had been before. I wasn't looking for sympathy nor was I expecting her to say anything but when I felt her hand on my shoulder, it felt as if some of the heavy weight had been lifted.

"You really cared about her," she said.

"Yes. She was my first and you were right that she was older. I was a stupid kid. I loved the attention at first, the fact she was older providing me with an entirely different experience than I likely would have had as an eighteen-year-old kid. Unfortunately, as with all boys of that age, I was ready to move on. I'd never thought of what we shared as forever, but she'd grown attached. I didn't see her overdose coming, although I learned later that she hid her drug use from me since I'd told her about my mother."

"Geez. You weren't to blame."

I lifted my glass, taking a sip as I thought about her words. "Yeah, I was. I could have handled the breakup better. I could have seen the signs. In hindsight, they were there all along. I chose not to see them. I don't know why I was so stupid."

"You weren't stupid, Maddox. You needed someone after your father abandoned you. This woman made her choice. Her choice. I understand how addictive drugs can be, but you didn't push her into what happened. They did. That's important for you to remember as well as the fact that not all women are that fragile."

I half laughed and turned to face her, brushing my knuckles down her cheek. "Since when did you get so smart?"

"When you weren't looking or caring."

"Ah, lady. I've cared for you more than you know. You are very special and I adore you."

"But you can't love me."

"I'm not certain I can love anyone," I told her honestly.

She leaned into my hand, pressing hers on top. "What was her name?"

"Lola."

"That's beautiful. Thank you for telling me about her. That means a lot."

Another awkward moment settled in but she didn't make a move to leave.

"Your dad will be okay. The two of you are forged from the same steel. So strong."

I could tell her eyes had misted over and it nearly crushed me.

"I hope so."

The quiet settling between us was different, as if my admittance had brought us closer. Sadly, I had to break the moment and the bubble surrounding us. "Zoe. I need to ask you some questions and I need you to be completely honest with me."

"Okay. What?"

"What happened today? You were terrified in a way I haven't seen before."

I sensed when she opened her mouth, she was prepared to provide the same canned answer as before. When she looked away, I was afraid she was shutting down.

"I thought you were behind me, squeezing my shoulders. Then I heard a dark and evil laugh. That's when I jumped up, but I didn't see anyone. I thought maybe I'd imagined it."

"Now, you don't."

She hesitated again. Then shook her head.

"That's because something happened when you were in New York. Right?"

"No."

Her clipped answer was just as I'd expected. "I know about the club."

"What club?" She jerked up her head and there was no doubt she was trying to search my eyes.

Now I was the one hesitating.

"Which club, Maddox? What are you talking about?"

"The one where you worked."

"How would you know that?"

I rubbed my jaw and felt a nightmare coming on. "Because I was there."

"In New York?"

"Yes."

"When?" Her voice was trembling.

"The two weeks before you graduated."

"What? You were following me? You were stalking me?"

What the hell was I supposed to say? "I was ensuring your safety."

"My father asked you to come, or did you do that on your own?" She was now shaking from anger.

"Arman asked if I'd check on you."

Zoe sucked in her breath, taking a long stride away from me. "Oh, my God. I thought my father appreciated my independence."

"He does, Zoe. He was just concerned about your safety."

"Why?"

"He didn't tell me."

"My father tells you everything."

"No, not everything. Now, as I said, I need you to answer the question. I intervened with the guy who gave you roses the day before you graduated. What did he say or do to you?"

The way she shook her head was a clear indication she was about ready to explode. "You fucking asshole. You didn't even have the nerve to tell me you were there? You watched me, followed me? It was you outside my dorm room? The place where I took classes. Wasn't it?"

"I was there."

"God. I thought someone was following me and all along it was you. I need to be left alone for a little while."

When she turned to go, I was forced to stop her.

"Don't walk away from me, Zoe. Were you threatened?"

She tried to jerk her arm away, but I held fast. "Let me go."

"Not until you tell me."

"You son of a bitch. Fine. Yes, I was."

"How?"

"Some asshole called me. He said something like I would always be his."

"Were those his exact words?" Her exasperation was growing.

"I don't remember. Let me go!"

"Not until you tell me." My voice was deeper, and I dragged her close to me, cocking my head as I peered down at her.

"He said... He said that I belonged to him now and always." With that, she jerked her arm free, backing away before I could catch her again. Once in the light, I could tell tears were streaming down her face. "Here I thought I could trust you and you trusted me. I was stupid and wrong. I thought we cared about each other. No. You don't even understand the meaning of the word friendship. I want to go home. If you won't take me, I will find a way off this godforsaken island. And when I get there, I never want to see you again."

With that, she walked away.

This time, I allowed that to happen.

CHAPTER 21

Zoe

Damn him.

Damn the man I adored, that I craved. I folded my arms from the chill that refused to leave even though it was still in the eighties outside. As I moved quickly through the house, racing down the stairs to my bedroom, I glanced over my shoulder twice. I wasn't honestly certain whether I was hoping he'd follow, demanding I talk to him or tossing me on the bed as a reminder I belonged to him.

Neither occurred and by the time I flew into the room, I slammed the door with enough oomph I was certain he could hear it from wherever he was lurking in the house. Fuming, I paced the room, trying to make sense of why my father would send his number one right-hand man to trail behind me. As if I couldn't protect myself.

Okay, so maybe I was acting naïve when I'd already chastised myself that I should have contacted my father. I'd simply wanted to continue proving that I could live on my own, no longer Daddy's little princess. I stomped toward the bathroom, flicking on the light. Even from standing in the doorway, the reflection of the woman I'd become stared back at me.

If I didn't know better, I'd say the girl was laughing at me, making fun of my ridiculous behavior and determination to remain behind rose-colored glasses. That's the one piece of advice that Raven had given me. She'd never tried to pretend that she could be a surrogate mother. She'd become more like a sister, but her advice had been damn good.

I'd just chosen to ignore it.

She'd told me that in continuing to deny who I was, I would eventually put myself in harm's way. I'd asked her how she planned on following her own advice and she'd told me that she'd learned very quickly that my father's instincts on security were spot on. She was a rule breaker like me, yet she'd managed to not only learn to obey my father's rules, she even seemed to value his strength and knowledge.

Why hadn't I been able to do the same?

I took two long steps toward the counter, slamming my hands on the surface, glaring at myself in the mirror. The truth was I didn't like what I was seeing, the foolishness and childish behavior more like temper tantrums than anything else. I wasn't asserting my authority because I had none. I wasn't highlighting my independence; I was making a fool of myself over and over again.

Especially with the man who'd remained centered in the forefront of my mind.

I was an idiot through and through.

"Damn you." I pointed my index finger at the girl then shook my head. The bullshit was going to stop right now. I wanted to work with Maddox to try to help. I needed to be a part of the solution so I could return home. I didn't want my father to die. I just…

A single tear slipped past my lashes and I watched as it slowly trickled down my cheek. Before it reached my chin, I furiously wiped it away, feeling more secure in who I was than just seconds before. It was time to act like a goddamn adult. As thoughts about Maddox drifted into the back of my mind, I tried to determine if what I was feeling was nothing more than a childish fantasy, something that I'd shove aside like he did with Lola.

Memories flowed, so many of them that I was able to laugh at more than one. When they shifted to the moment on the beach with him, the incredible picnic and the campfire, I realized I hadn't been lying or fooling myself. I loved him. He deserved to know that I wouldn't toss him aside.

That I wouldn't leave.

He'd risked everything, including his friendship to keep me safe. Now it was time I offered everything I had to the man I adored.

A naughty thought replaced the haunted ones, and I thought about what I'd brought with me in clothes. I'd tossed a couple of things into my suitcase on a whim, hopeful that

THE WISEGUY

Maddox would finally see me for the vixen I was. Yeah, right. Laughing, I threw *that* girl another look before almost skipping into the bedroom, locating the sexy nightie I'd brought with me. If the sexy crimson piece didn't help him understand exactly how I felt, then nothing would.

I hurriedly slipped into it, running my fingers through my curls then fluffing my hair when I was finished before opening the door. After taking a deep breath, I moved into the hallway, listening for any signs of where he might be. Hearing nothing, I eased up the stairs, heading toward the living room where we'd been standing.

He wasn't there.

He wasn't outside either.

The silence in the house was terrifying but he'd closed the back door. As I moved throughout the house, I noticed he'd set the alarm near the entrance, the beeping light an indication of his actions. He'd explained the security system after our arrival, cautioning me of where cameras were located throughout the house and the exterior.

The man was a consummate bodyguard. No, he was more than that. He was brilliant and organized, the only man worthy to be my father's right-hand man. I inched down the corridor to his office, noticing the light. He was forever working, trying desperately to solve the riddle.

When I moved to the doorway, I could tell how tense he was by his shoulders, his body rigid as he sat in front of a series of computer screens. He wasn't blinking and in truth, I couldn't tell if he was breathing. In my bare feet, I padded inside, surprised that he didn't notice my approach. I eased behind his chair, noticing he had a list of people and cities up on the screen.

There were weapons in an open duffle, the man ready for a war. This might be the first time I'd allowed myself to be impressed more so than incensed. He was very good at what he did.

I held my breath and placed my hands on his shoulders.

The exaggerated breath he let out was ragged, the sound as haunting as his face had become. When I squeezed his shoulders, kneading them in a gentle massage, he tensed for a few seconds.

"You should get some sleep," he said in a husky voice, even more so than before. I noticed a glass of liquor and a bottle of scotch on the desk beside him, as if he planned on drinking the night away.

"I'm not tired." I continued to massage him, shifting one hand to his neck, using my long fingers to try to knead out the kinks.

"You need your rest."

"No."

"Hmmm…" He didn't move yet his fingers remained poised on the keyboard, his chest rising and falling.

"You're tense."

"I have reason to be."

"Let me make it better." I slipped one hand down his chest, still caressing. He was as hot as I was, the rush of heat between us easily combustible.

He half chuckled and took a sip of his drink. "I don't think you can."

"You're doubting my skills?"

"You don't need me in your life, Zoe. That's evident."

"That's where you're wrong. You're exactly what I need. As the man protecting me. As the man I respect. And as the man I love. Hear me, Maddox Cormier. I love you and I don't intend on leaving you. I'm sorry I've acted like such a child. I've made your life miserable and that wasn't my intent. I just… I wanted to be someone I wasn't. Will you ever forgive me?"

When he said nothing, I knew in my heart it was too late. I'd fucked up. I'd lost the man I loved more than anything. I started to pull away, my heart aching.

He grabbed my hand, his grip firm.

"You're not going anywhere," he growled.

"I know I'm too much of a risk to your life. I understand."

"Fuck that, little lamb." Maddox swiveled in his chair, dragging me around the side, yanking me onto his lap. He was rock hard and throbbing, his thick cock pushing against my bottom. I was excited and terrified, filled with desire and such love that it clouded my judgment.

But I didn't care.

As he lifted my chin with his index finger, his nostrils flaring, there were a few seconds of awe at his size, of being mesmerized by not only his handsome features but also by the man himself. He was in control of everything.

My safety.

My environment.

And my heart.

"Baby, you belong to me. I never want to hurt or deceive you," he whispered gruffly. "You just need to trust me."

"I do trust you, with all of me." I wrapped my arm around his neck and shoulders, shifting on his lap, teasing him relentlessly until he smiled.

"Then show me, baby. Show me exactly the way you feel and what you want."

His command was dark and delicious, as dangerous as he was and in those few precious seconds where all time stood still, there was no doubt neither one of us would ever be able to retrace our steps, erasing what we'd shared.

As he cupped the side of my face, guiding our lips closer together, there wasn't a single inch of my body that wasn't quivering in anticipation. He was truly my everything. The way he captured my mouth was even more possessive than I'd experienced before, yet he took his time, as if savoring the moment was more important to him than anything.

As if what we shared could be stripped away at any moment.

The danger was real, the sense that I hadn't been wrong about someone touching and threatening me only hours before weighing heavily on my mind. Yet in giving up all sense of control to this powerful man, in accepting who and what I was, I felt a sense of peace like I had never before.

He swept his tongue inside, dominating mine as he tasted me, every action savage yet at the same time, his explorations were subtle. I wrapped my fingers around his long locks of hair, tethering myself to him. The electricity sparked in wave after wave, my pulse increasing with every passing second. He had no idea how much I adored the taste of scotch on his lips, the smooth yet powerful flavor quenching my thirst.

Although I wouldn't mind having his seed filling my mouth, the man drowning me with his cum.

His body shaking, he slid his hand to the back of my head, tangling his fingers in my hair, tugging until our lips parted. We were both breathing heavily, our needs rushing to the surface.

"You are so fucking beautiful, Zoe."

How could any woman feel as incredible or lovely as I did? As he jerked my head back, exposing my neck, I wrapped my fingers around his shirt, still wiggling on his lap. He was as aroused as I was, his cock throbbing in time to the rapid beating of my pulse.

The sounds he made as he pressed his lips against my heated skin were intoxicating, the man ready to devour me. I closed my eyes, still shivering even with the combined warmth of our bodies. As he dragged his tongue underneath my jaw, taking his time to nip and lick my skin, several moans escaped my mouth.

The way he took his time as he tickled the area near my pulse with the tip of a single finger, tracing my shoulder blade before sliding it down the length of my arm kept my skin prickling.

My heart thudding.

It was the anticipation of what he would do, of having his cock buried deep inside that made the moment explosive. There were no additional words to be said, no desire to burst the precarious bubble we were in. There was only the here and now, the incredible moments that we'd share completely together. The armor had been ripped aside, the walls shattered between us. We were both vulnerable for entirely different reasons, yet our worlds and concerns were so much the same.

He shifted his attention to my breast, slowly swirling the tip around my hardened nipple still covered by lace. When he finally yanked the material aside, exposing my naked skin, I moaned so loudly I almost laughed. It didn't matter how he touched me. Every time was the same, the sheer indulgence something fantasies were made of.

Chuckling in his usual dark and possessive way, he yanked both straps of my nightie down my arms, leaving both breasts completely exposed, the light breeze of the air conditioning creating one shiver after another.

Did he have any idea what he was doing to me? Did he know I was losing not only my soul but my heart as well? I shifted against his thick bulge, taunting him as he was doing to me. He countered by ripping off the thin material, tossing it aside as if it meant nothing. He pinched both nipples between his thumbs and forefingers until I cried out, lowering my head and gasping for air.

There was a maniacal look in his eyes, both dilated, the intensity of his expression allowing me to accept he was going to devour every inch of me.

And I couldn't wait.

His actions becoming more brutal, he pushed my back against his desk, forcing me to stare up at the ceiling. I struggled to hold onto his arms as he slowly lowered his head. I never thought his heated breath would scorch my skin, but I was wrong. Oh, so wrong.

"My God," I muttered, dragging my tongue across my bottom lip, smacking my hands against his desk to try to gain some leverage. All I managed to do was to create several beeping sounds, which finally pushed a nervous laugh from my lips. "I hope I didn't start a terrorist attack."

He growled his answer at first, his rough tongue tickling my skin as he dragged it down the side of my neck in between my breasts. His mouth was wet and hot as he pulled one nipple between his teeth, sucking before biting down not once but three times. The pain was electrifying, keeping my nerves on edge in the very best way.

I stared up at the ceiling, mewing loudly as I continued to undulate. I sensed he wanted to ensure I knew that he was in full control and always would be. I willingly gave in, no longer fighting anything. The fact I was naked on his lap, my pussy throbbing from his rough touch was pure sin. And I loved every second of it.

Maddox took his time bathing me with his tongue, licking under my other breast before pulling the tender bud into his mouth. Every inch of my skin was so sensitive, every nerve standing on end.

When he suddenly jerked me back into a sitting position, our lips dangerously close, our breathing was exactly the same. I laughed nervously, keeping my hands pressed against his shoulders. There was something so enthralling about the way he was holding me, but my hunger had increased, the need to feel his heated skin pressed against mine all consuming. I laughed again as I struggled to yank his shirt from the tight confines of his pants, every action becoming frantic.

After a few seconds, he pushed my hands away, the wry smile on his face matched by his twinkling eyes. He jerked off the polo from the back of his neck, pitching it all the way across the room.

I didn't waste any time, planting my palms on his chest, digging my nails in as I gave him a tongue bath, starting at his left ear. He chuckled again as I nipped his earlobe, immediately sliding just the tip of my tongue down the thick cords of his neck to his shoulder. I couldn't contain my exuberance, kneading his chest muscles as I fought to lower my head, even daring to push him back to gain more access.

"You're a hungry girl," he muttered, stating the obvious teasingly.

"Hell, yes." Purring, I crawled my fingers down to his abdomen, licking around my mouth in an exaggerated fashion before fighting with the button on his jeans. I sensed he was watching my every move, likely amused that I was struggling so much. The simple truth was the man continued to make me nervous, his power and prowess unlike any other boy I'd been around. His aura was godlike, keeping the electricity flowing and my mind on a slickened precipice.

He knew it too, the smirk one I would have wanted to wipe off only a few days before. But now, it was just something else to adore about him. Not that I didn't appreciate and crave every inch already. When I finally managed to unzip his jeans, he lifted his hips, which pushed me up by several inches. The move was surprising, making me laugh nervously.

"Lower my jeans, baby," he instructed.

"Why should I?"

"Because if you don't, I'll tie you down, teasing you relentlessly without giving you any relief."

"You wouldn't dare." I lifted my gaze, giving him a naughty girl look. I could tell by his dilated eyes that he meant every word. "Fine. Have it your way." I tugged on the dense material, fighting with the carved edges of his hips before managing to lower the jeans to his thighs, freeing his delicious cock. The glisten of pre-cum on his sensitive slit was a powerful draw, my mouth watering. Somehow, I knew he wasn't going to allow me to play but for so long.

Yet I couldn't help myself, sliding the tip of my index finger through the tangy beads, slowly bringing it to my mouth. I purposely rolled my eyes into the back of my head as I slipped it past my lips, sucking as if enjoying the finest cherry lollypop.

His scattered breathing was another sweet reward, his nostrils flaring as he lowered his gaze from my face to my chest. I adored every animalistic sound he made, the husky growls and near barks sparking even more desire.

I removed my finger, sliding the tip around his mouth, bursting into laughter when he nipped the end, easily able to drag the entire length into his mouth. My yelps continued as he sucked relentlessly. He was showing off his predatory skills, which kept me fully aroused, my blood pressure rising. But without warning, he yanked first one of my arms behind my back then the other, snapping the fingers of one hand around both wrists.

"What are you doing?" I demanded, although this time I was playing.

"Making certain you're reminded who's in charge." The grin on his face was positively evil and somehow, he managed to lift me from his knees, using his other hand to position the tip of his cock against my slickened folds. There was no hesitation on his part, the sense of urgency too great.

I moaned in happiness as he thrust every inch into my tight channel, both of us gasping for air as my muscles expanded. Almost instantly they started to pulse, clenching and releasing several times. He moaned his joy and satisfaction, never blinking as he locked eyes with mine. There was even more intensity buried deep in the dark man, which worried me. I'd seen the look before but for an entirely different reason.

It had been the moments just after something had occurred, he and my father discussing their alternatives, making decisions on how to handle whatever the ongoing situation. The electricity had soared then as well, but it had been all about his anger.

He was still enraged, as if the world had done him wrong, but he was using the energy to fuck me hard. The man was so muscular, his thighs powerful enough to lift and impale me at the same time.

I struggled in his tight hold but there was no getting out of his clutches until he wanted me to. Not that I ever did. I couldn't help envisioning myself tied to his bed, awaiting his return from work. The filthy thought was followed by lurid images. He kept his gaze explosive, his eyes hooded as he studied me, the same wry smile on his face as he drove his cock deep inside.

Everything about the moment was insane and beautiful, our coupling more passionate than I'd known was possible. There was no real way of explaining what the time spent inside his office with guns within my view, and a computer system able to rival any law enforcement agency or the military meant to me. Perhaps it was more about accepting the world we lived in or maybe it was an understanding that life was too short and that anything could happen at any time.

The party my father and his bride had thrown, every detail meticulously planned was the perfect indication, the truth to our reality. We had to seize the moment, the day, and our raging passion.

Maddox's chest continued to rise and fall, his eyes raking over me, feasting in an entirely different way. He finally let go of my arms, allowing me to slide my hands up and down his arms, squeezing his muscles as he gripped my hips, forcing me to buck against him. I marveled in how his skin felt to my touch, rolling my hands over his shoulders, catching the indentation where he'd been shot. The divot only added character to his sculpted body, another dimension of his character that I wanted to understand.

We continued staring into each other's eyes as I bucked hard against him, pressing the balls of my feet into the tile floor. I tossed my head back and forth, the rush of sensations pitching against the raging climax that was just starting to sweep through me.

Unable to hold back any longer, I threw back my head, whimpering and laughing nervously as tingling jolts of current sliced into every cell and muscle.

"That's it, baby girl. I adore the shimmer crossing your face when you come."

His words were scattered, the dark whisper of them almost as enticing as his perfect body. I closed my eyes once again, digging my fingernails into his back, rocking so hard against him that I was fearful we'd fall to the floor. I should have known better. He held my hips so tightly I had a sense my skin would bruise.

And I'd wear the marks proudly.

All time stopped, the thought of losing control all I could think about.

"Uh. Uh. Uh. Yes... Yes!" The scream erupting from my lungs as the orgasm powered into me was unrecognizable, my mind one foggy mess of dirty thoughts and images. And I loved the moment of letting go, of surrendering to the man I loved.

The climax refused to abate, the heated sensations keeping beads of perspiration over my lip. I felt his body tensing, every muscle tightening and knew that within seconds, he'd fill me with his seed.

And when he did, the roar he issued was as primal and dangerous as it could get.

This time he didn't need to remind me that I belonged to him.

Until the end of time.

CHAPTER 22

Maddox

Lucas Marciano.

It had taken me half the night to remember the asshole's name who'd almost accosted Zoe in New York. The reason was simple. I'd believed him to be nothing more than an enamored older man hungry for a taste of a beautiful girl. After learning about the threat she'd received, the feeling she'd been followed, even seeing a dark figure outside her dorm room, I'd stayed up all night until I'd remembered.

I wasn't the one she'd described, and I refused to tell her that her fears were real. While the kid we'd followed the day before wasn't the man who'd touched her on the outside patio, I was certain he remained on the island watching us, biding his time. Maybe I was imagining things myself, but my instinct had never failed me.

THE WISEGUY

The man wasn't likely a real player, merely someone paid to garner as much information about Zoe as possible. What I didn't understand was why she wasn't taken in New York if that had been the intention all along. There were too many things I didn't understand, which annoyed and angered me.

I stood on the deck drinking my third cup of coffee, my nerves even more on edge than before. I'd allowed her to go to the beach for a short swim, the phone app for the security system easily alerting me to anyone coming within close proximity of the house. Given both sides of the property were wooded, the house was not visible from the road and very few homes were within a few miles, random visitors had never occurred. If I was right and someone was on the island searching for us, unless I'd tripped up in my observation skills, there was no way we'd been followed to the house.

Yet I remained on edge, so much so that I was ready to lock her inside a room. I dragged my tongue across my lips, still able to taste her even after a few hours had passed. She'd changed dramatically in just a few hours, no longer fighting my orders. She'd even brought points and counterpoints regarding the lists I'd prepared of possible enemies. I'd been surprised that she'd had good ideas, including having our internal email system checked for any leaks.

I'd developed a quick and easy program to scan our secure system. While it might take a little while, as long as the internet connection held, I could learn more than I hoped within hours. I glanced at the sky, the clouds forming creating a malevolent atmosphere.

Another bad feeling pooled in the pit of my stomach and I backed into the house, moving toward the kitchen in search of the weather radio I'd purchased after the first weather event I'd endured years before. After searching the cabinets and finally finding it, I had to continue searching for batteries.

By the time I did, ten fucking minutes had passed, enough that I almost dropped them from being angry with myself. I glanced out the kitchen window, unable to see Zoe from where I was standing. The radio in hand, I headed back to the living room, immediately moving out to the deck. As I tried to find a station close, the reception crackling, I searched the beach, about ready to drop everything to hunt her down when I noticed her standing off to the right.

She was standing in the surf, her hand over her eyes as if searching for something. I breathed a sigh of relief, able to keep her in sight and the moment I heard a voice, the French accent was as I would have expected.

The connection was clear at first, the reporter mentioning something about a couple of events being cancelled, which forced me to listen more intently. It didn't take long to hear the reason for the cancellations.

A tropical storm was rolling in quickly. If the reports were true, it would arrive late the next day. I had no intentions of sticking around for it. The last thing I wanted to do was to get stuck on the island for an extended period of time.

"Fuck." Now I had to figure out if returning was in our best interest. If Zoe was the target, heading back to New Orleans could mean drawing the danger back to our hometown. Before I had a chance to make a single decision, my phone rang. I yanked it from my pocket, tossing another look toward the beach. She was now sitting in the surf. While the water didn't appear to be showing signs of the upcoming weather system, my hackles remained raised, my concern increasing.

I didn't like the dangerous situation whatsoever. It was as if karma had it out for us.

"Tony. What did you find on Zoe in New York? Anything on this Marciano guy?" I'd texted him the information, unable to find anything about him through use of the computer.

"First of all, there was a single unknown phone number who called her, everyone else family or the few friends she had in the city," he answered.

"Did you trace the number you found?"

"A burner phone."

I squeezed my iPhone. I wanted to turn her over my knee for not telling anyone. Her independent streak had placed her life squarely in danger. "What about this Marciano dude?"

"You've never heard of the name?" my soldier asked as if shocked I hadn't.

"Cut to the chase, bud. I'm not in any mood for crap."

"Don't worry. It sounded familiar from my days being in New York. But I ended up contacting a few buddies of mine who are heavy into the scene. You know what I mean."

He'd been a low-level soldier to the Russian Bratva in New York, moving to New Orleans to care for his dying mother. He'd stayed after her death, finding the climate more suitable to his Italian nature. Or so he'd told me. While the man irritated the hell out of me, he was good for certain things, including his knowledge base of almost all the syndicates in New York. The knowledge had been useful years before in preventing an Armenian crew from encroaching on our turf.

"That means you found something."

"You're not going to like it."

His voice sounded far off and when I didn't hear him reply within a few seconds, I jerked the phone away from my face, noticing the reception was shit. I moved into the house, heading toward the internet hub.

"Can you hear me?" Tony asked, his voice clearer.

"The reception is crap. There's a storm rolling in. Who is this guy?"

"I don't know who you think you saw but it wasn't Lucas Marciano, unless it was a pure coincidence."

"Meaning what?"

The crackling sound coming from the other end of the phone was loud.

"Meaning the guy is… enforcer for…"

"What did you say?" There was nothing but constant clicks, what little I could hear from him coming in syllables. "Tony. Call me back. I'm losing you." I pressed end, tossing the phone on the outside table, moving toward the railing and slamming my hands on the wooden surface.

What the hell had he been trying to tell me? An enforcer? For whom? While it was possible the guy had been faking his drunkenness, fabricating the reek of alcohol, I'd seen his bloodshot eyes, his cheap suit. Sure, even that could be faked but the man was at least sixty. I knew of no enforcers still in the job at that advanced age.

Landry's comment about made men not surviving past forty-five slipped into the back of my mind. I scanned the ocean, noticing she was swimming in the shallow waters. As I took another glance at the sky, I didn't like what I saw. In the short time I'd been on the phone, the clouds had darkened significantly. That had to mean squalls were on the way.

Seconds later, I heard her scream. I took off racing down the stairs, jumping over the thick rock wall to the sand fifteen feet below. She was struggling to get to shore but I couldn't tell what was holding her back. A rip current? The water was churning more than it should be.

Then I heard a noise and stiffened.

What the fuck? There was a speedboat powering toward the shore. I yanked out my weapon, continuing to race to the shore. By the time I reached the edge of the water, she was on her feet, heading toward me.

I lunged toward her and into the water. She flailed in my arms, finally wrapping them around my neck. "I got you, baby."

Zoe was shivering, clutching me as she tried to land her feet on the sand. "You came for me."

"You really thought otherwise?" I threw my arm around her and jerking her completely out of the water. Out of the corner of my eye, I noticed a glint of metal and pushed her to the sand.

Fuck me. They were after her.

"Stay down!"

Two people were on the boat and there was no doubt in my mind one of them was holding a weapon in his hand. As Zoe started to scream, I took aim.

Pop! Pop! Pop! Pop!

The boat came far too close for my comfort and I dropped down over her just as the captain spun it around in a tight arc, heading out into the deeper water of the cove. Gasping for air, I threw a look over my shoulder, realizing the shooter had been hit.

"Fuck. Fuck. Fuck," she cried, clawing her fingers into the sand.

"Jesus Christ. Are you okay?"

"Uh-huh. I think so. They came out of… nowhere. I was just swimming, and I heard a noise and…"

I turned her over, cupping the side of her face. "We need to get back to the house. We're getting off this island." I glanced back over my shoulder, the boat no longer easy to spot. The fuckers would be back. Of that I was certain. I helped Zoe to her feet, keeping behind her as we trudged toward the house. As soon as we were at the steps, I threw one last look at the cove. The boat had disappeared.

What in God's name was going on and how had we found?

"What's happening?" she asked as I started to guide her up the stairs.

"Get your stuff together. We're leaving as soon as you do."

As soon as we were on the landing, she turned to me, her eyes searching mine. She rose onto her tiptoes, kissing my cheek, her heated breath scintillating but her harsh whisper a reminder of my position and how seriously I needed to take it.

"Thank you, Maddox. I'm terrified but you make it easier." When she pulled away, she noticed the watch still attached to my wrist. "You ruined your watch."

"Oh, honey. I'd lose every fucking possession I had to keep you safe. You need to know that."

The way she cupped my face was different, so gentle yet her face was so forlorn. "I know you would. That's why I love you. Maybe one day you can love me back."

Goddamn the woman. Couldn't she tell how hard I'd fallen for her, how much I wanted to wrap myself around her, making passionate love to her for weeks on end?

She disappeared into the shadows, and I turned around to face the water once more, finally sliding my weapon back into my jeans. "I'm coming for you fuckers. And when I find you, I promise you that you will suffer."

* * *

The wind had picked up in intensity during the thirty minutes we remained at the house. I alternated looking out the window at the swaying trees and in the rearview mirror. While I couldn't detect we'd been followed, it was obvious the perpetrator knew exactly where we were. I kept my foot on the pedal as I roared through town heading toward the mostly private airstrip, the location used by the rich and famous when they arrived or departed. I'd been lucky to get one of the few storage facilities, bartering with a watch that had cost almost as much as the one she'd bought me.

I would find someone to repair it. The gift, like the woman, was far too precious to be ignored. I glanced in her direction as I rounded the last corner. Now her expression was blank, her hands folded in her lap as she stared out the windshield.

"We're almost there," I told her.

"What if they shoot us down? Did you think about that?"

"They won't."

"Don't make promises you can't keep. Cause I'll hold you to them." She tipped her head, offering a slight smile.

"Trust me, little lamb. I'm a damn good pilot."

"I haven't figured out anything you aren't good at, including saving damsels in distress."

I shook my head and accelerated through the open gate as I headed for the hangar where the plane was kept. It was a secure facility, manned by someone twenty-four hours a day. I paid a pretty penny for it, but in my mind, the money spent was worth every penny.

That's why when I noticed the regular door standing open, flopping back and forth in the wind, every muscle in my body tensed.

"Are you sure we're going to get off the island with this level of wind?" she asked, fortunately not honing in on my sudden stiffness.

"We'll get off this blasted island. Do me a favor and stay right here," I told her as I parked the Jeep, throwing it into park but leaving it running.

"What's wrong?"

"I just want to check with the guy inside. He handles the flight schedules. I might need to pay him a little extra to bump us in line. I'll be right back." I didn't give her time to offer any kind of rebuttal or argue with me, slipping onto the concrete and scanning the area. There was activity at one of the other hangars, a vehicle heading toward it. While I'd refused to listen to the radio on the way for fear of scaring her even more, the bad feeling refused to leave.

We were smack in the middle of hurricane season, the irregular weather patterns offering up storms at a moment's notice. I waited until I was close to the swinging door before yanking out my weapon, keeping it in both hands. As I moved toward the door, I listened for any sounds. The only damn thing I heard sounded like a leaky roof. Given it hadn't rained yet, I knew better than to think I was identifying the sound correctly.

I stepped backward, ensuring Zoe remained in the Jeep where I told her to stay. She was there but I sensed her nervousness. After taking a deep breath, I moved closer to the door, darting my head in. There was no one in sight, which wasn't necessarily unusual, but my sixth sense was overactive.

Keeping against the building, I entered, twisting my body one direction then the other, both hands firmly wrapped around the Glock. Even though I took cautious steps, the sound of my boots against the floor echoed. The closer I came to my Cirrus, the louder the dripping sound. I constantly scanned the area, refusing to call out to the attendant.

Something was wrong. I was certain of it. I bent down, noticing something that appeared to be either oil or gasoline dripped on the floor to the left of my plane. That wasn't good. If the plane had been sabotaged, then we were shit out of luck.

I took careful strides, moving to the front of the plane before shifting around to the side.

"Fuck." The dripping sound hadn't been a leaky valve. The employee of the airport was hanging from a rope attached to one of the tail wings of the plane, blood from someone slicing his neck open before hanging him finding its way down his arms, dripping onto the concrete.

"Maddox."

I heard Zoe's voice a split second before she burst into a scream. My reaction was the same as before, immediate. I turned and grabbed her, pressing her face into my chest.

"Jesus. You need to start listening to me," I told her, muffling her scream. After a few seconds, I pulled her head back enough to be able to look into her eyes. "What are you doing in here? Did something else happen?"

"I thought I saw someone dressed in black. I got scared."

Fuck. Fuck. Fuck.

"Okay, baby. This is getting dicey."

"Is he dead?" she asked, her voice small.

"Yeah, he's dead. I need to check the plane. Just turn around for me. I won't be a second. Can you do that?"

She lifted her head, nodding.

I kissed her forehead, waiting until she'd turned around. I moved toward the plane, looking around me before opening the door. There was no sudden movement, no oddity when I climbed in. I glanced at the console, trying to determine if the plane had been tampered with.

Seeing nothing, I moved to start the airplane. As soon as I did, I heard a distinct clicking sound. This time, I allowed my instinct to take over, jumping from the plane and running toward Zoe.

There was no time to waste. I threw us both out the door, half carrying her as far away as I could get us from the hangar.

She struggled in my hold but didn't try to get away.

As soon as I looked over my shoulder, I sensed the explosion before it happened.

Yet I wasn't ready for the power of the bomb.

Until it was too late.

Boom!

CHAPTER 23

Zoe

"Goddamn it. There must be a plane on this godforsaken island," Maddox said, barking into the phone.

I leaned against the wall, trying to remain calm when I couldn't stop shaking. In the several hours since we'd returned, the wind had kicked up tremendously, the weather system he had squawking several times in warning. He'd already tried to get a commercial flight out. There was none coming in or going out given the increasing windspeed.

The sky was turning pitch black, ominous and dark. At least we had power, but I had a terrible feeling that wouldn't last long. The black clouds weren't only outside. They were surrounding us like demons attempting to drag us straight to hell.

Laughing, I moved toward the drinks I'd made for us, preferring scotch to dull the pain. He'd barely touched his, pacing the floor as he'd tried to make as many outgoing calls as possible. At least he'd managed to get through to Francois. My father was stable although he'd yet to waken from the coma.

Maddox had tried to hide the details of the news from me, but I'd been able to read between the lines. He'd tried to pass off the infection running its course through my father's body as run of the mill, as if it could easily be cured by antibiotics. Maybe he'd forgotten my nursing training. But I knew if the doctors didn't get the situation under control, my father's organs could start shutting down one at a time.

While I trusted Uncle Louie implicitly, infections of that nature could easily get out of hand within hours. I pressed my fingers against my forehead, trying not to think the worst but it was so hard. I was an emotional wreck, longing to have one last chance at telling my father what he meant to me.

"No. I need to talk to a supervisor," Maddox snapped and jerked his drink off the table, eyeing me carefully. While he offered a smile, there was no hiding the intensity of his concerns. He was as haunted and angry as I was.

I knew him far too well by now, the loss of control he was feeling derailing a portion of his mind. Plus, he suffered from the ache of potentially losing his best friend. I took another sip of my drink, barely easing it to the table without dropping it.

With one last connection on the verge of failing, we'd be forced to hunker down in the middle of what was now expected to be a category one hurricane.

I was numb inside, shocked that he'd saved my life twice in one day. We'd been extremely lucky we'd gotten out of the blast zone, the hangar and everything inside completely demolished.

"No. That's not okay. That's…" As soon as he pulled the phone away, he cursed.

"The line is dead?"

"Yeah. I guess we lost the internet. Always the first to go in these kinds of storms."

"My God. We're stuck," I said as I closed my eyes.

"For now, little lamb. However, it'll be okay. The storm will pass."

"How? How is it going to be okay? For all we know there's a dozen more assholes trying to kill us. That man died just because he was in the wrong place at the wrong time. Because of us. Us!"

"How do I know? Because I have enough firepower to start a goddamn war."

I turned away from him on purpose.

"Look, Zoe. I think the young man at the hangar had been dead for at least a few hours, which likely means whoever is responsible killed him first then headed toward the house."

"How did they find us? How?"

"Because the government in St. Barts requires this address to be on file. My guess is that the employee was forced to open the files on the computer in the office, providing it."

"How do you know?"

"Just a guess but I'm pretty good at them."

"You have no soldiers to stand by your side. You're one man, Maddox. One. I can fire a weapon, but I doubt you'll allow me to use one." I threw up my hand with my index finger as I stared at him. He had cuts on his face from protecting me from the shrapnel, yet he'd refused to allow me to tend to his wounds.

As he walked closer, I found myself bristling, shaking all over again. "Do you really think I'm going to allow anyone to get inside this house?"

"You're not Superman. You won't wear the cape."

He chuckled. "Who says I need one? I have magic powers." As he pulled me into his arms, I could tell how tense he remained.

"What if the storm surge is bad?"

"We're in a protected cove. That will keep us from getting the brunt of the storm since it's coming from the opposite direction. However, it's time we batten down the hatches. Are you game for it?"

"Do I have another choice?" I pulled out of his arms, trying to control the anger and sadness. The fear that I couldn't seem to break free of from the notion not only was I going to lose my father but the man I loved as well. The despair was overwhelming, so much so that I had difficulty breathing.

"We'll be fine. And yes, I will allow you to have a weapon."

"What if we lose power?"

He rubbed his knuckles across my face. "I do have a small generator we can use. That will help. I also have plenty of flashlights. We'll make a picnic out of it."

I was shocked that he was making light of the situation. It wasn't like him. That meant he was more worried than he wanted to let on.

A generator. "Does it power the security system?"

When he took a deep breath, holding it, I shivered all over again. "Look, we're going to be fine. Okay?"

It didn't matter that he continued to tell me that. I'd almost been run down by a speedboat, had seen a dead man with his throat slit, and had almost blown up in a fiery explosion, all in just a few hours. Laughter bubbled to the surface. I was obviously losing all sense of rationality, drifting ever so close to la-la-land.

"I'm trying to believe you, but the storm is coming in so fast."

"I know but with it being a fast-moving storm, it'll get the hell out of here quickly as well. Think of it that way. However, we do need to get the shutters locked down. Is that something you can help me with?"

I stared into his gorgeous eyes, finally nodding. "Just tell me what I can do to help."

"Good girl. We can do this together. I'll show you how to latch one. That's all you need to do."

Together.

The thought burned into the back of my mind as I headed downstairs while he took the main floor.

I found myself moving through the house, trying to do what he asked, but I could no longer feel my feet, I felt so numb inside. I was sick to my stomach as I moved from room to room, struggling with the heavy wooden shutters. I still couldn't wrap my mind around everything that had happened, fighting the anger and nerves with everything I had.

When I was finished with the last one, I could still hear the wind howling through the windows. I backed away just as the light flickered for the first time. The last thing I wanted to do was be in the lower level if the power went off. It was a crazy little thing, a fear of the shadows but after today, I deserved to be worried to a point.

I raced up the stairs, finding him in the kitchen sliding batteries into a flashlight. The weather station was still going, the reports being alternated in French and English.

"Any additional news?" I asked as I moved closer.

"Nothing that you want to hear."

"Meaning what?"

He took a deep breath before answering. "They're upgraded it to a category two."

"You're certain we'll be okay?"

"Yes, Zoe. I am. Why don't we put together a bite to eat."

"I don't think I can." It was at that moment that adrenaline chose to flood my system, my breathing suddenly shallow, and I was unable to get enough air to breathe. It took a few seconds to realize I was having a panic attack. I gripped the edge of the counter, lifting my head to stare at him. I could swear I heard footsteps. I could swear I heard the robotic voice of the man who'd threatened me.

I couldn't have a meltdown. I just couldn't.

Thankfully, he wasn't paying attention, loading up another flashlight. I think he was droning on about how I needed to keep up my strength, but his words were suddenly all jumbled together.

As the light began to fade around me, my periphery of vision going first, I reached out for him. "Maddox. Maddox…"

"No!"

"I feel a kick," Maddox said as he lifted his gaze, grinning as his eyes darted back and forth across mine.

"It's only been three months. I don't think that's possible just yet."

"Are you kidding me, little mama? I know my son is kicking away, eager to come out into the world."

"Uh-huh." I removed his hand, but he pulled my arm, curling my fingers then rolling his thumb back and forth across my knuckles as he brought my hand toward his mouth. When he rolled his lips back and forth, I couldn't keep from shivering. He had that kind

of effect on me, so powerful in everything he did. "You better stop, or I won't make it to cooking our dinner."

"I am famished but not for food." *He lifted me off my feet and I squealed.*

"What are you doing?"

"Oh, nothing. Just fulfilling my needs. I am a growing boy."

"Growing boy, my ass. Put me down." *He was taking long strides down the hall toward the kitchen.* "I said put me down, you big lug, you!"

"Okay. With pleasure." *He plopped me down onto the floor and as soon as I tried to run away, he grabbed my arm, giving me his most heated defiant look.* "Not so fast. You deserve a spanking."

"For what? I'm a good girl."

"Uh-huh. Let me count the ways you haven't been good." *He tapped his index finger against his lips.* "Oh, yes. Backtalking. You refuse to follow my rules."

"What rules?" *I teased. I was a little vixen, constantly trying to get away with things.*

"You know exactly which rules. I've been too lenient with you. It's time that ends. I'm going to give you at least three spankings a week."

"Three? That's ridiculous!"

"Would you like it to be four?"

"You're a very bad man. Did anyone ever tell you that?"

He laughed and rubbed his hand down my arm. "My lovely wife all the time. Off with your dress and panties."

"That's not fair."

"I never said I was a fair man."

"Okay. True." I giggled seeing the stern look on his face. Somehow, I knew I wasn't getting out of this. When he reached for my dress, I pushed his hands away. "I can do it."

"Good girl. Then do it for me while I find the perfect implement."

"You mean you aren't using your hand?"

He wagged his finger, winking at me. "Not tonight. You need to remember this round of discipline for a long time. Perhaps that will keep you in line."

As he pressed the tip of his index finger against my nose, a trickling shiver skittered down my spine, but it had nothing to do with the anticipation of a hard spanking. The man just did that to me, pushing me into a puddle of desire and heat with the intensity of his looks, the tiny lines of wisdom crinkling around his eyes when he smiled. The hard line of his jaw and the exquisite muscular physique that stole my breath at least once a day.

Exhaling, I watched him head to the kitchen drawers, biting my lower lip before yanking the hem of my dress.

"When you're finished undressing, lie across the table for me, little lamb."

He had no idea what his pet name for me did every time he uttered the words. My breath was still shallow as I folded my dress, placing it over the back of one of the chairs. I slowly gazed over my shoulder, cringing just a little bit inside from seeing him twirling an evil-looking wooden spoon. The man was creative in his punishments, the implements selected not ordinary by any means.

Closing my eyes, I slipped my fingers underneath the elastic of my thong, for some crazy reason still attempting to be sexy when I lowered the fragile lace past my hips. Who could be sexy just before a spanking? I rolled my eyes, gently placing them on the table before doing as he asked. How many times had I been spanked draped across the kitchen table? I couldn't count them. There wasn't a room in the house that he hadn't taken advantage of.

I positioned my hands over my head, gripping the edge of the wooden surface so he wouldn't need to command me to do so. As I waited, I thought about how lucky I was to have such an incredible partner in life and in love. Just doing so made me hot and wet, my pussy throbbing. I couldn't believe I always became aroused when he spanked me. Who else in their right mind would experience something like that? Only this girl.

Maddox took his sweet time, which was just his way of kicking the anticipation into high gear. He wanted me trembling, ready to confess all my sins.

Which I usually did.

Why did he have such a tremendous effect on me?

When I finally heard his footsteps, the man whistling as he approached, I gritted my teeth. I had a feeling the spanking would be harsh.

Within seconds, I realized I was right. He wasted no time in bringing the thick wood down on my bottom, moving from one side to the other in a perfect rhythm. I wiggled and humped the table in my effort to remain in position. He'd started over a number of times because I'd refused to do so. Not today. Today, I would be a good girl.

After that, maybe I'd be able to suck his thick cock. I dragged my tongue across my bottom lip as the delicious and sinful thought lingered in my mind.

The cracks he issued were numerous, one coming right after the other. Finally, I couldn't keep from moaning, my breath stolen as the discomfort turned into raw yet blissful pain.

"See. You can be a good girl when you want to be." *The powerful man was teasing me, as he always enjoyed doing, driving me to the point of coming close to an enraptured climax. I used to hate him for it, but now... This was a slice of ecstasy that couldn't be explained.*

He issued a low and husky growl as he caressed my skin, gently rolling the rough pads of his fingers in circles from one side to the other. When he rolled a single finger down the crack of my ass, taking his time to open my legs, a waft of my desire floated all the way up to my nose.

"You're very wet, my perfect little lamb," *he mused, daring to taunt me by pushing the tip just past my slickened folds.*

I moaned and wiggled once again, opening my legs even wider. There was nothing like being completely exposed and vulnerable for him.

"Not yet, baby girl. Perhaps after your spanking." *He resumed the round of punishment, obviously enjoying his work given he was whistling the entire time. I used to long to rip out his eyeballs when he acted this way, so very much in control and loving it. Now? I took it in stride, knowing that in truth, I was the one in control. The man couldn't resist my feminine wiles.*

As the strikes became even more painful, I bit back a series of whimpers, but the longing remained, the wetness escalating. At this rate, I'd beg him to fuck me.

After doling out at least six more, he flung the spoon aside, yet allowing me to see the implement of doom only inches away.

"What am I going to do with you, bad little girl?" he asked as he planted his hands on either side of me, leaning over and blowing his hot breath across the back of my neck. "Let me think." He pressed his fingers against my spine, taking his time to roll them down to my aching and likely very red bottom. "I know. I am a thirsty man, hungry too. I think I'll enjoy a feast meant for a king."

He flipped me over on the table, immediately bending my legs at the knees, pressing them against the table. I was completely exposed, my mind spinning as he yanked one of the chairs forward, sitting down with a hard thump. The sound of him scooting the chair forward made me laugh.

"Something funny?" he asked in the deepest voice I'd heard to date.

"Yes. You."

"Hmmm..." He pressed his hands against my inner thighs, dragging his tongue from my kneecap up the length of my leg, teasing me as usual by almost dipping his tongue into my wetness.

I kept one arm over my head, lolling my other hand across my lips, doing my best to watch what he was doing. When he lowered his head, I sucked in and held my breath. He did nothing more than blow across my pussy, chuckling like the beast he was before lifting his heated gaze.

"My beautiful yet notoriously mischievous wife. I think I might tie you up naked today, forcing you to wait for my return."

"That's mean."

"You bet." He finally swirled his tongue around my clit several times, watching my reaction, a smirk on his face.

A part of me wanted to hold back any satisfaction, refusing to react in any way, but when he pinched my sensitive bud, I whimpered automatically. As he repeated it again, I issued a strangled moan. But the moment he cracked his fingers against my pussy not once but four times, I jerked up from the table with a sharp yelp.

"Be good, baby girl. I plan on soothing all your aches and pains." He smacked my pussy lips four more times then immediately dropped his head all the way down, licking my pussy feverishly while thrusting two fingers into my tight channel.

Maddox knew exactly what I preferred, always bringing me to the edge of a climax then pulling back, making me crazy and begging for him to lick me like the wild animal he was. I knew this afternoon wouldn't be an exception.

I tossed my head back and forth as he added a third then fourth finger, flexing them open as he thrust hard and fast. In contrast, he was sucking and licking my clit so tenderly. It was the combination that finally got to me, pushing me over the edge within seconds.

He could sense I was close to coming, finally burying his face into my wetness.

I reached for him, snagging his thick locks of hair with my fist, jerking up from the table as white-hot heat tore through me, the orgasm pushing up from my curled toes.

"Oh... yes. Oh. Oh." The high-pitched scream floated toward the ceiling as my pussy clenched and released around his fingers, pulling them in even deeper. The rapturous moment left sparkling lights floating in front of my eyes, my mind a beautiful haze of filthy images and thoughts.

There was nothing like being lost in pure ecstasy, every savage sound he made keeping me floating on a cloud. As one climax drifted into a second, all I could hear was the rapid beating of my heart.

Thump. Thump. Thump...

CHAPTER 24

Zoe

Thump. Thump. Thump.

Maddox...

I opened my eyes, blinking several times, a cold shiver sliding down both legs. For a full minute I tried to adjust to what I was seeing. What had happened? It was dark, so fucking dark. Except for a single light. Where was that coming from? I tried to rationalize what had happened, why I couldn't remember. As the fog in my mind started to lift, another shiver coursed down my spine.

I'd blacked out. That had to be it. I'd experienced a panic attack.

"Maddox?" I whispered. Where was I? I eased my hand down, feeling a blanket covering me. When I twisted my body, I also figured out I wasn't lying in a bed. I tried to sit up, my eyes finally getting used to the shadowed light.

I was in the living room. He'd placed me on the couch after I'd fainted. From a panic attack. I was horrified even as a series of images tickled the back of my mind as I remembered the dream I'd had. No wonder my nipples ached, my pussy throbbing. A wet dream? Now? I wanted to laugh except I continue to hear thumping sounds coming from all around me as well as howling wind. The storm. How long had I been out?

"Maddox?" I whispered again, tossing the blanket aside. Where was he?

Fear replaced every other sensation, my pulse racing.

When he didn't answer, I was immediately tossed into a moment of utter chaos. While I knew a portion of the terror coursing through me had to do with the fact I'd blacked out and the darkness, there was also a gut feeling in addition to the power being out, there was something very wrong.

Cautiously, I rose from the couch, hating the fact my legs were shaking, making it almost impossible to take a step forward. When I did, the second I heard another sound, I let out a sharp cry before realizing the limb of a tree or maybe flying debris had hit the exterior of the house. The pounding rain seemed to increase with every passing second, which added to the sense of danger.

"Maddox!" My voice was more insistent but was still met with silence. If you could call an approaching hurricane silence. As I headed toward the flashlight, accepting the fact he was likely trying to get the generator going, I couldn't get over the sensations of my skin crawling.

The darkness ate at me even when I'd reached the flashlight, the ominous shadows in the room whispering from the depths of my soul. As if there were demons waiting in the darkest corners of the room, prepared to devour not only my soul but my body as well.

Of course that was ridiculous given the level of security, but I was still nervous, trying my best to find patience, which usually eluded me. I swung the light around the room, thankful that Maddox hadn't carried me downstairs to another level of darkness.

My mouth was dry, whether from nerves or how long I'd been convulsing in a sea of vivid and dirty, sinful images. I allowed myself a smile as I tried to make my way toward the kitchen.

The slight sound from behind me drew my attention and I stopped short before reaching the hallway. "Maddox?" After a few seconds, I slowly tipped my head over my shoulder, shining the flashlight into the living room. Seeing nothing, I reminded myself the storm was creating unrealistic scares, my nerves remaining on edge. I hadn't experienced a panic attack since I was a child. They'd been fairly often then, a doctor telling my father they were because I felt the loss of my mother so intensely.

Why now?

Because not only did Maddox feel out of control, so did I, just like I'd felt as a child, my world turned upside down. I had to remind myself the man I adored would return soon.

Then there'd be light, at least enough to chase away the demons. For now, I was thirsty. I did what I could to ignore the trickling fear, grabbing a bottle of water from the refrigerator before returning to the living room.

With the windows being shuttered, I couldn't see how bad the storm had gotten but I could feel it, the cold chill of the whipping wind sliding through the cracks, underneath the doors.

Clunk.

The sound was more startling than before, as if the roof was caving in. After gently easing the bottle onto a bookshelf, I folded one arm across my chest as I lifted the flashlight beam to the ceiling, inspecting for any leaks.

Another strange sound assaulted my senses seconds later and I swung the light around the room. "Maddox?" Maybe I could at least find out where he was. That would give me a level of reassurance that he wasn't lying dead somewhere, struck by a tree. Great. Now my mind was drifting into another level of uncontrollable thoughts.

As soon as I headed for the front door, hair on the back of my neck stood up on end. "Maddox?" I asked again, although my voice now sounded haunted.

"I'm afraid Maddox isn't coming to rescue you."

The dark voice was evil, unrecognizable. But I was certain without a shadow of a doubt that the person standing in the living room was the same one who'd threatened me on the phone months before, and also the same person responsible for terrorizing me outside the ice cream shop.

I held my breath, doing my best to capture my angry resolve. "Who the fuck are you?"

"We'll just say someone you're going to become acquainted with very soon." His laugh was just like before, horrible in the inflection. "Before I take you to your new master."

Master?

Without moving, I scanned the area around me, fearful that he'd moved closer. When I was certain he had, I grabbed the only thing I could see using as a weapon.

A lamp.

I had a feeling this was the fight for my life, my bloodcurdling scream sounding more like a warrior princess than a frightened woman. The moment I managed to connect the thick piece of metal with the asshole trying to ruin our lives, I dropped the flashlight. As it bounced across the floor, I was provided with a single clear shot of the man's face no longer hidden behind a hoodie or mask.

Maybe the terror skittering through me added to the moment, but the man's eyes were pure evil. He lunged toward me as I jerked backward, able to grab a portion of my hair. There was a ripping sound as strands of hair were yanked from my head.

As I was pitched backward, the force enough to pummel me into the couch, I almost dropped the lamp.

But I didn't.

When he came after me again, I smashed it not once but twice against the perpetrator's head, shocked when I felt warm liquid splash against my cheek. The man's blood. Good. He bellowed then jumped forward, tackling me to the floor, easily ripping the lamp from my hand. The harsh smash as it hit the wall stifled the strangled sounds erupting from my throat as I struggled to scream.

"Your boyfriend is dead, sweetheart," the bastard said as he wrapped his hands around my throat.

"Who. Are. You?"

"Your boyfriend's worst nightmare. Redemption."

Redemption. What the hell did he mean? I wiggled and tried to kick out but he was too strong.

The feeling of suffocation was immediate, the weight of the man's heavy body crushing me against the floor, but it didn't matter. Nothing mattered any longer if Maddox was dead.

As I struggled in the attacker's hands, dim lights flashing in my mind's eye, memories and images of the man I was so desperately in love with floated in front of me. While I'd never believed in the afterlife, heaven nothing more than a beautiful story given I'd begged for my mother to show me a sign and never received one, I could swear she was now standing under a bright sun beckoning for me to join her.

But I wasn't ready.

Not until I killed the bastard first.

I fought him, doing everything in my power to get away, reaching for the lamp even as I felt the life ebbing away, my throat closing.

As I started to pray, slipping into a dark silence, another noise dragged me back to reality, just as the man determined to end my life was tossed aside. Was I dreaming or had the man I loved, the one I'd called a hero more than once come to my rescue?

* * *

Maddox

Her scream had cut through me like a knife, the blood pumping in my brain pushing me into action. As I'd bolted into the house, chastising myself for leaving her alone for even one second, I realized just how in love with Zoe I truly was.

Her agonizing sounds would forever haunt me, and I reacted without a second thought, wrapping my hand around the neck of the man assaulting her. Whether it was adrenaline or simply rage, I was easily able to toss the fucker away. But as expected, he came out swinging, attempting to pound my face with his fist.

I was too quick for him, dodging easily, issuing three brutal jabs in a row.

Zoe coughed and rolled, the strangled sound only adding gasoline to the fire. But she was alive. And I would keep her that way.

No one fucked with my woman.

The limited light was just enough to allow me to see the man who'd attacked us, not that I could recognize him. That didn't matter. I took another hard swing, my fist connecting with his jaw. As he grunted, I noticed he was reaching for a weapon. I threw out my leg, catching him just under the chin.

"Maddox!" Zoe exclaimed.

"Stay down, baby." When the fucker decided to target her again, lunging in her direction, I smashed my Glock against the side of his face, pummeling him backward. The horrific sounds of the quickly moving storm added to the distortion of light, the near tragedy of the moment.

He came at me again, gripping his weapon and preparing to fire. I threw my arm out, pitching his aside a split second before the gun went off. Fortunately, the asshole dropped it. The surprise was enough to force his eyes away and I wrapped my other hand around his throat, using the momentum and force of the fight to enable me to slam him against the bookcase next to the wall.

As books and other objects fell around us, I squeezed my hand, cutting off his air supply. Zoe had found the light, showering the beam in my direction.

"What do you want?" I asked, my gut telling me I wouldn't get an answer even though I let off on my solid hold. "You might live if you tell me."

"Ask yourself who you fear the most, Boogeyman."

What the fuck?

The stream of light allowed me to see into the fucker's eyes. When he grinned, even daring to laugh, I easily realized that he was nothing more than a hired gun, a man sent to throw me off.

And to send me a message.

What the hell was the worthless piece of garbage trying to tell me? That this charade was all about me, something that I'd done in my life, an act of revenge that no one had considered? I dug my fingers into his neck once again, enjoying his choking sounds.

When I sensed she'd moved closer, I hissed under my breath.

"Get away, Zoe. This isn't something you need to see," I told her as I pressed the barrel against his temple.

"Not a chance. End this. Kill him," she said.

Very slowly, I turned my head, able to see the eagerness on her face.

While that moment was cathartic, the act I was about to perform something I should regret, I knew better than to think I would.

After all, I was nothing but a cold-blooded killer.

So I did my job.

I pulled the trigger.

CHAPTER 25

Maddox

Three fucking days.

It had taken that long to have a jet flown in to pick us up. I toughed it out several times before, but the lack of electricity and the fallen trees shutting down roads had made investigation basically impossible. We'd been back only a few hours and I'd finally gotten some sleep, although I doubted that I'd feel rested for days, maybe weeks to come.

If ever.

While the house itself had received only minor damage from the category three hurricane, the shoreline had been littered with debris, the water churning the entire time we'd remained. I'd dragged the body of the assailant into the deepest part of the forest, doing my best to bury him. I'd scoured his person, ensuring there were no traces of either Zoe or myself. I'd also searched the area, finding his vehicle a mile and half from the house. As anticipated, the assailant had been careful to avoid leaving even a single detail that might help shed light on the mystery.

That had kept my anger level high, my patience low and both Zoe and me on edge. I'd barely gotten any sleep, determined to keep watch over the woman who'd turned into perhaps the strongest young lady I'd ever met.

The events of the last few months had changed her dramatically, specifically the last week. She was no longer hiding behind rose-colored glasses, although I was grateful to see she hadn't completely lost her verve for life.

She'd been able to laugh, to provide comfort and even fleeting moments of passion. But as soon as we'd landed, Francois coming to the airport, she'd resumed her dutiful daughter role without asking any questions or making any demands.

The lies would eventually consume us, although until I had a chance to clear the air with Arman regarding the supposed arranged marriage, I wouldn't rest. Nor would I allow him to learn about our budding relationship. I rubbed my tired eyes, the bright sun slicing through the clear window adding to the ache in my temples.

At least Arman's condition in the days of our zero communication had drastically improved, enough so he'd insisted on coming home the night before. There had been no sepsis, only a secondary infection masking itself as something more severe.

The fact he'd refused to remain at his father's house was interesting.

It was also telling.

Whatever secret Arman held close in the dark reaches of his mind had something to do with his father. Maybe that's why I'd tasked my soldiers with attempting to check into Jean Baptiste's recent phone calls and whereabouts. It was risky and against protocol, but I needed to know what we were dealing with quickly.

What troubled me more than anything were the words the last attacker had thrown at me. My greatest nightmare? Shit. I had none, except for the anxiety about not being there when I was needed. That couldn't have anything to do with why the assailant had shadowed our movements, he and his companions enjoying the game of cat and mouse. One thing was certain and not easy to allow to remain in my mind. This entire situation was about something I'd done or not done.

Other than talking with Zoe, I hadn't mentioned it to anyone yet. I'd wanted time to process if nothing else. However, the clock was ticking and I was set to meet with Arman.

Zoe had told me what the last assassin had said to her and that had only added to the mystery. I had a feeling if we didn't figure it out soon, there would be no method of redemption.

I glanced at my watch, the one Zoe had gifted me. After two days it had dried out from the water excursion, choosing to keep perfect time. While it was only three in the afternoon, it was five o'clock somewhere. Right? Chuckling, I moved away from the window toward the bar, fighting the strange series of nerves that had formed early that morning.

I wasn't a good liar. Then again, I'd had very little reason to tell a fib in my life, priding myself on being truthful. Even to those I was preparing to exterminate. For some reason, the thought of expounding on my feelings for Zoe left a bad taste in my mouth. So, I allowed the anger I felt regarding being kept in the dark to fuel the fire burning deep within.

Arman's house still showed signs of the tragedy, several windows boarded up, bullet holes in the walls in his office. I hadn't been able to walk to the greenhouse and Raven and Gabriel had yet to return. I wondered if anyone would feel comfortable here again. I certainly didn't.

As I was pouring a drink, I heard voices behind Arman's closed office door. When it opened, I expected to see my old friend, not Tony. He'd tracked me down. Hopefully, that meant he'd discovered something useful. I was still uncertain about him, questioning his loyalty, although at this moment, everything about my life was being scrutinized.

"Hey, boss. I wanted to finish the conversation we started," Tony said as he walked closer.

"Yeah, please do." With the internet being down on the island, the only time I'd spent researching had been on the plane. Even that time had been limited, my ability to concentrate in the toilet.

"I confirmed what I was trying to tell you. Whoever you had dealings with in New York wasn't the Lucas Marciano I was talking about."

"And who were you talking about?" I turned to face him, leaning against the credenza.

"He was an assassin out of New York when I was there. At the time he worked for the Gambino family. He was one bad dude."

"How are you certain it's not the same man?"

He handed me a photograph of a much younger man. "Because the man I knew was a couple years younger than me. Didn't you describe the man you saw as much older?"

"Sixty at least." I took the photograph, my chest tightening. "Where is this Lucas now?"

"My buddy still living in New York mentioned he's working for some bigwig rancher in Texas. That's what he was told anyway."

My hackles were immediately raised given Devin Carlos ruled a portion of Texas. "Your buddy is certain? This dude is someone you can trust?"

Shrugging, he glanced out the window. "Mickey encouraged me to get the fuck out of New York. He was the one who suggested the Thibodeaux family. That's why I moved here. I know you don't trust me, Maddox, but I am loyal to the family. More than you realize."

His attempt to assure me of his loyalty was because I'd raised the point to Francois more than once, including the moment I'd finally managed to get the man on the phone after the hurricane.

"Can you track this guy?"

"I can try, although Lucas' reputation is to stay in the shadows. Just like the Boogeyman." Tony grinned as he referenced my other name.

I sucked in my breath, taking a few seconds to exhale. When the door opened again, both Tony and I shifted our attention.

Arman.

He studied me as if he didn't know who I was, finally nodding in respect as he walked in. While I could swear the man lost twenty pounds during his hospital stay, he was alive and walking without the need for assistance.

"I'll see what I can do, Maddox. I can't promise anything."

"Let me know," I told Tony, waiting as he acknowledged Arman before walking out, closing the door behind him.

Arman walked closer, eyeing me carefully, slowly lowering his gaze to the drink in my hand. When he walked closer, I noticed a strange expression on his face. As he stuck out his arm for a handshake, I was suddenly more awkward than I'd ever been around my good friend.

The hesitation was as strange as the moment.

"What's wrong, my friend?" he asked. "You don't appreciate gestures of thanks?"

I felt like a shit, lower than low. When I finally accepted his gesture, he pulled me into a hug, which was something he'd never done before. My reaction was to stiffen.

"You save my daughter's life not once but four times in less than a week. You're a real hero."

When he backed away, I immediately pulled my hand free. "I'm no hero and you know it. I was doing my job." I'd told both Francois and Thomas what had transpired with the attacks, although the conversation at four-thirty in the morning less than thirty minutes after we'd landed had seemed more like a debriefing.

Or an inquisition.

"Is that all there is?"

"Meaning?" I asked, taking a purposeful step away.

"No man goes through that kind of peril if they don't have strong feelings for the people or persons they're protecting. You truly are a member of this family. You are without a doubt my closest friend. There isn't anything I wouldn't do for you. Name your price for keeping her safe."

Ah, shit. The guilt continued to rise like bile in my throat. "As I said, I was doing my job, and yes, I do care about your family. You all are my family."

"I know that. Lighten up, buddy. We're getting closer to getting to the bottom of this nightmare. I don't know if Francois told you but the reason that we haven't seen Raphael Arturo's ugly face is that he was diagnosed with a rare form of leukemia several years ago. He finally came to the United States for treatment but from what I've heard, and it will be confirmed, he's on his deathbed. We can rule him out."

While I hadn't been told, I knew what we were going through had something to do with Devin, especially after what Tony had just informed me of. I had no reason to disbelieve him, although I had asked Thomas to have both his and Landry's recent activities checked as well.

"It would appear Devin Carlos is behind at least a portion of what happened."

He laughed, the sound becoming bitter. "So it would seem."

"Meaning?"

"Meaning that's what I suspected all along."

The man was lying. It would appear both of us were. It was time to end the charade before things got out of hand.

"I need to ask you a question, Arman. That might change your mind about our friendship."

He moved slowly toward the leather chair near the window, wincing when he sat down. "I doubt anything will, but you do have me curious."

I shook my head before I could ask him what was vital for me to learn. "Did you arrange for Zoe to be married to someone important to the family and the operations?"

While anger flashed in my friend's eyes, it wasn't before the slight hint of shock, one he didn't want me to see. But I had.

He leaned forward, steepling his hands after placing his elbows on his knees. "Why in God's name would you suggest something so ridiculous?"

"Because of something Zoe mentioned and because of certain details I learned." And had left out with Francois on purpose. I wanted the element of surprise intact when I talked with Arman. Sadly, I knew whatever contract he'd entered into had come back to bite him. When he remained quiet, his stare cutting through me, I was forced to press him. "If I remember correctly, Devin has a son destined to take over from his father at some point. Did you determine it was in your best interest to establish a strong connection just like your father would do?"

I was shocked when he jerked up from the chair, taking two long strides then wrapping his fingers around my shirt.

"How fucking dare you, Maddox. You might be my friend and my right-hand man, but you have no right to question anything I do with regard to my family. My family. Not yours. Remember? You don't have one."

While I sensed his venom wasn't based on his anger at what I'd just accused him of, that didn't mean my own rage didn't surface. "Fuck you, Arman. You're right. I had a father who abused my mother, enjoying threatening and terrifying his own son after beating him for sheer practice. And I had a drug addict for a mother, the heroin she stuck in her arm and the pills she popped helping her deal with my violent father. Do you want another look at the scars the fucker left behind? Will that make you feel like a better father yourself for selling off your own daughter?"

There was no doubt the words I said would end our friendship, but at this point, I would not allow the atrocity to continue. Not for a fucking second. I jerked away, resisting punching him, doing my best to remind myself he was recovering from a life-threatening injury that was my fault and mine alone.

"What the hell is it to you? You've made it a point not to care about anyone. Isn't that right, Maddox? You shut down after Lola died, acting as if everything in this fucking world is your fault. That chip on your shoulder is weighing you down, brother."

"What is it to me? Let me tell you something, *brother*." I threw the family word in his face. "That beautiful girl you sold off like cattle is special, a bright star in a sea of sharks and piranhas, the reason the sun rises in the morning. If you spent any time around her, you'd understand just how amazing she is."

As soon as I ended the tirade, I noticed his eyes were open wide.

The quiet and tension settling between us was more difficult than I'd imagined.

"My God," he half whispered. "How did I not see it? You're in love with her."

I closed my eyes, looking away.

"Answer me," he demanded.

"Yes, Arman. I'm in love with Zoe and I won't allow you to take her away from me." While I glared him in the eyes, trying to remain as controlled and defiant as I was capable of, he shocked the hell out of me by issuing a single hard punch.

I tumbled backward, almost stumbling to the floor, slapping my hand on my jaw. While I managed to keep my hold on the drink, I watched as scotch splashed on the crystal dial.

All I could think about was that the beautiful gift would soon be destroyed.

Along with my desire to be with Zoe.

He took a deep breath, moving slowly once again as he returned to the chair. This time as he eased onto the seat, I was certain he'd aged another five years. His coloration was as close to gray as I'd seen it before. When he placed his head in his hands, I felt even more like a shit.

The seconds ticked by.

"I didn't arrange the marriage with Devin and his son, Maddox, but you're right as you always are."

"Then who the fuck did?"

He lifted his head, glancing at the door before answering. "My father."

"What?" Now I was the one who needed to sit down.

He nodded. "It's true. Documentation was sent to me providing proof the night of the graduation party. I was trying to get to Devin, but he ignored my calls. I was prepared to buy out the contract with every cent of money I had."

"You got wind of this supposed arrangement prior to her return to the city, which is why you not only demanded she come home but had me shadow her until you could bring her here yourself."

He nodded, looking as forlorn as I'd ever seen him. "I wasn't certain what to make of anything, but I wasn't going to allow Devin to get his hands on her without a fight."

"Fuck. Why would your father do something like that? Jean Baptiste expressed his hatred of the man more than once."

"I honestly don't know except business is business, billions of dollars at stake and things aren't quite as rosy in Texas as Francois has led us to believe. In fact, they're on the verge of imploding. Devin's hold in Texas with the state legislators has him locking out various avenues, construction taking three times as long and at least twice if not four times the expense we planned. Francois had tried to put a finger in the dike but if something doesn't change, our spinoff corporation will go bankrupt within six months."

Jesus Christ. I had no idea. None.

Texas had been fully and completely in Francois' control, but there'd been no red flags that I'd seen or heard of. "Your father was trying to protect the entire family."

"And our holdings. Maybe in the old days it was a viable solution, but my daughter isn't for sale. To anyone."

The way he was looking at me was a further indication he didn't approve of my relationship with her. "Understood."

"Maybe you do, but I sure as fuck don't. We invested a hell of a lot of money in the various resorts and other business holdings in the Lone Star State. I was also in the process of trying to determine how bad it was before the party. But to do something so egregious without talking to me is… unimaginable."

I bristled seeing the cloud covering his face. I wasn't entirely certain he wouldn't have considered entering into the same contract, no matter the conviction in his earlier statement.

"That's why you didn't talk to me about the situation and why you begged me to take her away."

"Yeah. Had I known the lengths Devin would go to in his attempt to keep the contract in effect, I never would have asked you to put your life on the line not once but three additional times. For that, I'm sorry."

"Have you tried to double check the contract? Signatures can be faked."

"Thomas found out my father and Devin have been nice and cozy on the phone over the last few months."

Another surprise. That would never have occurred before. Still, I wasn't convinced.

I thought about what he'd just told me, and something didn't jibe with me. Even if what Tony had said was true, leaving the possibility that Lucas had hired someone to bring her roses in the club, keeping an eye on what was supposedly a done deal, there were too many missing pieces. "I don't buy it."

"Which part?"

"That your father sold you out to protect your brother. You're certain the contract is with Jean Baptiste?"

He pointed toward his desk. "You can see for yourself. The contract is in the top drawer where I left it the night of the party. Why are you suggesting otherwise?"

Before answering him, I wanted to see the contract for myself. I pulled it into my hands, flipping through it quickly. While it would appear on the surface that Jean Baptiste had signed the very legal contract, a nagging sensation remained in the back of my mind. "The asshole who attacked us inside my house in St. Barts said something about facing my greatest nightmare. That certainly makes it seem as if the shit that went down is about me."

As I glanced at him, he turned his head. "You've had only a few dealings with Devin. Why the fuck would he target you along with my daughter?"

"For one, because your daughter has had a crush on me for years. However, that's not my point."

Arman rose to his feet a second time, walking toward me slowly. I stood my ground, allowing him to take out whatever aggression he felt he needed to. I was a big boy. I'd been the one to open Pandora's Box. I could take the heat.

And would continue to do so if necessary.

Because I loved her.

"Then what are you suggesting?"

"That we have a frank conversation with your father before heading to Texas to discover the truth."

He nodded a few times then took the nearly empty drink from my hand, powering it back. "You're right as always. Let's do this. It's time we take full control."

Full control.

Somehow, the words held an entirely different meaning.

CHAPTER 26

*M*addox

In a world where cloaks and daggers should have been a thing of the past, armor only needed on rare occasions, subterfuge had caused far too much deception. I wasn't immune to the fact I had a part in it, Arman saying nothing about my relationship with Zoe on the way to his father's house.

She'd been anxious when I'd left, uncertain what I had planned or if I'd tell her father we were involved. In truth, I hadn't known at that point when I'd slipped into the room I'd given her in my house, kissing her goodbye. I'd wanted nothing more than to hold her all night long, but with soldiers keeping watch, the last thing I'd needed was anyone spouting off damning news before I could come clean with my friend.

While I wasn't certain it had been a good idea, I did feel as if a weight had been lifted. For good or for bad, I wasn't certain.

We'd told no one we were coming, including Francois. I still wasn't certain the contract was legal, although without getting the family's attorney involved, we wouldn't know the actual ramifications. That would come later if we didn't determine the contract was bogus.

As I climbed from the car, a flash in the window above caught my eye. I looked up, noticing Zoe standing in front of the window. She pressed her hand on the glass, providing a sense of solidarity.

Arman noticed, slowly tilting his head. He didn't look at me or say a word, moving toward the front entrance instead. We were both tense, just for entirely different reasons.

I took a deep breath, glancing at the woman I adored one last time. A significant part of me dreaded telling her we'd be leaving for Texas by the morning if not sooner. It all depended on how Jean Baptiste handled the accusations and our conversation with him. I shifted my gaze to the file, a copy of the contract inside. The other had been secured in Arman's safe to ensure not only did we have evidence but that if anything happened to him, I could still discover the truth one way or the other.

He'd made me promise on Zoe's life that I would keep her from marrying Devin's son. It was a promise I intended on keeping.

Exhaling, I headed inside, noticing Arman was headed toward the back. I followed, noticing Arman had found his father out on the screened-in porch, a location Jean Baptiste loved on sunny days.

As I moved into the room, I gave the patriarch a nod of respect as I always did. He immediately stood, obviously delighted to see his son.

"Arman. I am so glad to see you're alright," Jean Baptiste said. "Although I was surprised you chose to return home. Your wife and son need you."

"And I need them. I also need the truth." Arman shoved his hands in to his pockets, glancing in my direction before heading to one of the screen panels, staring outside at nothing.

"Truth about what?" Jean Baptiste barked, obviously noticing the look we'd shared.

I moved closer to his father, handing him the file, keeping my fingers in position. "About your promise made to Devin Carlos."

"What promise?" he growled, but as with Arman, I could tell he was holding something back. He glared at me before snatching the file from my hands.

Both Arman and I gave him time to both look through and digest the terms of the contract. For Zoe's hand in marriage, Devin had agreed to share partnership in both the Thibodeaux holdings in Texas as well as a similar percentage of Devin's holdings in Texas and New Mexico. If the alliance had been agreed to under any other set of circumstances, it would have been considered a damn good situation. However, this wasn't just an ordinary business deal.

Jean Baptiste almost faltered, his chest rising and falling as he read it over more than once. "What the fuck is this?" he finally asked.

"You tell me, Pops." Arman didn't bother facing his father.

"Is this some kind of joke?"

I took a deep breath as I studied Jean Baptiste. He was genuinely shocked, which is what I'd expected, or maybe what I'd hoped would occur. "So you did not enter into this agreement with Mr. Carlos?"

"Are you fucking out of your mind?"

He words held an air of truth regarding his granddaughter, but he was still hiding something.

"Then the bullshit phone calls you had with Devin were made by an imposter. Right, Dad?" Arman hissed.

Jean Baptiste's eyes opened wide. He carefully placed the folder on the table and headed toward the back of the porch himself. "I talked to Devin."

"About my fucking daughter!"

"No! That is not the kind of man I am."

"Then what the fuck were you talking to Devin Carlos about and why in God's name is your signature on that contract selling off my daughter as if she was a commodity and nothing else?"

Jean Baptiste cursed in French under his breath, words that didn't need a translator to understand. He was as angry as both of us were. "I was trying to keep our investments from going south in Texas. Francois is a good businessman yet even he can't fight Devin and his hold on the politicians, lawmen, and ranchers in that fucking state. Devin and I were close to an agreement."

"When the fuck were you going to tell me, Pops? Huh? I'm the CEO, the Kingpin of this fucking family organization. If you didn't want me to take over, then why the fuck did you hand me the regime in the first place?"

"Because you deserved it. And because… because my doctor told me if I didn't slow down, I was going to have a stroke. Your mother insisted."

Arman turned to face his father, shaking his head. "You had so much pride you didn't want to tell me?"

"I don't know, son. What I do know is that the contract was forged."

"So you don't think Devin was trying to have the deal sweetened?" I asked. "And did you sign anything with him?"

"We both signed a nondisclosure and in truth, I can't believe Carlos would stoop this low. There might be other people involved. That needs to be determined."

I believed the man. Whether or not Arman did remain to be seen. "While you're right, Jean Baptiste, and we're still double checking to ensure no mistake has been made, Devin needs to be dealt with. Whether he's responsible for the contract is only part of the issue. He needs to fully understand and embrace that the business situation in Texas will no longer be tolerated."

"You're a damn good man, Maddox. But you need to be careful. Things could get out of control easily, our business in Texas destroyed."

"This isn't about the money," I countered.

"My best friend is right," Arman stated after a few seconds. "We will handle this, Pops. My fucking way. The time for caution is done. My daughter will not be getting married. To anyone." When issuing the last two words, he made certain he locked eyes with mine.

The message was loud and clear.

Out of the corner of my eye, I noticed Zoe standing just outside the sunroom. As I tipped my head, it was obvious she'd heard at least a portion of the conversation.

She walked closer and when I tried to stop her, she threw out her arm.

Jean Baptiste noticed her before Arman, but he gave his son a look that forced Arman to shift toward his daughter.

"Baby. I didn't see you standing there," Arman said.

"I love you, Daddy. Very much. You are my rock and the thought of losing you tore me up inside."

"I love you too, baby girl."

"That's just the thing, Daddy. I'm not a baby or a little girl any longer. I'm a grown woman who can and will make her own choices. I don't know whether or not what I heard is truthful or a lie, but I won't be sold off like a possession to anyone. I've already made my choice regarding the man I'm in love with. And if that bothers you, Daddy, then I'll walk away from the family, my trust fund, and the name, but I will not give up the man who makes me happy, who makes me feel alive."

"Who the fuck are we talking about?" Jean Baptiste asked.

"Maddox," Arman said as he shook his head. "It would seem my daughter and my best friend are involved."

"What. The. Fuck?" Jean Baptiste hissed.

"Don't go there, Grandpa. This is none of your concern and if you think you're going to retaliate against the man who protected me and who saved my life at the risk of his own, then think again. He would die to protect this family. He would do anything in his power to protect every single member of this family. Do you hear me? He's taken a bullet for you, Dad. Hasn't he? He almost died to save your life?" She glared at her father.

Arman's jaw remained as clenched as mine, both of us staring at each other as if ready to start a fist fight.

"This is ridiculous," the patriarch said under his breath.

"Is it, Grandfather? Really?" Zoe continued. "From what I heard, Maddox also saved your life way back when he was a teenager, just a kid. In doing so, he secured a place in this family. He's been a part of us all along. Yet he's not blood. There is nothing illegal about the fact I'm in love with him. If I want to marry him, then by God neither one of you are going to stop me. And if you dare think you're going to excommunicate Maddox, fire him, or even for one second think you're going to physically hurt him, so help me God I will find a way to destroy this entire family. Do you hear me? Do you?"

For all the times that the beautiful girl had taken a back seat to her father's desires, playing the good girl and following the rules, a feisty lioness lay hidden under the lamb's clothing. She was truly a formidable woman and one that I admired.

"Answer me, Father."

Arman had a slight twinkle in his eyes. "I hear you, daughter."

She took a deep breath and by God, the girl could still surprise the hell out of me. When she turned sharply in my direction, gripping my chin and dragging my head down by a few inches, it was all I could do not to laugh. Yet as she captured my mouth for a change, the swell of desire refused to be denied.

I slipped my arm around her, lifting her off her feet. As she threw her arms around my neck, I sensed an audience behind us.

When I heard not one but three squeals, I eased my little lamb away, giving her a stern look.

"I told you so," Delaney stated with a gleam in her eyes.

"My God. This is fantastic. This is exactly what Raven and I hoped for!" Edmee said as she clapped her hands together, both she and Raven bounding into the room as if we weren't still facing a crisis.

Raven was drained, her face drawn yet there was a sparkle to her eyes as well as she wrapped her arm around her tense husband.

"You knew about this... this... thing?" Jean Baptiste asked.

"We hoped, Pops," Edmee answered.

"Unbelievable," Arman said under his breath.

"That's what was said about us, honey bunny. Remember?" Raven teased.

While I appreciated the support of certain members of the family, it didn't mean that the danger was over or that what Zoe and I had shared had a chance.

"She's your daughter, son," Jean Baptiste growled his response.

"Yes, she is. Very much so. A strong and very vibrant woman." Arman nodded, suddenly becoming a proud papa.

"Thank you, Daddy. Maybe we can become more of a family now. Even closer."

"We will. Unfortunately, we need to leave for Texas," Arman told me in particular.

Zoe pulled away. "What do you mean you're leaving for Texas? I am not marrying the son of our enemy."

"No, you're not," I answered. "However, we need to make that clear to the person responsible."

"I don't want you to go. What if something happens to you?"

I glanced at the family and sighed before leading her from the sunroom.

"What? I don't want you to leave right now."

I kept my hand on the small of her back, guiding her out of sight of the others. When she backed against the wall, her expression highlighting her rebellious side, my cock throbbed. I pressed my hand beside her head, leaning in so only she could hear.

"You made quite a scene in there," I told her.

"And I would do so again and will if necessary. Don't change the subject."

I slipped a finger under her chin, lifting her head and forcing her to look into my eyes. "First of all, you're not in charge. I am. Second, that's your family in there, people who love you very much. You need to try and remember that."

"Not if they go against you. You protected me. Now, I'm going to protect you."

Amusement and adoration spiraled all through me, enough so it was all I could do not to toss her over my shoulder, taking her upstairs to an empty room. "Listen to me, baby. I can take care of myself. This nightmare is coming to an end one way or the other. But this is something we have to do."

She clutched my shirt, managing to slide a finger through the space between the buttons. Just the simple touch was enough to push the electricity we shared back and forth. "I know you do. I just... I don't want you hurt."

"Baby. Don't underestimate me. I'm pretty damn powerful when I want to be."

A smile crossed her face. "I know you are. That's partially why I love you."

"You're going to stay right here under tight security. Yes?"

"I will."

"If I find out you disobeyed me, you will not be able to sit down for a week solid."

"Promises. Promises."

Leaning down until our lips were almost touching, I drank in her perfume, fearful it would be the last time I would be allowed. But it wasn't about Arman forbidding me to see her. I had a bad feeling that I wouldn't return.

As I captured her mouth and heard her instant moan, my heartbeat increased. She was the most amazing woman, something special, and I was grateful I'd been given the time to get to know her. If it meant dying, I would go to my grave to ensure she had a bright future.

And I would do so happily.

As I swept my tongue inside, she arched her back, pulling me even closer. There was no denying our chemistry or the need we both shared.

When I pulled away, I brushed my knuckles down her cheek. "Take care of yourself, little lamb. You're one incredible woman." I backed away before I changed my mind.

"Don't die on me, Maddox."

"I have no intention of it. That much I promise you."

"This time, I'm going to hold you to that promise. Come back to me. I will be waiting for as long as it takes."

If I were a decent man, I never would have allowed things to get this far, but I'd proven more than once that while I was many things, decent wasn't one of them.

She was mine.

All mine.

CHAPTER 27

Maddox

"You're lost in a train of thought," Arman said as he sat down in the seat opposite me, handing me a drink.

We were on his private plane, the one that had come to rescue Zoe and me, landing in Texas within the hour. I had been deep in thought, still trying to get a better understanding of what we would be walking into. We'd had a rather terse meeting with Francois, the man defensive about how hard he'd worked to try to salvage the business in the Lone Star State. From everything I'd looked at, the only holdup was Devin's buddies keeping the projects from being approved, finding a way to sabotage both construction crews and materials coming in by railroad and tractor trailer.

It would seem the warning he'd been given several years before hadn't stuck.

However, Francois had made some damn good decisions, acquiring other pieces of land that would make us a fortune if we were able to get the monkey off our backs.

Yet the nagging remained. The question of if he was behind the bogus contract weighed on all our minds.

Tony had learned that the real Lucas Marciano had been murdered. To date, no one had been arrested for the crime. It was just another part of the mystery.

"Yeah, well, it's hard not to be," I answered, accepting the drink and immediately taking a sip. I'd also found it impossible to drive Zoe out of my mind. She'd retreated to whatever bedroom she'd been given, staring at me as we'd left. I didn't need to be close to realize she was nervous I wouldn't return.

"Agreed. We go in with guns a-blazing, my friend." He laughed after making the statement. While two dozen soldiers remained guarding the house, we'd also brought a full brigade with us to prevent Devin from doing anything stupid. Francois had been convinced to remain behind to handle business. Just in case things didn't go well.

We certainly couldn't have every member of the family in harm's way. I feared for Arman given his injury but there was no stopping the man when he insisted on doing something. He and I were very much alike.

"I can't stop thinking we're missing something," I told him, glancing over at Thomas. What I hadn't told Arman was that I'd seen him in a private conversation with Jean Baptiste. That wouldn't ordinarily be considered odd except for the timing.

"We will figure it out. We're close. I can feel it. Whatever the case, you're right in that we won't accept Devin's bullshit with our business any longer."

I nodded and threw back a gulp, wishing the liquid would burn the back of my throat.

He stared out the window and the elephant remained in the room. However, I wasn't going to be the one who brought it up. It really wasn't my place to do so. At least just yet.

"You were right that my daughter is no longer a little girl. She's a woman with a mind of her own. It's funny. She reminds me of her mother so much more the older she gets. Do you remember how she was, becoming the light when she entered any room?"

"Yeah, I do, but Zoe got her hard head from you."

He narrowed his eyes as he glanced in my direction, the first real smile I'd seen crossing his face. "Okay, I'll accept that. She really does love you. Doesn't she?"

Yet another awkward moment settled in. "It would appear so, Arman."

"Well, she has questionable tastes but maybe I can buy what she sees in you." He laughed when I didn't say anything. "Look, I wish you'd told me."

"It's not something that was planned, Arman. When I saw her in New York, everything changed."

"I heard what my daughter said, the conviction with which she said it. She's right in that I owe you my life several times over. So does Pops and Francois as well."

"You are my family."

"I'm so sorry what I said about your birth parents. That was shitty of me."

"You weren't saying anything that wasn't the truth."

"Maybe, but stooping that low was crass as fuck. I can't imagine the horrors you went through. I'm just glad that fucker is behind bars for the rest of his natural life."

I snickered. "Yeah, I know." As Thomas looked over, I could swear the man appeared more uncomfortable than before. He'd said only a few words since getting on the plane.

"I'm only going to say this to you once. I'll give you my blessing, but you will make her an honest woman. And if you ever hurt her in any way, I will kill you. It's that simple."

"An honest woman, huh? Is that even possible in this family?"

"You're a son of a bitch but I do love you like a brother. Let's make sure this asshole knows we are the most powerful family in the entire United States."

"You got it, brother."

* * *

Devin's ranch was exactly as I remembered, the location sprawling yet the house aging. We hadn't called ahead, although we'd learned through several of the Thibodeaux employees located near the man's estate that he was home.

We arrived in five different vehicles, only a few of our men required to maintain direct watch over Devin's few men. He was a larger-than-life figure within Texas, under the false assumption that no one would dare threaten or cross him.

He'd soon learn how wrong he was.

And how stupid.

With Tony and Landry behind us, Thomas, Arman, and I headed for the front door. There was no need to knock, Devin answering the door himself. That meant he had cameras positioned on his property, something new and different since the last time.

He glanced from one to the other of us then did his best to look outside.

"Your men are surrounded, Devin. They're not coming to your assistance," Arman told him.

"What the hell are you doing here?"

"We need to talk," I told him. "We're not leaving until we do."

The way he eyed us carefully meant he realized that we were going nowhere. Good for him. I unbuttoned my jacket, allowing him to see the handle of my Glock just so he knew our intent if he didn't comply.

Backing up, he opened the door wider. "Come in, gentlemen. We are all businessmen here. Yes?"

Arman smirked as I laughed. That was one way of looking at it.

Devin led us through the house to his office. "You'll need to forgive the mess. When my wife is away, I tend to ignore the house."

As if we gave a shit.

Once inside his office, the moment he attempted to move behind his desk, I walked toward him. I'd learned years before he'd had a panic system installed, including a button under his desk as well as a room located in an unknown area of his house. It wasn't unlike the security both Jean Baptiste and Arman had created, although now the rooms were used for weapons storage more than anything.

"Don't do anything stupid, Devin," I told him.

Devin eyed my approach, slowly moving both hands on top of his desk. "What is so urgent that you couldn't call me by phone?"

I was the lead on the start of our conversation, immediately tossing the file on his desk. I moved to the wall behind him, leaning against it and folding my arms while he took a few seconds to look it over. I was fascinated by the fact he had the same facial expression as Arman's father had when reading the signed document.

As if he was innocent of all charges.

I glanced at Arman who was doing his best to control his anger, often something he wasn't very good at. Just like myself. We'd always been the yin to each other's yang. When one was enraged, the other would compensate with logic and vice versa. Not tonight. Tonight we were both on edge, refusing to accept any additional lies or bullshit from anyone.

"What is this crap?" Devin asked, tossing the file as if the papers had seared his fingers. "Some lazy attempt to combine our businesses?" The way he glared at Arman was interesting. Either the man truly had no clue, or he had balls the size of watermelons. Either way, his reaction incensed Arman to the point he whipped out his weapon, pointing the barrel at Devin's head.

"You fucking lying sack of shit," Arman hissed. "If you think for a moment that I'm not onto your lies then you're a fucking moron."

Devin was smart enough to raise his arms instead of attempting to grab his weapon, which I assume was located inside one of his drawers. He was a Texan after all. He had ancient rifles and animal heads on his office wall, proud of his trophies and his ancestry. I'd boned up on the man's heritage and his business practices prior to leaving New Orleans. His great-grandfather had been vital to the growth of San Antonio, Houston, and Dallas, his grandfather and father following in the man's footsteps. He'd been given legacy at an early age, only eighteen.

I suspected the brutal man had killed his own father in order to grab the reins so young. I wondered if he realized his own son was in the same position. Perhaps I should tell him to watch his back when we left.

Of course, I was assuming the man would still be alive.

"That's not my signature," Devin insisted.

"Then how did it get there?" I demanded.

"I don't fucking know. I sign a lot of crap. Anyone could have forged that." Devin half turned in my direction. The hint of fear was mostly masked but not his indignation.

"You'll need to prove that you didn't make this arrangement. One which would allow you to easily grab a significant portion of my business instead of wasting your time using your buddies to derail us." Arman watched the man's reaction, shaking his head.

Devin exhaled. "Look. We are businessmen. You and your goddamn brother charged onto the scene just like your father did. You ignored my offers. You acted as if you were going to drive me out of my own state. You bet I came out fighting."

"That's going to end right now. You will work together with the Thibodeaux estate," I stated as Arman and I had discussed.

"Why should I do that?" Devin turned toward me, cocking his head. I sensed true curiosity in his eyes, a hint of amusement that we were suggesting working together.

"Because you and your family get to live if you back off your bulldogs." I said the words matter-of-factly. "If not, your daughter will suddenly disappear first."

"You wouldn't do that!"

"As of this moment," Arman stated, "your daughter is surrounded. We'll take her, your grandchildren far away and you'll never see them again. That's just for starters.

That's in retaliation for trying to marry off my daughter to your son."

"I'm telling you. I did not sign that goddamn contract!" Devin slammed his fist on his desk, the force knocking the papers and contract to the floor.

The moment was interrupted by Thomas' phone ringing. He'd been extraordinarily quiet for hours, pensive without offering any reason why.

I glanced in his direction and without looking at either Arman or me, he walked out of Devin's office to take the call. That surprised the hell out of me.

Arman used the interruption to take a few long strides forward, wrapping his hand around Devin's throat and jerking him halfway over the desk as he jammed the barrel into the man's temple.

I inched forward, giving my best friend a hard glare. Killing Devin wasn't part of the plan. At least not unless absolutely necessary.

"You'll need to convince me that you didn't enter into a bogus contract," Arman said.

Devin's face paled as he gripped Arman's arms. I walked closer to ensure things wouldn't get out of hand, eying both Tony and Landry to ensure they were in position if things got ugly.

"It's just not possible," Devin said with full sincerity in his voice.

"Why?" I intervened.

Arman squeezed his fingers, forcing Devin to choke. I could tell my buddy's anger was getting out of hand.

"Because…" Devin started, his voice strangled.

"Go on," I encouraged. Thomas returned to the room, his demeanor entirely different than when he left. "Talk. Now!"

"Because my son is gay." The words flew from Devin's mouth, spit out as if disgusted by being forced to admit it.

Arman's expression didn't change for a full ten seconds. When he glanced in my direction, he started to laugh, releasing his hold. "You're kidding me."

Thomas walked to my side, his face imploring. "We need to talk," he said to me only.

I threw up my hand, glaring at him. That he'd chosen this minute to interrupt the situation was unusual. And very disconcerting.

"No, I'm not kidding you. My son wouldn't touch your daughter. He's already… involved with some guy out in Houston. Which is why he's no longer a part of my business."

The man had driven his own son away because of the kid's sexual preference? I was incensed myself, disgusted with the man and his world. In my mind it didn't matter how powerful he was or where he lived and his reputation. Blood was blood, family more important than anything. I wanted to put a bullet in the man's brain myself.

"Listen to me," Thomas hissed. "I know who did this to the family. Devin has nothing to do with it."

"Then who?" I said, furious at everything that had transpired.

Pop! Pop! Pop!

The gunfire came from outside. Suddenly, there were shouts.

"Go find out what the hell is going on," Arman barked, once again pointing the weapon at Devin. I yanked out my Glock as well as both Landry and Tony raced from the room holding their weapons in their hands.

Thomas rushed to the door, jerking out his weapon as well.

"What the fuck is going on?" Arman demanded as additional gunfire could be heard, including coming from more than one assault rifle.

"Your father did this," Thomas snapped.

Arman and I stared at each other, uncertain what the hell Thomas was getting at.

All hell broke loose before he had a chance to explain, an explosion occurring in another part of the house.

"Get down," Arman yelled, yanking Devin across the desk to the floor. "If you move, you die, you fucker."

For once the powerful Texan allowed his fear to show, crawling behind the couch, staring up at me as if I could be his savior.

Arman rushed to one side of the door while I moved beside Thomas. "Jean Baptiste did not do this."

"No!" Thomas said. "It's—"

THE WISEGUY

The second explosion was close, driving all three of us to the floor, debris falling from the ceiling. I rolled, trying to keep my aim on the door. After a few seconds of yelling, additional gunfire, a quiet settled in.

The sound of footsteps put us on edge. Both Arman and Thomas crawled closer, all three of us pointing our weapons at the door.

"Jack is out of prison," Thomas said through clenched teeth.

Jack.

Jack Cormier.

My father.

I'd spent my life building back from nothing, from begging and stealing in the streets as a young child. From hating the world because of my losses to finding joy again. I'd learned to become the Boogeyman when I'd longed to find peace and solace because of the wounds that dug deep. It was at that moment that everything came crashing down around me, the past colliding with the present, the ache of losing so much returning.

Redemption. My greatest nightmare. I should have figured it out.

The range of emotions continued to expand, morphing and changing with every passing second.

Including red-hot rage. I was full of anger, refusing to allow my real family to be hurt because of my past. I struggled to my feet, moving toward the door, ignoring the smoke and continually falling debris. And I aimed my weapon toward the center of the entryway, prepared to end this charade myself.

"What the hell is going on?" Arman said from behind me as a figure moved into the entryway.

My father's laughter echoed in my ears, dark and foreboding and exactly as I remembered when he'd come for me, finding me hiding in my closet or under my bed.

"Come here, you little fuck."

"Don't, Daddy. Please don't."

"You need to take your beating like a man. You'll thank me one day."

"No, Daddy. No!"

The memory was bittersweet, the images rushing into the back of my mind ones I'd refused to acknowledge after finding a new family.

As the man who'd sired me walked through the door, four men flanking his side, I took aim between his eyes.

Jack Cormier looked the same except for the ugly scars covering one side of his face, his hair gray where it used to be thick and black like mine. It was obvious he'd been in a fire, the mottled skin and the difficulty he had blinking with one eye indicating he'd endured horrific pain.

Only I didn't give a damn. After what he'd put me and Mother through, I hoped he suffered for weeks, months.

And I wished that I could continue his agony. Maybe I'd introduce him to the Boogeyman, something he'd helped create with his violence and brutality. The ugly memories threatened to derail me, but I refused to allow it to happen.

That's exactly what the man wanted.

Arman and Thomas were right beside me, Devin finally rising to his feet as well.

I'd never experienced the moment where all time stopped, where the air was sucked out of a room. While smoke continued to sweep into the room, the eerie quiet was a perfect backdrop for the moment.

Jack glanced from one man to the other before smiling as he locked his gaze on me. He threw out his arms as if making a gesture of endearment. "What's wrong, son? Aren't you happy to see your old man?"

"I'm going to ask again. What the fuck is going on?" Arman asked, taking a single step closer. That forced the men my father had hired to lift their assault weapons. They were dressed in black exactly as the ones I'd seen both at Arman's house and in St. Barts. My father had exacted revenge. Why? Why did he want to destroy what I'd found?

"The bastard is trying to destroy me just like he did to my mother," I answered.

"Please, son. You are my flesh and blood. You want to know why, Arman? All you need to do is ask your father for the real answer." Jack wore a smile, the same one he did every time he beat my mother and me all those years ago.

When he took a step closer, I did everything I could to relax, even allowing the same calculated smile to cross my face as my father had.

"Did you like how I forged the signatures? All I had to do was steal the nondisclosure your father signed, Arman. Oh, did you know your father was in talks with Mr. Carlos here?" Jack laughed again and it was all I could do not to fire my weapon. "How about when I tipped off that sexy reporter that something juicy was going to happen at the party?"

"You broke into my house and stole the nondisclosure paperwork? What the hell is going on here?" Devin demanded.

"It would seem all of us in this room are at an impasse, Mr. Carlos. Incidentally, I'm sorry about your estate and the loss of your men but it's just business." Jack laughed once again, taunting all of us.

"Your father was released from prison a few months ago," Thomas said with almost no emotion. I knew there was a significant story behind his words. "Jean Baptiste had me search to try and find out his whereabouts, but he disappeared."

Jack grinned. "Yeah, I learned that was a necessity. I wanted to surprise you, son."

Surprise? I wanted to kill him. There was little keeping me from it except the fact there were five against four. I couldn't risk Arman's life or Thomas' either. Even if the fact Thomas had kept this knowledge from me was the worst betrayal by someone close I'd experienced in the entire time I'd been with the Thibodeaux family.

"Fine, Jack. Why target my real family?" I asked, as if I really gave a shit. All I wanted was to end the fucker's life as I should have done as a child. Before my mother had basically taken her own life. Before I was forced onto the street.

"Your real family? You had a real family. You don't really know. Do you?" Jack asked, shifting his angry gaze to Arman.

"I don't care," I answered.

"Let me enlighten you, my son," he said in a dark voice. "I was Jean Baptiste's right-hand man before he tossed me aside like trash. Didn't you know that?"

The news hit me hard. I quickly threw a glance in Arman's direction. He had no clue either. Was it even possible what the sperm donor was saying was true? If Thomas' face was any indication, for once my father wasn't lying. What in God's name had been kept secret from me for almost thirty years?

"So the fuck what?" I taunted.

"So, the treacherous bastard betrayed me, especially when he accepted my own son as his. He had me tossed in prison. He was the reason for my face being set on fire." Jack rubbed the disfigured side of his face, half laughing, the sound even more maniacal than before.

I sensed Devin shifting to the side, trying to get a better vantage point. "You forged the contract. Didn't you?" I barked, half laughing myself. The man had taken a ruse to an entirely different level. I had to give him some credit. I hadn't given a shit what prison he'd been shoved into, never going to visit, never making a single phone call. He'd used the time against me as he'd done everything else.

Whether or not he'd worked for Jean Baptiste would be determined. Not that it really mattered at this point.

"It was all in fun."

My birth father was a fucked-up human being. If you could call him that.

"Jack was in New York when Zoe graduated," Thomas stated. "He was tracked to St. Barts then to Texas."

"Very good," Jack said, his face full of amusement.

"You targeted my daughter," Arman growled. "Why? Tell me before I blow your head off."

Jack tapped his finger across his lips. "Well, she has been in love with Maddox for years. I know my son. I also knew it was only a matter of time before he couldn't keep his cock in his pants. Being told you fucked her in that greenhouse was the best news in the world. That set the entire plan into beautiful motion. I don't think you want to blow my head off, Arman. If you attempt to do so, I'll need to kill that beautiful daughter of yours. After I make her mine."

I knew the rules of war, the games that were often played when two sides were brought together in conflict, pretending as if they wanted to work out a deal to prevent bloodshed. While the intelligent side of me had reminded me more than once that with a man as crazy as my father, I needed to be very careful with my actions.

THE WISEGUY

But the moment he'd threatened the woman I loved once again, I'd reached a point of no return. Firing a single shot, I caught him between the eyes, the look of shock on his face providing some level of satisfaction. The surprise at my actions expressed by my father's men also allowed two seconds of assessing the situation before following the training I'd been put through by Jean Baptiste.

I yanked Devin down to the floor before lunging in front of both Arman and Thomas, pummeling all three of us to the floor a split second before shots were fired. I rolled, the Glock still firmly planted in both hands, firing off indiscriminately.

As the sounds of gunfire from all four of us echoed into the room, another series of images rushed into the forefront of my mind.

My mother before she'd succumbed to her addiction. Her laugh. The few times she'd read to me, promising to keep the boogeyman away. Jean Baptiste praising me, calling me his son so long ago.

The man I considered my brother during high school. Football games. Homecoming dances.

And the woman I'd vowed to protect and would now honor in love.

As the smoke cleared, I rose as if from the ashes, the moments of slow motion and muffled sounds remaining as I walked to my father's lifeless body. As I peered down into the man's vacant eyes, I realized that I no longer considered myself the Boogeyman.

Arman flanked my side, gripping my shoulder. "It's over, my brother. It's time to go home."

Home.

I'd hated the world for thirteen years of my life, acting as if I didn't care about anything or anyone except for my mom. Then Jean Baptiste had come into my life, a driving force in not only surviving the horrors of what I'd been through but in also learning to thrive.

Yet I'd been dead inside until Zoe had awakened my soul and my heart.

Maybe my fucking bastard of a father had done me a favor after all. He'd given me a reason to live.

I glanced at Arman, who gave me a respectful nod, before spitting on my father. It was as close to spitting on the man's grave as I would come. The bastard didn't deserve to have me waste another moment of my life on someone so evil.

As I turned away, I felt stronger and more alive than I had in a long time.

It was time to return to my family and maybe for the first time in years, I'd visit my mother's grave. After all, I had a story to tell, one I knew she'd appreciate. And maybe she'd be able to give me her blessing on my upcoming marriage.

CHAPTER 28

"Familial betrayal is, to me, the most heartbreaking kind—because if you can't trust your family to love you and protect you, who can you really trust?"

—Alexandra Bracken

Maddox

I'd read the quote somewhere a long time before, so long that it had taken me a minute to remember the person responsible for saying it. I don't know why it felt important to repeat it over in my mind several times other than to finally put my past where it belonged.

In a coffin, the lid nailed down for all eternity.

Maybe I'd always known my birth father would exact revenge on the fact I'd survived. How many times had he told me over the years that I should never have been born, that I was worthless? And how many times had he threatened to end my life because I'd complained that I was hungry or when I'd tried to protect my mother with my frail body?

As I watched the heavy torrent of rain beating against the window of Arman's office, I was reminded that the sun would shine again tomorrow. It was all about enjoying the beautiful rays after the rain had helped make the flowers and grass grow. It was one of the few things I remembered my mother telling me when I very young.

We'd lost several good men in Texas, too many of them.

I felt Arman's presence beside me seconds later. So much had occurred since we'd left the Lone Star State. Devin had been thankful that I'd saved his life, agreeing to enter into business with the Thibodeaux family. It would increase both empires by billions eventually.

Not that it mattered to me other than I wanted the family to succeed. My family. I would remain wary of the alliance, but it was a good business decision.

"Thomas did what my father asked, trying to find out if the threats he'd received had any merit," Arman told me.

"I'm not angry with Thomas. He was not only following orders but protecting a family much like you and I've done."

"My father had his reasons."

"I never really told you, but I always considered your father mine as well. After what Jack put me through, what he did to my mom, the only reason I survived without succumbing to drugs was because he picked me up. I'm ready to put the past behind me. I just want to know why Jean Baptiste never told me there was a connection to my birth father."

"That's something only Pops can answer. Just know that he does love you like a son."

There was no animosity in Arman, Francois, or Louie for the way I'd been treated over the years, always welcome at family gatherings and holidays. For being a family of ruthless, savage men, they had big hearts. That was evident in the way they loved their women and children.

And each other.

I had them to thank for the man I'd become, for the love I was able to shower over Zoe. The future that I knew would entail a large family. I almost laughed thinking about it. Zoe had no idea how much I wanted children. God willing, we'd have several.

He clapped me on the back before heading to the door. "You've always been my brother. Now, you'll be my son-in-law."

I couldn't help but laugh. "Well, you are older than me."

"By six fucking months."

"I'm never going to let you forget it."

"I'm sure you won't, you bastard." His laughter boomed into the room, driving out the sounds of hard rain.

I was left alone for only a few minutes, the sound of the door opening once again forcing me to suck in my breath. I sensed Jean Baptiste had entered. He hadn't shied away from wanting to talk with me in private the same as I did with him. It was time to clear the air about the past and to simply let it go.

When he said nothing for a full minute, I tried to relax, turning my head slightly so I could catch a glimpse of his face. He seemed pensive, which was what the entire family had expressed since our return a few days before.

"Is it true that my birth father worked for you?" I finally asked.

"It's true. In the early days, I considered him an important asset, someone I could trust."

"What happened?"

"Your father was an angry man, violent. More so than even I was at the time. I'd believed he could be controlled, but when he started using drugs, his brutality became intolerable. I was forced to clean up after him several times at the risk of my family." He walked closer. "I cared about Jack. I tried to get him help, including getting him into one of the best rehabs in the county, all expenses paid. After three months of extensive treatment, he returned a changed man. You were maybe eight or nine at the time."

"I was eleven. It was the last time my mother was lucid most of the time. We also healed during his absence. We thought he was gone for good."

Jean Baptiste exhaled, the haunted look in his eyes letting me know how much the situation troubled him. "I didn't know much about you or your mother at the time. I'll be honest with you. I didn't give a shit. I had my own family to deal with, my business right on the edge all the time. I was a selfish prick back then and I hate myself for it. When Jack returned, he proved himself for months, a year or so maybe. He moved up in my organization, holding a place of trust."

"So what happened?"

"He betrayed me, stealing four hundred thousand dollars that we never found. He would have gotten away with the treachery had he not made a single mistake. I wanted to kill him but was convinced to have him thrown in jail instead. The whole situation bothered me. I'd even believed that somehow, I'd failed Jack. I didn't learn how dire the situation was with your mother or what he'd done to you. I did hear your mother died and the day I caught you in my restaurant, I knew I'd been given a second chance on saving a life. Your life."

"Why didn't you tell me what happened?"

"The truth was that you were so disturbed for the first couple of years that I knew it could destroy you or push you into becoming a carbon copy of your father. The day you saved my life, I committed to raising you as my own, determined to let the past stay in the ugliness of what it was. As the years passed, it became easier to do so."

"He threatened you through the years?"

"Every once in a while, I heard he'd issued some threat, most of which I didn't take seriously. But I learned a few months ago that he'd used that money he'd stolen that I'd never found to amass himself an army of supporters. I have enough enemies that it wasn't hard for him to do. When I received a threat, I asked Thomas to look into his whereabouts. I found out he'd been released from prison, but he remained in New York."

"Who was Lucas Marciano?"

"He was the illegitimate son of a man considered an enemy, someone I'd ousted from New Orleans. Had I known what happened to my granddaughter, I would have had Jack tracked and killed. Unfortunately, by the time I asked Thomas to track him, your father had disappeared. I admit it. I never anticipated the attack at Arman's estate. I've no doubt the guilt in not confiding in you and the rest of my family will always be with me."

"My father hated me."

"He hated that you took his place when it was no one's fault but his own. However, you are not your father. Not in a single way."

I nodded, realizing that I was more like my mother, although she had a good soul. Mine was black.

"I hope that one day you'll find it in your heart to forgive me for not confiding in you." Jean Baptiste moved closer, staring me directly in the eyes.

"It's about forgiveness. And Jack Cormier is not my father. You are."

As with every cloud and every rainstorm, there was always sunshine waiting for the dawn of a new day, a bright spot in dark skies allowing for hope and the prospect of a brighter future. As Jean Baptiste's face lit up from what I'd said, relieving the tremendous guilt he'd felt, I noticed a rainbow in the distant sky.

It was a sign of forgiveness and encouragement sent from my mother.

And now, I was ready and eager to move into the future, embracing love for the first time in my life.

My heart was suddenly full.

* * *

Four months later...

Zoe

I stood staring at my reflection in the mirror, turning from one side to the other, making faces as I'd done so often. The last few months had been a whirlwind of activity, including a breathtaking wedding at my father's house. Between Raven, Delaney, and Edmee along with my grandmother, I'd had to do almost nothing to prepare for the incredible event.

I'd been searching for a new house, a bigger one like my darling husband had demanded we move into, followed by furniture purchases, and working with painters and other contractors to make our newly purchased estate a dream home. I hadn't had time to think about anything else, including what I wanted to do for the rest of my life.

When a little seed had been planted, I'd had a feeling my career would be placed on hold for a little while. A grin crossed my face at the thought.

Suddenly, a series of tickling sensations sent a wave of electricity all the way to my toes. As my sexy, rugged husband came into the room, he took my breath away, as always. This was a day off for him, which had surprised me given how busy my father's company had gotten. Although I couldn't really call it my father's any longer. Even my uncle Louie had a vested interest in the corporation's success, a gift from Arman for saving his life.

Maybe one day I'd shake things up and become the first female vice president. I bit my lip as my husband approached, his nostrils flaring as he took a deep breath. He was dressed more casually than I was used to in an open shirt untucked paired with the sexiest pair of tight-fitting jeans I'd ever seen.

I longed to brush my fingers against his muscular chest. When I turned sideways again, placing my hand on my stomach, I gave him a pouting look. "Does this dress make me look fat?" At three months pregnant, I was just starting to show.

The day I'd told him I was pregnant, he purchased cigars for every single male in the corporation. Every one of them. I'd chastised him playfully until he'd reminded me that he was very much in charge.

Just the way I liked it.

He wrapped his arms around me, kissing the top of my head. "I think you look perfect. I want to see you barefoot and pregnant for years to come," Maddox said before issuing a dark growl.

"That's very sexist of you."

"Just being honest."

I pulled away, giving him a pouting look. "Bad boy."

He leaned against the dresser, folding his arms. "Speaking of bad. You are a very bad girl."

I pointed at my chest, blinking several times. "I'm a very good girl. What are you talking about?"

He wagged his finger, issuing a tsking sound. "Nope. You're hardheaded and stubborn, ignoring the rules."

"What rules?"

"My rules, little lamb."

"Oh, those." I looked away, playfully sliding my hand between my breasts.

"Well, I think you need a hard spanking to remind you that I am in charge of this household."

The grin on his face kept quivers trickling down the backs of my legs. "Not fair."

"Who said anything in life was fair? And I think given your bad behavior, I'm going to develop a maintenance program, spanking you two or three times a week. Now, let's go."

A sudden flash swept through my mind. The dream I'd had months before when we were in St. Barts. This was remarkably like it. I was concentrating so hard on remembering every little detail of the filthy dream that I'd ignored his command.

Not a good thing.

Maddox swept me off my feet, tossing me over his shoulder. "You're coming with me."

"This won't be good for the baby."

"Uh-huh. Nice try."

I laughed even though I pummeled his back as he headed down the long hallway toward the kitchen. "I'll get you for this."

"I'd really love to see you try."

Whoever said love was a many splendored thing certainly knew what they were talking about. My heart was as full as my life, the closeness I felt to my family extraordinary. My grandfather and grandmother had remained in the city and every birthday and holiday, every achievement had been a celebration of family and close friends. The fullness of my life and my heart was something I would never have believed possible only a few months before.

Yet here I was with the man of my dreams, our little family ready to expand in a few short months. I was truly blessed.

He eased me onto my feet, cupping both sides of my face as he so very often did. Unlike the dream, as he lowered his head, brushing his lips across mine, it caused me to swoon, the heat building between us. When he finally kissed me, it was tender at first, allowing my heart to soar. As it became more passionate, I clung to him, fisting his shirt and arching my back.

But with all good things, it was time for the intimate moment to shift into something else. Maddox took a step back, giving me a stern look. "Remove your clothes while I find the perfect implement."

I bit my lower lip, watching as he moved toward the kitchen drawers. Of course, I knew exactly what he was going to choose. One big wooden spoon. He even whistled, the joy in his heart making mine burst with happiness.

"When you're finished undressing, lie across the table and grip the edge. This spanking is going to hurt."

Grinning, I did what he asked, folding my clothes as neatly as I'd done in the dream. As I leaned over the table, I couldn't help but be thankful that we'd both taken a chance on love.

As the powerful man approached, he twirled the identical wooden spoon I'd seen in my dream, something he'd only recently purchased out of the blue. I suddenly remembered my father had told me so long ago that my mother had believed in karma. She'd had a favorite quote that she'd handwritten in a poem to my father, something he'd placed behind the picture I'd kept of her on my nightstand.

"Every action of our lives touches on some chord that will vibrate in eternity." The beautiful thought had been said by someone named Edwin Hubbell Chapin, a man I didn't know but his words held a new meaning for my life and my future.

My mother was with me, blessing the future.

Maddox's mother was looking down on us from heaven with a smile on her face.

As the man of my dreams brought the spoon down, the crackle of electricity sparked again, allowing me to feel more alive than ever before.

All because we'd taken a chance on believing in karma.

The End

AFTERWORD

Stormy Night Publications would like to thank you for your interest in our books.

If you liked this book (or even if you didn't), we would really appreciate you leaving a review on the site where you purchased it. Reviews provide useful feedback for us and our authors, and this feedback (both positive comments and constructive criticism) allows us to work even harder to make sure we provide the content our customers want to read.

If you would like to check out more books from Stormy Night Publications, if you want to learn more about our company, or if you would like to join our mailing list, please visit our website at:

http://www.stormynightpublications.com

BOOKS OF THE SAVAGE EMPIRE SERIES

The Kingpin

When I caught her sneaking into my home, I thought Raven was just a girl doing a silly sorority dare, so I set her bare ass on fire with my belt and then taught her a much more shameful lesson.

My seed was already dripping down her thighs before I learned she's my enemy's daughter.

That's when I decided I would be keeping her.

And that I'd be making her my bride.

The Capo

By the time I knew the beautiful little firecracker who snuck into one of my clubs was my best friend's daughter, I'd already reddened her bare ass with my belt and ravaged her thoroughly.

But now that I've claimed her, I'm keeping her.

Forbidden fruit just tastes sweeter…

BOOKS OF THE RUTHLESS EMPIRE SERIES

The Don

Maxwell Powers swept into my life after my father was gunned down, but the moment those piercing blue eyes caught mine I knew he would be doing more than just avenging his old friend.

I haven't seen him since I was a little girl, but that won't keep him from bending me over and belting my bare backside… or from making me scream his name as he claims my virgin body.

He's twice my age, and he's my godfather.

But I know I'll be soaking wet and ready for him tonight…

The Consigliere

As consigliere of New York's most ruthless crime syndicate, Daniel Briggs rules with an iron fist. But here in Los Angeles, he's just my big brother's best friend, forbidden in every way.

This stunningly handsome billionaire may be the most eligible bachelor on the West Coast, but to him I'm still just a little girl in need of protection from men who would ravage her brutally.

Men like him.

But he'll soon realize I'm all grown up, and then it won't be long before my teenage crush finally shows me the side of him he's kept hidden from me—the savage side that will blister my bare ass for talking back and then take what has always been his with my hair gripped in his fist.

I don't know what comes after that. I just know everything he does to me will be utterly sinful…

The Underboss

When Francesco Arturo helped me escape an unwanted arranged marriage three years ago, I didn't know he was the underboss of the most powerful mafia organization in New York.

I was just an eighteen-year-old virgin on the run, and he was the handsome savior mesmerizing me with eyes the color of the Aegean Sea before carrying me off to his bed to make me his.

He could have taken my innocence that day, but he didn't.

I gave it to him.

But this isn't a fairy tale. When that perfect night came to an end, I was still the daughter of a Chicago crime boss with a father set on marrying her off to whatever vile man paid the most.

Now he's finally found a suitor for me, but there is something the brutal bastard doesn't know.

I already belong to someone else, and he's coming to take me back.

BOOKS OF THE TAINTED REGIME SERIES

Cruelest Vow

D'Artagnan Conti was born into poverty, raised to be a soldier in my father's savage regime. I grew up in luxury, longing to escape my family's cruel machinations, and the young man with sapphire eyes and the voice of an angel became not just my forbidden crush but my everything.

Then he was taken from me, killed in a brutal attack by our enemies. Or so I was led to believe...

For twenty years I did my best to forget him, until a devilishly handsome stranger awakened my desire in a way that I hadn't thought possible, baring my body and soul and setting them both ablaze with passion so intense it burns hotter than the lash of leather across my naked backside.

Every taste of his lips, every whisper in my ear, and every quivering climax pulled me deeper into this dark, twisted rapture, and only when I was already under his spell did I learn the truth.

The man I thought I'd lost is the one who has made me his.

Twisted Embrace

Enzo Lazaro is my best friend's brother, yet the fact that it was taboo only left me even more desperate for him to undress me with those piercing eyes and then strip me bare and ravage me.

But until he found out a secret I hadn't even known myself, I never thought I'd be screaming his name in bed with my belted ass still burning because he decided I needed a lesson in obedience.

...or that he'd be claiming me as his bride.

It turns out I'm the daughter of a Russian mobster, and even though my adopted parents never told me, that means I have dangerous enemies. He says he's making me his wife to protect me.

But we both know he would have taken what he wanted eventually anyway.

Captured Innocence

When Mattia DeLuca paid my father handsomely for the right to claim me as his bride, it didn't matter that I wanted nothing to do with my own Cosa Nostra family, let alone someone else's. Long before he put a ring on my finger, my own screams of climax told me I was his forever.

Even when I ran away, hoping to leave my family's mafia world behind, I always knew Mattia would track me down one day and take his belt to my bare ass before taking me to his bed again.

But when he came for me, it wasn't just to punish, ravage, and then wed me.

It was to rescue me.

BOOKS OF THE CARNAL SINS SERIES

Required Surrender

My first mistake was agreeing to participate in a charity auction. My second was believing I could walk away from the commanding billionaire with a brogue accent and dazzling green eyes.

It was supposed to be one date, but a man like Lachlan McKenzie plays by his own set of rules.

As the owner of Carnal Sins, DC's exclusive kink club, his reputation is as dark and demanding as his desires, and before I knew it I ended up his to enjoy not for just one night but a full week.

I fought his control, but I knew I wouldn't win… and in my heart I don't think I even wanted to. Not after he called me his good girl, stripped me bare and spanked me with his belt, and then made me blush and beg and come so hard I forgot all about being his only for a few more days.

That didn't matter anyway. We both know he's keeping me forever.

Demanded Submission

When he came to my aid after a head-on collision that seemed not to have been an accident, Jameson Stark offered me a ride, help with my car, and a job at the most exclusive club in town.

He also bared me, spanked me until I knew better than to argue with him again, and then showed me what it means to be in the debt of a billionaire who isn't afraid to take everything he's owed.

But as the owner of the Miami branch of Carnal Sins, it isn't just Jameson's wealth and good looks that draw attention, and I knew a man like him must have enemies. I just didn't care.

Not when his every smoldering glance all but demanded my submission...

Compelled Obedience

Grant Wilde is as arrogant as he is rich and powerful, and if I didn't need his help so desperately I'd tell him exactly where he ought to shove his money, his exclusive club, and his cocky smirk.

But I do need his help, and it will come at a price...

BOOKS OF THE KINGS OF CORRUPTION SERIES

King of Wrath

After a car wreck on an icy winter morning, I had no idea the man who saved my life would turn out to be the heir to a powerful mafia family… let alone that I'd be forced into marrying him.

When this mysterious stranger sought to seduce me, I should have ignored the dark passion he ignited. Instead, I begged him to claim me as he stripped me bare and whipped me with his belt.

He was as savage as I was innocent, but it was only after he made me his that I learned the truth.

He's the head of the New York Cosa Nostra, and I belong to him now…

King of Cruelty

Constantine Thorn has been after me since I saw him kill a man nine years ago, and when he finally caught me he made me an offer I couldn't refuse. Marry him and he will protect me.

Only then did I learn that the man who made me his bride was the same monster I'd feared.

He's a brutal, heartless mafia boss and I wanted to hate the bastard, but with every stinging lash of his belt and every moment of helplessly intense passion, I fell deeper into the dark abyss.

He's the king of cruelty, and now I'm his queen.

King of Pain

Diego Santos may be wealthy, powerful, and sinfully gorgeous, but his slick veneer doesn't fool me. I know his true nature, and I had planned to end this arranged marriage before it even began.

But it wasn't Diego waiting for me at the altar.

By all appearances the man who laid claim to me was the mafia heir to whom I'd been promised, but I sensed an entirely different personality, one so electrifying I was swept up by his passion.

A part of me still wanted to escape, but then he took me in his arms and over his knee, laying my deepest, darkest needs bare and then fulfilling them in the most shameful ways imaginable.

Now I'm not just his bride. I'm his completely.

King of Depravity

When Brogan Callahan swept me off my feet, I didn't know he was heir to a powerful Irish mafia family. I didn't find that out until after he'd taken me in his arms... and over his knee.

By the time I learned the truth, I was already his.

I went on the run to escape my father's plans to marry me off, but it turns out the ruthless mob boss he had in mind is the same sinfully sexy bastard who just stripped me bare and claimed me savagely.

He demands my absolute obedience, and yet with each brutal kiss and stinging lash of his belt I feel myself falling ever deeper into the dark abyss of shameful need he's created within me.

At first I wondered if there were bounds to his depravity. Now I hope there aren't...

King of Savagery

I knew Maxim Nikitin was a man to be reckoned with when I went undercover to help the FBI bring him down, but nothing could have prepared me for his raw power... or his icy blue eyes.

He caught me, and now he's determined not just to punish me, but to tame me completely.

Every kiss is brutal, every touch possessive, every fiery lash of his belt more intense than the last, yet with every cry of pain and every scream of climax the truth becomes more obvious.

He doesn't need to break me. I belong to him already.

King of Malice

When I met Phoenix Diamonds, I didn't know anything about him except that he had a body carved from stone and a voice that left me hoping he'd order me to strip just so I could obey.

By the time I learned he's the head of a Greek crime syndicate intent on making me pay for the sins of my father, he'd already mastered me with his touch alone, belted my bare ass for daring to come without permission, and ravaged me thoroughly both that night and the next morning.

All I can do is try to pretend he isn't everything I've always fantasized about...

But I think he knows already.

BOOKS OF THE SINNERS AND SAINTS SERIES

Beautiful Villain

When I knocked on Kirill Sabatin's door, I didn't know he was the Kozlov Bratva's most feared enforcer. I didn't expect him to be the most terrifyingly sexy man I've ever laid eyes on either…

I told him off for making so much noise in the middle of the night, but if the crack of his palm against my bare bottom didn't wake everyone in the building my screams of climax certainly did.

I shouldn't have let him spank me, let alone seduce me. He's a dangerous man and I could easily end up in way over my head. But the moment I set eyes on those rippling, sweat-slicked muscles I knew I needed that beautiful villain to take me long and hard and savagely right then and there.

And he did.

Now I just have to hope him claiming me doesn't start a mob war…

Beautiful Sinner

When I first screamed his name in shameful surrender, Sevastian Kozlov was the enemy, the heir of a rival family who had just finished spanking me into submission after I dared to defy him.

Though he'd already claimed my body by the time he claimed me as his bride, no matter how desperately I long for his touch I vowed this beautiful sinner would never conquer my heart.

But it wasn't up to me…

Beautiful Seduction

In my late-night hunt for the perfect pastry, I never expected to be the victim of a brutal attack… or for a brooding, blue-eyed stranger to become my savior, tending to my wounds while easing my fears. The electricity exploded between us, turning into a night of incredible passion.

Only later did I learn that Valentin Vincheti is the heir to the New York Italian mafia empire.

Then he came to take me, and this time he wasn't gentle. I shouldn't have surrendered, but with each savage kiss and stinging stroke of his belt his beautiful seduction became more difficult to resist. But when one of his enemies sets his sights on me, will my secrets put our lives at risk?

Beautiful Obsession

After I was left at the altar, I turned what was meant to be the reception into an epic party. But when a handsome stranger asked me to dance, I wasn't prepared for the passion he ignited.

He told me he was a very bad man, but that only made my heart race faster as I lay bare and bound, my dress discarded and my bottom sore from a spanking, waiting for him to ravage me.

It was supposed to be just one night. No strings. Nothing to entangle me in his dangerous world.

But that was before I became his beautiful obsession…

Beautiful Devil

Kostya Baranov is an infamous assassin, a man capable of incredible savagery, but when I witnessed a mafia hit he didn't silence me with a bullet. He decided to make me his instead.

Taken prisoner and forced to obey or feel the sting of his belt, shameful lust for my captor soon wars with fury at what he has done to me… and what he keeps doing to me with every touch.

But though he may be a beautiful devil, it is my own family's secret which may damn us both.

BOOKS OF THE BENEDETTI EMPIRE SERIES

Cruel Prince

Catherine's father conspired to have my father killed, and that debt to the Benedetti family must be settled. Just as he took something from me, I will take something from him.

His daughter.

She will be mine to punish and ravage, but when she suffers it will not be for his sins.

It will be for my pleasure.

She will beg, but it will be for me to claim her in the most shameful ways imaginable.

She will scream, but it will be because she doesn't think she can bear another climax.

But when she surrenders at last, it will not be to her captor.

It will be to her husband.

Ruthless Prince

Alexandra is a senator's daughter, used to mingling in the company of the rich and powerful, but tonight she will learn that there are men who play by different rules.

Men like me.

I could romance her. I could seduce her and then carry her gently to my bed.

But that can wait. Tonight I'm going to wring one ruthless climax after another from her quivering body with her bottom burning from my belt and her throat sore from screaming.

She will know she is mine before she even knows she is my bride.

Savage Prince

Gillian's father may be a powerful Irish mob boss, but he owes a blood debt to my family, and when I came to collect I didn't ask permission before taking his daughter as payment.

It was not up to him… or to her.

I will make her my bride, but I am not the kind of man who will wait until our wedding night to bare her and claim what belongs to me. She will walk down the aisle wet, well-used, and sore.

Her dress will hide the marks from my belt that taught her the consequences of disobeying her husband, but nothing will hide her blushes as her arousal drips down her thighs with each step.

By the time she says her vows she will already be mine.

BOOKS OF THE MERCILESS KINGS SERIES

King's Captive

Emily Porter saw me kill a man who betrayed my family and she helped put me behind bars. But someone with my connections doesn't stay in prison long, and she is about to learn the hard way that there is a price to pay for crossing the boss of the King dynasty. A very, very painful price…

She's going to cry for me as I blister that beautiful bottom, then she's going to scream for me as I ravage her over and over again, taking her in the most shameful ways she can imagine. But leaving her well-punished and well-used is just the beginning of what I have in store for Emily.

I'm going to make her my bride, and then I'm going to make her mine completely.

King's Hostage

When my life was threatened, Michael King didn't just take matters into his own hands.

He took me.

When he carried me off it was partly to protect me, but mostly it was because he wanted me.

I didn't choose to go with him, but it wasn't up to me. That's why I'm naked, wet, and sore in an opulent Swiss chalet with my bottom still burning from the belt of the infuriatingly sexy mafia boss who brought me here, punished me when I fought him, and then savagely made me his.

We'll return when things are safe in New Orleans, but I won't be going back to my old home.

I belong to him now, and he plans to keep me.

King's Possession

Her father had to be taught what happens when you cross a King, but that isn't why Genevieve Rossi is sore, well-used, and waiting for me to claim her in the only way I haven't already.

She's sore because she thought she could embarrass me in public without being punished.

She's well-used because after I spanked her I wanted more, and I take what I want.

She's waiting for me in my bed because she's my bride, and tonight is our wedding night.

I'm not going to be gentle with her, but when she wakes up tomorrow morning wet and blushing her cheeks won't be crimson because of the shameful things I did to her naked, quivering body.

It will be because she begged for all of them.

King's Toy

Vincenzo King thought I knew something about a man who betrayed him, but that isn't why I'm on my way to New Orleans well-used and sore with my backside still burning from his belt.

When he bared and punished me maybe it was just business, but what came after was not.

It was savage, it was shameful, and it was very, very personal.

I'm his toy now, and not the kind you keep in its box on the shelf.

He's going to play rough with me.

He's going to get me all wet and dirty.

Then he's going to do it all again tomorrow.

King's Demands

Julieta Morales hoped to escape an unwanted marriage, but the moment she got into my car her fate was sealed. She will have a husband, but it won't be the cartel boss her father chose for her.

It will be me.

But I'm not the kind of man who takes his bride gently amid rose petals on her wedding night. She'll learn to satisfy her King's demands with her bottom burning and her hair held in my fist.

She'll promise obedience when she speaks her vows, but she'll be mastered long before then.

King's Temptation

I didn't think I needed Dimitri Kristoff's protection, but it wasn't up to me. With a kingpin from a rival family coming after me, he took charge, took off his belt, and then took what he wanted.

He knows I'm not used to doing as I'm told. He just doesn't care.

The stripes seared across my bare bottom left me sore and sorry, but it was what came after that truly left me shaken. The princess of the King family shouldn't be on her knees for anyone, let alone this Bratva brute who has decided to claim for himself what he was meant to safeguard.

Nobody gave me to him, but I'm his anyway.

Now he's going to make sure I know it.

BOOKS OF THE MAFIA MASTERS SERIES

His as Payment

Caroline Hargrove thinks she is mine because her father owed me a debt, but that isn't why she is sitting in my car beside me with her bottom sore inside and out. She's wet, well-used, and coming with me whether she likes it or not because I decided I want her, and I take what I want.

As a senator's daughter, she probably thought no man would dare lay a hand on her, let alone spank her thoroughly and then claim her beautiful body in the most shameful ways possible.

She was wrong. Very, very wrong. She's going to be mastered, and I won't be gentle about it.

Taken as Collateral

Francesca Alessandro was just meant to be collateral, held captive as a warning to her father, but then she tried to fight me. She ended up sore and soaked as I taught her a lesson with my belt and then screaming with every savage climax as I taught her to obey in a much more shameful way.

She's mine now. Mine to keep. Mine to protect. Mine to use as hard and as often as I please.

Forced to Cooperate

Willow Church is not the first person who tried to put a bullet in me. She's just the first I let live. Now she will pay the price in the most shameful way imaginable. The stripes from my belt will teach her to obey, but what happens to her sore, red bottom after that will teach the real lesson.

She will be used mercilessly, over and over, and every brutal climax will remind her of the humiliating truth: she never even had a chance against me. Her body always knew its master.

Claimed as Revenge

Valencia Rivera became mine the moment her father broke the agreement he made with me. She thought she had a say in the matter, but my belt across her beautiful bottom taught her otherwise and a night spent screaming her surrender into the sheets left her in no doubt she belongs to me.

Using her hard and often will not be all it takes to tame her properly, but it will be a good start…

Made to Beg

Sierra Fox showed up at my door to ask for my protection, and I gave it to her… for a price. She belongs to me now, and I'm going to use her beautiful body as thoroughly as I please. The only thing for her to decide is how sore her cute little bottom will be when I'm through claiming her.

She came to me begging for help, but as her moans and screams grow louder with every brutal climax, we both know it won't be long before she begs me for something far more shameful.

BOOKS OF THE EDGE OF DARKNESS SERIES

Dark Stranger

On a dark, rainy night, I received a phone call. I shouldn't have answered it... but I did.

The things he says he'll do to me are far from sweet, this man I know only by his voice.

They're so filthy I blush crimson just hearing them... and yet still I answer, my panties always soaked the moment the phone rings. But this isn't going to end when I decide it's gone too far...

I can tell him to leave me alone, but I know it won't keep him away. He's coming for me, and when he does he's going to make me his in all the rough, shameful ways he promised he would.

And I'll be wet and ready for him... whether I want to be or not.

Dark Predator

She thinks I'm seducing her, but this isn't romance. It's something much more shameful.

Eden tried to leave the mafia behind, but someone far more dangerous has set his sights on her.

Me.

She was meant to be my revenge against an old enemy, but I decided to make her mine instead.

She'll moan as my belt lashes her quivering bottom and writhe as I claim her in the filthiest of ways, but that's just the beginning. When I'm done, it won't be just her body that belongs to me.

I'll own her heart and soul too.

BOOKS OF THE DARK OVERTURE SERIES

Indecent Invitation

I shouldn't be here.

My clothes shouldn't be scattered around the room, my bottom shouldn't be sore, and I certainly shouldn't be screaming into the sheets as a ruthless tycoon takes everything he wants from me.

I shouldn't even know Houston Powers at all, but I was in a bad spot and I was made an offer.

A shameful, indecent offer I couldn't refuse.

I was desperate, I needed the money, and I didn't have a choice. Not a real one, anyway.

I'm here because I signed a contract, but I'm his because he made me his.

Illicit Proposition

I should have known better.

His proposition was shameful. So shameful I threw my drink in his face when I heard it.

Then I saw the look in his eyes, and I knew I'd made a mistake.

I fought as he bared me and begged as he spanked me, but it didn't matter. All I could do was moan, scream, and climax helplessly for him as he took everything he wanted from me.

By the time I signed the contract, I was already his.

Unseemly Entanglement

I was warned about Frederick Duvall. I was told he was dangerous. But I never suspected that meeting the billionaire advertising mogul to discuss a business proposition would end with me bent over a table with my dress up and my panties down for a shameful lesson in obedience.

That should have been it. I should have told him what he could do with his offer and his money.

But I didn't.

I could say it was because two million dollars is a lot of cash, but as I stand before him naked, bound, and awaiting the sting of his cane for daring to displease him, I know that's not the truth.

I'm not here because he pays me. I'm here because he owns me.

BOOKS OF THE CLUB DARKNESS SERIES

Bent to His Will

Even the most powerful men in the world know better than to cross me, but Autumn Sutherland thought she could spy on me in my own club and get away with it. Now she must be punished.

She tried to expose me, so she will be exposed. Bare, bound, and helplessly on display, she'll beg for mercy as my strap lashes her quivering bottom and my crop leaves its burning welts on her most intimate spots. Then she'll scream my name as she takes every inch of me, long and hard.

When I am done with her, she won't just be sore and shamefully broken. She will be mine.

Broken by His Hand

Sophia Russo tried to keep away from me, but just thinking about what I would do to her left her panties drenched. She tried to hide it, but I didn't let her. I tore those soaked panties off, spanked her bare little bottom until she had no doubt who owns her, and then took her long and hard.

She begged and screamed as she came for me over and over, but she didn't learn her lesson…

She didn't just come back for more. She thought she could disobey me and get away with it.

This time I'm not just going to punish her. I'm going to break her.

Bound by His Command

Willow danced for the rich and powerful at the world's most exclusive club… until tonight.

Tonight I told her she belongs to me now, and no other man will touch her again.

Tonight I ripped her soaked panties from her beautiful body and taught her to obey with my belt.

Tonight I took her as mine, and I won't be giving her up.

MORE MAFIA AND BILLIONAIRE ROMANCES BY PIPER STONE

Caught

If you're forced to come to an arrangement with someone as dangerous as Jagger Calduchi, it means he's about to take what he wants, and you'll give it to him… even if it's your body.

I got caught snooping where I didn't belong, and Jagger made me an offer I couldn't refuse. A week with him where his rules are the only rules, or his bought and paid for cops take me to jail.

He's going to punish me, train me, and master me completely. When he's used me so shamefully I blush just to think about it, maybe he'll let me go home… or maybe he'll decide to keep me.

Ruthless

Treating a mobster shot by a rival's goons isn't really my forte, but when a man is powerful enough to have a whole wing of a hospital cleared out for his protection, you do as you're told.

To make matters worse, this isn't first time I've met Giovanni Calduchi. It turns out my newest patient is the stern, sexy brute who all but dragged me back to his hotel room a couple of nights ago so he could use my body as he pleased, then showed up at my house the next day, stripped me bare, and spanked me until I was begging him to take me even more roughly and shamefully.

Now, with his enemies likely to be coming after me in order to get to him, all I can do is hope he's as good at keeping me safe as he is at keeping me blushing, sore, and thoroughly satisfied.

Prey

Within moments of setting eyes on Sophia Waters, I was certain of two things. She was going to learn what happens to bad girls who cheat at cards, and I was going to be the one to teach her.

But there was one thing I didn't know as I reddened that cute little bottom and then took her long and hard and oh so shamefully: I wasn't the only one who didn't come here for a game of cards.

I came to kill a man. It turns out she came to protect him.

Nobody keeps me from my target, but I'm in no rush. Not when I'm enjoying this game of cat and mouse so much. I'll even let her catch me one day, and as she screams my name with each brutal climax she'll finally realize the truth. She was never the hunter. She was always the prey.

Given

Stephanie Michaelson was given to me, and she is mine. The sooner she learns that, the less often her cute little bottom will end up well-punished and sore as she is reminded of her place.

But even as she promises obedience with tears running down her cheeks, I know it isn't the sting of my belt that will truly tame her. It is what comes next that will leave her in no doubt she belongs to me. That part will be long, hard, and shameful… and I will make her beg for all of it.

Dangerous Stranger

I came to Spain hoping to start a new life away from dangerous men, but then I met Rafael Santiago. Now I'm not just caught up in the affairs of a mafia boss, I'm being forced into his car.

When I saw something I shouldn't have, Rafael took me captive, stripped me bare, and punished me until he felt certain I'd told him everything I knew about his organization… which was nothing at all. Then he offered me his protection in return for the right to use me as he pleases.

Now that I belong to him, his plans for me are more shameful than I could have ever imagined.

Indebted

After her father stole from me, I could have left Alessandra Toro in jail for a crime she didn't commit. But I have plans for her. A deal with the judge—the kind only a man like me can arrange—made her my captive, and she will pay her father's debt with her beautiful body.

She will try to run, of course, but it won't be the law that comes after her. It will be me.

The sting of my belt across her quivering bare bottom will teach Alessandra the price of defiance, but it is the far more shameful penance that follows which will truly tame her.

Taken

When Winter O'Brien was given to me, she thought she had a say in the matter. She was wrong.

She is my bride. Mine to claim, mine to punish, and mine to use as shamefully as I please. The sting of my belt on her bare bottom will teach her to obey, but obedience is just the beginning.

I will demand so much more.

Bratva's Captive

I told Chloe Kingstrom that getting close to me would be dangerous, and she should keep her distance. The moment she disobeyed and followed me into that bar, she became mine.

Now my enemies are after her, but it's not what they would do to her she should worry about.

It's what I'm going to do to her.

My belt across her bare backside will teach her obedience, but what comes after will be different.

She's going to blush, beg, and scream with every climax as she's ravaged more thoroughly than she can imagine. Then I'm going to flip her over and claim her in an even more shameful way.

If she's a good girl, I might even let her enjoy it.

Hunted

Hope Gracen was just another target to be tracked down… until I caught her.

When I discovered I'd been lied to, I carried her off.

She'll tell me the truth with her bottom still burning from my belt, but that isn't why she's here.

I took her to protect her. I'm keeping her because she's mine.

Theirs as Payment

Until mere moments ago, I was a doctor heading home after my shift at the hospital. But that was before I was forced into the back seat of an SUV, then bared and spanked for trying to escape.

Now I'm just leverage for the Cabello brothers to use against my father, but it isn't the thought of being held hostage by these brutes that has my heart racing and my whole body quivering.

It is the way they're looking at me…

Like they're about to tear my clothes off and take turns mounting me like wild beasts.

Like they're going to share me, using me in ways more shameful than I can even imagine.

Like they own me.

Ruthless Acquisition

I knew the shameful stakes when I bet against these bastards. I just didn't expect to lose.

Now they've come to collect their winnings.

But they aren't just planning to take a belt to my bare bottom for trying to run and then claim everything they're owed from my naked, helpless body as I blush, beg, and scream for them.

They've acquired me, and they plan to keep me.

Bound by Contract

I knew I was in trouble the moment Gregory Steele called me into his office, but I wasn't expecting to end up stripped bare and bent over his desk for a painful lesson from his belt.

Taking a little bit of money here and there might have gone unnoticed in another organization, but stealing from one of the most powerful mafia bosses on the West Coast has consequences.

It doesn't matter why I did it. The only thing that matters now is what he's going to do to me.

I have no doubt he will use me shamefully, but he didn't make me sign that contract just to show me off with my cheeks blushing and my bottom sore under the scandalous outfit he chose for me.

Now that I'm his, he plans to keep me.

Dangerous Addiction

I went looking for a man working with my enemies. When I found only her instead, I should have just left her alone… or maybe taken what I wanted from her and then left… but I didn't.

I couldn't.

So I carried her off to keep for myself.

She didn't make it easy for me, and that earned her a lesson in obedience. A shameful one.

But as her bare bottom reddens under my punishing hand I can see her arousal dripping down her quivering thighs, and no matter how much she squirms and sobs and begs we both know exactly what she needs, and we both know as soon as this spanking is over I'm going to give it to her.

Hard.

Auction House

When I went undercover to investigate a series of murders with links to Steele Franklin's auction house operation, I expected to be sold for the humiliating use of one of his fellow billionaires.

But he wanted me for himself.

No contract. No agreed upon terms. No say in the matter at all except whether to surrender to his shameful demands without a fight or make him strip me bare and spank me into submission first.

I chose the second option, but as one devastating climax after another is forced from my naked, quivering body, what scares me isn't the thought of him keeping me locked up in a cage forever.

It's knowing he won't need to.

Interrogated

As Liam McGinty's belt lashes my bare backside, it isn't the burning sting or the humiliating awareness that my body's surrender is on full display for this ruthless mobster that shocks me.

It's the fact that this isn't a scene from one of my books.

I almost can't process the fact that I'm really riding in the back of a luxury SUV belonging to the most powerful Irish mafia boss in New York—the man I've written so much about—with my cheeks blushing, my bottom sore inside and out, and my arousal soaking the seat beneath me.

But whether I can process it or not, I'm his captive now.

Maybe he'll let me go when he's gotten the answers he needs and he's used me as he pleases.

Or maybe he'll keep me…

Vow of Seduction

Alexander Durante, Brogan Lancaster, and Daniel Norwood are powerful, dangerous men, but that won't keep them safe from me. Not after they let my brother take the fall for their crimes.

I spent years preparing for my chance at revenge. But things didn't go as planned…

Now I'm naked, bound, and helpless, waiting to be used and punished as these brutes see fit, and yet what's on my mind isn't how to escape all of the shameful things they're going to do to me.

It's whether I even want to…

Brutal Heir

When I went to an author convention, I didn't expect to find myself enjoying a rooftop meal with the sexiest cover model in the business, let alone screaming his name in bed later that night.

I didn't plan to be targeted by assassins, rushed to a helicopter under cover of armed men, and then spirited away to his home country with my bottom still burning from a spanking either, but it turns out there are some really important things I didn't know about Diavolo Montoya…

Like the fact that he's the heir to a notorious crime syndicate.

I should hate him, but even as his prisoner our connection is too intense to ignore, and I'm beginning to realize that what began as a moment of passion is going to end with me as his.

Forever.

Bed of Thorns

Hardened by years spent in prison for a crime he didn't commit, Edmond Montego is no longer the gentle man I remember. When he came for me, he didn't just take me for the very first time.

He claimed my virgin body with a savagery that left me screaming… and he made me beg for it.

I should have run when I had the chance, but with every lash of his belt, every passionate kiss, and every brutal climax, I fell more and more under his spell.

But he has a dark secret, and if we're not careful, we'll lose everything… including our lives.

Morally Gray

Saxon Thornburg is known to the world as a reputable businessman, but I knew his true nature even before he kidnapped me, bared, bound, and punished me, and then shamefully ravaged me.

He is not just the billionaire boss of a powerful crime family. He is the Patriarch.

Women drop to their knees on command for him, but he chose me because I didn't surrender.

Until he took off his belt…

Vicious Intentions

Cain, Hunter, and Cristiano were heirs to some of the richest and most powerful families in the world, men who might as well have been kings. Ten years ago they caught me eavesdropping, and when they were done setting my bare ass on fire with a belt they claimed and ravaged me.

Or at least that's what happens in the fleeting memories I still have left after the car accident…

Though I'm a successful musician now, wealthy and famous myself, in my heart I know if one of those brutes—let alone all three—ordered me to strip and surrender to them in the most shameful of ways, I wouldn't even need the threat of another humiliating punishment to obey immediately.

I never expected to see them again, of course… or to find myself naked, wet, and blushing as a ruthless Chicago crime boss takes his time enjoying me along with two of his closest friends.

But even before the memory of their faces returned, my body remembered its masters.

Scandalous Liaison

Recently divorced from my cheating ex, the last thing I needed on the flight home for my brother's wedding was a too-hot-for-his-own-good asshole sitting by me in first class.

But when I escaped to the bathroom to hyperventilate in peace, Mr. Tall, Dark, and Surly followed me. Then he made me forget all about the turbulence with a punishing kiss, a hard spanking, and a series of screaming climaxes loud enough for everyone on the plane to hear.

It wasn't until after our deliciously shameful tryst that I learned the truth.

The man who ravaged me is my father's greatest enemy… and he's willing to help me take control of the company my father has used for his ruthless schemes for far too long already.

All it will cost is my complete surrender.

Ruthlessly Mine

She was on the run from bastards like me, desperate to leave the brutal world of assassins and mob bosses behind. But she was drawn to me like a moth to a flame, and I'm a bad, bad man…

That's why she's not just wet, well-used, and sore from my belt and what came after.

She's mine.

Ruthlessly mine.

Scandal

When a mysterious, dangerously sexy stranger led me back to his hotel room for a night of no-strings-attached passion, I didn't expect to end up with my bare ass thoroughly spanked.

But the real shock came the next day. That's when I discovered that the gorgeous, violet-eyed brute who made me scream in bed last night is one of the most powerful mafia bosses in the city.

…and as the future district attorney, I've just been tasked with putting him behind bars for life.

Caught in a web of lust and scandal, I know only one thing for certain.

I belong to him now.

BOOKS OF THE MISSOULA BAD BOYS SERIES

Phoenix

As a single dad, a battle-scarred Marine, and a smokejumper, my life was complicated enough. Then Wren Tillman showed up in town, full of sass and all but begging for my belt, and what began as a passionate night after I rescued her from a snowstorm quickly became much more.

Her father plans to marry her off for his own gain, but I've claimed her, and I plan to keep her.

She can fight it if she wants, but in her heart she knows she's already mine.

Snake

I left Missoula to serve my country and came back a bitter, broken man. But when Chastity Garrington made my recovery her personal crusade, I decided I had a mission of my own.

Mastering her.

Her task won't be easy, and the fire in her eyes tells me mine won't either. Yet the spark between us is instant, and we both know she'll be wet, sore, and screaming my name soon enough.

But I want more than that.

By the time my body has healed, I plan to have claimed her heart.

Maverick

When I found her trapped in a ravine, I thought Lily Sanborn was just another lost tourist. Then she tried to steal my truck, and I realized she was on the run… and in need of a dose of my belt.

Holed up in my cabin with her bottom burning and a snowstorm raging outside, there's no denying the spark between us, and we both know she'll soon be screaming my name as I take her in the most shameful of ways.

But when her past catches up to her, the men who come after her will learn a hard lesson.

She's mine now, and I protect what's mine.

BOOKS OF THE MONTANA BAD BOYS SERIES

Hawk

He's a big, angry Marine, and I'm going to be sore when he's done with me.

Hawk Travers is not a man to be trifled with. I learned that lesson in the hardest way possible, first with a painful, humiliating public spanking and then much more shamefully in private.

She came looking for trouble. She got a taste of my belt instead.

Bryce Myers pushed me too far and she ended up with her bottom welted. But as satisfying as it is to hear this feisty little reporter scream my name as I put her in her place, I get the feeling she isn't going to stop snooping around no matter how well-used and sore I leave her cute backside.

She's gotten herself in way over her head, but she's mine now, and I protect what's mine.

Scorpion

He didn't ask if I like it rough. It wasn't up to me.

I thought I could get away with pissing off a big, tough Marine. I ended up with my face planted in the sheets, my burning bottom raised high, and my hair held tightly in his fist as he took me long and hard and taught me the kind of shameful lesson only a man like Scorpion could teach.

She was begging for a taste of my belt. She got much more than that.

Getting so tipsy she thought she could be sassy with me in my own bar earned Caroline a spanking, but it was trying to make off with my truck that sealed the deal. She'll feel my belt across her bare backside, then she'll scream my name as she takes every single inch of me.

This naughty girl needs to be put in her place, and I'm going to enjoy every moment of it.

Mustang

I tried to tell him how to run his ranch. Then he took off his belt.

When I heard a rumor about his ranch, I confronted Mustang about it. I thought I could go toe to toe with the big, tough former Marine, but I ended up blushing, sore, and very thoroughly used.

I told her it was going to hurt. I meant it.

Danni Brexton is a hot little number with a sharp tongue and a chip on her shoulder. She's the kind of trouble that needs to be ridden hard and put away wet, but only after a taste of my belt.

It will take more than just a firm hand and a burning bottom to tame this sassy spitfire, but I plan to keep her safe, sound, and screaming my name in bed whether she likes it or not. By the time I'm through with her, there won't be a shadow of a doubt in her mind that she belongs to me.

Nash

When he caught me on his property, he didn't call the police. He just took off his belt.

Nash caught me breaking into his shed while on the run from the mob, and when he demanded answers and obedience I gave him neither. Then he took off his belt and taught me in the most shameful way possible what happens to naughty girls who play games with a big, rough Marine.

She's mine to protect. That doesn't mean I'm going to be gentle with her.

Michelle doesn't just need a place to hide out. She needs a man who will bare her bottom and spank her until she is sore and sobbing whenever she puts herself at risk with reckless defiance, then shove her face into the sheets and make her scream his name with every savage climax.

She'll get all of that from me, and much, much more.

Austin

I offered this brute a ride. I ended up the one being ridden.

The first time I saw Austin, he was hitchhiking. I stopped to give him a lift, but I didn't end up taking this big, rough former Marine wherever he was heading. He was far too busy taking me.

She thought she was in charge. Then I took off my belt.

When Francesca Montgomery pulled up beside me, I didn't know who she was, but I knew what she needed and I gave it to her. Long, hard, and thoroughly, until she was screaming my name as she climaxed over and over with her quivering bare bottom still sporting the marks from my belt.

But someone wants to hurt her, and when someone tries to hurt what's mine, I take it personally.

BOOKS OF THE EAGLE FORCE SERIES

Debt of Honor

Isabella Adams is a brilliant scientist, but her latest discovery has made her a target of Russian assassins. I've been assigned to protect her, and when her reckless behavior puts her in danger she'll learn in the most shameful of ways what it means to be under the command of a Marine.

She can beg and plead as my belt lashes her bare backside, but the only mercy she'll receive is the chance to scream as she climaxes over and over with her well-spanked bottom still burning.

As my past returns to haunt me, it'll take every skill I've mastered to keep her alive.

She may be a national treasure, but she belongs to me now.

Debt of Loyalty

After she was kidnapped in broad daylight, I was hired to bring Willow Cavanaugh home, but as the daughter of a wealthy family she's used to getting what she wants rather than taking orders.

Too bad.

She'll do as she's told or she'll earn herself a stern, shameful reminder of who is in charge, but it will take more than just a well-spanked bare bottom to truly tame this feisty little rich girl.

She'll learn her place over my knee, but it's in my bed that I'll make her mine.

Debt of Sacrifice

When she witnessed a murder, it put Greer McDuff on a brutal cartel's radar… and on mine.

As a former Navy SEAL now serving with the elite Eagle Force, my assignment is to protect her by any means necessary. If that requires a stern reminder of who is in charge with her bottom bare over my knee and then an even more shameful lesson in my bed, then that's what she'll get.

There's just one problem.

The only place I know I can keep her safe is the ranch I left behind and vowed never to return.

BOOKS OF THE DANGEROUS BUSINESS SERIES

Persuasion

Her father stole something from the mob and they hired me to get it back, but that's not the real reason Giliana Worthington is locked naked in a cage with her bottom well-used and sore.

I brought her here so I could take my time punishing her, mastering her, and ravaging her helpless, quivering body over and over again as she screams and moans and begs for more.

I didn't take her as a hostage. I took her because she is mine.

Bad Men

I thought I could run away from the marriage the mafia arranged for me, but I ended up held prisoner in a foreign country by someone far more dangerous than the man I tried to escape.

Then Jack and Diego came for me.

They didn't ask if I wanted to be theirs. They just took me.

I ran, but they caught me, stripped me bare, and punished me in the most shameful way possible.

Now they're going to share me, and they're not going to be gentle about it.

BOOKS OF THE DARK WOLVES SERIES

His to Claim

For centuries my kind have hidden our feral nature, our brute strength, and our carnal instincts. But this human female is my mate, and nothing will keep me from claiming and ravaging her.

She is mine to tame and protect, and if my belt doesn't teach her to obey then she'll learn in a much more shameful fashion. Either way, her surrender will be as complete as it is inevitable.

His to Possess

Stone Keeler is a six-foot-four hunk who could win any girl's heart and then make her scream in bed, but as he claimed my quivering body for the first time the look in his eyes was terrifying.

It was dark and savage, as if at any moment he might lose control completely and take me like a beast takes his mate, mounting and rutting me and marking me as his with every brutal climax.

I ran from him… but I couldn't stay away for long.

Not when I belong to him already.

BOOKS OF THE ALPHA DYNASTY SERIES

Unchained Beast

As the firstborn of the Dupree family, I have spent my life building the wealth and power of our mafia empire while keeping our dark secret hidden and my savage hunger at bay. But the beast within me cannot be chained forever, and I must claim a mate before I lose control completely…

That is why Coraline LeBlanc is mine.

When I mount and ravage her, it won't be because I want her. It will be because I need her.

But that doesn't mean I won't enjoy stripping her bare and spanking her until she surrenders, then making her beg and scream with every desperate climax as I take what belongs to me.

The beast will claim her, but I will keep her.

Savage Brute

It wasn't his mafia birthright that made Dax Dupree a monster. Years behind bars and a brutal war with a rival organization made him hard as steel, but the beast he can barely control was always there, and without a mate to mark and claim it would soon take hold of him completely.

I didn't know that when he showed up at my bar after closing and spanked me until I was wet and shamefully ready for him to mount and ravage me, or even when I woke the next morning with my throat sore from screaming and his seed still drying on my thighs. But I know it now.

Because I'm his mate.

Ruthless Monster

When Esme Rawlings looks at me, she sees many things. A ruthless mob boss. A key witness to the latest murder in an ongoing turf war. A guardian angel who saved her from a hitman's bullet.

But when I look at her, I see just one thing.

My mate.

She can investigate me as thoroughly as she feels necessary, prying into every aspect of my family's vast mafia empire, but the only truth she really needs to know about me she will learn tonight with her bare bottom burning and her protests drowned out by her screams of climax.

I take what belongs to me.

Ravenous Predator

Suzette Barker thought she could steal from the most powerful mafia boss in Philadelphia. My belt across her naked backside taught her otherwise, but as tears run down her cheeks and her arousal glistens on her bare thighs, there is something more important she will understand soon.

Kneeling at my feet and demonstrating her remorseful surrender in the most shameful way possible won't bring an end to this, nor will her screams of climax as I take her long and hard. She'll be coming with me and I'll be mounting and savagely rutting her as often as I please.

Not just because she owes me.

Because she's my mate.

Merciless Savage

Christoff Dupree doesn't strike me as the kind of man who woos a woman gently, so when I saw the flowers on my kitchen table I knew it wasn't just a gesture of appreciation for saving his life.

This ruthless mafia boss wasn't seducing me. Those roses mean that I belong to him now.

That I'm his to spank into shameful submission before he mounts me and claims me savagely.

That I'm his mate.

BOOKS OF THE ALPHA BEASTS SERIES

King's Mate

Her scent drew me to her, but something deeper and more powerful told me she was mine. Something that would not be denied. Something that demanded I claim her then and there.

I took her the way a beast takes his mate. Roughly. Savagely. Without mercy or remorse.

She will run, and when she does she will be punished, but it is not me that she fears. Every quivering, desperate climax reminds her that her body knows its master, and that terrifies her.

She knows I am not a gentle king, and she will scream for me as she learns her place.

Beast's Claim

Raven is not one of my kind, but the moment I caught her scent I knew she belonged to me.

She is my mate, and when I claim her it will not be gentle. She can fight me, but her pleas for mercy as she is punished will soon give way to screams of climax as she is mounted and rutted.

By the time I am finished with her, the evidence of her body's surrender will be mingled with my seed as it drips down her bare thighs. But she will be more than just sore and utterly spent.

She will be mine.

Alpha's Mate

I didn't ask Nicolina to be my mate. It was not up to her. An alpha takes what belongs to him.

She will plead for mercy as she is bared and punished for daring to run from me, but her screams as she is claimed and rutted will be those of helpless climax as her body surrenders to its master.

She is mine, and I'm going to make sure she knows it.

MORE STORMY NIGHT BOOKS BY PIPER STONE

Claimed by the Beasts

Though she has done her best to run from it, Scarlet Dumane cannot escape what is in store for her. She has known for years that she is destined to belong not just to one savage beast, but to three, and now the time has come for her to be claimed. Soon her mates will own every inch of her beautiful body, and she will be shared and used as roughly and as often as they please.

Scarlet hid from the disturbing truth about herself, her family, and her town for as long as she could, but now her grandmother's death has finally brought her back home to the bayous of Louisiana and at last she must face her fate, no matter how shameful and terrifying.

She will be a queen, but her mates will be her masters, and defiance will be thoroughly punished. Yet even when she is stripped bare and spanked until she is sobbing, her need for them only grows, and every blush, moan, and quivering climax binds her to them more tightly. But with enemies lurking in the shadows, can she trust her mates to protect her from both man and beast?

Millionaire Daddy

Dominick Asbury is not just a handsome millionaire whose deep voice makes Jenna's tummy flutter whenever they are together, nor is he merely the first man bold enough to strip her bare and spank her hard and thoroughly whenever she has been naughty. He is much more than that.

He is her daddy.

He is the one who punishes her when she's been a bad girl, and he is the one who takes her in his arms afterwards and brings her to

one climax after another until she is utterly spent and satisfied.

But something shady is going on behind the scenes at Dominick's company, and when Jenna draws the wrong conclusion from a poorly written article about him and creates an embarrassing public scene, will she end up not only costing them both their jobs but losing her daddy as well?

Conquering Their Mate

For years the Cenzans have cast a menacing eye on Earth, but it still came as a shock to be captured, stripped bare, and claimed as a mate by their leader and his most trusted warriors.

It infuriates me to be punished for the slightest defiance and forced to submit to these alien brutes, but as I'm led naked through the corridors of their ship, my well-punished bare bottom and my helpless arousal both fully on display, I cannot help wondering how long it will be until I'm kneeling at the feet of my mates and begging them take me as shamefully as they please.

Captured and Kept

Since her career was knocked off track in retaliation for her efforts to expose a sinister plot by high-ranking government officials, reporter Danielle Carver has been stuck writing puff pieces in a small town in Oregon. Desperate for a serious story, she sets out to investigate the rumors she's been hearing about mysterious men living in the mountains nearby. But when she secretly follows them back to their remote cabin, the ruggedly handsome beasts don't take kindly to her snooping around, and Dani soon finds herself stripped bare for a painful, humiliating spanking.

Their rough dominance arouses her deeply, and before long she is blushing crimson as they take turns using her beautiful body as thoroughly and shamefully as they please. But when Dani uncovers the true reason for their presence in the area, will more than just her career be at risk?

Taming His Brat

It's been years since Cooper Dawson left her small Texas hometown, but after her stubborn defiance gets her fired from two jobs in a row, she knows something definitely needs to change. What she doesn't expect, however, is for her sharp tongue and arrogant attitude to land her over the knee of a stern, ruggedly sexy cowboy for a painful, embarrassing, and very public spanking.

Rex Sullivan cannot deny being smitten by Cooper, and the fact that she is in desperate need of his belt across her bare backside only makes the war-hardened ex-Marine more determined to tame the beautiful, fiery redhead. It isn't long before she's screaming his name as he shows her just how hard and roughly a cowboy can ride a headstrong filly. But Rex and Cooper both have secrets, and when the demons of their past rear their ugly heads, will their romance be torn apart?

Capturing Their Mate

I thought the Cenzan invaders could never find me here, but I was wrong. Three of the alien brutes came to take me, and before I ever set foot aboard their ship I had already been stripped bare, spanked thoroughly, and claimed more shamefully then I would have ever thought possible.

They have decided that a public example must be made of me, and I will be punished and used in the most humiliating ways imaginable as a warning to anyone who might dare to defy them. But I am no ordinary breeder, and the secrets hidden in my past could change their world… or end it.

Rogue

Tracking down cyborgs is my job, but this time I'm the one being hunted. This rogue machine has spent most of his life locked up, and now that he's on the loose he has plans for me…

He isn't just going to strip me, punish me, and use me. He will take me longer and harder than any human ever could, claiming me so thoroughly that I will be left in no doubt who owns me.

No matter how shamefully I beg and plead, my body will be ravaged again and again with pleasure so intense it terrifies me to even imagine, because that is what he was built to do.

Roughneck

When I took a job on an oil rig to escape my scheming stepfather's efforts to set me up with one of his business cronies, I knew I'd be working with rugged men. What I didn't expect is to find myself bent over a desk, my cheeks soaked with tears and my bare thighs wet for a very different reason, as my well-punished bottom is thoroughly used by a stern, infuriatingly sexy roughneck.

Even though I should have known better than to get sassy with a firm-handed cowboy, let alone a tough-as-nails former Marine, there's no denying that learning the hard way was every bit as hot as it was shameful. But a sore, welted backside is just the start of his plans for me, and no matter how much I blush to admit it, I know I'm going to take everything he gives me and beg for more.

Hunting Their Mate

As far as I'm concerned, the Cenzans will always be the enemy, and there can be no peace while they remain on our planet. I planned to make them pay for invading our world, but I was hunted down and captured by two of their warriors with the help of a battle-hardened former Marine. Now I'm the one who is going to pay, as the three of them punish me, shame me, and share me.

Though the thought of a fellow human taking the side of these alien brutes enrages me, that is far from the worst of it. With every searing stroke of the strap that lands across my bare bottom, with every savage thrust as I am claimed over and over, and with every screaming climax, it is made more clear that it is my own quivering, thoroughly used body which has truly betrayed me.

Primitive

I was sent to this world to help build a new Earth, but I was shocked by what I found here. The men of this planet are not just primitive savages. They are predators, and I am now their prey…

The government lied to all of us. Not all of the creatures who hunted and captured me are aliens. Some of them were human once, specimens transformed in labs into little more than feral beasts.

I fought, but I was thrown over a shoulder and carried off. I ran, but I was caught and punished. Now they are going to claim me, share me, and use me so roughly that when the last screaming climax has been wrung from my naked, helpless body, I wonder if I'll still know my own name.

Harvest

The Centurions conquered Earth long before I was born, but they did not come for our land or our resources. They came for mates, women deemed suitable for breeding. Women like me.

Three of the alien brutes decided to claim me, and when I defied them, they made a public example of me, punishing me so thoroughly and shamefully I might never stop blushing.

But now, as my virgin body is used in every way possible, I'm not sure I want them to stop…

Torched

I work alongside firefighters, so I know how to handle musclebound roughnecks, but Blaise Tompkins is in a league of his own. The night we met, I threw a glass of wine in his face, then ended up shoved against the wall with my panties on the floor and my arousal dripping down my thighs, screaming out climax after shameful climax with my well-punished bottom still burning.

I've got a series of arsons to get to the bottom of, and finding out that the infuriatingly sexy brute who spanked me like a naughty little girl will be helping me with the investigation seemed like the last thing I needed, until somebody hurled a rock through my window in an effort to scare me away from the case. Now having a big, strong man around doesn't seem like such a bad idea…

Fertile

The men who hunt me were always brutes, but now lust makes them barely more than beasts.

When they catch me, I know what comes next.

I will fight, but my need to be bred is just as strong as theirs is to breed. When they strip me, punish me, and use me the way I'm meant to be used, my screams will be the screams of climax.

Hostage

I knew going after one of the most powerful mafia bosses in the world would be dangerous, but I didn't anticipate being dragged from my apartment already sore, sorry, and shamefully used.

My captors don't just plan to teach me a lesson and then let me go. They plan to share me, punish me, and claim me so ruthlessly I'll be screaming my submission into the sheets long before they're through with me. They took me as a hostage, but they'll keep me as theirs.

Defiled

I was born to rule, but for her sake I am banished, forced to wander the Earth among mortals. Her virgin body will pay the price for my protection, and it will be a shameful price indeed.

Stripped, punished, and ravaged over and over, she will scream with every savage climax.

She will be defiled, but before I am done with her she will beg to be mine.

Kept

On the run from corrupt men determined to silence me, I sought refuge in his cabin. I ate his food, drank his whiskey, and slept in his bed. But then the big bad bear came home and I learned the hard way that sometimes Goldilocks ends up with her cute little bottom well-used and sore.

He stripped me, spanked me, and ravaged me in the most shameful way possible, but then this rugged brute did something no one else ever has before. He made it clear he plans to keep me…

Auctioned

Twenty years ago the Malzeons saved us when we were at the brink of self-annihilation, but there was a price for their intervention. They demanded humans as servants… and as pets.

Only criminals were supposed to be offered to the aliens for their use, but when I defied Earth's government, asking questions that no one else would dare to ask, I was sold to them at auction.

I was bought by two of their most powerful commanders, rivals who nonetheless plan to share me. I am their property now, and they intend to tame me, train me, and enjoy me thoroughly.

But I have information they need, a secret guarded so zealously that discovering it cost me my freedom, and if they do not act quickly enough both of our worlds will soon be in grave danger.

Hard Ride

When I snuck into Montana Cobalt's house, I was looking for help learning to ride like him, but what I got was his belt across my bare backside. Then with tears still running down my cheeks and arousal dripping onto my thighs, the big brute taught me a much more shameful lesson.

Montana has agreed to train me, but not just for the rodeo. He's going to break me in and put me through my paces, and then he's going to show me what it means to be ridden rough and dirty.

Carnal

For centuries my kind have hidden our feral nature, our brute strength, and our carnal instincts. But this human female is my mate, and nothing will keep me from claiming and ravaging her.

She is mine to tame and protect, and if my belt doesn't teach her to obey then she'll learn in a much more shameful fashion. Either way, her surrender will be as complete as it is inevitable.

Bounty

After I went undercover to take down a mob boss and ended up betrayed, framed, and on the run, Harper Rollins tried to bring me in. But instead of collecting a bounty, she earned herself a hard spanking and then an even rougher lesson that left her cute bottom sore in a very different way.

She's not one to give up without a fight, but that's fine by me. It just means I'll have plenty more chances to welt her beautiful backside and then make her scream her surrender into the sheets.

Beast

Primitive, irresistible need compelled him to claim me, but it was more than mere instinct that drove this alien beast to punish me for my defiance and then ravage me thoroughly and savagely. Every screaming climax was a brand marking me as his, ensuring I never forget who I belong to.

He's strong enough to take what he wants from me, but that's not why I surrendered so easily as he stripped me bare, pushed me up

against the wall, and made me his so roughly and shamefully.

It wasn't fear that forced me to submit. It was need.

Gladiator

Xander didn't just win me in the arena. The alien brute claimed me there too, with my punished bottom still burning and my screams of climax almost drowned out by the roar of the crowd.

Almost...

Victory earned him freedom and the right to take me as his mate, but making me truly his will mean more than just spanking me into shameful surrender and then rutting me like a wild beast. Before he carries me off as his prize, the dark truth that brought me here must be exposed at last.

Big Rig

Alexis Harding is used to telling men exactly what she thinks, but she's never had a roughneck like me as a boss before. On my rig, I make the rules and sassy little girls get stripped bare, bent over my desk, and taught their place, first with my belt and then in a much more shameful way.

She'll be sore and sorry long before I'm done with her, but the arousal glistening on her thighs reveals the truth she would rather keep hidden. She needs it rough, and that's how she'll get it.

Warriors

I knew this was a primitive planet when I landed, but nothing could have prepared me for the rough beasts who inhabit it. The sting of their prince's firm hand on my bare bottom taught me my place in his world, but it was what came after that truly demonstrated his mastery over me.

This alien brute has granted me his protection and his help with my mission, but the price was my total submission to both his shameful demands and those of his second in command as well.

But it isn't the savage way they make use of my quivering body that terrifies me the most. What leaves me trembling is the thought that I may never leave this place… because I won't want to.

Owned

With a ruthless, corrupt billionaire after me, Crockett, Dylan, and Wade are just the men I need. Rough men who know how to keep a woman safe… and how to make her scream their names.

But the Hell's Fury MC doesn't do charity work, and their help will come at a price.

A shameful price…

They aren't just going to bare me, punish me, and then do whatever they want with me.

They're going to make me beg for it.

Seized

Delaney Archer got herself mixed up with someone who crossed us, and now she's going to find out just how roughly and shamefully three bad men like us can make use of her beautiful body.

She can plead for mercy, but it won't stop us from stripping her bare and spanking her until she's sore, sobbing, and soaking wet. Our feisty little captive is going to take everything we give her, and she'll be screaming our names with every savage climax long before we're done with her.

Cruel Masters

I thought I understood the risks of going undercover to report on billionaires flaunting their power, but these men didn't send lawyers after me. They're going to deal with me themselves.

Now I'm naked aboard their private plane, my backside already burning from one of their belts, and these three infuriatingly sexy bastards have only just gotten started teaching me my place.

I'm not just going to be punished, shamed, and shared. I'm going to be mastered.

Hard Men

My father's will left his company to me, but the three roughnecks who ran it for him have other ideas. They're owed a debt and they mean to collect on it, but it's not money these brutes want.

It's me.

In return for protection from my father's enemies, I will be theirs to share. But these are hard men, and they don't just intend to punish my defiance and use me as shamefully as they please.

They plan to master me completely.

Rough Ride

As I hear the leather slide through the loops of his pants, I know what comes next. Jake Travers is going to blister my backside. Then he's going to ride me the way only a rodeo champion can.

Plenty of men who thought they could put me in my place have learned the hard way that I was more than they could handle, and when Jake showed up I was sure he would be no different.

I was wrong.

When I pushed him, he bared and spanked me in front of a bar full of people.

I should have let it go at that, but I couldn't.

That's why he's taking off his belt…

Primal Instinct

Ruger Jameson can buy anything he wants, but that's not the reason I'm his to use as he pleases.

He's a former Army Ranger accustomed to having his orders followed, but that's not why I obey him.

He saved my life after our plane crashed, but I'm not on my knees just to thank him properly.

I'm his because my body knows its master.

I do as I'm told because he blisters my bare backside every time I dare to do otherwise.

I'm at his feet because I belong to him and I plan to show it in the most shameful way possible.

Captor

I was supposed to be safe from the lottery. Set apart for a man who would treat me with dignity.

But as I'm probed and examined in the most intimate, shameful ways imaginable while the hulking alien king who just spanked me looks on approvingly, I know one thing for certain.

This brute didn't end up with me by chance. He wanted me, so he found a way to take me.

He'll savor every blush as I stand bare and on display for him, every plea for mercy as he punishes my defiance, and every quivering climax as he slowly masters my virgin body.

I'll be his before he even claims me.

Rough and Dirty

Wrecking my cheating ex's truck with a bat might have made me feel better… if the one I went after had actually belonged to him, instead of to the burly roughneck currently taking off his belt.

Now I'm bent over in a parking lot with my bottom burning as this ruggedly sexy bastard and his two equally brutish friends take turns reddening my ass, and I can tell they're just getting started.

That thought shouldn't excite me, and I certainly shouldn't be imagining all the shameful things these men might do to me. But what I should or shouldn't be thinking doesn't matter anyway.

They can see the arousal glistening on my thighs, and they know I need it rough and dirty…

His to Take

When Zadok Vakan caught me trying to escape his planet with priceless stolen technology, he didn't have me sent to the mines. He made sure I was stripped bare and sold at auction instead.

Then he bought me for himself.

Even as he punishes me for the slightest hint of defiance and then claims me like a beast, indulging every filthy desire his savage nature can conceive, I swear I'll never surrender.

But it doesn't matter.

I'm already his, and we both know it.

Tyrant

When I accepted a lucrative marketing position at his vineyard, Montgomery Wolfe made the terms of my employment clear right from the start. Follow his rules or face the consequences.

That's why I'm bent over his desk, doing my best to hate him as his belt lashes my bare bottom.

I shouldn't give in to this tyrant. I shouldn't yield to his shameful demands.

Yet I can't resist the passion he sets ablaze with every word, every touch, and every brutally possessive kiss, and I know before long my body will surrender to even his darkest needs…

Filthy Rogue

Losing my job to a woman who slept her way to the top was bad enough, and that was before my car broke down as I drove cross country to start over. Having to be rescued by an infuriatingly sexy biker who promptly bared and spanked me for sassing him was just icing on the cake.

After sharing a passionate night, I might have made a teensy mistake in taking cash from his wallet in order to pay the auto mechanic, but I hadn't thought I'd ever see him again...

Then on the first day at my new job, guess who swaggered in with payback on his mind?

He's living proof that the universe really is out to get me... and he's my new boss.

Captive Mate

When the fearsome alien warrior who invaded my dreams came for me in the flesh, he did more than just spank my bare ass and then make me scream his name as he mounted and rutted me.

He marked me as his.

Then, with the imprint of his teeth still red on my skin, he carried me off with him.

Because he isn't just my fantasy. He's my mate.

ABOUT PIPER STONE

Amazon Top 150 Internationally Best-Selling Author, Kindle Unlimited All Star Piper Stone writes in several genres. From her worlds of dark mafia, cowboys, and marines to contemporary reverse harem, shifter romance, and science fiction, she attempts to delight readers with a foray into darkness, sensuality, suspense, and always a romantic HEA. When she's not writing, you can find her sipping merlot while she enjoys spending time with her three Golden Retrievers (Indiana Jones, Magnum PI, and Remington Steele) and a husband who relishes creating fabulous food.

Dangerous is Delicious.

* * *

You can find her at:

Website: https://piperstonebooks.com/

Newsletter: https://piperstonebooks.com/newsletter/

Facebook: https://www.facebook.com/authorpiperstone/

Twitter: http://twitter.com/piperstone01

Instagram: http://www.instagram.com/authorpiperstone/

Amazon: http://amazon.com/author/piperstone

BookBub: http://bookbub.com/authors/piper-stone

TikTok: https://www.tiktok.com/@piperstoneauthor

Email: piperstonecreations@gmail.com

Made in the USA
Middletown, DE
19 April 2024